LOLA
DELPHINE

A Novel By
NAOMI BARKER

LOLA
DELPHINE

Oysters and pearls are intertwined with lunar forces. The iridescent pearl is like a tiny shining moon lying at the bottom of the ocean, reminding us of the beauty and strength something so delicate can hold.

CHAPTER ONE

Jack Alistair pulled up behind her convertible at the Casino de Monte-Carlo. Interesting, he thought, the lady likes to gamble. He was intrigued by how she would look. By chance, he had followed her through the winding streets for the last mile or so. She drove with a determined air that suggested she was a local and used to navigating the tourists and mopeds. He found himself captivated by her unruly blonde hair, which blew freely in the amber light of the Mediterranean sunset. He idly wondered if she was meeting someone. She waited while the valet attendants opened her door.

"Good evening, *Mademoiselle* Delphine."

She swung her golden legs out of the Porsche 911 and straightened out her white silk dress. He couldn't help but notice the way the luxurious fabric clung to her body. Unlike many women he usually saw around here, she was a natural beauty; he was attracted to the messy hair. As she turned to walk up the stairs, he suddenly saw it—a small but obvious crescent-moon-shaped scar on her right lower leg. In an instant, he remembered that scar and the lovely girl who went with it. Could it really be? Suddenly, he was brought out of his daydream by the valet tapping on his window.

"*Monsieur* Alistair, welcome."

The valet opened his door as Jack scrambled to have another look, but she had already gone inside. He felt shaken to the core. At last, he had found her. Lola Delphine.

Jack had done very well for himself. He had carved his own path and had proudly built a small fortune. Through hard work and sheer determination, he had become the most respected art dealer in England and possibly the whole of Europe. Jack's business, Alistair Fine Art International, had been growing over the years and his portfolio of clients expanding. He mainly focused on modern masters, and lately, some amazing pieces had come into his grasp.

The business was growing so much that he was expanding into a new office space. His estate agent had been looking for the last six months and finally, a converted tea warehouse along the River Thames on Wapping High Street had come on the market. Jack snapped it up. A more prominent place for his headquarters would have been Knightsbridge or Mayfair, but he preferred the character of the East End. His offices were over 5,000 square feet, and he had completely renovated the space. The exterior of the building still had the rustic appeal of a warehouse, but when you entered the gleaming doors, you were hit with a shiny white-marble floor and sleek furnishings. Perhaps the most stunning features were the magnificent arched windows overlooking the Thames. Jack had left exposed brickwork that added warmth to the otherwise contemporary interior. Feeling completely at home, he had added a penthouse residence with a roof terrace and had moved in a few weeks ago.

Jack sipped his espresso and idly thought back to that short moment in Monte Carlo when he had seen Lola. Could it really have been Lola or had his mind been playing tricks on him? He had searched for her in the casino to no avail. The valets refused to reveal her name due to the casino's privacy policy. They did tell him, however, that she had left a few minutes after arriving so unfortunately, he must have missed her. It amazed him that those few seconds had jolted him back to when he was a teenager and all the years of heartbreak and guilt that came after that. Jack had given up trying to communicate with her a long time ago after she constantly refused to answer his endless letters and phone messages. He couldn't ignore his feelings any longer. It had taken over his mind in the days since that Friday sunset on the Côte d'Azur, and he could think of nothing else but her. A crack of thunder brought him back to reality, and he knew what he had to do.

Jack picked up his phone. "Fiona, could you come in here, please?"

"Sure thing, Jack."

CHAPTER TWO

J ust over there on the right, please."
"Red door, luv?"
"Yes, that's it!"

As the cab came to a stop, Lola looked up at the three-story Georgian home she had grown so fond of since her parents sold the family country estate and she moved to the South of France. Paying the cab driver, she stepped onto the pavement. A chill wind hit her face. Wow, she thought, quite a change from the Côte d'Azur. Lola looked down at her Louis Vuitton weekender bag and hoped she had remembered everything; she had been so distracted when she had left France. Seeing Jack again was such a shock. Of course, she had pretended she didn't notice him, but as hard as she had tried over the years, she simply could not forget those sparkling blue eyes that followed her up the stairs to the casino. Blending into a large group of people in the foyer, she had waited until he strode in, obviously looking for her. At that moment she left abruptly, jumped into the Porsche, and hurried home to the sanctuary of her villa, which was situated in the hills above Sainte-Maxime in the Sémaphore area. Lola had been happy to make the long drive home; it had given her time to think and try to bury yet again the memories of that fateful summer years ago.

The door opened.

"Lola, what are you doing standing outside?"

"Hi, Dad, great to see you," Lola said.

Her dad, Oliver, often called Ollie by his family and close friends, embraced his daughter in a tight hug. She smelled the familiar scent of Givenchy Gentleman, which her father had been wearing for as long she could remember. Suddenly, she was nearly knocked over by Richard Chamberlain, the family's Labrador retriever, who had been named that because Lola's mother had been obsessed with the sexy priest in *The Thorn Birds*. The chocolate lab simply went by Rich. Kneeling, she spent a moment rubbing his head and petting him before following her dad into the black-and-white-tiled hallway.

She could hear her mum in the kitchen. "Is that you, Lola darling? Come here! I can't wait to give you a hug!"

Lola dropped her bag at the bottom of the staircase. Richard Chamberlain sniffed it and wagged his tail. The lab followed her as she walked into the spacious, beautifully updated kitchen, which was bathed in the last light of the September sun.

"So great to see you! It's been too long. I'm so glad you're home."

"Hi, Mum. Great to be here."

Lola's mum, Roberta, was standing behind the Aga stirring a large pot of marinara sauce. In her other hand, she held a glass of *Château La Nerthe*, her favourite red wine since her summer in the South of France when she was in her twenties. Lola gave her mum a big kiss on the cheek. At sixty-five, she was a beautiful woman and had such an understated sexiness that Ollie got jealous when younger men would flirt with her. Lola had definitely taken after her mother in so many ways, and at forty-three could still pass for someone ten years younger, but it was the confidence that Lola exuded that was so alluring. She was a natural beauty and her blonde hair, which she often let dry in the wind, constantly looked beachy. She loved to exercise and always travelled with a pair of running shoes so she could keep her five-foot-ten-inch athletic figure in good shape.

"Wine?"

"I'll get it, Mum."

"Lola, I'll take some, please," Ollie said. He settled onto one of the barstools opposite Roberta. He couldn't help but admire her figure in the crisp white shirt she was wearing. He could see her lace bra through the fabric. There was a splash of marinara sauce on her delicate rib cage. He began to get lost in thought, so he gave himself an imaginary slap, remembering his daughter on the far side of the kitchen pouring two glasses of *Château la Nerthe*.

"That's a huge pot of sauce," said Lola.

Roberta looked up. "Ben and Tabitha are coming over for dinner tonight. They might bring Fabian if his plane lands in time. They were so excited when I said you were coming, and it's such a coincidence that Fabian is flying in from Paris today."

* * *

Ahh, Fabian, Lola thought. How long had it been? The Whitecliffs had been friends of the Delphine family since Lola had competed against Fabian in equestrian events. The childish flirtation had begun when Lola was thirteen or fourteen; Fabian was two years older. He was definitely her first crush. Athletic and smart with a wicked sense of humour, it was hard not to love Fabian. They only saw each other during school holidays, as Fabian was away at boarding school, and following that, the University of St Andrews. Lola remembered the summer she turned eighteen; he had come home for the holidays, and the two families had met at the Stoneleigh Classic National Horse Show, where Lola and Fabian had entered a couple of events. Her mind drifted back to that summer.

While their parents had been busy catching up over Pimm's Cups and *Moët & Chandon* in the VIP tent, she and Fabian had some free time together. The next part still made her blush years later, but it was a moment she would never forget. It played out in her mind exactly the way it had happened. She was eighteen, and it started when she and Fabian had a break between events. They had tied the horses to the trailer to give them a bit of rest. She was tending to Tally when, out of the blue, it happened. Fabian brushed his hand across the small of her back. Thinking about that moment, it was such a subtle move but it sent an electric bolt through her young body. Then he moved her long blonde braid to the side before gently kissing the back of her neck. Seductively, he brought his lips around to her ear, which he caressed with his tongue. Lola remembered the moment she had turned around to see the look of desire in his eyes as he pulled her to him, the teenage years of frustration being fed by his hungry lips. His tongue had been eager as she felt his growing excitement through the tight fabric of his jodhpurs.

They slowly opened the horse trailer's side door into the front stall. Fabian took a blanket that was folded over a storage nook and put it down on the straw. Wanting this so much, she felt she was ready. He had been cheeky and playful as, one by one, the buttons came undone on her starched white shirt. A small groan left her lips as he stood back to admire her perfect breasts. For a few seconds, she remembered being in a trance but had been brought back to reality when Fabian's dad, Ben, started yelling for them outside the door. Thinking back to that short conversation, she was frustrated that they had been interrupted.

"Fabian, are you in there? We are going to have some lunch and wanted to see if you and Lola want to join us," Ben said. Lola tried desperately not to let out a squeal while frantically buttoning her shirt. Thankfully, Fabian had been quick to answer, so his dad hadn't opened the door.

"Coming, Dad. We were just, umm, giving the horses a rest, but lunch sounds great. I think we have an hour and a half before the next event."

Mr. Whitecliff seemed to believe the explanation and said, "We will see you both at the Harbour tent. I hear they have delicious crab sandwiches brought in from the Norfolk coast."

They heard him turn and leave.

She smiled to herself, thinking back to what she said to Fabian at that moment.

"Fabian, what have you done to me, you bad boy."

Then she had winked at him while straightening out her shirt and jacket. He held her for a moment and said, "You really are quite special, Miss Delphine."

After all that, they had walked over to meet their parents for lunch. Those few stolen moments with Fabian had changed her from a girl into a woman. It was the first time she understood the power of her sexuality, which now seemed like a secret weapon she never knew she had. The thought had lasted only a second as they entered the tent. Lola's parents and the Whitecliffs greeted them with plates of sandwiches and a bottle of Champagne, and they made their way to an empty table near the bar. She thought back to her mother's comment and replayed it in her head.

"You are quite flushed, Lola. Are you okay?"

Today the comment almost made her laugh out loud. Her dad had saved her from having to respond when he stood up to greet an old friend, Max Valentine-Smithe. Ollie introduced everyone. Lola had been a little confused because Max had held her gaze a long time, which made her feel both nervous and excited, even though he looked to be the same age as her parents. Max had the lightest blue eyes she had ever seen and short, cropped white-grey hair. He had a certain swagger about him and was wearing an outfit that looked like it had spent the night on the bedroom floor. However, you knew by the quality that it had probably cost thousands and come from Armani or somewhere similar. Lola had also noticed his slight East London accent. There had definitely been something alluring about him.

Her mother asked how Ollie knew Max, and It turned out Ollie had met him on a hunting trip a few years back with Max's brother Neville, a business acquaintance. Their main course arrived, and Max excused himself after pulling a small gold card case from his breast pocket. She remembered it because it had a four-leaf clover engraved on the front. He handed her father a business card and suggested that they come to his stables to see a new foal that had just been born. There had been something puzzling about her mother's reaction to being introduced to Max. She had looked almost ashen as she sat staring at her lunch. Afterwards, she stayed behind, claiming to need relief from the midday sun.

A couple of weeks later, her dad had driven her to Max's farm to see the new foal, and that's the day her life changed forever. She met Jack Alistair.

* * *

A knock on the door brought Lola out of the past and back to the present. Ollie had just set the last Baccarat wine glass on the dining table. They had decided to dine in the expansive kitchen tonight, as the views to the communal gardens were so fabulous this time of year. Even in September, the light was lovely at seven.

Ollie stepped back to admire the table, appreciating the contrast between the old rustic Tuscan farmhouse table and the contemporary dining chairs they had found in a design shop in Cambridge last year. This room was his favourite place to dine. He could hear his wife in the hallway greeting the Whitecliffs and showing them the new Claire Cusack sculpture they had recently commissioned. He wondered if Fabian had come with them; it was always a pleasure to see him. These days, it was rare to see Fabian with the amount of travelling he did as a top executive for Banque du NKB, one of France's largest banks.

Lola could hear the Whitecliffs downstairs as she fastened the strap of her Valentino kitten heel. Choosing to wear the softest leather trousers in fawn, she paired them with a mocha silk charmeuse camisole top that set off her Riviera tan very nicely. Just in case Fabian was able to come to dinner, she wanted to look effortlessly sexy. At the last moment, she rubbed some amber oil, her favourite scent, through her hair. She glanced in the mirror before heading down to see the Whitecliffs.

For a moment, she was disappointed. Tabitha and Ben were discussing the new Cusack sculpture with her parents, but there was no sign of Fabian. Probably for the best, she thought. After all, he does have a new girlfriend in Paris, and she didn't need any more complications in her life right now, especially after nearly running into Jack last Friday. She hadn't seen Fabian since a mutual friend's birthday party last year, and thankfully, they both had dates, although Lola's was more of a friend than anything else.

"So great to see you, Lola," Tabitha said. "You look beautiful and so tanned."

She embraced Lola, and Ben gave her a peck on both cheeks.

"How is everything? Your mum keeps us up to date on what you are up to. It all sounds very glamorous living in the South of France, along with all that jet-setting you do. We're so impressed with the success of your accessories company."

"Thank you both so much. It's wonderful to see you."

They walked back into the kitchen, and Ollie busied himself fixing everybody's drinks. The Whitecliffs sat down at the large island, and Richard Chamberlain wagged his tail and waited for a stray peanut to come his way.

"So glad Fabian can make it," Ollie said, as he poured the wine.

"Yes, he's just running a little late due to his flight being delayed, but he said he would come straight here from Heathrow."

Lola tried not to look too excited as she downed half a glass of wine and felt the elixir calm her mind and body. Fabian had always had this effect on her, even after all these years, but she wished she could turn the clock back to before the summer of the Stoneleigh Classic Horse Show and that fateful meeting of Max Valentine-Smithe.

*   *   *

There was a knock on the door. Rich let out one loud bark, then wagged his tail and headed into the hallway, followed by Ollie. "Fabian must be here," he said. Lola could hear her dad opening the front door.

"Please, come in. We're so happy you can join us," he said, embracing Fabian in a big hug. "Let me help you with your bags; you can leave them in my study if you like. Everyone is in the kitchen. Please go on through."

As all the greetings were made, Lola held back. She heard Tabitha say to Fabian, "Look, Fabian, isn't it amazing timing that Lola just happens to be in London this week?"

Fabian broke away from all the hugs and turned to face Lola. Their eyes locked onto one another for a moment, and Fabian pulled Lola into a friendly hug. She could smell his still-boyish scent lingering on his chiselled neck. All those years of riding and college sports followed by his interest in hiking and sailing had undoubtedly kept his body in fantastic shape. She noticed how well they still fit together.

"Nice to see you, Lola," Fabian said. "You look lovely as ever."

Fabian couldn't help the intense attraction he felt for Lola. He still wanted her badly even though he knew it would never work between them. Realistically, he knew he should push her out of his heart entirely, but for some reason, he never could. Not to mention she had hurt him so terribly all those years ago when she became infatuated with Jack Alistair.

Lola pulled back, and she could have sworn she saw Fabian gaze at her now-hardened nipples. She couldn't deny the intense sexual attraction she still felt for him.

"You look well, Fabian. How's Paris? Your mum mentioned you were getting quite serious with a lovely French girl."

Fabian was so handsome, still looking like the boy of her teenage fantasies. A little grey had appeared at the edges of his thick mop of sandy hair and a few laugh lines around his eyes, but she liked this older Fabian. He seemed more confident, and he looked fabulous in a faded pair of jeans, slightly wrinkled Paul Smith shirt, and Tod's driving shoes, which had always been a favourite of his.

"Paris is fine. Work's busy as usual, and we have just moved into a larger apartment in the Third Arrondissement, about a ten-minute walk from the Picasso Museum. Anais is very excited and is making the place look spectacular."

Lola couldn't help but be a little jealous of Anais. She was ten years older than Fabian and had that *très chic* elegance only a French woman can have, not to mention she had been a top model for many years and still was very much in demand at fifty-five.

"I forgot how you two met."

"I was invited to the opening of a new contemporary art gallery called Galerie Raphael, which is just a short walk from our new apartment in the Marais. Anais is friends with the owner, who is more of a silent partner—an American guy, a Texan. Would you believe he's called Riggs Howard? Turns out the three of us have a passion for horses. After Riggs retired from the oil business, he bought a racehorse yard just outside of Houston. He's the backing behind the gallery, which is being run by his son Bentley. Riggs is quite the character and drives a DeLorean in Paris. Apparently, he's a huge fan of *Back to the Future*."

Lola hoped her jealousy didn't show. She couldn't even understand why she felt like this. Fabian had been nothing more than an old family friend for years now.

"Dinner is served," Roberta said.

Lola turned to the table to see a steaming bowl of spaghetti Bolognese, a large salad, garlic bread, and a new bottle of *Château la Nerthe*. They sat down, and the meal flowed nicely, as it does with old friends who laughed as they reminisced about holidays they had taken together.

All of a sudden, Richard Chamberlain, who had been waiting for an opportune moment to grab a piece of bread, made his move and managed to tip a glass of wine over on Lola's leather trousers and the side of Fabian's jeans.

"Rich, down! Bad boy," Lola said. While she was busy mopping up the wine with her serviette, Roberta grabbed some paper towels from the kitchen and started mopping up the mess. "I'm going to go and change," Lola said, standing up from the table.

"Me too." Fabian walked back to Ollie's study to dig another pair of jeans out of his suitcase.

Shutting the bedroom door, Lola pulled off the leather trousers and walked into the bathroom. She filled the sink with cold water, hoping it would get the red wine stain out. She noticed that the wine had gone through the fine leather and stained her lace Coco de Mer panties. Better soak them too, she thought.

Fabian opened Lola's bedroom door. She heard the door open and turned away from the sink. Fabian stood there with a pair of clean jeans over his arm. He moved toward her, noticing how unbelievably beautiful she was in the camisole and stained white-lace panties. Silently, he threw the jeans on the bed and pulled Lola to him with such passion it almost knocked her over. He thrust his tongue into Lola's mouth. She quickly unbuttoned his shirt, and he lifted her camisole over her head. The light silk fell to the floor like an autumn leaf. Fabian paused, took her hand, and led her to the bed. He sat hypnotised as she climbed on top of him, and their mouths became one again. Feeling his mounting excitement through the denim, she started unbuttoning his jeans.

Lola couldn't remember the last time she had wanted anything so badly, but her body told her so in every way. Fabian was kissing her neck and slowly making his way down to her hard rosebud nipples. He caressed one round and round with his tongue. Lola let out a loud groan of desire. Feeling her pleasure grow, she sat in his lap, rocking slightly, the waves of passion controlling her. All of a sudden, Fabian popped her nipple in his mouth and sucked so hard that Lola came with such force she cried out Fabian's name. It surprised both of them how quickly it had all happened. Taking her in his arms, he held her for a moment. He could feel her quivering body as he took in her scent for the last time, putting his own desire aside for now. Thankfully, his jeans had stayed in place. A wave of guilt spread over him as he thought of his life in Paris with Anais.

Lola felt him stiffen slightly. "Fabian, are you okay?"

"Oh, Lola, I'm just very confused. I'm in love with this wonderful woman in Paris. It's just that you've always had the most amazing power over me. Seeing you after all this time, I guess it stirred up a lot of old feelings."

Lola could hear her parents laughing downstairs. She looked at her watch, and thankfully they had only been gone about fifteen minutes.

"We should go back down before they wonder what's going on," Lola said. "Do you want to meet for lunch tomorrow so we can talk this over?" Lola felt a little guilty, too. She wasn't in the habit of messing around with taken men, but with Fabian, it was just different. She also needed some time to think and process her feelings.

"That sounds like a good idea," Fabian said. "How about The Ivy at one?"

CHAPTER THREE

Lola heard her phone buzz and groaned as she rolled out of bed. She headed to the bathroom to splash some cold water on her face; her leather trousers and panties still sat in the sink in wine-stained water. Taking them out, she placed them in the bathtub. The cold water hit her face and brought her fuzzy mind a bit more into focus. She looked at herself in the mirror; the eyes don't lie, she thought—too much red wine for me last night!

After she and Fabian had made their way back downstairs, the evening had run pretty smoothly. She had drunk too much, trying to mask the regret of her lust getting the better of her. He had definitely come on to her first, but she should have resisted. Even a small romantic encounter with a man who had a girlfriend or wife never appealed to her. Thank goodness we didn't go any further than we did, she thought. Fabian's jeans had stayed in place; unfortunately, his tongue had not! I'm not going to beat myself up anymore, she said to herself. After all, it was Fabian who had invited himself into her bedroom.

Lola got back between the luxurious Egyptian cotton sheets. She knew she would feel more clarity once the red wine blur had worn off a bit. It was seven-thirty, early for a Saturday. There was a text message from her business manager, Ingrid Ashton, who also happened to be her best friend.

Hi Lola, so glad you're in London. Let's get together for lunch today. We can talk about some exciting new business opportunities for Jetset Delilah and, of course, have a catch-up gossip! Let me know what time and place work for you.

At the end of the text was a line of hearts and Champagne emojis. Perfect, just what I need, she thought. Ingrid was always the best medicine; they were like sisters and knew practically everything about each other. Plus, in the last five years, she had helped take Lola's company, Jetset Delilah, to the next level with her incredible business sense. There was absolutely no jealousy between them. Each woman played an equally important part in the company. Lola was the creative side, while Ingrid handled the day-to-day running of the home office based in London's Covent Garden area.

Even before seeing Ingrid's text, Lola had decided to cancel lunch with Fabian. Enough had been said already by their actions last night. She thought it was a good idea to put some time and space between them. He was returning to Paris next week, so she probably wouldn't see him again for a long time, which was probably better for them both. Picking up her phone, she wondered whether to call or text him and what to say, not wanting it to be weird or uncomfortable. Suddenly, her phone rang; it was Fabian! Lola took a deep breath and answered.

"Hi, Fabian, how are you feeling this morning?"

"Lola, I'm okay. To be honest, I'm a little confused by my actions last night. Was it a full moon or something?" he joked.

"Could have been," Lola said. "Truth be known, I deliberately trained Rich to knock over my glass at that moment, leading me to undress." He could probably tell she was nervous from how fast she spoke, but he was glad the conversation was light-hearted between them. "Or maybe it's just the effect I have on men these days."

He took a serious tone for a moment. "You have always had that effect on me, Lola, ever since we were kids." Lola was silent for a minute. She could almost feel the sensual touch of his hand. As he spoke, she realised now last night had been very powerful for both of them; it had been impossible to ignore his advances.

"Lola, are you there?"

"Yes, yes, sorry! Look, Fabian, I think it's better for both of us if we cancel lunch today. I feel like I need some time to process this, and you are going back to your life in Paris with Anais. The last thing I want to do is interfere with your relationship with her. Let's not make this any more complicated than we already have."

"That's probably a good idea. Can we keep last night our secret, please?"

"Of course, Fabian, I promise I will. You take care."

"You, too." They hung up at the same time.

Lola lay back on the down pillows and took a few deep breaths. She was glad the phone call was over, and she had the distraction of her lunch with Ingrid this afternoon. Where would it be fun to go? I know, she thought, picking up the mobile phone again to text Ingrid back.

How about Scott's in Mayfair at 12.30? I'll make a reservation for the bar. I'm ready for a fun lunch. Can't wait to see ya!

Almost immediately, the phone buzzed with a response.

Perfect! See you there!

The doorman greeted Lola as she walked into Scott's. She turned heads in her high-waisted faded flared jeans and white silk shirt, which she had paired with tan suede booties. The look was finished with a vintage Gucci horse-bit bag and one of her signature Jetset Delilah scarves tied around the handle. It was, in true Lola style, effortlessly chic.

Spotting her best friend at the bar, Lola waved. Ingrid was the polar opposite in looks to Lola. She was five feet six inches in heels, which she always wore, even in the snow. Her beautiful, almond-shaped, dark-brown eyes were the kind you could get lost in, complemented by almost black raven hair, not to mention a curvaceous figure that could give Eartha Kitt a run for her money. Ingrid had always joked about feeling lucky to have been given the best body bits and pieces from her Jamaican father and Spanish mother.

"Hi, it's so fabulous to see you. How are you?" The two women embraced before settling at the bar.

"I was here a bit early, so I took the liberty of ordering a bottle of *Veuve Clicquot*. I hope you don't mind," Ingrid said with a wink.

"Do I ever?" Lola laughed. "To be honest, I was a little overserved last night at my parents' house. You know how my mum loves her French wines; they were on a roll, especially since the Whitecliffs joined us for a very fun dinner."

"Including Fabian?" Ingrid, of course, knew Lola's history. Fabian had been her first real boyfriend. The bartender poured a glass of Champagne for Lola. As she took a sip, she felt the bubbles warm her cheeks, or was it a flashback to last night's tryst with Fabian that warmed her body? As much as she usually shared everything with Ingrid, she decided to keep last night a secret to honour Fabian's wishes, as they had agreed.

Luckily, the bartender interrupted. "Are you ready to order something to get started?"

Ingrid turned to Lola. "Shall we just order what we normally do?"

"Sounds good to me."

"We will start with a dozen Jersey oysters, and then we'll split the Dover sole." The bartender took their order and refilled their Champagne flutes.

Ingrid couldn't wait to inform Lola. "So, I have some exciting news for you. I just got an email from the buyer of Deux Margaux in Paris, and they want to do a large order of Jetset Delilah scarves. They will also take some for their St. Tropez and Monte Carlo boutiques and La Petite Deux Margaux in the Hotel du Cap-Eden-Roc."

"That is fabulous news! When do they want them?"

"As soon as possible!"

They had been trying to get Jetset Delilah into Deux Margaux for years. It was one of the most prestigious fashion stores in Paris, and the boutiques on the French Riviera were often visited by celebrities, especially during the Cannes Film Festival. If film stars were photographed wearing these accessories, Jetset Delilah would undoubtedly be thrust into the global market.

"Let's try and get the order filled by the end of next week before I go back to France."

A dozen oysters arrived. Lola wondered, as she always did when she ate oysters, if today she would finally discover a pearl. She watched as the bartender put two fresh glasses of *rosé* Champagne in front of them.

"Sorry, but we didn't order these," Lola informed the bartender. "We still have some of the Veuve left."

"The gentleman across the bar sent them to you," the bartender responded. "He said if you were eating oysters, you simply must pair them with a glass of *Cristal Rosé*."

Lola and Ingrid giggled together and looked up coyly to see a man on the other side of the bar waving at them. They raised their glasses to thank him. Lola did a double-take. Memories she had ignored and pushed away deliberately came back instantly. She knew the man; she was pretty sure of it. The short white-grey hair and the light blue eyes. He was a lot older now, but he still had that certain something that was incredibly attractive. What a coincidence, Lola thought. Of all people, Max Valentine-Smithe.

"Ingrid, I know him," she said in a hushed tone. "His name is Max Valentine-Smithe; he was an old acquaintance of my dad's. I haven't seen him in years, but I visited his big horse farm in Hertfordshire when I was eighteen or something."

Ingrid didn't have a lot of time to respond because Max was making his way over to them.

"What a surprise," said Max. Lola turned. Yes, it was definitely Max draped in Armani with those amazingly sparkling eyes you could hardly look away from.

"Max, wow, this is a coincidence; it's been years. Let me introduce you to my best friend, Ingrid Ashton."

Ingrid shook his hand. He really was attractive. She felt his eyes drift slowly over her body. She was glad she had decided on the peach skin-tight leather pencil skirt and matching silk shirt, which she had left unbuttoned just enough to show off her spectacular curves.

"I saw you two come in, and it took me a minute to figure out how we know each other. It must be over twenty years ago since you came to the stables. By the way, do you ever see or hear from that stable lad who worked for me back then, Jack Alistair? He called years ago and was looking for you; he wondered if I had your number or whereabouts."

At the mention of Jack, Lola froze. Her thoughts went back to that fateful moment a few weeks ago in Monte Carlo. Over the years, she had tried and done an excellent job of avoiding all contact with him. Jack had called her office many times, but her executive assistant, Jill, had been given strict orders not to put him through. Thankfully, her office had excellent security, and it was impossible to get in the front door or use the lift without a special key card.

"Eh, no, I haven't had any contact with him, and that's how I would like to keep it."

Thankfully, the Dover sole arrived, so Max began to excuse himself. "We should exchange numbers."

Lola didn't want to; instead, she made a weak excuse. "Unfortunately, I didn't bring any business cards with me."

At that moment, Ingrid chimed in. "I did. Here." She pulled a card out of her bag and handed it to Max. He, in turn, gave each of them one of his.

"Thank you for the Champagne." Lola hoped he didn't notice her shaky voice.

Turning to Ingrid, he took her hand. "And it was a pleasure meeting you," Max said, undressing her with his eyes as he took one last lusty gaze over her body.

As soon as he was out of earshot, Ingrid turned to Lola. "He's very hot, don't you think?"

Lola looked at her friend and could see that Max's charms had worked. "If I were you, I'd stay clear of him. Our family has a history with him; some I know and some I'm pretty sure I don't."

"That sounds intriguing."

"If you don't mind, I don't want to talk about it; it's old gossip. Let's move on. I want to hear about your date last week with George."

Ingrid usually took Lola's advice, but she was conflicted. There was such an instant connection with Max, and she knew from the way he looked at her that he found her very attractive. She wondered why Lola had warned her about him. In a way, it made him seem even more exciting. It was interesting that Max had brought up Jack Alistair. She knew a bit about Lola's history with Jack because she had been given strict instructions never to take any calls from him. Lola had just said he was an ex-boyfriend from years ago. That bothered her, as Ingrid always knew there was more to it than that. She figured if Lola ever wanted to tell her the whole saga, she would. Well, we will see if he calls, she thought. What Lola didn't notice was that Ingrid had also slipped Max her own business card. She would leave it up to fate; if he called, she would figure it out then. Could one date really hurt?

CHAPTER FOUR

The next few days were a whirlwind at Jetset Delilah. They were working extra-long hours to fill the order for Deux Margaux and were going to send everything to the flagship store in Paris. Then the Paris buying department was going to decide what to send to the three smaller boutiques in the Côte d'Azur. Lola was very excited about it and was in the middle of checking a long list of emails when Ingrid knocked on the door.

"I'm going to run out and grab a sandwich from Pret A Manger. Do you want anything?"

Lola looked at the time on her phone. "Wow. Half-past two already! Yes, that would be great. I'll have the avocado pine-nut wrap. That sounds very good right now; I'm starving! Thank you."

Ingrid grabbed her Burberry Mac, and she was glad she had. As she stepped out onto the pavement, a chill wind, not uncommon for September, hit her face. It was good to get out of the office for a few minutes.

As she made her way down Long Acre, the cool air felt good. Feeling like a bit of a walk, she decided to go to a different Pret A Manger at the end of St. Martin's Lane instead of the one closest to the office. She passed the St. Martin's Lane Hotel, laughing to herself and remembering all the good times she had had at the bar there. She was lost in thought when her phone rang. She dug it out of her Mac's pocket. It was a number she didn't recognise, probably someone trying to sell something. A minute later, it pinged with a voicemail. Ingrid walked into Pret A Manger and picked up her favourite, a California club and the avocado wrap for Lola. There was a bit of a line, so she listened to the phone message while she was waiting.

Hi Ingrid, this is Max Valentine-Smithe. We met the other day at Scott's restaurant. I was wondering if you are free Friday night because a good friend is performing at Ronnie Scott's jazz club. It's kind of a surprise; he's just going to sit in with the band for a couple of songs. You may have heard of him—Francis Williams. Call me when you get a chance."

Ingrid listened to the message again. She couldn't believe he was friends with Francis Williams, probably one of the most famous rock stars in the world. She had loved the Fuzz, the band he had fronted in the eighties. Ingrid loved musicians, but Lola deliberately had forgotten to tell her this juicy piece of information, as it would have made Max even more attractive. She was giddy at the thought of hanging out with a famous rock star.

I have to go, she thought. It's just one night, and I would be stupid to turn down a meeting with Francis. Plus, just the sound of Max's voice made her pulse race. But what to tell Lola? She thought it was better not to mention it, as Lola would be annoyed and probably hurt that she had gone against her wishes.

After paying for the sandwiches, Ingrid headed back to the office. Not wanting to risk that Lola would overhear, Ingrid decided to call him back before returning to work. Nipping into the St. Martin's Lane Hotel lobby, she sat down on a small sofa and picked up her phone to call Max. He picked up right away.

"Hello, this is Max."

"Hi, it's Ingrid Ashton. I just got your message."

"Great to hear from you, Ingrid. So, are you free Friday night?"

"Yes, I am!"

"How about we meet for dinner beforehand at the bar at J.Sheekey at seven-thirty. Afterwards, we can walk or take a pedal cab to Ronnie Scott's."

"Perfect. I'll see you there!"

Funny, she was practically on the other side of the street from J.Sheekey right now. As she gathered up her bag and walked out of the hotel, she felt a sense of elevated excitement at the thought of a hot date rolled into meeting a famous rock star. It was a shame she had to keep it from her best friend. At the same time, she hoped Lola wouldn't ask her to do something Friday night.

* * *

Friday came quickly. It had been a successful work week. The orders had been sent to Paris, and they had received a call from Harvey Nichols luxury department store in Knightsbridge about potential interest, with a meeting set for next week. Lola appeared in Ingrid's office.

"Hey, do you want to have a relaxed night in tonight? I could come to your flat, and we could order a pizza or something."

Ingrid had already planned a good excuse if Lola happened to ask. "I already told my mum I would talk to her tonight, and you know that is no short call. Plus, I'm absolutely exhausted after our week." Ingrid's Spanish mum lived in Madrid. They didn't see each other very often, so Lola knew how valuable their phone calls were.

"I'm pretty tired, too. I guess I will head home and spend some time with my parents. It's probably a nice thing to do since I leave for the Côte d'Azur on Monday."

Ingrid was relieved; she hated lying to Lola, especially using her mum as an alibi, but she thought it was for the best.

* * *

They decided to wrap up their work a little earlier than usual after such a busy work week. Both women stood on the street to hail cabs, Lola to Montagu Square, Marylebone, and Ingrid to the South Bank. Ingrid's flat was located very close to the London Eye. She couldn't wait to get home and start getting ready for her date. Max had texted her today to confirm he had made a reservation for the bar at J.Sheekey. Thankfully, traffic was not too bad, and she got home swiftly.

Ingrid loved her flat. She had bought it a couple of years ago when Jetset Delilah had started to do well, and her salary had increased. She opened the fridge, took out a nicely chilled Sancerre, poured herself a large glass, and turned on the music system. Francis Williams' "Late Night Owl" started playing. She had been listening to Francis since she knew she was going to meet him. Must stay calm, she thought. I need to be sophisticated and not act like a crazed fan.

Ingrid walked out onto her small balcony. It had just enough room for a café table and two chairs. She was taken in by the smell of the River Thames—not a bad smell, just a musky river smell that always brought her heart home. Sipping the chilled Sancerre, she watched as a couple leaned against the railing of the Queen's

Walk, the wide paved path that ran by the river all the way to Tower Bridge. As she watched, they began to kiss passionately. She looked at her watch. It was time to get ready.

Ingrid's bedroom was her favourite room in the small flat. Painted the palest shade of seagrass, it looked almost iridescent in certain light. She had really splashed out on her bedding, which was pure white except for a fine grey embroidered border on the pillowcases and duvet cover. On the opposite wall hung the most beautiful abstract painting that she loved to get lost in while lying on her bed. It was the colour of the Mediterranean, but most importantly, it reminded her of her mum in Spain. She had purchased it there on a visit a few years ago.

Stepping into the closet, she pulled out the Victoria Beckham dress she had planned to wear and laid it on the bed. It was from a collection a few years ago, but it was so sexy—the deepest red with an exposed zipper going all the way down the back. It paired perfectly with her sky-high Louboutins. She unbuttoned the crisp white shirt and tailored pinstripe trousers she had worn to work and hung them in the closet.

Turning to face the cheval glass mirror, she was wearing white-lace French knickers and a white-lace bra. Ingrid pulled her stomach in, put her hand under the lacey fabric, and stroked the thin landing strip of hair she had dyed fuchsia for fun. Lingering there for a moment, she felt aroused. After slipping out of the fine scraps of lace, she opened the top drawer of a small chest and spotted her favourite black La Perla lingerie; she laid them down next to the dress. Max is in for a treat, she thought, even though she planned on being on her best behaviour tonight. After a quick time check, she stepped into the shower.

Ingrid enjoyed a long hot shower. After towelling off, she rubbed lotion all over her body and finished with a spritz of her favourite perfume from Fragonard—a sexy sandalwood scent. Lola had bought it in France and given it to Ingrid last year as a birthday gift. She dried her hair slowly and spent time with her makeup before slipping into the Victoria Beckham dress. Ingrid checked her phone; thankfully, there were no texts from Lola. She didn't want to have to lie again. It was just after seven, and she planned to leave in a few minutes. She took one last look at her hair in the mirror. She had left it wild and free tonight and gone with a very natural makeup palette. Easing her feet into the Louboutins, she grabbed a fitted black moto jacket and took a final look in the mirror. Yes, you look hot tonight, she thought. The jacket added a bit of rock and roll to the outfit, which she loved. Ingrid locked the door and walked down Queen's Walk. She intended to hail a cab on Westminster Bridge. Heads turned as she walked along the river in the six-inch heels. She felt exhilarated at the evening to come. Luckily, she only waited a couple of minutes for a taxi.

"Where to, luv?"

"J.Sheekey, please."

The cabbie looked at Ingrid in the rear view mirror. She was a beauty all right; she looked like that film star Thandiwe, Thandiwe somebody who had been in *Mission Impossible*. He couldn't remember the star's last name.

He made idle conversation. "Having a good evening, are we?"

"Yes, great, thank you, and I think it's about to get better."

The cabbie laughed. "Good for you, luv."

They were now on St. Martin's Lane and would be arriving shortly. Ingrid pulled a small compact out of her YSL clutch and reapplied her lipstick. She was a little nervous but more excited than anything else. The cab pulled up as close as he could to the restaurant, which was just a couple of doors down on the left.

"Here we go then. Have a good evening. Don't do anything I wouldn't do," he joked.

Ingrid giggled as she handed him the fare and closed the taxi door. The phone pinged with a text; she dished it out of her clutch in case it was Max saying he was running late or something. It was Lola, and she decided not to open the message. It could wait until later. Lola probably wanted to persuade her to come out tonight. She felt just a tiny bit guilty as the maître d' welcomed her to J.Sheekey.

* * *

Lola finished up the text to Ingrid. As she sat drinking wine at the kitchen island with her mother, she could hear her father on the phone calling J.Sheekey for a last-minute reservation. The fish pie was his favourite, and it seemed like a fun, spontaneous idea to go out for dinner before Lola returned to France. She looked at her phone to see if Ingrid had responded; she hadn't. Maybe she's still chatting with her mum in Spain, thought Lola.

Roberta topped up their glasses and poured some Marcona almonds into a small bowl while Richard Chamberlain wagged his tail. Lola laughed at him and rubbed between his ears. That dog is always hungry, she thought.

Ollie walked back into the kitchen. "Well, unfortunately, J.Sheekey is all booked up tonight. Any other ideas, ladies?"

"How about we just walk around the corner to the Chiltern Firehouse restaurant. You know Henry will always squeeze us in," Roberta said.

"Good idea, darling. I'll give them a ring right now. Lola, you better text Ingrid back to let her know the change in plans just in case she decides to show up."

Picking up her phone, Lola texted Ingrid the update and apologised for the confusion. What she didn't realise was that she forgot to hit send on the text, so the newest message sat waiting in her phone unsent.

"Will you two be ready to leave in thirty minutes? I'm getting very hungry; I made the reservation for eight forty-five."

Lola looked at the kitchen clock. Eight, just enough time to do a quick change. She headed upstairs. Seeking comfort tonight after her long week in the office, she fancied wearing jeans. I know, she thought, black jeans, suede over-the-knee boots, and a cream cashmere sweater would be perfect. She still hadn't noticed that she had forgotten to send Ingrid the new text about the change of plans. Lola had no idea that her mistake would put Ingrid into a state of panic, thinking she was going to run into her at J.Sheekey tonight and catch her red-handed dining with Max.

Ingrid, meanwhile, still hadn't looked at Lola's text. She thought she would do so during the next bathroom break. Upon arriving at the restaurant, the maître d' had shown her to the square bar area, where she spotted Max. He was talking to the man next to him whose face she couldn't quite see.

The maître d' announced Ingrid to the two gentlemen. "Mr. Valentine-Smithe, your guest has arrived." They both turned around; Ingrid couldn't believe it. Max was sitting there with Francis Williams! Max stood up and greeted her. "Ingrid, great to see you again." He gave her a quick embrace. "Let me introduce you to my good friend, Francis Williams."

Rising from his seat, Francis shook her hand. Ingrid hoped she appeared calm because inside, she was bubbling with excitement. "Lovely to meet you, Ingrid. Max tells me he met you through Lola Delphine."

"Yes, that's right. Max was very kind to send us some Champagne when he saw us sitting at the bar at Scott's last week. Lola is my best friend, and we work together."

She wondered what the connection was between the Delphine family and these two men. Lola had definitely wanted to avoid any further questions, and she certainly had never mentioned that she knew Francis Williams, which was strange.

Max interrupted, saying, "I think you should sit between us. I just ordered the *plateau de fruits de mer* for us to share. What would you like to drink?"

"I'd love a glass of Champagne, thank you."

The bartender stood in front of them, waiting. Max said, "Great idea! Can we have a bottle of *Bollinger Extra Brut*, please? Three glasses?" He looked at Francis.

"No, I'm going to have a dirty Grey Goose martini with blue-cheese olives, please. I will probably move on to wine after that."

While the bartender began to shake the martini, Francis apologised for crashing their date. He had called Max this afternoon to see about dinner, not knowing about his plans with Ingrid. Wow, she was a beauty; he could see why Max fancied her.

"Max tells me you are going to play a few songs tonight at Ronnie Scott's."

"Yes, some old friends of mine are playing tonight and asked if I'd like to join them. The audience will have no clue, which is always fun. I'm going to play "Late Night Owl," "Sleepwalk Pantomime," and my newest song, "Old Friend, New Lover.""

"That's exciting; I'm looking forward to it."

The bartender put the martini down in front of Francis and poured the Champagne.

"Well, cheers, and here's to new friends." They clinked their glasses, and Ingrid took a long sip. When she glanced across the bar, she caught several people taking a few cheeky photos of Francis when they thought he wasn't looking. A couple of ladies across the bar looked like they were trying to decide whether they should come over. It made Ingrid feel amazing to be sitting in the middle of these two. She was thoroughly enjoying the attention. She could really get used to this.

"Will you excuse me? I want to go to the ladies before the *fruits de mer* platter arrives."

The two men stood up. Perfect manners, she thought. One of the benefits of being with an older man, perhaps. She made her way to the bathroom. As soon as the door closed, she pulled out her phone to look at Lola's message. She froze. It read:

Hi, hope you had a fun talk with your mum. We are going to J.Sheekey tonight, as my dad is craving the fish pie. Meet us, please! It is Friday after all. XX

Looking at the time Lola had sent the text, Ingrid saw that it had been an hour ago. She wondered if they were at a table and she hadn't seen them yet, or if they were on the way. What to do? Maybe there was a possibility they wouldn't see her at the bar. Ingrid pulled out her lipstick and reapplied it. Fluffing her hair, she went into the stall to think for a minute. Well, there's no choice. I will deal with what comes next. How upset can Lola really get?

Ingrid pulled herself together as she left the restroom. Please don't be here, she thought. She didn't want anything to tarnish this fun night or, more importantly, her friendship with Lola. Thankfully, there were no Delphine sightings on the way back to the bar. The seafood platter sat there waiting.

Max stood and pulled out Ingrid's seat and waited as she sat down. Francis was busy typing something on his phone, so she turned to Max.

"So, do you live in London or the countryside? I think I heard you mention something at Scott's about having horses."

"I still have a place in the country in a village called Ashwell in Hertfordshire. I did have a horse yard close to Ashwell for many years after I retired from the music business. Lately, I've been spending a lot of time in London at my flat in St. Katharine Docks."

Ingrid popped a chilled shrimp in her mouth and savoured the flavour; it was so juicy. She took a sip of Champagne and asked, "So, did you work with Francis?"

"Yes, I was his tour manager for many years. I started with him when he was with his band, The Fuzz, so it must be at least thirty years. We ended up knowing pretty much everything about each other, which happens when you spend so much time travelling together. I just needed a life change; it's intense being on the road constantly. The good news is that Francis and I are best friends; he's more like a brother, really."

Francis was now off his phone and reached to grab an oyster from the platter.

"To cut a long story short, I was his boss, ha-ha." He loved to tease Max about it.

Ingrid could tell how close the two men were. Francis turned to Ingrid. "So, tell me about you."

Ingrid started to tell him about her job and the fact that she had grown up in Madrid until the age of fourteen. He really was so attractive—green-blue eyes and blonde hair. Dyed, she assumed, for a man of his ilk. His body was incredibly fit and toned. He had a fashion sense similar to Max's and wore a stylish jacket that Ingrid knew after working for years in the fashion business had to be Armani. The three of them chatted their way through the seafood platter and the bottle of *Bollinger*.

The bartender returned. "Would you like to order anything else?"

Ingrid looked at the menu, and Max spoke up. "Another bottle of Champagne, please. Francis, what are you having?"

"I'll join you in a glass, thanks."

"Would you like to order a second course?"

Max turned to Ingrid. "What else would you like, darlin'?" When he said the word darlin,' his East End accent was very obvious; she thought it was super sexy. She hesitated, looking over the menu quickly.

"Ingrid, how about we get a couple of small plates?"

She nodded. "You pick; it all looks good."

"We'll have the char-grilled Cornish squid, gravlax, and how about a side of french fries?"

Ingrid smiled. "Sounds tasty to me."

Francis shook his head. "All that sounds wonderful, but I think I'll have the bisque. I don't want to eat too much before going on stage tonight."

Ingrid's phone suddenly pinged. Freezing for a second, she wondered if this meant that Lola was here somewhere. She looked around the bar area; it was hard to see most of the restaurant from where they were sitting.

"Everything okay?" Max had noticed Ingrid's face change when her phone pinged.

"Yes, I think I'm going to visit the restroom before all that wonderful food gets here."

She made her way toward the bathroom and stopped dead in her tracks as she saw a swish of blonde hair identical to Lola's. Her mind was reeling. What to do? Maybe she could pass without being noticed. Ingrid studied the woman. Then the woman turned to face her dining companion, and Ingrid let out a sigh of relief. It wasn't Lola, after all. She could see that now; the hair was identical, and that was it. Thank goodness, she thought. Making her way to the safety of the bathroom, she took her phone out of her clutch. Indeed, the text was from Lola. Ingrid held her breath as she read the text:

Hi, so sorry for the confusion, but we couldn't get a table at J.Sheekey. They were all booked up tonight, but we are at the Chiltern Firehouse. I meant to send this text at 8 but forgot to hit send. Sorry!! Hope to see you there. XX

Ingrid was so relieved and began to relax and not worry. She decided to send a quick text back:

Thanks for the update, but I'm in tonight. X

Meanwhile, Francis turned to Max at the bar. "So, you saw Lola the other day?"

"Right, last Sunday at Scott's. She and Ingrid were having lunch at the bar."

"How'd she look?"

"Very beautiful, just like her mother."

Francis was lost in thought as he remembered all those years ago. Roberta had been absolutely gorgeous. She was unique in her looks, almost like a blonde Jane Birkin.

As Ingrid came back to the bar, Max stood up and pulled out her seat. As he did, he touched the small of her back, letting his hand linger there for a few long seconds. She looked up at him, and their eyes met. She felt a rush of pure lust burn through her body. If he could have this much effect on her with a slight touch, what was going to happen next? She could only imagine.

They finished their dinner and the *Bollinger*, which was spectacular. Francis put his credit card down on the bar and looked at the time on his phone. "We better get going; I have a car waiting outside." Ingrid and Max thanked Francis for the meal while he signed the bill.

Getting out of the restaurant took a bit longer than expected as a few people wanted to stop Francis on the way. He was very gracious and shook hands with some of the diners. Ingrid noticed how Max suddenly took charge and steered them all out the door in a quick, smooth move and into the black Range Rover that awaited them on St. Martin's Lane. She noticed a couple of people taking photos as they climbed into the Rover.

The driver spoke up. "Where to, gov?"

"Ronnie Scott's please, Harry."

The Rover took off for the short drive to Soho. As she looked out the window, Ingrid could see that they were now heading down Frith Street. Soho was buzzing with people having fun on a Friday night. She could see the neon Ronnie Scott's sign just ahead. Harry, the driver, slowed down. "Do you want me to pull up at the front entrance?"

"Yes, that will be great. Thank you, Harry."

The Rover pulled up, and Harry got out and opened the door for them. They stepped onto the pavement and quickly moved to the entrance of the club. Recognising the gentlemen, the doorman greeted them and swiftly led them to their seats. They were seated front and centre at a small table close to the stage. This place was legendary. Ingrid looked around. She loved how the table lamps cast a warm red glow over the room, helping to illuminate the photographs of famous jazz musicians that lined the walls. She shrugged out of her moto jacket, and Max put it on the back of her chair.

The waitress approached to take their drink orders, and Max looked over the wine list. "How about a bottle of *Veuve Clicquot*? Is that good for you, Francis?"

"I may have a glass after I go on stage, but can we get a bottle of still water, please?" Francis stood up and excused himself. "I'll be right back."

As Max turned to Ingrid, she could feel the intense electric chemistry between them. He whispered into her ear. "You look gorgeous tonight. I hope you're glad you came out."

She looked at him coyly. "Of course, Mr. Valentine-Smithe, I'm having a smashing time."

He leaned over and put his mouth very close to her neck, right under her ear, and lingered there for a moment. She wanted him to kiss her badly, but he hovered a fraction away from her; she could feel his breath.

"Not only that, but you also smell gorgeous."

As Ingrid turned to him, he moved forward and lightly brushed his lips over hers. She was utterly lost in the moment and parted her lips as their tongues met. It turned her on; she knew now she was in trouble, and there was no going back. They smiled at each other, both knowing what was inevitable. In unison, they took a sip of the Champagne that had just been delivered.

Francis came back to the table. "I just went backstage to talk to the guys one more time about the arrangement of one of the songs. They should be coming on in five minutes. I'm going to play halfway through the first set."

Ingrid thought Francis was such a nice, humble person (and extremely attractive!), considering who he was. Just incredibly gracious and like any other new friend you may meet—quite refreshing for someone so famous.

The crowd started to cheer and clap as the band walked on stage.

"Thank you all for coming tonight. We are looking forward to a couple of hours of playing a lot of our old favourites and some new stuff from our recent album, plus we have an old friend of ours joining us on stage tonight to play a few songs, so please enjoy!"

The crowd clapped again as they started to play the first song, a smoky melody that reminded Ingrid of the type of sounds she had heard on Frenchmen Street when she had visited New Orleans a few years ago.

Ingrid whispered to Max, "How does Francis know them?" When he moved closer to her, she could smell his cologne, which was very subtle but sexy.

He whispered, "The percussionist, Bill Swanson, and Christoph Harper, the sax player, who are some of the best musicians in the world, have toured with him on and off over the years." He softly kissed her ear. The small gesture heated her body. They gave each other another knowing glance.

After the band had played four or five songs, they stopped to introduce Francis to the stage. Ingrid watched as they brought out a stool and a Henman guitar.

"We have a very special guest for you here tonight. Let me introduce Mr. Francis Williams." The crowd erupted into cheers and stood as Francis rose. He gave them both a quick wink as he left the table. He sat down on the stool, and the crowd grew quiet in anticipation of which songs he would sing. Ingrid could feel the excitement of the audience. They probably couldn't believe Francis Williams was playing tonight.

"Hello there! So, tonight I'm going to play three songs. The first one is a song off my new album, *Old friend, New Lover*, which is about when someone you knew years ago shows up in your life again and, without knowing it, opens a window in your heart that leads you on a beautiful new journey together. So, ladies and gentlemen, here it is. I hope you enjoy it!"

Ingrid adored his music and was sad when the third song, "Late Night Owl," finished. The crowd stood and cheered as Francis took a bow. He turned to the band. "Thank you so much for letting me sit in with you tonight." As he walked off the stage, he waved and thanked the audience as they continued to clap.

The band started their next song, and the crowd settled down. Francis joined Max and Ingrid, who congratulated him on his performance in hushed voices. Thanking them quietly, he grabbed the bottle of Champagne from the ice bucket on the table and poured himself a glass. The first set came to an end, and Francis stood up. "Well, it was lovely to meet you, Ingrid." He gave her a friendly kiss on the cheek. "I'm heading out."

Max got up and said to Ingrid, "I'll be right back—just going to help the boss make a smooth exit."

"Sure." She smiled and said goodbye to Francis and told him how much she had enjoyed meeting him. Ingrid assumed a part of

Max's job when he had worked for Francis was almost like being security and monitoring crazed fans who came too close. Max returned to the table a few minutes later. "Sorry about that; part of my job years ago was helping to navigate him in and out of places quickly."

"That's what I thought."

Max lifted the bottle to pour another glass, but there was only a drop left. "Should I order another bottle, or do you fancy a change of scenery?"

Ingrid turned to him, and at that moment he pulled her closer, and their lips met. Thank goodness it's dark in here, she thought. His tongue gently explored her mouth; she was hungry for his touch. Ingrid pulled back slightly and wondered if he could see the desire in her eyes. "Yes, how about a change of scenery?"

Max paid the bill with cash. As he always liked to do, he left a large tip for the waitress. They stood up, and he took her hand as he led her out of Ronnie Scott's to Frith Street. "Would you like to come to my place in St. Katharine Docks for a nightcap? I have some Champagne in the fridge or, if you'd prefer, a lovely bottle of red."

Ingrid knew she should get in a cab and go home, but she was torn. She wanted this so much, and they were having so much fun, it seemed a shame to end the night now. "Okay, just one drink now, Mr. Valentine-Smithe; don't try to tempt me with anything else." She giggled as she said this.

Max nodded, and she could have sworn he winked at her while he stood on the street looking for a cab. Within a minute at most, they spotted the yellow light on an available taxi making its way toward them. It stopped, and Max opened the door. "St. Katharine Docks, please."

"Which side, sir?"

"If you can drop us off on Thomas More Street, that would be perfect."

The cab took off down the very busy Frith Street. Soho was always hopping on the weekends; in fact, it was most of the time. There were people everywhere, standing outside pubs, drinking, or dining *al fresco*. Lots of girls were teetering in heels and stumbling around from too many drinks. People were waiting in line at various clubs, and the atmosphere was very festive. Max put his hand on Ingrid's knee. For the twenty-minute drive, they made light conversation as the taxi made its way through the streets of London.

"Here we are, Thomas More Street."

"If you can pull up right there, that will get us close enough."

They thanked the cab driver, and Max paid. Feeling the chill from the river Thames, Ingrid pulled her jacket around her. As they walked into the former docks area, he took her hand. Ingrid loved it here. She scanned the gorgeous marina with its fancy sailboats and small yachts. They walked past the Dickens Inn, a fun place to have a drink, especially in the summer.

Max turned to her. "Well, here we are then, this is me." He opened the door to Ivory House Apartments. While they waited for the lift, his hand rested on her lower back.

She turned to him. "I also live on the river, on the South Bank, close to the London Eye."

Max looked at her and brought her closer. "Maybe I need to get a speedboat then." He laughed when he said it, and so did she.

The lift arrived, and they travelled up to Max's penthouse apartment. He held her hand, and she felt hungry for his touch. He opened the front door and led her in.

CHAPTER FIVE

D own the river to the east, about a mile away, Jack Alistair sat in his offices on Wapping High Street. He could hear the wind blowing the old sign next door at the Captain Kidd pub. The creaking back and forth reminded him of a boat rocking in choppy water. Jack had worked late tonight but was very excited to have found a buyer for a George Stubbs painting a client had asked him to sell. He loved Stubbs; the beautiful horse paintings reminded him of his childhood and his time working as a stable hand for Max Valentine-Smithe. The job helped pay for his tuition and bills when he was studying at London's Courtauld Institute of Art. Max had had several Stubbs prints around his house, and Jack had always admired them. He opened the bottom drawer of a large cabinet that ran alongside the exposed brickwork wall of his office. Aha, there it was.

Jack pulled out a folder. He smiled when he looked at it. That folder must be at least twenty-five years old, he thought to himself. The folder was covered in doodles that he had done while sitting in various art history classes when he was a student at The Courtauld. He spread the contents of the folder on the desk— various newspaper clippings and photographs lay in front of him. Jack felt his heart sadden as he picked up a photo of a twenty-year-old Lola sitting on her beloved first pony. Penny had long been retired from rides due to her age and some underlying health issues. Lola looked so beautiful and natural as she sat bareback on the pony, whose head was turned toward the camera. Lola was laughing in the picture taken that summer in the paddock in front of the Delphines' estate in Hertfordshire. The barefooted Lola wore an old blue-and-white Benetton rugby shirt with the sleeves rolled up and a pair of denim cut-off shorts. Jack's heart ached when he looked at the photo. He knew now that he would never be at peace until he could tell Lola what really happened that afternoon, one week after the picture was taken.

For years he had tried to talk to Lola about what happened that day, but she had built a wall around herself as the years went on. His endless phone calls and letters went unanswered. One day he had even appeared at Lola's parents' house in London, and they shook their heads and said Lola refused to see him. He heard through a friend years ago that she had moved to the South of France, which somehow made it a bit easier for him. Knowing she was out of the country, he stopped constantly wondering if he would run into her somewhere in London.

As a result, his business became his obsession. He had built himself an incredibly successful career as a highly respectable art dealer. He loved his job and the lifestyle it afforded. The work helped fight the demons and guilt he had lived with all these years. He knew it had affected any relationship he considered. The girlfriends came and went, always complaining he was distant and unable to commit to a relationship. So he just battled on with work, which was the only thing that seemed to bring him some kind of peace.

Jack looked at the desk and the contents of the folder. He picked up a cutting from a newspaper and saw Lola holding a trophy above her head. She had become quite an accomplished horsewoman, and there were several similar clippings on the desktop. A magazine article caught his eye. There she was, the forty-year-old Lola interviewed for *Town and Country* magazine about her accessories company, Jetset Delilah. She was stunning in the photo, wearing a simple silk dress with one of her signature scarves tied around her neck. He wondered if she ever thought of him. He felt like he had done a good job of putting his feelings aside, but that all came crashing down that Friday evening when, in the most unbelievable twist of fate, he had seen her again at the casino in Monte Carlo. Knowing that he was determined to make things right, he had to find a way to talk to her. There was no choice because he still loved Lola with all his heart. The rawness of it shocked him. Even if she would never forgive him, he needed to let her know how he still felt after all these years.

Sitting back in his chair, Jack glanced up at the antique maritime clock on the wall. Twelve-thirty; he was tired. It had been a long day, but suddenly he felt quite calm. Devising a plan, he sent a text message to his personal assistant.

Fiona, please book me on a flight leaving Sunday afternoon to Nice, and book me into the Hotel du Cap-Eden-Roc.

Jack thought for a moment; how long should he stay? He could certainly do a lot of his work from there, and he could visit his collector, Claude Laurent, again in Monte Carlo. Going back to his text, he added that he would need to stay two weeks. That should be a good start; he could always stay longer. Jack put the phone down and climbed a small spiral staircase to his private apartment. He paused at the top to look across the river through the big arched window. Lost in thought, he was sure this time it was the right thing to do. I'm coming for you Lola Delphine, he whispered to himself.

CHAPTER SIX

Ingrid sat perched on a barstool in Max's kitchen. It was a very open-plan layout with an expansive window facing the marina. He had given her a quick tour of the three-bedroom penthouse, and she was impressed with his taste. The place was furnished in almost a Scandinavian style—very light and crisp but with some beautiful elements of colour here and there. Primarily large abstract paintings hung on the walls. Max was busy pouring her a second glass of Opus One, a gift from Francis, who had visited the Napa Valley winery last year. The wine was so smooth. Ingrid was beginning to feel quite tipsy in a happy, relaxed type of way.

"I love your paintings. Do you collect art?"

Max put the wine bottle on the island. "I guess a little here and there. I have some Stubbs prints at my place in the country; they're supposed to be worth something. But I decided I wanted this place to be a bit more contemporary for a change."

Ingrid took a long sip of the Opus, and Max came around to join her. He pulled his barstool closer to her, and for a moment, they just took each other in. She giggled softly as he leaned in to kiss her, his tongue caressing every part of her mouth. It was so intense that it almost took her breath away. He pulled back slightly. "Ingrid, would you like to stay tonight?" She nodded. It was impossible to refuse; she was burning with desire. He stood and picked up the wine bottle and their two glasses and said, "Follow me."

Max led her into his bedroom, which was really more of a suite. She noticed it had a wall of windows and a glass door leading to a long balcony. He put the wine and glasses on the nightstand. Ingrid was dancing a little to the soft music Max had turned on; he sat on the bed watching. She motioned for him to come to her, and as he did, she rubbed her body up against his in a very seductive way. They danced like that for a few minutes. She could feel his hardness mounting beneath his grey jeans. He whispered in her ear, "Why don't I help you out of this dress?"

Ingrid turned around and brought her hair up to a quick top knot, all the time swaying her hips to the beat of "Until We Sleep." He unzipped the wide exposed zipper on Ingrid's dress, and she stepped out of it. The six-inch Louboutins still enhanced her height. He took the dress, laid it neatly over a chair, and went back to the bed as she continued to dance in the black-lace La Perla lingerie. Max watched intently, his excitement growing.

"Come here, Ingrid."

She danced her way over to him and pushed him down on the bed. He undid his shirt and slipped out of it quickly and then attacked his jeans. Ingrid quickly pulled the jeans off, and they landed on the floor in a crumpled heap. She climbed on top of him, and while he watched, she undid her bra. Groaning with desire for her, Max was thoroughly enjoying the show. Playfully, she lifted his arms and pinned them down above his head. As she rubbed her large breasts up and down his chest, her nipples hard and needy, she could feel that his cock had escaped from his boxer shorts.

Ingrid hovered seductively over him, their tongues meeting again. She wanted to feel him deep inside her. Max brought his arms down and grabbed her from behind. He slid a couple of fingers inside the scrap of black lace; she was dripping wet. Ingrid encouraged Max, saying, "That feels so good." He carried on circling and teasing her, playing with the dripping pearl inside. Ingrid was getting so close she moaned, "Oh Max, yes, that is so incredible." Her pleasure was mounting, and she was on the verge of coming so hard she cried out, "I want you inside me now." She shifted back quickly, slipped on the condom he had discreetly put on the bed and guided his rock-hard cock into her, taking him as deep as she could. His excitement was growing quickly, and he knew he could not hold on much longer. As she rode him hard, she cried out.

As the final waves of pure pleasure hit her, he was quick to follow, and with one last deep thrust, he let out a loud groan of contentment. They lay entwined in each other's arms for a short while, and he kissed her neck softly. "How about a little wine, and we can get cosy under the covers."

"Smashing. Do you, by chance, have a spare toothbrush I could use, please?"

"Yes, there's one in the top left-hand drawer, I think, and also a variety of products from various hotel spas."

As Ingrid bounced out of bed, Max commented, "By the way, Miss Ashton, I noticed that your collar and cuffs don't match. The question is, are you a natural brunette or a natural hot pink?"

"Well, Mr. Valentine-Smithe, I'm full of surprises, you know," she said with a cheeky grin. "I'll be right back; don't go anywhere."

He admired her body as she sashayed her way to the bathroom. She probably had the most fabulous breasts he had ever had the pleasure of meeting. As he thought about them, he felt his cock starting to wake up again.

Ingrid splashed cold water over her face and used some lotion. It revived her a bit. She fixed her hair a little, went back out to the bedroom, and climbed into bed.

"That was pretty amazing, Miss Ashton."

She took a large gulp of chilled water that he had placed on the nightstand while she was in the bathroom.

"It really was. Just imagine how good it will be after more practice." She laughed as she said it. They lay close together and drifted off into a deep satisfying sleep.

* * *

Max woke up the next morning and looked at the beautiful Ingrid sleeping. He pulled on some jeans and a tee-shirt as Ingrid stirred and opened her eyes.

"Hi," she said in a drowsy voice. "What time is it?"

"Around seven. I'm going to grab us a little coffee and some croissants. What kind of coffee do you like?"

"I'd love a cappuccino, please."

"I'll be right back. There's a coffee shop just across the dock."

"Thank you."

She heard the door close, so she got up and headed for the bathroom, where she cleaned her teeth and tried to make herself look halfway presentable. There was a white towelling robe on the back of the door. As she put it on, she noticed the logo embroidered on the breast pocket, which read The Tides Hotel. Walking around Max's bedroom, she gathered up all her things and put them on the chair with her dress. She blushed a little as she remembered the seductive dance she had performed.

Max walked into the *café* and waited in a short line to order the coffee. As he did, he looked at a small newsstand that displayed the morning newspapers. The front page of one caught his eye; it read, "Francis Williams plays at Ronnie Scott's." Max picked up the paper and turned the pages until he came upon the story. There was a large photo of the three of them entering the club and a short article about how Francis had played three songs, one of them being his newest, "Old Friend, New Lover." Funny, he hadn't noticed any paparazzi last night. As he ordered the coffee and croissants, he folded the newspaper and put it under his arm. He paid for everything, including the newspaper, as he thought Ingrid would enjoy seeing it.

When Max got back home, Ingrid was sitting at the kitchen island in his bathrobe looking at her phone. "Here we go." He put everything down. "I see you found my robe." "Yes, I hope you don't mind; it's very comfy. Where is The Tides Hotel?"

"It's in Miami's South Beach. When I was on tour with Francis, we always stayed there. They have a room called the Goldeneye Suite that is simply fabulous. Oh, by the way,

I thought you might want to look at this."

He opened the newspaper to the article and noticed that Ingrid froze as she looked at nearly a full-page photo of the three of them outside Ronnie Scott's. She studied it for a second. At least it was a profile picture, but anyone who knew her well would certainly know it was Ingrid. She knew at that moment that the secret of her evening would be revealed to Lola but hoped that her friendship would not be shattered. She sat for a moment looking at the article and wondered if that most amazing evening really had been worth it.

Max noticed the change. "How are you doing this morning, Ingrid?"

"Oh great, thank you. I would like to take a quick shower, and then I'll head home and let you get on with your day."

"Okay, I can give you a lift if you like."

She got up and gave him a quick kiss on the cheek. He pulled her in for more, but the newspaper story had certainly frayed her mood, and she swatted him off playfully. All she wanted to do was get home and think about what to tell Lola.

"A lift would be great, thank you," Ingrid said as she picked up her cappuccino and headed toward the bathroom for a hot shower. The water felt good. She let her mind wander over different scenarios about how to tell Lola. Would it be better to wait until Lola called her or make the first move? She would figure it out when she got home. Ingrid had decided not to mention it to Max today; men typically didn't like that kind of drama. Her concern was that she might hear something she didn't want to know and thought talking to Lola first would be a better move. They had been friends for ten years and worked together for five. She thought she knew a lot about Lola's childhood, but there must be more. Mr. and Mrs. Delphine had often included her in family dinners and holiday celebrations. Ingrid did notice that there were some things Lola kept very private, though, and would sometimes shut the conversation down immediately if she ever asked or got too inquisitive. Somehow Max played a part in all of this; the question was, what could it be?

Ingrid dried off. Putting the red Victoria Beckham dress back on felt completely over-the-top for a Saturday morning. At least Max was giving her a lift so she wouldn't have to stand on the pavement to hail a cab, her wild night revealed to the streets of London. They rode the lift down to the parking garage. "That's me," he said, pointing to a black Aston Martin DB11. "An Aston for Miss Ashton," he mused.

"Very nice," Ingrid said as he held the door open for her. They made light conversation as the Aston sped over Tower Bridge and headed west, following the river for about ten minutes.

"Thank you for the lift and such a great evening," she said as he pulled up to her building. Their lips met for a few moments as he kissed her goodbye.

"I'll call you, Ingrid."

Her hips captivated him as she walked away from the car. Max expected her to turn and wave goodbye, but she didn't look back as she opened the door to the foyer of her building. Waiting for the lift, she looked at her phone with dread—already two missed calls from Lola.

CHAPTER SEVEN

Ollie walked into the hallway and picked up the newspapers that had been delivered that morning. Very little gave him more pleasure than looking through them slowly over his morning coffee. He took them back into the kitchen, where Roberta was making scrambled eggs for breakfast.

He looked over the front headline of the top paper. In the right column, it said, "Francis Williams plays at Ronnie Scott's." He turned to the page and saw the photo of Francis going into the club with two other people. He read the short article. "Friday night's performance at Ronnie Scott's was quite a lucky surprise for the audience. Francis Williams stepped on stage to play three songs with some good friends who happened to be the main show at the club last night. The three songs were 'Late Night Owl,' 'Sleepwalk Pantomime,' and his new song, 'Old Friend, New Lover.' Williams arrived with his former tour manager and close friend Max Valentine-Smith and an unnamed woman." The story then discussed his new album and the upcoming world tour. Ollie looked at the picture again. Max, whom he hadn't seen in years, still looked very fit. Suddenly, something about the woman looked very familiar; she looked exactly like Lola's friend Ingrid.

"What a strange coincidence," he said, looking up at Roberta. "You'll never believe who is in the paper today." Roberta paused from buttering the toast as he continued. "Max Valentine-Smithe, Francis Williams, and Lola's friend Ingrid Ashton."

One name sent a shockwave through her body as memories came back from years ago. All she could muster was a nod of acknowledgement as Ollie continued. "Francis Williams was playing at Ronnie Scott's last night; the three of them were photographed outside the club, and there is a short blurb on Francis' new music."

Roberta reached for the newspaper so she could have a closer look. A flood of memories that she had pushed into a private compartment in her mind came back as she looked at the two men she had known all those years ago. Next, she studied the woman and looked up. "Yes, that's definitely Ingrid. I wonder how she knows Max and Francis." Roberta turned away for a moment to regroup.

"Listen, Roberta, I know this is difficult, but I think it's time you faced your past. I'm not going to push you into it; I just think for everyone involved, it's the right thing to do."

She tried to compose herself. Even after all these years, it never got any easier. As she spoke, he could see the sadness in her eyes. "You are right; I just need a bit more time."

Ollie had heard this before, but he knew that this was her decision and hers only. Standing up, he came around to where she stood serving the scrambled eggs and took her in his arms, saying nothing.

* * *

Lola finished tying her running shoes and headed downstairs. She wanted to get going before the forecasted rain arrived. She was just opening the front door when she heard her dad yelling at her from the kitchen. "Good morning, Lola. Do you want any breakfast before you leave?"

"Thanks, Dad, but I really want to get started before the rain starts."

"Okay, enjoy your run."

"Bye," Lola yelled as she closed the front door behind her. She checked her phone one more time to see if Ingrid had responded to her two calls this morning. She hoped to get together for dinner tonight or brunch tomorrow before returning to France on Monday. Her best friend usually got back to her right away, so Lola thought it was a little strange. She zipped her phone into her Lululemon hoodie and took off down the road at a warm-up pace. She would try Ingrid again when she got home.

* * *

Roberta pulled herself together as she served the scrambled eggs. Knowing that his wife needed a distraction today, Ollie asked, "What would you like to do today, darling?"

She looked at her gold Tank Solo watch with a brown alligator strap from Cartier. It had been a twentieth-wedding anniversary gift from Ollie. It was half-past ten, and Mrs. Bell, the cleaner, would be coming soon; she did half days on Saturday. "I'd like to go to Borough Market and do some shopping, and then we could have a late lunch there or somewhere on the river."

"That sounds perfect."

Borough Market was always bustling, and it was fun to pick up unusual food items from the different vendors. They finished their breakfast as Richard Chamberlain waited patiently for a treat. Ollie threw him the last corner of toast. As Rich gulped it down, Ollie laughed and gave him a long pat. Standing up, he tidied up the newspapers and stacked them into a neat pile to the side next to a collection of *Horse and Hound* and *Town and Country* magazines that had featured Lola.

Roberta went to the coat closet in the hall and pulled out a quilted beige Burberry jacket that would be perfect over her tight-fitted polo neck and skinny jeans. She pulled on some Gucci trainers and was ready to go. Ollie grabbed his favourite Barbour jacket, and they headed out of the door just as Mrs. Bell arrived. They greeted her and were on their way.

"I hope she doesn't throw away that newspaper," Ollie said. I want to show it to Lola later."

Mrs. Bell doesn't usually throw things like that away without asking, darling."

A cab pulled up, and they jumped in. "Borough Market, please." The cab sped off. Roberta was glad to be out of the house. She felt that she could escape her memories if she kept moving today. The question remained—how did Ingrid know the two men?

* * *

Forty-five minutes later, Lola walked the last few minutes of her run to cool down. She felt great and was looking forward to a hot shower and something to eat. She unlocked the front door and was met by a happy Rich wagging his tail. She could hear the roar of the vacuum cleaner coming from somewhere upstairs. Of course, Mrs. Bell must be here, she remembered. Lola sat on the bottom stair and untied her shoes; she pulled her phone out of her pocket. Finally, she thought, Ingrid had sent a text.

Hi, sorry it took a while to get back to you. Call me when you can.

Lola thought the text sounded a little weird, and she was just about to call Ingrid back when the vacuum cleaner stopped, and she heard Mrs. Bell say hello.

"Hi, Mrs. Bell, it's Lola. I just came back from a run; is everything okay?"

Mrs. Bell came halfway down the stairs. "I was wondering if you could tell me if your dad is finished with his newspapers. I know Roberta always gets sick of them piling up on the kitchen island, and I'd like to finish cleaning the area."

"Why don't I have a look right now?"

Lola walked back into the kitchen and saw the stack of papers that concerned Mrs. Bell. She put her phone down and looked at the first paper. It was from yesterday, so she assumed her father had already read it since he usually spent a couple of hours in the morning reading them. She put that one aside and looked at the next one, which was dated today, and laughed. On the side of the major headline, it said, "How my goats made me a millionaire." She turned to Rich and wondered if he had that potential; this paper was definitely a keeper! There were a couple more old newspapers that she gathered up to throw out. Assuming the last one was also older, she didn't bother to look at the date. She picked up her phone and the old newspapers and opened the recycle bin. Suddenly, Rich started barking and growling at a squirrel in the garden a few feet away from the large sash windows that lined one side of the kitchen.

"Rich, stop it!" she yelled, but he wouldn't stop pawing at the glass. The squirrel continued to taunt him from the other side of the window. Not paying attention, she threw the papers toward the bin along with her phone and ran to grab Rich, who by now was in a heightened state of excitement. The phone clattered to the wooden floor along with the papers. She grabbed the dog and pulled him away from the window and into the hallway, where she gave him a stern telling off. Looking rather sheepish, he wagged his tail, trotted into Ollie's study, and promptly curled up on his dog bed.

Lola went back into the kitchen and picked up her phone, checking to see if the face had cracked. Fortunately, it was still in good shape. She zipped it back into her pocket for safekeeping and knelt to gather up the newspapers when one of the headlines caught her eye. She looked at the date to see if it was an older paper. No, it was this morning's; it must have been under the stack of old ones. She tossed the others in the recycle bin, picked up today's paper, and laid it out on the island. Lola read the small headline out loud to herself. "Francis Williams plays at Ronnie Scott's." Lola turned the pages until she came to the story and the large photograph that went with it. What she saw took her breath away, and there was not a shadow of a doubt who was in the picture with Francis Williams and Max Valentine-Smithe. It was Ingrid.

CHAPTER EIGHT

Ingrid had tortured herself all morning about what to do and what to tell Lola. She had already had several text messages from other friends who had seen the article. Most of them just wanted to hear the juicy gossip of the night, but Ingrid wanted to keep it to herself for a while, at least until she sorted things out with Lola. Eventually, she had plucked up enough courage to ring after avoiding her phone calls all morning. Now she was receiving no response, and she was sick with worry that Lola had seen the article and was really hurt by the deceit.

Ingrid paced around her flat, not knowing what to do. I know, she thought, I will go over to the Delphines' and talk to Lola in person. She grabbed her Burberry Mac and a tote bag, locked the door, and headed down the three flights of stairs to the car park. She fancied a drive. Even though it was a little chilly, she decided to have the roof down on her black Mercedes SLK. She tied her hair into a high ponytail and turned the music up loud as she eased out onto the street and headed toward Montagu Square, Marylebone.

The drive felt so refreshing; she wished it could have been longer, especially since she dreaded what was about to happen. Finding a parking spot close to the Delphines' Georgian townhome, she almost forgot to feed the meter in her anxious state. Ingrid crossed the square and walked up to the Delphines' home. She stood for a moment staring at the shiny red front door and took a few deep breaths. Using the brass lion door knocker, she knocked twice. As Rich barked on the other side of the door, she looked around nervously while waiting for someone to answer, not knowing, of course, if Lola was even at home. The door swung open, and Mrs. Bell stood there.

"Hello Mrs. Bell, how are you? I was just wondering if Lola was home, by chance." Ingrid had met Mrs. Bell on and off over the years, as she had worked for the Delphine family for a very long time.

"Hi, Ingrid. Yes, she's here. I think she's still in the shower, but you are more than welcome to come in and wait."

"That would be great, thank you." Ingrid followed the housekeeper into the hallway, pausing briefly to pet Rich.

"Why don't you wait in the kitchen? I just made a pot of tea, if you fancy a cup."

"That sounds lovely, thank you." Mrs. Bell poured Ingrid a cup of PG Tips and gave her a small jug of milk and some sugar.

"Right, I'll let her know you are here." Mrs. Bell wandered off, and Ingrid could hear her going up the stairs in search of Lola. Looking around at the familiar kitchen, she recalled the many evenings spent here drinking wine and eating fabulous home-cooked food. Roberta was such a great cook, and they had been so generous with their hospitality over the years. She felt her heart sadden at the thought that she might have destroyed her friendship with Lola over a man she barely knew. Now that she had had plenty of time to think about it, it really wasn't worth it, of course.

While sipping the tea and looking out at the lovely communal garden in Montagu Square, she heard her phone buzz with a new text message. She dug it out of her tote bag. It was from Lola; she read it slowly.

> *Mrs. Bell told me you are downstairs. I don't want to see you. Please leave.*

Ingrid gulped, and the tears started to fall down her face. She texted back.

> *Please let me apologise. I'm so sorry I have hurt your feelings.*

Not knowing what to do, she felt she just had to see Lola. She couldn't leave without having some resolution. She wiped the tears away on the arm of her Mac and put the teacup in the sink. Picking up her bag, she walked out of the kitchen and began to climb the stairway to Lola's room. It was all she could think of doing right now. She knocked on Lola's door. "Lola, it's me. Please, can I come in?" Not getting a response, she turned the door handle and the door swung open. Lola was sitting on the bed in a bathrobe, her wet hair hanging around her shoulders. Ingrid could see the newspaper lying open to her photograph. "Look, Lola, I'm so sorry. I never meant to hurt your feelings like this."

Lola just stared at her in disbelief. "Ingrid, first of all, you lied to me. I asked you to stay clear of Max, remember?"

"Yes, of course, I remember, and I shouldn't have lied to you. It's just that I found him so attractive, and when he called me about going to Ronnie Scott's, I got carried away in the moment." The tears rolled down Ingrid's face while Lola sat like an ice queen on the bed.

Taking a few steps to the bed, Ingrid looked down at the newspaper, pointing at it. "Lola, what is it with Max? And you never told me you know Francis Williams either. You mentioned some kind of history. I just don't understand any of it."

As Lola spoke, her voice sounded shaky. "As I said at Scott's, there's some family history with Max and Francis; some I know and some I'm pretty sure I don't. I can't tell you anything else, especially now that I feel you have betrayed my trust."

Ingrid held onto the bed frame to steady herself. She felt like she had been punched so hard in the gut that all the wind had been taken out of her. "I hope there is something I can do or say to fix this. You know your friendship is so important to me, and I can't imagine not being friends anymore. If I could go back and do things differently, I would." There were a few seconds of painful silence. The atmosphere in the room was intense.

Lola looked up at Ingrid. "Don't worry about your job; I'm very good at separating our friendship issues and working relationship, and I can always use Jill as a go-between." Jill was Lola's executive assistant.

Through her tears, Ingrid managed to speak. "Thank you, Lola. I will make this right; I promise." She turned and walked toward the door and was just about to open it when Lola spoke again.

"Ingrid, just tell me one thing." Ingrid turned around and faced Lola. "Did you sleep with him?" Lola knew the answer instantly as she watched Ingrid cast her eyes down to the floor.

"I did. I'm sorry, Lola." Ingrid opened the door and ran down the staircase and through the hallway. She couldn't wait to get to her car, so she carried on running across the square with tears streaming down her face. Opening her car door, she slumped into the seat and sobbed uncontrollably. She rocked back and forth, trying to calm herself. How could she ever fix this?

CHAPTER NINE

Jack looked at the large maritime clock on his office wall. It was just after ten-thirty. He had a couple of hours before he needed to leave. The car service was picking him up at twelve-thirty. It was a quick drive to City Airport, especially on Sunday. Fiona, his assistant, had managed to get him on a 2.15 p.m. British Airways flight. It was a bit later than he would have liked, but there were fewer flights available since it was Sunday. He would get to the Eden-Roc Hotel in plenty of time for dinner.

The old manila folder had sat on his desk since Friday evening. Jack was lost in a daydream. So many painful memories he had fought for years were coming back to him. Suddenly, he remembered something and opened the folder and emptied it onto his desk again. After looking through everything carefully, he did not find what he was looking for, so he picked up the photo of Lola sitting on Penny and studied it carefully. There it was around her neck, the small gold horseshoe pendant he had given her for her twentieth birthday. He searched the clippings again; it wasn't hiding among them. Jack lifted the folder and smiled a little as he looked at all his scribbles and doodles covering it. He opened the flap and put his hand inside, even searching the corners. There was nothing on one side, and then, suddenly, he felt it wedged into the other corner. His fingers fumbled around; it must be jammed in there, he thought. Jack opened the drawer of his desk and pulled out a pair of scissors, carefully snipped the corner off the folder, and there it was—the gold horseshoe pendant still attached to the broken chain.

Jack had bought the necklace from Alex Monroe, a boutique jeweller in Covent Garden. It amazed him that something so small could represent so much. After climbing the spiral staircase to his apartment, he went to the nightstand. Opening the drawer, he pulled out a little velvet drawstring pouch containing some cufflinks; he swapped them for the necklace, pulled the drawstring tightly, and put the pouch in his breast pocket. The car would be here soon, so he carried his suitcase down the stairs, gathered up the folder, and put it in his bag. Jack sent one last quick email to Fiona before taking the lift down to the waiting car.

*   *   *

After a smooth two-and-a-quarter-hour flight, Jack walked out of the Nice airport terminal and was excited to feel the warm breeze that felt wonderful after chilly London. He jumped in the waiting car the hotel had arranged. His rental car would be brought to the Hotel du Cap-Eden-Roc tomorrow. That was the most convenient plan because the Nice airport had a horrible reputation for long lines when hiring a car. As the car made its way to Cap d'Antibes, he looked out the window at the majestic umbrella pines that grew everywhere on the Riviera.

Jack started to put a plan together in his head; just being here made him feel closer to Lola. Reaching into his breast pocket, he pulled out the velvet pouch and held the delicate pendant in his hand, trying to figure out his next move. He sat looking at it for a couple of minutes before returning it to his pocket. Jack was tired of running away from his heartbreak. It had been with him for years, and he was certain that it had affected the man he could have become. He took the old folder out of his laptop bag and pulled out a few of the photos, hoping to find some kind of clue. The first one was a picture of Lola kneeling to pat a tiny foal. Jack had taken the shot at Max Valentine-Smithe's stables. He had invited her over to see the new foal born a week earlier to one of Max's prized mares.

The next photo was a shot of the Delphine family sitting in the garden at their estate in Ashwell, about a twenty-minute drive from Max's stables. Jack had been invited to lunch because Roberta's mother, Delilah, was visiting from the South of France and had come to celebrate her eight-fifth birthday. In the photo, Lola held her grandmother's hand, and everyone was laughing as they sat around the table covered with the remains of the birthday lunch. She had been incredibly close to her grandmother and was devastated when, a few months after her birthday, Delilah had taken a fall and passed away from complications shortly afterwards. Jack had enjoyed meeting the sweet French woman who shared many entertaining tales about her life on the Riviera.

Delilah had been a successful artist with patrons all over the world. Lola had named her accessories company Jetset Delilah to honour her memory, which he knew her grandmother would have loved. He returned the two pictures to the folder and looked at the last one, which he had kept tucked away in his wallet for years until the memory got too painful. Lola had sent him the photo from France. She was sunbathing in a white bikini at Delilah's pool when she had visited for ten days that summer. Looking gorgeous, she was very tanned, and her hair was almost white from being bleached by the Côte d'Azur sun. She was pointing at the stunning view of the Mediterranean that was shimmering in the distance. Jack had been tempted to accept Lola's invitation to join her for a couple of days, but he was taking summer classes and couldn't get away. He flipped the photo over, and there it was, his first clue to where she might be. On the back, it read, "Sexy in Sainte-Maxime—XXX." He smiled when he read her flirty note. Something else was written in the corner, but it was hard to make out, as the ink had faded over the years. He lifted his sunglasses and squinted at the writing. Holding the photo up to catch the light, he could just make out the faint letters. It read "Villa Bonne Chance" and was dated July 23. The irony of the name made him laugh a little. It was as if Grandmother Delilah was watching and sending him a sign. It gave him more hope than he had had in a while.

CHAPTER TEN

L ola zipped her Louis Vuitton bag closed and took one last look around the room. She walked downstairs to find her parents sitting in Ollie's study, drinking coffee and looking through the Monday morning newspapers. Roberta stood up to greet her daughter.

"Are you sure you are okay, Lola?" she said. Her dad looked at her with concern. They had come home on Saturday from Borough Market to find Lola sobbing in her bedroom, and nothing they could say would persuade her to open up. The only thing she had said was that she and Ingrid had fought. Lola realised that when Jack had pushed her to confront her mother, it was all too much. She simply was not ready to face the truth.

"Yes, Ingrid and I just had a disagreement about something private that I don't want to talk about right now."

Roberta was sad for her daughter, as she knew how close the two friends were. Her dad spoke up. "Does it have anything to do with the newspaper article?"

"Look, Dad, I know you two are worried about me, but please don't be. I will be fine. It will be good to get back to France. I'm going to be busy checking on my new collections, which have just been sent to three boutiques there."

"Well, okay then. If you ever want to talk about it, we are always here."

Her mum gave her a big hug, followed by Ollie. Lola gave Rich one last pat on the head and headed out the front door to the waiting car. The previous month had opened a lot of old wounds, first seeing Jack at the casino, her tryst with Fabian, and now the most devastating—discovering Ingrid had lied to her. Of course, only Lola knew there was so much more to this than the deceit. She needed time to think.

Lola had a flashback of Jack watching her from his car in Monte Carlo. Just the thought of him tugged on her heartstrings; she had been so in love with him all those years ago and had fought returning any of his calls or letters because she was so terrified of opening that window to her heart again. The letters had dried up the last few years, but she had seen pictures of him in the press, and he had been interviewed on television recently talking about a famous Stubbs painting he had sold. Instead of facing her demons, Lola had focused on building her fashion empire. She had had boyfriends on and off but nothing serious, and she wondered if she would ever find a true soulmate again.

Arriving at Heathrow Airport, Lola thanked and tipped the driver who helped her with her bag. Fortunately, the security lines at Heathrow were short, and she made it to the club lounge in no time. Glancing at her Rolex, a fortieth-birthday present from her parents, she saw that it was eleven. She was trying to stick to coffee, but a Bloody Mary on one of the many tables around the club offering a selection of alcoholic beverages was more appealing. She settled into one of the armchairs, took a long sip, and felt the spicy vodka drink work its magic. Lola was busy checking emails on her phone when she heard a man with an American accent ask her something.

"Is this seat taken?" She looked up to see a very tanned, athletic-looking man who was probably about ten years her senior.

"No, it's all yours," she said, watching him as he put a newspaper and his phone on the armrest.

"So, I see you are a fan of Bloody Marys, too," he said, smiling as he picked up his drink.

"Yes, I'm a bit of a nervous flyer, and it takes the edge off."

"I agree! Where are you heading today?"

"To the Riviera, flying into Nice."

"Wow, that's a coincidence. Me too." He smiled at her again, and she noticed that he was very attractive. "I'm Chase Campbell. Nice to meet you."

"Lola Delphine. Nice to meet you, too."

They chatted for a few minutes, and she discovered he was an actor from California and had just flown in from Los Angeles this morning. It was fun to talk to him and, for a while, it helped her forget the stressful few weeks she had just experienced.

"Are you staying in Nice?" Lola asked.

"No, I'm going to a friend's wedding in Saint-Paul de Vence. They are getting married at La Colombe d'Or Hotel next weekend, so I'm staying there as well. How about you?" he said, turning to Lola.

"I actually live in the South of France; my place is in the hills by Sainte-Maxime. Have you been to France before?"

"Only Paris. This is my first time to that region."

"Well, you are definitely staying in the right place. La Colombe d'Or is fabulous, and Saint-Paul de Vence is also home to the Fondation Maeght, a modern art museum designed by Joan Miró that was his studio. It's surrounded by lovely gardens that overlook the village."

He nodded. "I have a guidebook, and I'm going to rent a car at the airport, so I'm looking forward to doing some sightseeing." Lola looked at her watch. It was probably time to get moving to the gate. She was unsure if they should walk together, but Chase made the decision for her. "How about we walk together and see if they can seat us next to each other, if you don't mind?" She didn't mind and enjoyed his easy company, plus it didn't hurt that he was incredibly handsome in a rugged type of way. "Sure, why not?"

They walked side by side out of the club lounge and headed toward the gate, which was only a short distance away. When they got there, they asked the agent at the gate if they could be seated together. Luckily, business class was not that full, so it was easy.

Lola wished she could text Ingrid and tell her about her new American friend and how hot he was. She knew Ingrid would have made some joke about joining the mile-high club, but she pushed the feeling out of her mind and instead turned her attention to Chase. They ordered a couple more Bloody Marys and settled into the flight, chatting and laughing the whole time. It really was a lot of fun.

As the plane was landing, Chase turned to Lola. "Would you like to have lunch or dinner this week sometime?"

She thought about it for a second. Did she need any more possible complications at the moment? Probably not, but it was so refreshing to chat with someone who knew nothing of her weighted heart.

"Yes, that sounds great," she said, digging a business card out of her bag. Suddenly, the plane bounced as it hit the runway, and Lola, not thinking, squeezed his arm in a short burst of fear. He lay his hand on hers and said, "Don't worry, that sometimes happens when they come in too hard or something." He kept his hand on Lola's; she could feel that the attraction was mutual. The plane came to a halt, and they retrieved their bags. Both of them had travelled only with hand luggage, so they walked together toward the exit. Lola's housekeeper, Claudette, was picking her up since she didn't like to leave her car at the airport when she travelled. They were nearing the passenger pick-up area when Chase stopped for a minute and turned to Lola. "Miss Delphine, it was an absolute pleasure meeting you."

She looked into his eyes. "And it was delightful to meet you too, Chase Campbell."

They stood for a moment, and Chase reached up and pushed a strand of Lola's blonde hair behind her ear. It was such a subtle touch, but Lola still felt her body quiver slightly. He touched her cheek and moved closer. Leaning in, he brushed his lips against hers with the lightest, most sensual kiss. Lola stood stuck to the spot, smiling at him, mesmerised by her desire. He was the first to speak. "I am looking forward to seeing you again."

She nodded. "Goodbye for now, Mr. Campbell."

Lola made her way outside. She had just received a text message from Claudette saying she was waiting in the arrival area as usual. Looking for her, she wondered if she appeared flustered from her encounter with Chase. Immediately, she spotted the old red Citroën deux chevaux that Claudette drove. She must have had the car for thirty years, but it still was running strong. Claudette was like family. She had started working for Lola's grandmother, Delilah, when she was eighteen. Growing up in Paris, her parents had expected her to go to law school, but her desire was to write poetry and get it published. She had bolted to the South of France to pursue her dream, and working for Delilah was perfect because she had plenty of time to write.

Over the years, Claudette had had three books published, so when Delilah passed away and left Villa Bonne Chance to Lola, she was thrilled that Claudette wanted to continue working at the house, which worked perfectly for both of them. She came in when needed to do general house and garden work and was happy to cook occasionally. Her specialty was the Provençal dish bouillabaisse, which was a real treat.

Lola waved at Claudette as she put her bag in the back of the car. "*Bonjour, ça va?*" they said in unison and kissed each other once on each cheek as they settled in the car for the hour or so journey. Lola was looking forward to getting home; she couldn't wait to jump in the pool to cool off. They whizzed past familiar landmarks while Claudette chatted away, inquiring after Mr. and Mrs. Delphine and then spending time bringing Lola up to date on local news and anything that had happened in the area while she had been in London.

When they were nearing Villa Bonne Chance, Lola lowered her window and took in the magnificent fragrance of the Côte d'Azur, a blend of Mediterranean Sea breeze, lavender, and rosemary, which grew everywhere here. She looked across at the Bay of St. Tropez, where she saw various yachts enjoying the glorious late afternoon. She could just make out *Les Bateaux Verts*, which were the fast boats that could take one to Les Issambres, Sainte-Maxime, Port Grimaud, and St. Tropez. To the north of Sainte-Maxime was the Massif des Maures mountain range that protected the area from the cold winds of the mistral.

Claudette drove around the last bend and down the winding driveway shaded by the umbrella pines that lined the gravel entry.

As they pulled in to park, Lola looked up at the glorious Villa Bonne Chance. It was always so good to come home. It was a traditional Mediterranean villa that Lola had updated completely last year. The one-story home was L-shaped with a separate small art studio on one side of the pool. Lola had converted the studio into her office when she had inherited the villa from her grandmother.

"Thank you so much for picking me up, Claudette," Lola said as she lifted her bag out of the car and opened the front door. Claudette followed her.

"Do you want me to make dinner tonight, Lola? I did get a selection of cold meats and cheeses, fresh bread, et cetera, if you just fancy something simple."

"Simple sounds perfect. I'm going to unpack quickly and take a swim. Why don't you finish for the day?" Lola heard Claudette shout "goodbye" as she headed into the bedroom.

"Okay! *Merci, à demain.*"

Lola's bedroom featured large floor-to-ceiling windows with breathtaking views of the Mediterranean on one side and the pool on the other. She put her bag on the floor and went over to the bed to stroke her Siamese cats, Domino and Solitaire, who were named after two famous Bond women. They woke up and meowed for attention. After she petted them for a while, they rolled on their backs, wanting more. As she sat there talking and playing with the cats, she pulled her phone out to check the time; it was just after four. Suddenly, she fancied a chilled glass of *rosé*, which would go very nicely with the cheese plate Claudette had left for her.

Lola noticed she had received some voicemails, so she began to listen. The first two were from her assistant, Jill, in London, and there was one from her mum checking to see if she had arrived home safely. Usually, Ingrid would have called, either for business reasons or for a gossip, but Lola had instructed Jill to tell Ingrid that everything would be conducted through her for the time being or by email. It was still too raw to hear Ingrid's voice. Thankfully, Jill had not asked too many questions. The last message was from a withheld number, but the voice made Lola smile instantly.

"Hi, this is Chase. Just wondering when you would like to have lunch or dinner or hopefully both this week."

She could hear his nervousness and anticipation, which she found alluring. He finished the message with his mobile phone number and contact details at the Colombe d'Or. She felt a wave of lust as she remembered the passionate and suggestive kiss at the airport. Lola decided to wait until she had swum and had a glass of wine to call him back. She didn't want to appear too keen, even though she was. She looked at her bag on the floor and decided it could wait, so she pulled a white bikini from her armoire and changed quickly. Gazing at herself in the large antique wall mirror, she noted that the white bikini had gold details on the side, and it reminded her of one she had loved years ago.

Lola walked barefoot to the kitchen, which was an open plan with only a large white Carrara island separating it from the living area. She opened the wine fridge, scrolling for just the right *rosé*. Ah, there it was, the magical pink potion of the Riviera, *Château de Selle*. Grateful that Claudette had stocked both fridges while she was in London, she poured herself a large glass and took a minute to look around her newly decorated home.

She had gone with a natural aesthetic, allowing the brightness of the outside to flow in. Large, comfortable, sand-coloured linen sofas were placed around the beautiful eighteenth-century marble fireplace Lola had found in the Porte de Clignancourt, the most famous antique market in Paris. In front of one of the large windows was a simple farmhouse table and chairs that seated eight, but what took centre stage, besides the Steinway baby grand piano, were the beautiful paintings Lola had inherited with the house. Her grandmother had been an avid art collector, and the collection was an eclectic mix of classics and contemporary paintings and sculptures. Lola's favourite, of course, was the large collection of her grandmother's paintings.

The villa was the perfect size for her, about 2,500 square feet, just two bedrooms and three bathrooms. It was a manageable size, especially since she travelled so much. Lola stepped out to the patio, which was shaded by a large umbrella, and admired the new wicker sofa accented with classic navy-and-white Breton Stripe cushions. On the other side, facing the pool, were four matching sun loungers she had just purchased from a design shop in Les Issambres. It really was the perfect setting.

Lola placed her *rosé* and phone on the side of the infinity pool and dove in. The cool water felt so good that she swam a couple of laps and stopped to look at the stunning view of the Bay of St. Tropez. It was easy to run away here, and Lola remembered again why she had chosen to live in the South of France full time. Swimming back over to her wine, she took a sip and decided to listen to Chase's message again. After a few more sips, she picked up the phone to call him back. She listened as the U.S. phone took a minute to connect.

"Hello, this is Chase."

"Hi, this is Lola, the girl from the plane."

He laughed when she said that. "Funny girl, how could I forget you? So, what's your schedule look like this week?"

"Since you're visiting, is there anywhere you've read about that you would like to see?"

"Lola, I have a feeling you're the expert."

She had a think for a split second. "How about Wednesday at around ten? You could come to my place, and we can drive together to St. Tropez and do a little sightseeing, then head on to Club 55 in Ramatuelle for a late lunch. I will text you my address after we get off the phone."

"I'm looking forward to it, Lola. See you Wednesday!" She was about to hang up when he said one last thing.

"And Miss Delphine?"

"Yes?"

"I just can't stop thinking about that kiss in the airport."

She laughed for a second and hung up the phone to text him her address. Well, what a perfect elixir to make you forget the woes of the last month, she thought, as she sat on the side of the pool sipping the chilled *rosé*.

*   *   *

Lola awoke early Tuesday morning and headed out for her daily three-mile jog after a quick coffee. She loved running in her neighbourhood. It was fun to look at the pretty villas that lined the streets with the Mediterranean backdrop. It would be impossible to tire of this view, she thought. She loved her morning runs; it gave her time to think, and she always joked that it was cheaper than therapy. The phone suddenly interrupted her thoughts. She saw that it was Jill. Since she was nearly home, she answered.

"Hi Jill, how's everything going?"

"Hi, good. I'm just calling to let you know I just got an email from Deux Margaux, and the shipment to the Riviera stores arrives

Thursday. The buyer in the region, Clemence Dubois, would like to meet with you once they have Jetset Delilah displayed in the stores. She also wants to know if you are free on the twentieth because she would like to invite you to a *soirée* at the Hotel du Cap-Eden-Roc.

"Sounds fun. Forward the email to me, and I will personally reach out to her this afternoon. Thank you, Jill."

They hung up just as Lola was opening her front door. Domino was there to meet her and appeared to be ready for breakfast. She picked her up, and the cat purred loudly. Lola sat her down on a barstool and opened a can of food. "Here you go, kitty," she said as Domino jumped down to start her breakfast; her sister Solitaire quickly joined her. Lola moved into the kitchen, heated a croissant, and had another coffee. She started to go through the post, separating the business post from the other stuff, which consisted of a couple of magazines and an invitation to attend a charity gala at the Hôtel Martinez in Cannes.

After a quick shower, she headed out to her poolside office. It was such a lovely space. Delilah had added it after she purchased the villa and had designed it deliberately to catch the optimum light she needed for her painting. There was still the lingering smell of oil paint that always reminded Lola of when she would visit her grandmother all those years ago. Lola sat down at her desk and opened the computer. First, she responded to Clemence Dubois's email. She attached her mobile phone number so they could decide on a good time to meet next week. She also gladly accepted the invitation to the Eden-Roc *soirée*, which Deux Margaux was hosting; it was a thank you to all their most loyal customers. It was taking place in the Champagne Lounge, which sat above the hotel's legendary pavilion. It would be an excellent opportunity for her to promote her brand, and she was glad to get one last visit there before they closed for the winter months. Lola's day flew by, mostly returning emails and talking on the phone to the London office. Since she was taking time off tomorrow to spend with Chase, she felt the need to work late. Finally, at around eight, she wrapped up for the day. She stood up and stretched, and for some reason, her grandmother's old wooden art box caught her eye. She had found it a few years ago in a small storage space above the studio. It mostly contained old paints and brushes, but she couldn't bear to part with it, so it sat on the bottom of a bookshelf for a few years. Lola had never looked through it properly, as she assumed it was just old art supplies. She was compelled to take it with her so she could have a proper look.

Lola walked by the now-illuminated saltwater pool that looked so inviting at dusk and over to the main house carrying the box, which she set on the kitchen island. She turned on some lamps and admired the vase of white roses that Claudette had very thoughtfully arranged. They sat on the coffee table in her favourite crystal vase, which she had found at the weekly antique market in Antibes.

Pouring a glass of Châteauneuf-du-Pape, one of her favourite red wines, she heated some quiche Lorraine and made a small salad; it was all she felt like eating tonight. Lola sat on a barstool and enjoyed a sip of wine. She ate a bite of quiche and started to look through the box, taking the paint tubes out one by one and lying them on the kitchen island. She could see something wedged to the side of the box, but it appeared to be stuck there. Lola got a butter knife out of the drawer and gently eased it away from the wood. She managed to get it out with very little damage.

It was a photo of something. She picked it up to have a closer look and couldn't believe the memories that came flooding back.

It was a photo of her sunbathing in a white bikini and pointing at the view here at the villa when she was probably only twenty. She remembered she had made a couple of copies, one to give to her grandmother and one to send to Jack in England. Lola recalled that she had written Jack a saucy message on the back of the photo. She picked it up and took it over to a table lamp in the corner so she could see it more clearly in the light. Inspecting it closely, a great stream of unlocked emotion suddenly filled her. Lola immediately recognised the gold horseshoe pendant around her neck. She hadn't thought of that pendant in years. As the tears rolled down her cheeks, she thought back to when Jack had given it to her for her twentieth birthday. After that, she has never taken it off until that devastating day later that summer.

Sitting quietly, Lola wondered where the necklace was today. She got up, put the paints back in the box, and set it on the floor next to the door so she could take it out in the morning. She put the photo on the table. It amazed her that something as small as an old pendant could have such an impact on her. She had completely lost her appetite, so instead she poured another large glass of wine, grabbed the bottle, and sat down on one of the comfortable sofas.

The two Siamese cats jumped up to join her. She was glad for the comfort as they both snuggled next to her, wanting to be petted. She thought about cancelling her day with Chase tomorrow, but it seemed that he would be a perfect escape plan for her troubled mind, and she was looking forward to seeing him. It will be all right, she said to herself, but she couldn't help the guttural feeling deep inside that Jack Alistair still held a large piece of her heart.

CHAPTER ELEVEN

Fabian opened the balcony door. The air felt good after being in an office all day. He looked down at rue de Turbigo, which was busy for a Tuesday night, and wondered when Anais would be home. She had done a cover shoot for French *Vogue* today, so he knew she might be late. He loved living in Paris; it was charming, and it never ceased to amaze him that one could stumble on so many undiscovered jewels in the city. He shut the balcony door and sat down on the sofa. Picking up the wedding invitation that was on the coffee table, he read it out loud.

Please join us for the wedding of Scarlet Jones and Riggs Howard.

Scrolling down to the details, Fabian saw that it started at two with an intimate ceremony followed by a reception and dancing. There was also going to be a small dinner on Friday night and a brunch on Sunday at *Château Eza*, which was in the stunning medieval hilltop village of Èze. He was looking forward to going to the South of France and was excited to talk to Anais about extending their trip for a few days. He was also looking forward to meeting Scarlet finally. He and Anais had gotten to know

Riggs quite well, and they were flattered to be included in the wedding celebrations. They always made an effort to support the art gallery he was backing, and Fabian had already bought two paintings that were hanging in their hallway.

The phone in his pocket started to vibrate. He pulled it out and saw that it was Anais. "Hello, darling. How did it go?"

"Hi. We were in the Rodin Museum for most of the day shooting. I'm pretty tired but very excited; this is a big deal having a fifty-five-year-old model on the cover. As you know, in this industry, they typically use very young girls."

"Well, you look like a young girl, darling."

She laughed when he said that. "Thank you, Fabian, you're good for my ego! Listen, do you mind if I meet Nadine for a late dinner at Frenchie? You know, the one on rue du Nil."

"No, not at all. I might have an early night tonight. It's been a long day at the office, but can we talk about last-minute details for our trip in the morning? I think that after the wedding, we should tag a few more days onto the trip. You know how beautiful the South of France is this time of year. I'll contact the Colombe d'Or to see if they have availability past the weekend; otherwise, we could always find another hotel."

"Yes, let's talk about it in the morning. *Salut.*"

Fabian looked at the time. It was nine-thirty, so he decided to get in bed and watch a film. He figured Anais would be at least a couple of hours with Nadine, who notoriously always seemed to have man problems. She wanted to meet with Anais at weird times because of some drama or other. He had never met Nadine; apparently, she was a fashion photographer, and that's how the two had met. He walked into their bedroom and started flipping through the TV guide until he found something that looked half decent. Settling on the bed, he yawned and started to doze off with no idea what Anais was really up to.

* * *

Simultaneously, across town at the George Cinq Hotel, Anais opened the bathroom door and walked back into the bedroom, holding her glass of wine. "Well, I just bought myself a couple more hours with you, Riggs. Fabian thought my photoshoot ran late, and I just told him I was having dinner with Nadine, but after you get married on Saturday, all this has to stop."

Riggs Howard looked at the commanding, nearly six-foot naked woman standing in front of him. He knew she couldn't give him up. She had tried many times and always came back. Her peroxide blonde hair was cut almost like Twiggy's famous do from the sixties, and he could see her enormous green eyes staring at him from beneath the long fringe. Their arrangement had suited him perfectly. He had been alone in Paris for six months while his fiancé, Scarlet, stayed in Houston to pack up the house and sort out a few loose ends before moving to be with him.

Riggs wondered if he was making a mistake getting married again. He already had a son, Bentley, with his first wife, and at sixty-five, he had no intention of having more kids. Bentley was in his late thirties now, and Riggs had enjoyed helping him get the art gallery up and running. Scarlet had threatened to leave him if he didn't commit to her completely, so Riggs had acquiesced. There was just something about having a thirty-year-old woman hanging on his arm that stroked his ego in a big way.

"Come here, lovely." He patted the down duvet as she walked over to him. She was so willowy and had the longest legs he had ever seen. He looked down at her beautiful muff, as he called it.

There was only the slightest fluff of blonde hair that barely covered her moist lips. He felt himself beginning to get hard. Anais stood over him and pulled the covers back. He was still in decent shape for a man of his age. She seductively flicked his cock with her long red fingernail; instantly, he was rock hard. She reached for her oversized handbag, which she always carried to model shoots. She unzipped it and pulled out a pair of handcuffs and a small black-leather riding crop. In one swift move, she cuffed Riggs's hands above his head. He laughed a little nervously. "Does this mean I've been a bad boy then?"

"Shh, no talking, and I mean that." She took the riding crop and slowly started to circle the base of his cock with it. She could tell he wanted to make a noise, but it amused her that she was in total control, and he kept quiet, not knowing what she might do. She ran the crop up and down his body slowly and positioned herself on top of him, her wet muff suspended a few inches from his hungry cock. Gradually, she started to increase the strokes to small lashes. Riggs muffled a groan of pleasure. Watching her hover over him was too much; he was desperate to pull her down and ram himself into that wet heavenly place. Anais lowered herself down and let the tip of his cock enter her for a split second, then jumped off and stood looking down at him. "Beg me for more, Riggs." She had the crop pointed at him and a look of pure control in her eyes.

"Please, more, Anais. Please, I'll do anything."

"Now, that's what I want to hear." Anais was dripping wet with excitement herself as she climbed back on top of him, squatting above his needy cock, this time facing the other way, so he had the view of entering her from behind. Very slowly, she eased down on him; she felt the smooth tip begin to enter her and suddenly, she came down on his cock so fast he let out a sound of complete rapture. Anais rose up and down on his cock, riding him as deeply as she could. Focusing now on her own ecstasy, she was getting close as the waves of euphoria started to take over. She could tell he was about to explode, so with one last deep thrust, she screamed out in pleasure as the final wave engulfed her. He was seconds behind as he cried out her name, and she felt the warm juice fill her up.

Anais climbed off him, walked to the bathroom, and turned on the shower.

"Well, aren't you going to unlock me first?" he yelled. He could wait, she thought as she smiled and closed the shower door, enjoying the warm water on her tired body. After five minutes, Anais turned off the shower and dried off quickly. While she was getting dressed, she could hear Riggs begging her. "Please unlock me, Miss Anais. My wrists are hurting, and I don't think I can feel my right arm."

"Did I say you could talk? You broke the rules; you only talk when I say so." Anais put the riding crop back in her bag and smiled.

"That was great; thank you, Riggs. See you on the Riviera."

"No, really, Anais, this is not funny anymore. You do remember we are in a hotel, right? What if housekeeping finds me like this?"

Anais closed the door and walked down the hallway to the lift. As she rode down to the lobby, she laughed to herself. That will teach him, she thought. The doors opened, and she walked over to the front desk.

"*Bonsoir, madame.* How can I help you?"

"*Bonsoir, monsieur.* I was wondering if I could order room service to be taken up to room 333. Last name Howard. My husband is up there, and he asked if it could be brought up immediately and for the server to bring in the food. No need to knock. He has a bad back and is resting it at the moment."

"Absolutely, *madame*. Would you like to see a menu?"

"No, I looked at it before I came down. He would like the chateaubriand, extra bloody, *s'il vous plaît*. Oh, and would the waiter please give this to him? I forgot, and I don't really have time to go back up." She gave him the key to the handcuffs along with a huge cheeky grin.

"Of course, *madame*. I assure you that it will be taken care of immediately."

"*Merci beaucoup.*" Anais walked out the door of the George Cinq Hotel and didn't look back. She jumped into a waiting cab and headed home to rue de Turbigo.

* * *

Anais let herself into the apartment quietly in case Fabian was sleeping. She walked softly down the hallway to the bedroom, saw that Fabian had dozed off, and turned off the television. He stirred as she put her bag down.

"Hi, darling, how was your dinner? What time is it?"

"Dinner was fine. You know Nadine; always some kind of man problems with that one." She looked at her watch. "It's just after eleven." Anais started to undress, laying her clothes neatly on the ottoman at the end of the bed. He watched her and considered if he had enough energy for a bit of naughtiness. She climbed in, and he snuggled behind her, kissing the back of her neck.

Out of the blue, he suddenly said, "You smell different somehow." Anais tried not to let her body tense up. He was probably smelling the hotel products she had just used. She should have been smarter and just let the water run over her body.

"Well, you know how much makeup they put on you on these photoshoots, so it could be that. Also, one of the other models was showing me her new perfume, and I sprayed some on myself."

Fabian was silent, making Anais very nervous. She turned over to face him and realised from his heavy breathing he had fallen back to sleep. A wave of guilt came over her; she really intended to give up Riggs. This had been going on for nearly six months, and there were only so many times she could use her imaginary friend Nadine as cover. This weekend in the Côte d'Azur is going to be very interesting indeed, she thought. Anais was beginning to doze off when a quote from Somerset Maugham drifted into her mind; it perfectly summed up what she was thinking about the French Riviera—"a sunny place for shady people."

CHAPTER TWELVE

L ola woke up early Wednesday morning after having slept poorly. She opened her eyes slightly to see Solitaire sleeping on the other pillow and reached over to stroke her and, in turn, got rewarded with a loud purr that made Lola smile a little. She lay there for a moment thinking about the photo, wishing she could tell someone her story, but she didn't trust anybody with that much of her heart. Despite feeling fatigued, she got up, made a quick pot of coffee, and changed into workout clothes. A run was just what she needed. It was half-past six, so she had plenty of time before getting ready for her date at ten with Chase.

Running out of her driveway, Lola made a left onto the street. Besides greeting a couple of people taking their dogs on an early morning walk, it was very quiet and peaceful. The sun was just coming up, and the quality of light threw a dusty-rose glow over everything that was absolutely beautiful. She was constantly reminded why so many artists had chosen to make the Riviera their home over the years. After about two miles, she stopped for a moment and looked out across the Bay of St. Tropez. The cool sea air revived her spirit, and she already felt better than last night. She decided to head back so she could check emails and have a light breakfast, plus she needed to figure out what to wear for her hot date.

The thought of Chase made her sprint half the way home. She slowed to a walk as she made the last bend and noticed as she walked through the open gate of her villa that she really should get the villa's Bonne Chance sign restored or have a new one made. Age had gotten the better of it in the last few years. Claudette's Citroën was parked in the driveway; as Lola got closer, she could see Claudette watering the big tubs of lavender and rosemary beside the front door.

"*Bonjour,* Lola." She smiled and waved as she continued to water various plants around the entryway.

"*Bonjour.*" Lola walked into the villa and poured herself a coffee and a large glass of water. She grabbed a *pain au chocolat*, which was still warm. Claudette must have stopped at La Tarte Tropézienne in Les Issambres on her way in.

Lola checked emails on her phone. She had already told Jill she was taking most of the day off and to forward anything important so she would take care of it tomorrow. She scrolled down, and there was one from Ingrid. She debated not opening it now, but Ingrid did run the London office, and it could be something important. It read:

Dear Lola,

I miss you. I want you to know that I have not returned any of Max's messages. Our friendship is very important to me. I wanted to let you know that in case it makes a difference. Love, Ingrid.

Lola read the message again and didn't know how she felt about it. Seeing his name in print sent a shiver through her body. She put the phone down and walked over to the table where the photo still sat from last night. She looked at it one last time and brought it with her to the bedroom, where she put it in the nightstand drawer in between the pages of an old childhood Beatrix Potter book, *The Tale of Jemima Puddle-Duck*, for safekeeping.

She threw her running clothes into the laundry hamper and stepped into the shower. Spending a long time soaping her lean body and getting lost in the moment, she felt her nipples harden as she massaged each one lightly until the suds had washed away. After showering, she felt revived and fresh. Somehow, the sleepless night was forgotten for a while. She walked into the closet, which was just beyond the bathroom. She had added the spacious closet when the villa had been newly decorated last year. Such a closet was considered a luxury since not many older houses in the area had any kind of closet at all.

Looking around, Lola ran her hands across some of her dresses, trying to decide what would be perfect for today. The weather was still quite warm, as it often was in September. She decided on a short silk olive-green slip dress and natural-coloured gladiator sandals. She pulled out her tan Hermès Evelyne crossbody bag, perfect for St. Tropez. To finish off the look, she wore a leather necklace with a large baroque pearl attached to it. As she tied the leather cord in the back, she remembered the last time she had worn it was the fateful evening at the casino when she had seen Jack. It was the first time she had seen him in over twenty years. She quickly shut down the memory and carried on getting ready.

Lola rubbed lotion on her legs, spending time massaging it into the crescent-moon-shaped scar on her lower leg. She took some tinted concealer and skilfully applied it throughout the area. She wanted to make the scar invisible today, so she wouldn't have to answer any questions about it. Next, she applied minimal natural-looking makeup and let her hair dry naturally, giving it a very sexy beachy effect. She looked at herself in the mirror and was happy with the ensemble. It felt good to get ready for the fun day ahead. Chase would be here in fifteen minutes, so she walked into the main living area and made sure everything looked exactly as she liked it. The white roses still looked beautiful, and she leaned down to take in their scent.

At five minutes before ten, there was a knock on the door. Lola admitted to herself that she was a little nervous as she opened the door.

"Hi, Lola. How are you?" he said, looking at her intensely. "You look fabulous."

"Great to see you, Chase. Please come in." He followed her in and shut the door behind him. "Wow, this place is stunning," he said, looking around.

"Would you like a quick coffee before we leave?"

"That would be great, thank you!" He sat down on one of the barstools at the marble island while she fixed them each a coffee.

"Milk, sugar?"

"No, black is great for me," he said, giving her a film-star smile.

He looked as handsome as she remembered and was wearing a white Lacrosse shirt, faded distressed jeans, and a pair of saddle-coloured suede drivers. The look was incredibly sexy.

Lola put the coffee in front of him and said, "I made the reservation at Club Cinquante Cinq for half-past one. That way, we will have a bit of time in St. Tropez before lunch. Have you heard about the place?"

"No, but I'd like to."

"It's on Pampelonne Beach and has been there since 1955, hence the name. When Brigitte Bardot filmed *And God Created Woman*, the cast and crew would frequent what used to be an old fishermen's hut. A local couple, Bernard and Geneviève de Colmont, would serve simple meals to them. Over the years, it developed from a beach shack into a very chic beach club and restaurant."

"That sounds very cool," Chase said, looking around the room. He stood up and looked at the painting that was hanging above the dining table. "This is beautiful."

"Thank you. My grandmother, Delilah Cornel, painted it. She was quite a well-known artist around here. Many of the big hotels commissioned paintings from her, even the famous Hotel Eden-Roc. I think they have six or seven pieces hanging in some of their suites."

"That's interesting; you'll have to tell me more over lunch," he said, smiling again. He stood, looking out over the pool. "That view is amazing!"

Lola smiled at his enthusiasm. "I know. I never tire of it and feel fortunate that I get to live here most of the year. We should get going," she said as she put the coffee cups in the dishwasher.

He followed her out the front door. His rental car, a silver BMW SUV sat in the driveway. She didn't see Claudette's Citroën; she must be at the supermarket. She had told Lola she would leave her special *bouillabaisse* in the fridge for dinner tonight.

"Why don't I drive?" Lola said. "I know the way like the back of my hand."

"Are you sure?"

"Yes, of course." Her white Porsche 911 was parked on the side of the villa underneath an awning. Chase went around to open the door for her. As he did that, his hand grazed the curve of her figure. She turned to him, and for a second, their eyes met. It was a very subtle touch but just enough to get Lola's attention as she climbed into the Porsche. They decided to keep the roof on so they could talk on the journey. As they were pulling out of the driveway, Chase looked back at the gate as they made a left onto the main street.

"I noticed your villa is called Bonne Chance; that means good luck, right?"

"Yes, my grandmother used to own the villa, and she named it that because she said it made her happy when she was here. I inherited the villa when she passed away many years ago."

"Was she French, then?"

"She was born here but grew up spending her time between London and Paris where her family owned a music shop. She is my mother's mother. The villa had been in her family for many years, so when I was growing up, we came here often. My grandfather died when I was just a baby, so she moved here full time to paint. I really miss her; we were very close."

He put his hand on her knee in a comforting way. She thought it was a very sweet gesture. The scenic drive along the winding coastline offered inspiring views of the Mediterranean. Fortunately, traffic wasn't too bad today.

They chatted constantly about their lives. She was intrigued by his acting career, so she asked him, "Are you in anything at the moment?"

"Yes, I'm in a night-time soap opera called *Balderdash*. It's about a large wealthy family in Los Angeles who have a British butler with the same name. It's your typical soap opera with affairs, murder, and conflict all wrapped up in a glamorous package," he said laughing. "I play the dad, Blake Baron."

"*Balderdash*, that's hilarious! I think the only person who would ever say that is Mr. Darcy or maybe one of the older gentleman members of the Garrick Club in London."

"I may have to start bringing the word back in your honour, Lola," he said, laughing.

Chase really was pleasant company, and she was glad she had not cancelled. It was fun to show someone new around, and it certainly helped that he was very easy on the eyes. They parked on the edge of St. Tropez's Old Town, *La Ponche*, and walked through the charming cobblestone alleyways, stopping to look in the windows of various art galleries and boutiques.

Lola guided them toward the Vieux Port, St. Tropez's famous harbour lined by *cafés* and shops. They were just across the street from the Hermès store when Lola pointed, saying, "There's Deux Margaux, the store I told you about that is going to sell my collection."

"Can we go in and see it?"

"It's not there until tomorrow, and then it will probably take a few days to get the display together. I am excited to have Jetset Delilah in all three Deux Margaux stores, plus they are having a fun *soirée* at the Eden-Roc Hotel. All their best customers have been invited."

They walked along, looking at all the boats and superyachts docked along the quay. Lola looked at the time. "Well, we have time for a little drink here, if you like, and then we should head to Cinquante Cinq."

"Sure, a cold beer sounds really good right now."

"I know just the place, La Petite Plage. It's just over there," she said, pointing at a charming-looking restaurant completely open on one side, offering fantastic views of the water and an array of superyachts. They made their way to the restaurant. Chase noticed the light covering of sand on the floor, and the ambience was very beachy with wicker-and-linen seating and Rotan light fixtures hanging over the tables. They were seated at the perfect table with an excellent view; it was certainly a good spot for people-watching. They were looking at the drinks menu when the waiter came to take their order.

"Bonjour monsieurs-dames, avez vous décidé ce que vous aimerait boire?"

Lola ordered for both since her French was impeccable.

"Bonjour, je voudrais un verre de rosé, et mon ami voudrait une bière, s'il vous plaît."

Chase sat back and looked at Lola, smiling. He touched her hand slightly as she looked at him. The drinks arrived, and they toasted each other and took a sip. It was so enjoyable to sit and watch as the day unfolded before them. "I really can't believe I've never been to the South of France before; it's so magical."

Lola was happy that he felt that way. He obviously saw the enchantment here.

"I think it's an extraordinary place with so much history and so much mystery!"

She laughed at the accidental rhyme. "I just have such a connection with the area. I feel that I'm meant to be here. It's kind of perfect working between here and London. I think I have the best of both worlds."

He could tell she was excited when she talked about the area, and he found her passion alluring. "I did have a chance to come down here a few years ago. I have a friend Stefan van Carson. You probably have heard of him; he is one of the most prominent movie directors in the world."

Lola nodded as Chase continued. "He was here for the Cannes Film Festival and was throwing a weekend party on his superyacht, *Lekker Kontje.*"

Understanding a bit of Dutch, Lola laughed at the name.

"Unfortunately, I had work commitments, so couldn't I go. He sent me some pictures of *Lekker Kontje,* and she is quite the beauty. Even comes with a personal helicopter."

"Oh, I'm sure; some of the yachts around here are incredibly extravagant," Lola said as she lifted her half-empty glass of *rosé.*

"I didn't think to reach out to Stefan about my trip. I wonder if he is anywhere in the area. Could be fun to take a little boat ride! Maybe I'll give him a call tomorrow."

"It's always good to have friends with superyachts," Lola said with a twinkle in her eye.

The waiter came by to see if they needed anything else. They were enjoying everything so much, they decided to have another round. Chase leaned forward, and she smelled a lingering trace of cologne as he gently parted her hair and gave her the softest kiss on the neck. There was no doubt about it; there was definite chemistry between them. He pulled back, leaving Lola longing for more as the waiter brought the drinks, placed them on the table, and retrieved the old glasses. They sat in silence for a minute, enjoying each other's company. Lola could hear light music in the background—the jazz sounds of "Writing Letters to You in My Sleep." Lola felt relaxed and happy. She didn't feel like leaving, and she wondered if Chase would mind missing out on Club Cinquante Cinq. They could have a marvellous lunch here instead.

"Chase, I have an idea. What if we blow off Club 55 and just stay here and have lunch?"

"I thought that myself, as I saw the waiter walk by with a huge bowl of steamed mussels and french fries. I don't even need to look at the menu."

Lola put her hand on his arm, turned to him, and said seriously, "Mr. Campbell, I have to confess something...I like a nice mussel."

"You are funny, Miss Delphine." They lifted their drinks and laughed as they toasted one another.

They ordered *moules-frites* for two, along with a bottle of *rosé*. Lola hesitated about having more wine because of the drive, but Chase said he would only have half a glass and drive them back to Villa Bonne Chance. They spent the next two hours swapping stories and laughing. Their worlds were so different, but Lola enjoyed hearing the tales from the various films he had been in and all the shenanigans the actors created. He paid the bill and stood to pull out Lola's chair.

"Thank you so much, Chase. That was such a spectacular lunch. When we get back, would you like to take a late afternoon swim?"

He said nothing but just stood a few inches away, taking in her beauty. She waited for him to answer or kiss her, but instead, he gently took her hand and led her out of La Petite Plage.

They decided to take the roof off the car for the drive home. Lola gave directions as Chase drove them out of St. Tropez. They were nearing her villa when he turned the music down for a minute and said, "I have a proposition for you, Lola. Would you like to accompany me to the wedding on Saturday? I know it's short notice, but I talked to Riggs, my friend who is getting married, and he said a couple of people had cancelled last minute, so I can bring you as my date if you are free."

She thought about it for a minute; she did love La Colombe d'Or, and he was great company. "That would be lovely, thank you! You can fill me in on the details when we get home. It's weird because the name Riggs sounds so familiar to me. It's kind of an unusual name."

"Well, his real name is Randall Howard, but his friends all call him Riggs, perhaps because of his years in the oil business in Texas." She thought hard for a moment and simply couldn't remember. She met so many people in her line of work, and the chance of her knowing someone Chase was connected to was a distinct possibility.

When they arrived at the villa, Lola noticed that Claudette had already left for the day. Chase parked the car and came around to open her door for her. She held his hand as they walked through the front door and were met with a flood of light from the floor to ceilings windows, which revealed a breathtaking late-afternoon view.

Chase paused. "I have some swim shorts in the back of my car from the other day at the beach; I'll grab them." He turned and walked out to his car.

Lola put her bag on the barstool and petted the two cats that were circling her legs. "Great, I'll feed these hungry felines." She finished with the cats as Chase returned. "What would you like to drink? I have a wide variety of choices. I think I fancy Champagne," she said, pulling a bottle of *Veuve Clicquot Brut Rosé* out of the fridge.

"That sounds great. I'll join you in that." He came around to open the bottle for her while she took two Champagne flutes and a silver ice bucket out of a small antique cellarette opposite the dining table.

"I tell you what, why don't we take this outside? I'm going to change into my bikini. You can use the guest room to change if you like." She pointed at a door just beyond the dining area.

Lola decided on a simple yellow string bikini, tied a pale blue sarong around her slender waist, and walked back to the kitchen. He was waiting for her outside on one of the sofas. The Champagne sat in an ice bucket on the table. Chase stood up as she came toward him. He had one of the most amazing physiques she had ever seen, not surprising considering the type of roles he usually played. He had just the perfect amount of muscle and tone in all the right places.

She stopped in front of him, and he put his hands on hers and pulled her to him. Their lips parted as they began to explore each other's mouths with such passion and lust Lola had to hold onto the arm of the sofa to steady herself. He untied the sarong, and his hands cupped her peach-shaped bottom as he pulled her in tightly, their mouths never stopping to take a break. Lola could feel his mounting excitement under the swim shorts. She slowly released herself from his lips and looked into his wanting eyes.

"Why don't we have a glass of the bubbly," she said gently to Chase, catching her breath as she regrouped after the incredibly passionate embrace.

They toasted, and he said, "Lola Delphine, you are so beautiful, you could certainly catch a guy's heart, especially this guy."

"I'm really having fun with you, Chase."

He seemed a little disappointed in the way she said it, so to change the mood a little she said, "Why don't we get in the pool? It's going to feel so good, especially since I turned on the heater this morning."

Diving in unison, they raced to the other end of the pool and laughed at their impromptu mini-competition. They swam back to the other side and Lola quickly got out, handed Chase his glass, and got back into the warm water. She sat with him on a shallow step at one end of the pool. They were enjoying the wonderful combination of the Brazilian sounds of Bebel Gilberto mixed with the Riviera courtship calls of the cicada symphony that were a typical sound in the area. They were playing late this year, Lola thought. She always wondered where they all went for the winter.

The pool lights suddenly switched on, illuminating the turquoise water. It looked so inviting that Lola put her glass down and pushed herself into the water, lay on her back, and looked at the last tangerine light of the sunset. Chase followed her. As she drifted, he scooped her up and held her, slowly bending his head to meet her lips, which tasted slightly salty from the pool. Lola let herself go for a second; she desperately wanted to feel lost in the moment because it felt so perfect. As hard as she tried, however, the piece of her heart she had kept locked away for so long refused to be released in this tender moment with this gorgeous man.

"Would you like some dinner? Claudette made some *bouillabaisse* earlier, and I can heat it up." She wondered if Chase sensed her withdrawal.

"Lola, I have had a lovely day with you, but I think I'm going to head out. I'm driving to Gordes in the morning, and I want to get an early start."

She could tell he had felt her resistance and appreciated even more that he was allowing her space without pushing her with questions. "You will love it there," she said. "It's probably one of the most stunning hilltop villages in the area."

They got out of the pool and dried off before going back inside so he could change and gather his things. Lola wrapped the towel tightly around herself while waiting for him to come out of the guest bedroom. He held her in a tight embrace and kissed her lightly. Lola looked into his eyes, seeing a hint of disappointment. "I move slowly, Chase," she said, not knowing what else to say. As he tightened his embrace, she could feel his heart beating through his thin cotton shirt. She felt safe in his arms. "It's okay, Lola, you don't owe me any explanations at all. I have thoroughly enjoyed our time together. It's been wonderful, and whatever happens after that will be very special." She nodded, and they walked hand in hand out the front door.

Lola waved as he drove down the driveway. She felt bewildered. He was the perfect gentleman, and she had enjoyed spending the day with him. She locked the front door behind her, noticing the time on the grandfather clock that stood on the right side of the entry, which said eight. She went into the kitchen and poured herself a glass of *Châteauneuf-du-Pape*, which was left over from the other night. On the way to the bedroom, she stroked Domino and Solitaire, who were rolled up in a furry ball together on the linen sofa; they purred softly but didn't stir.

Lola put the wine glass down by the side of the bed, went into the bathroom and turned on the shower. She hung her bikini over the bathtub taps to dry out and stepped into the hot shower. She thought about the last few days. It was as if there was a shift taking place in her heart. She didn't understand it yet, but she felt it was important not to ignore it. It terrified her, but there seemed to be some greater force pushing her along on her journey.

Lola stepped out of the shower and dried off. She slipped into a peach-coloured silk robe, leaving it open to let the breeze cool her after the hot shower. The bed looked so inviting, she pulled the duvet back and lay down, remembering the deep passionate kisses from earlier. She began to explore her body with both hands, her fingers arriving on one nipple, which she started rubbing and tweaking until it stood to attention. She could feel her moistness growing as she imagined Chase's tongue from earlier. She circled the other one for a moment, feeling lost in the moment; she reached over, opened the nightstand drawer, and pulled out her toyfriend Nigel. She switched it on, and it began to hum and vibrate softly. She slowly started circling the very top of her inner thigh, enjoying the sensation running through her core, the other hand continuing to tease each nipple, one by one.

Lola couldn't take it anymore; she eased the toy in between her now-dripping lips, all the time thinking about Chase's tongue licking her all over. She began to climax very quickly, her breathing getting heavier all the time. The toy continued to circle her sopping jewel; she couldn't hold on for much longer as the waves of pure ecstasy pushed her to an almost painful heightened level of pleasure. The toy moved into her parted lips, and she felt the final wave sweep over her as her subconscious mind took over. In that instant, she saw not Chase but Jack's eyes looking deep into her soul. She cried out his name with a guttural sob, "Jack!"

Lola felt deeply relaxed and satisfied. She lay back, thinking about what had just happened. She hadn't thought of Jack like this in years. She barely knew the grown man, Jack of today, only the snippets of knowledge from news clippings and art journals over the last twenty years or so. Lola picked up Nigel and put him to sleep in the nightstand drawer. She switched off the lamp, covered herself with the cosy down duvet, and quickly drifted into the deepest sleep she had in years.

CHAPTER THIRTEEN

L ate Thursday afternoon, Jack was pacing around his suite at the Eden-Roc. He was on the phone with Claude Laurent in Monte Carlo. Claude was very interested in a Kandinsky painting that had sold at Christie's a few years ago. He wanted Jack to find out if the owner of the painting, Annika Barinov, a Romanian billionaire, wanted to sell it. Of course, he would pay an inflated price. He was insistent because it was his wife's favourite piece since she had seen it on their honeymoon on the cover of a coffee-table book in their room at the Cipriani Hotel in Venice. It was their wedding anniversary next month, and Claude thought it would be the perfect romantic gesture after twenty years of marriage. What he didn't tell Jack was that his wife had caught him in bed with another woman last week and was threatening to leave him. He thought this was a good peace offering.

"I will do my best, Claude. You know there are some other Kandinsky paintings I can probably get my hands on and…"

Claude cut him off mid-sentence. "I don't want any others; that's the one Helena wants, and I intend to get it for her, with or without you."

Jack took a deep breath. He didn't want to lose Claude, probably one of his best clients. "I will see what I can do and let you know how it goes in the next few days."

"*Merci, Monsieur Alistair. Jusque-là au revoir,*" he said with a clipped French accent.

Jack sat on the comfortable sofa; he was unsure how to proceed. Annika Barinov was impossible to deal with, and she never sold any of her collection simply because she didn't have to. She owned one of the most impressive private art collections in the world and, as rumour had it, some of it was kept in her penthouse in Monte Carlo. Claude would probably go over there himself if he knew how close the Kandinsky actually might be. The thought amused Jack a little.

He searched Annika online and immediately several photos came up of her at various charity events and society galas. She looked younger than he had imagined and was beautiful, with straight, sleek blonde hair cut into a classic bob that set off the piercing grey-green, almost wolf-like eyes and Slavic cheekbones. When he scrolled down, there was a picture of her on a yacht on her birthday, sitting next to what looked like the famous film director Stefan van Carson. There was an enormous tiered birthday cake on the table that said, "Congratulations 50!" in large gold letters. She was smiling as she unwrapped a classic egg-shell blue Tiffany box.

Jack's phone rang, so he put the laptop on the coffee table; it was Fiona, his assistant. "Hi Fiona, is everything okay?"

"Yes, I just wanted to know how everything is going out there and if you need anything."

"Well, I just got off the phone with Claude Laurent, and he wants me to ask Annika Barinov a question. You know of her, right?"

"Yes, yes, a Romanian billionaire with an art collection that rivals the Louvre," she joked.

"Well, she has a Kandinsky called *Piano Notes* that Claude wants to buy for his wife for their wedding anniversary. I have a feeling there's more to it than that. He probably screwed up somehow. I think Claude has somewhat of a playboy reputation, should we say."

"I've heard she's not an easy person to find, constantly moving among her large portfolio of real estate, including the cruise-ship-sized superyacht, *Miroslava*. I just looked it up, and that name is interpreted as 'a very independent sensual woman who is a winner and a great lover of intrigue.' You better be careful, Jack," she said, laughing.

"No need to worry about that; my heart is in other places," he said, thinking immediately back to Lola, who had completely taken over his mind in the last few weeks. "Thanks, Fiona. I'm going to wrap it up for the day. Let's talk tomorrow; maybe you can start some research on Miss Barinov." After a brief goodbye, they hung up.

Jack sat back. He needed to put together a plan. It was good that he was here in the South of France and able to handle Claude. He hoped and prayed that by some fluke, Annika Barinov was somewhere nearby. To begin with, he needed to get a list of the most glamourous upcoming galas and events she might attend. That would definitely be a good start. Looking at her pictures online, he could tell she was not one to miss a glittering party.

He thought back to the last time he was here; he had arranged to meet Claude at the Casino de Monte-Carlo. It was the magical night when he pulled up to the casino entrance, and Lola had stepped out of her car in front of him. After almost twenty minutes of searching for her, the valet had informed him that she had left five minutes after arriving. Feeling heartbroken, he had struggled through cocktails with Claude, who had introduced him to a close Italian friend and up-and-coming artist, Violetta Martini, who needed some art contacts in London. There was something about Violetta; she seemed so familiar, like he knew her from his childhood. However, that was impossible because she was probably only in her twenties. At the time, Jack suspected that Claude was sleeping with Miss Martini, but he never got involved with his clients' personal lives.

The evening had gone by in a haze after the incredible chance sighting of Lola. At that moment, he had known he couldn't run from his heart any longer. She still held way too much of it, and he finally understood what he must do to find true peace. Jack was now sure that Lola was his soul mate, and after all these years of running, it was finally the right time.

The sun was setting and casting a soft tea-rose tint over the room. Jack decided it would be a marvellous evening to visit the Champagne Lounge and experience the sweeping views over the Mediterranean and the pool. It was the perfect place to catch the sunset. He watched as the light caught the crystal chandelier and sent dancing rainbow spectrums around the room like a disco ball. One of them positioned itself on a painting opposite where he was sitting. Something about the painting pulled him off the sofa to have a closer look. It was in a gilded frame, and the colours were muted and calming somehow. He now stood in front of it and could see that it was a classic Mediterranean villa typical of the area. Tall cypress trees lined the entrance, with the house in the distance down a short gravel drive. Somehow, the painting made him want to open the front door to see what was on the other side. Jack looked at it for a few minutes, taking in the details. It was probably painted by a local artist, he thought, as he glanced down to the bottom right-hand corner to read the small title and name. What he read instantly took his breath away: *Bonne Chance* by Delilah Cornel.

Jack couldn't believe it. What an amazing coincidence and stroke of good luck. He went over to his laptop bag leaning against the sofa and pulled out the old folder of photos and clippings, spreading them out on the table. Ah, there it was, the one of Lola in her white bikini out by the pool. He turned it over and reread the message, which said, "Sexy in Sainte-Maxime" and had the name Villa Bonne Chance written in the corner.

Jack dug out the Swiss army knife he always travelled with and opened its small magnifying glass. Approaching the painting, he held it over a faint sign on the right of the entry gate. It had been hard to read with the naked eye, but there it was again: Villa Bonne Chance. Jack pulled his phone out of his pocket and took some pictures of the painting. It could have been painted forty years ago or longer, so he knew the trees would be a lot taller now. He wondered if it still had the same name. From reading one of the articles about Lola, he knew that she lived in her grandmother's old villa on the French Riviera, so he was pretty sure that being as sentimental as she was about her grandmother, Delilah, the name would not have changed. The question was, would it still be possible to find this villa from the picture, knowing that it was in the Sainte-Maxime area?

Jack needed a drink. He grabbed a light jacket and his mobile phone and made his way to the Champagne Lounge. The bar area was full, so he made himself comfortable on one of the cream-coloured sofas. He still couldn't believe what he had just discovered in his room. The last few days, he felt like he had been waiting for a sign or some help with his search. He wished he could hug Grandmother Delilah and thank her with all his heart because it felt like she was watching out for him from above. His favourite waiter, Alberto, came over.

"*Bienvenue, Monsieur Alistair, que puis-je vous faire boire ce soir?*"

"*Salute, Alberto, ça va?*"

"*Oui, ça va bien merci, monsieur.*"

"I would like a glass of *Ruinart Blanc de Blancs*. Also, I have a quick question. You've worked here for over thirty years, right?"

"Yes, that is correct. I started working here when I was eighteen, so it has been almost thirty-six years now."

"I wanted to ask you about a painting in my room. By any chance, have you heard of the artist Delilah Cornel, or would anyone who has worked at the Eden-Roc for a long time know of her?"

"Let me have a think about it. I will ask some of the older staff. Also, I wonder if there is some kind of record of the paintings acquired that long ago. May I ask why? Were you interested in purchasing it?"

"No, Alberto, the painting is of a villa called Bonne Chance. It's somewhere in the Sainte-Maxime area. What the villa represents to me is like a closed oyster; inside waits a beautiful pearl I've been searching for all my life."

Alberto nodded; he could see the tenderness in Jack's eyes. "I will see what I can do, *monsieur.*" Jack thanked Alberto, who turned and went to the bar, coming back a couple of minutes later with a glass of *Blanc de Blanc*.

Jack was tired from the emotional rollercoaster he had been on the last few weeks. Lost in thought, he caught a final glimpse of the sun setting over the Mediterranean. Taking a long drink, he turned to check out the other lucky people who had joined him up here. Jack noticed that the Champagne Lounge was busy tonight. He surveyed the area and saw the DJ who was playing the sultry sounds of Ibrahim Maalouf and thought it must be nice to work in this stunning environment and play music every night. He smiled at a small group of young women perched on the middle sofas, looking like they were dying to dance but were too nervous to make a move in this sophisticated setting. They had the appearance of models, beautiful and all lithe limbs, displaying a kind of innocent confidence while realising their power. A couple of men in suits were ogling them, probably debating whether to make their move. Jack watched as one of the men signalled Alberto to bring the ladies another bottle of Champagne, on them of course.

While silently debating whether to go and have a bite at the Louroc Restaurant in the hotel, a young, good-looking couple sat on the sofa opposite him and put their drinks on the small table that divided them.

The young lady asked, "Do you mind if we sit here?"

"No, not at all." Jack detected an Australian accent. They were exceedingly tanned and obviously excited to be having drinks in such a prestigious setting. Alberto came and took their drink order and asked Jack if he would care for another. He nodded yes. For some reason, something about the young couple gave him hope and made him feel happy. They were so relaxed with each other and incredibly tactile; it was very sweet and refreshing. Three new glasses of Champagne arrived, and they all thanked Alberto. Jack smiled at them and raised his glass slightly before taking a drink.

The young woman spoke in an animated way and could not wait to share her news. "We just got engaged today!" As she said it, she couldn't help but show Jack her ring finger, which boasted a small cushion-cut diamond on a gold band.

"Congratulations," he said, lifting his glass again to toast them.

"I'm Hannah, and this is Charlie," she said.

"Jack. Nice to meet you both. Are you on holiday here?"

Charlie answered. "No, we work together and have a couple of days off. I have always wanted to come to the Hotel du Cap-Eden-Roc after reading about its glamorous history. We are spending the night in Juan les Pins. How about you?"

"I'm down here from London for business and some pleasure. I'm lucky to come here quite often."

Hannah chimed in. "You are so lucky; the Côte d'Azur is one of my favourite spots. Out of all the places we get to go, it's still my favourite." Her energy was infectious, and Jack was happy he had stayed for another drink.

Intrigued, he couldn't help but ask, and she seemed so open to conversation. "What is it that you do that involves so much travel, if you don't mind my asking?"

"We're crew on a large yacht that's docked in the Antibes harbour."

"That's interesting. I always wondered what it would be like working on a boat and getting to see the world like that. How long are you docked here?"

"Just a few days, then it's off to Portofino. We feel pretty fortunate to be on this particular yacht, as it is one of the biggest in Europe. The woman who owns it can be very demanding, but the owners of these luxury yachts always are. You've probably read about it before."

"Maybe. What's it called?"

Charlie took over the conversation. "*Miroslava*. It's owned by Romanian billionaire Annika Barinov."

Jack could not believe it! What a stroke of luck. He didn't want to give the game away, so he asked casually, "Where in the harbour are you docked? Sometimes I like to take a walk out there. It would be interesting to see one of the biggest yachts in Europe."

Charlie gave him the general location. "Well, if you do come out there and you see someone on deck, tell them you know us, and we'll come out and wave if we can," he said in a friendly way.

"Thank you!" Jack stood up and congratulated them one more time on their engagement and excused himself from the festivities. On the way out, he stopped to talk to Alberto for a minute. "Good night, Alberto. I would like to take care of that young couple's bill tonight and add a Champagne bottle. They are celebrating their engagement."

"Of course, *monsieur. Bonne nuit.*"

The Australian couple had no idea the importance of their conversation tonight and the valuable information that had just saved Jack a lot of work. The timing could not be better. He walked quickly back to his suite to plan his day at Port Vauban Antibes harbour tomorrow.

CHAPTER FOURTEEN

The rain was coming down hard in London on Friday morning. Ingrid stood looking out her glass balcony door at the River Thames. The different shades of grey washed together, looking like a muted watercolour painting. People were hurrying down the Thames path, wrangling their umbrellas in the wind as they made their way to work. She looked at her phone; it was eight-thirty. Time to go, she thought. She was putting on her Burberry Mac when her phone buzzed; it was a text from Max.

I would really like to talk to you, Ingrid. I have a feeling I know why you haven't returned any of my messages. Please think about it. XX.

She had to give him credit for being so persistent. He had called or texted her every day since their date, and it was getting tough to ignore because the truth of the matter was that she really did like him a lot. Ingrid needed time to think. Lola had not responded to her messages unless it was business. Maybe Max had an idea about what had happened all those years ago, and perhaps there was something he knew that could help her find a way to fix her relationship with Lola. Ingrid decided to wait until later to figure out if she was going to respond.

Tightening the belt on the Mac, she headed out into the rain to find a taxi. Thankfully, she was able to climb aboard a taxi quickly and head toward Floral Street in Covent Garden to the Jetset Delilah offices. The cab dropped her off on Long Acre, right in front of the entrance to Langley Court. She hurried along in the drizzle, reached Floral Street, took a quick left, and arrived at the entrance to the building in a couple of minutes. It was located opposite the Paul Smith store.

Ingrid stepped out of the lift and greeted Rebecca, the receptionist, who handed her some post. She walked back to her large office, waving at Jill, whose desk was positioned right outside. She took off the damp Mac, hung it on a coat rack in the corner, put the post down on the desk, and turned on the computer. As she started going over the barrage of emails, there was a knock on the half-open door. Ingrid looked up; Rebecca stood there smiling, holding the most enormous arrangement of white roses Ingrid had ever seen.

"These just came for you," she said excitedly.

"Wow! Why don't you put them down right there," she said, pointing at a small occasional table that sat on the opposite wall between two armchairs. "Thank you, Rebecca." Ingrid walked over to the beautiful arrangement and opened the card that accompanied it. Very tasteful, she thought. They were from Blooming Haus, which she knew had done floral design for Bulgari and many other iconic brands. It was a thoughtful decision, she decided, knowing her history in fashion. She read the note.

Miss A,

I know we barely know each other, but I just can't stop thinking about you.--Max, X

She sat on the armchair for a moment, reading the note over. The roses were perfect, and she leaned over to take in the scent. Her heart was torn; it was difficult to know what to do. Ingrid stood up, walked over to her desk, and sat down in the chair. She just had to call him. The pull on her heartstrings was simply too much. She nervously picked up the phone, and he answered after one ring.

"Hi Max, it's Ingrid."

"About time! What took you so long?" he joked.

"I wanted to call and thank you for the gorgeous flowers that just arrived."

"You are more than welcome. Look, how about an early dinner tonight? Maybe we can figure some things out together."

Ingrid thought about it for a minute. The silence seemed to go on forever. "Okay, well, just dinner. That's it, right?"

"Of course, darlin'. How about Langan's Brasserie in Mayfair? Let's meet after work at five-thirty."

"See you then." Ingrid hung up and sat for a while, lost in thought. She felt like her world had been turned upside down in the last couple of weeks. There were so many different emotions running through her, and she didn't know which one to trust. She couldn't help feeling excited about seeing Max again, and she hated to admit to herself that his voice alone had brought her back to that intoxicating night at St. Katharine Docks.

The day flew by. Ingrid spent a lot of time on the phone with the U.S. talking to the head buyer of Saks Fifth Avenue, who was interested in buying Jetset Delilah accessories for their flagship store in New York. If the line did well, the rest of the stores in the country would carry them. She forwarded some information to Lola and an outline of the conversation with Saks before closing the computer down for the day. She had deliberately absorbed herself in work today and didn't even take a lunch break. Occasionally, she glanced up at the beautiful white roses and wondered if seeing Max again was the right decision.

Around four forty-five, Ingrid headed to the restroom to reapply some makeup and fix her hair a little. She wished she had time to go home and change, but rush hour traffic would be heavy now, and there was no time. She looked at the navy-blue tight pinstripe pencil skirt and white silk charmeuse shirt, deciding to undo one extra button. Spraying some Fragonard on her wrist, she gave herself one more glance and walked back to her office to get her bag and Mac. "Bye, Jill, see you tomorrow. Do you have any questions or need anything before I leave?"

Jill waved and signalled she was on the phone, so Ingrid made her way to the lift and out to Floral Street, then on to Long Acre to find a cab. It was a damp chilly evening, and Ingrid was happy when she saw the yellow light on the cab that slowed to a halt in front of her. "Langan's Restaurant, please." The cab took off. Ingrid was happy the driver was not chatty; it gave her time to think. She decided that the best approach with Max would be to let him do the talking to see if he opened up. Hopefully, he had some insight into why Lola was so against their seeing each other and why she had reacted so negatively when she found out. It just didn't make sense to Ingrid; she was almost nervous about finding out.

She got to Langan's right on time. Max had texted a few minutes ago to say he was waiting in the bar area. He stood up when she walked in and greeted her with a kiss on the cheek, his musky cologne bringing back memories of their night together. "Ingrid, you are as gorgeous as I remember." When he stood back a little, his eyes lit up as he looked at her. "Shall we go to our table?"

"Yes, that would be great." Ingrid slipped off her Mac and accepted the waiter's offer to hang it up for her. They were seated against the wall under a large colourful print of the *Folies Bergère, Fleur de Lotus*. Max smiled at her warmly. She couldn't believe how nervous she felt in his presence. It was weird and exhilarating all at once. She hadn't expected to feel like this.

Since it was still early, there were just a few diners in the restaurant. Ingrid smiled when she glanced off to the side and saw a large table of raucous businessmen who had obviously carried on drinking after a lengthy lunch.

"What would you like to drink, Champagne?"

"I fancy a nice glass of red wine. Maybe it's the grey weather or something."

Max looked at the wine list and decided quickly on a bottle of *Château Talbot Sainte-Julien*, which he ordered right away. He turned to Ingrid. "So, how are you? I was beginning to think you didn't like me or something."

"No, it isn't that silly." She couldn't help touching his hand at that moment. "Unfortunately, it's a lot more complicated than that."

Max held her gaze for a moment. He picked up her hand and kissed it lightly, saying, "I really like you, Ingrid. I haven't stopped thinking about you, and I want to do whatever it takes to make this right."

The sommelier broke the moment when he arrived at the table with the *Château Talbot*. They watched as he opened it and described a little of the history of the wine as he gave Max a taste, then poured them both a glass and swiftly left, probably sensing their need for privacy. Ingrid looked at Max, wondering if she really wanted to open Pandora's box tonight. There was no going back once she started.

"The thing is Max, when you sent the Champagne over to Lola and me at Scott's that Sunday, she warned me about you and said I should stay away from you due to some family history, and in her words, 'some I do know, and some I don't.' I'm just really confused as to what to do about it all. The newspaper photographs confirmed that we had gone out, and now she has basically cut me out of her life other than essential business communication." It was a relief to talk about this with someone. She had been so upset the past week.

Max said nothing for a moment; instead, he leaned forward and kissed her. It was so spontaneous that it took her breath away. It was impossible to stop the flood of desire that pulsed through her body. He sat back again in his chair. Ingrid could tell his wheels were spinning, and he looked like he was thinking hard before he spoke.

"First, Ingrid, I'm so sorry I caused you all this stress and upset. I suppose I did know it would probably not sit well with Lola." He took a long sip of wine and reached for her hand again. "The thing is, when we met that first time at Scott's Restaurant, there was something about you I couldn't ignore, and I just had to see you again."

Ingrid could feel the heat in his hand. She looked into his eyes and could tell he was sincere. He continued after a long pause. "I don't know where to begin, and there are some things that Lola will have to tell you herself because I only know part of the story. I can only tell you what I know."

Ingrid felt like she was in a trance, locked into this intimate moment with a man she hardly knew. She couldn't say anything, so she just nodded, and he continued.

"I was in my mid-twenties and on tour with Francis Williams. He had just done his first solo album, which was more of a jazz sound than his previous music. Because of this, he was playing at the Jazz à Juan Festival in Juan-Les-Pins on the Riviera. It was a beautiful balmy July night, so after the show, we went back to the Eden-Roc, where we were staying, and headed up to the Champagne Lounge for a drink to wind down a bit. That's where we met her."

Ingrid waited as the moment grew more intense. She picked up her wine glass and took a drink of the lovely French wine. She couldn't stand the interlude, so she finally found her voice. "Who did you meet?"

"Roberta Cornel, Lola's mother."

CHAPTER FIFTEEN

Jack walked out on his private terrace holding a crystal rocks glass filled with an icy gin and tonic with a lemon wedge. It was another beautiful Riviera evening. He sat down on one of the plush sun loungers and stretched out his legs. He could see the flickering lights of a yacht in the distance. It seemed to be anchored behind the hotel. The day had gone well, and he felt he had moved in the right direction as far as making initial contact with Annika Barinov. He went over the morning again in fine detail and even jotted down precisely what Jimmy, from the crew of *Miroslava*, had said so that later he could relay to Claude what had happened. He had only been able to leave a message today with his assistant. Jack sat back with his refreshing cocktail and reviewed the conversation.

He had put together a letter for Annika Barinov that he hoped to get to her through his new Aussie crew friends. He had driven to Antibes this morning and parked as close as possible to Port Vauban, where *Miroslava* was docked. Jack had walked the short distance in the direction Charlie had told him. It was not difficult to spot her; she stood out against all the other fabulous yachts because of her sheer size. He had done some research on her last night and discovered that she had eight decks, including a helipad, swimming pool, squash court, two thirty-three-foot chase boats, and twelve jet skis. He spotted the helicopter on the back. It really was an impressive yacht. He could see a number of crew members walking around. They all wore the same uniform—a navy-blue polo shirt with *Miroslava* embroidered on the pocket and crisp white shorts. He stood there for a moment, watching all the activity, and waited until he thought he could get someone's attention. Suddenly, the moment was perfect. Two crew members came around on one of the lower decks and seemed to be taking a break. They rested side-by-side, leaning on the railings. Jack hated doing this, as it made him feel a bit ridiculous like he was a fan or something, but he saw no other way to get Annika Barinov's attention. But because of Claude's insistence and pressure, time was definitely of the essence.

He waved the envelope at the two crew members, and amazingly, one of them came down to the yacht's stern just above the swim platform, which had a long row of sun loungers on it. There was a sloping gangplank that came down onto the dock. The crew member, a young man probably in his early twenties, stood at the top of the gangplank. "Can I help you, sir?" He sounded Australian.

"I was wondering if Charlie and Hannah happen to be around? I have a letter I'd like to pass on." Jack could tell the guy was unsure of what to do; he was probably already breaking some kind of security protocol.

"They are still on shore leave and will not be back until this afternoon."

Jack thought about what he had said for a second and decided he better take this moment and run with it. "Is there any way you can get this to Annika Barinov?" he said, holding up the envelope.

"I guess I could pass it on to her executive assistant; she can decide what to do. Miss Barinov is very selective about how she devotes her time. Rumour has it she is spending a few days on film director Stefan van Carson's yacht."

Jack nodded, surprised that the man had shared the information so freely. He decided not to question it and just said, "That would be very helpful, thank you."

The guy walked down the gangplank, and Jack introduced himself. He shook the young man's hand warmly. "I'm Jack Alistair. I really appreciate your doing this for me. Please tell Charlie and Hannah I came by." Jack handed him the envelope.

"No problem, mate. I'm Jimmy, by the way. Charlie and I went to school together in Sydney, so we all signed up for this crew. How do you know them?"

"I met them last night at the Eden-Roc hotel. We had some drinks together, and they said I should come by to see this beauty," he said, gazing up at *Miroslava*.

Jimmy smiled and put the envelope in his back pocket. "Well, I better get back before someone misses me; they run a tight ship here."

Jack quickly remembered something and reached in his pocket and pulled out two one-hundred Euro notes folded together. He shook Jimmy's hand again, giving him the notes discreetly in case someone was watching.

Jimmy looked surprised. "That isn't necessary," he said, smiling at Jack's generosity.

"Take it; you can use it on your next shore leave." Jimmy relented and thanked Jack. As he walked up the gangplank, he waved one more time and disappeared through a door.

* * *

Jack finished up the detailed account for Claude and contemplated what he wanted for dinner when he thought he heard a knock. He turned and looked through the open terrace door, half expecting someone to be standing there. Jack stood up, walked into the suite's lounge area, and walked over to the door. He figured it was housekeeping coming to do their nightly turn-down service. He opened the door and was greeted by Alberto, who immediately apologised for coming unannounced.

"Please come in, Alberto," he gestured.

"Good evening, sir. Sorry to bother you, but I have some information on the artist Delilah Cornel, and I wanted to give it to you as soon as possible." He handed Jack a small yellowed page that looked like it had been torn out of a book in haste. Alberto explained, "I figured out where they kept all the old accounting books. There is a small office, more of a closet really, that is shelved all around. On the bottom shelf, in the corner, I found a leather-bound notebook that contained records of furnishings and artwork purchased from 1950 to 1970. I looked through them and guess what I found—a record of when the painting was purchased and who from. They actually purchased several of Miss Cornel's paintings for their suites."

Jack looked at the torn page, and Alberto pointed at the writing that said, "*Bonne Chance* by Delilah Cornel, purchased 1965." Under that, there was a list of other works they had purchased from Delilah and the prices paid. What caught Jack's eye, though, was the side note written next to the prices. He translated it into English and read aloud. "Ah-ha, this could be just what I'm looking for," he said, showing it to Alberto. It read, "Augustin and Marceau Art Installation and Picture Hanging Services to pick up and deliver seven paintings from Delilah Cornel." There was a stamp indicating they had collected all the paintings from Delilah and installed them in the hotel.

Alberto turned to Jack. "When I looked through some of the pages, it looked like Augustin and Marceau handled the installation of all the Eden-Roc's artwork between 1960 and 1975."

Jack read Alberto's mind. "I wonder if they are still in business; maybe a family member still runs it." He couldn't wait to get out his laptop to see what he could find. "How can I thank you, Alberto? I hope you didn't put your job at risk by doing this." Jack was excited but also concerned.

"It's okay, *monsieur*, no one looks through the old logs anymore. I could tell from the thick layer of dust covering them. Besides, I quite like doing some detective work now and again," he said with excitement. Jack smiled at his enthusiasm. He took a photo of the page and handed it back to Alberto.

"You keep it, *monsieur*. I don't want to risk going back in there again, and as I said, they are never going to miss it."

Jack turned and walked over to where his wallet sat on the coffee table to retrieve some money to give Alberto for all his help. "No, please, you have taken great care of me all these years that you have stayed at this hotel and, as I said, I enjoyed the detective work. It made me feel like Inspecteur Wens," he said laughing.

"You don't know how much I appreciate this; it means a lot to me that you went to this much trouble."

"It's no trouble, *monsieur*. I can tell how important this is to you, and if I can help you open that door again, it's worth it." He turned to Jack. Facing him, he paused for a minute; Jack could detect a sparkle in his eyes. "*Bonne chance, Monsieur* Alistair, *bonne chance*." Alberto turned and walked out the door, closing it softly behind him. Jack stood on the spot, not moving as a tear rolled down his cheek.

CHAPTER SIXTEEN

Lola looked at her phone for the hundredth time. She didn't know what to do about the wedding tomorrow in Saint-Paul de Vence. Chase had called and texted her several times since Wednesday. For some reason, she kept changing her mind, even though he had assured her they could go at her pace. The phone started ringing while she was staring at it, making Lola jump. She couldn't believe it; Chase was calling her again. She finally decided to talk to him; he didn't deserve to be ignored any longer. "Hello, Chase." She was a little nervous that he may be upset with her for not returning his calls.

"Hi, Lola. How are you? I just wanted to let Riggs and Scarlet know if you are coming tomorrow."

There was silence at the end of the line. "Lola, are you there?"

"Yes, I would like to come with you. Sorry it's taken me so long to confirm. I've just had so much going on this week."

"No problem, sweetheart. As I said, we can go slowly with all of this, and at the end of it, I'm willing to take that chance with you." She smiled down the phone; he was doing everything right. "Would you like me to pick you up?"

"No, I can drive. As you know, it's over an hour to get there from here." They went over the details, and Lola agreed to meet

Chase in the bar of the Colombe d'Or at one. They could have a drink before the ceremony at two. "Bye, Chase, see you tomorrow, and thank you for being so patient."

They hung up, and Lola walked outside and looked out at the midnight-blue Mediterranean. She could see lights from various yachts shimmering in the evening darkness. Lola looked around her pretty pool area and back at the house; again, she was so grateful that Grandmother Delilah had left her Villa Bonne Chance. There was just something so magical about the place. She decided she wanted to have an early night tonight so there would be enough time to do her daily morning run and get ready at a leisurely pace for the wedding. Lola walked back inside and closed the patio door behind her. She sat at the kitchen island to finish a glass of wine from earlier, deciding to check her work emails one last time before going to bed.

There were a couple from Jill and the one from Ingrid containing all the information from the Saks Fifth Avenue buyer. Lola was pleased about Jetset Delilah being in Saks in the near future; it was the perfect place to expand into the American market. She was just about to shut the laptop down when another message from Ingrid popped up on the screen. Lola looked at the time; it would be eight-thirty in London right now. She wondered what Ingrid could want at this time on a Friday night. It was impossible not to open the email. Curiosity got the better of her, and she clicked on it. It read:

Lola, I'm going to be completely honest with you, so I want to tell you about tonight. Max and I had an early dinner at Langan's. I agreed to meet with him again because he wanted to share some information he thought might help resolve some issues for us. Do you think it's possible for us to talk about this? Please, I really miss you, Lola.

Lola almost slammed the laptop shut; she was mad at Ingrid all over again. How dare she go snooping around into her family business? What made Lola extra angry was that she didn't even know all the details herself, mainly because she had always been so terrified of discovering the truth and unlocking that place in her heart that she had slammed shut over twenty years ago. She took a big chug of wine and sat for a minute, trying to calm down. She was annoyed at herself for opening the email. In her fuming state, she knew a martini and some loud music would be the only way forward. Lola walked over to the cellarette, grabbed the martini shaker and some dry vermouth, and brought it back to the island. She opened the freezer, retrieved a large bottle of Grey Goose, and poured a couple of large shots into the shaker along with some ice cubes. She shook until her hands were numb.

After dancing away to thunderous eighties music, Lola paused for a moment to pour the chilled martini into a glass. She danced like a madwoman for an hour or so, feeling like she was trying to dance away all the memories and pain. Sadly, Lola knew that a couple of martinis and loud music was only a temporary fix. She danced her way to the bedroom and switched off the music from a pad on the wall. Undressing clumsily, she threw the clothes at the chair in the corner and got into bed naked. She remembered toyfriend Nigel sleeping in the nightstand peacefully and wondered if he was ready for some fun tonight. But in her tipsy state, she decided, "Not tonight, Nigel. I have a headache."

*   *   *

Lola opened her eyes slightly to see the bright morning sunshine streaming into the room. She put the duvet over her face for a second to assess the level of her headache. Not too bad, considering the two huge martinis she had polished off last night after the red wine. Sitting up slightly, she took a slug out of a water bottle that lay on the pillow next to her, not remembering how it got there.

Domino and Solitaire were washing each other at the end of the bed, and when they saw that she had woken up, they stopped and came over for some attention. Lola petted them for a while and looked around for her phone, which was not in its usual place on the nightstand. She had no idea what time it was, so she eased out of bed and walked over to the pile of clothes that were half on the chair and half on the floor, chuckling a bit as she remembered the wild dance party last night. Ah, there it was, in the back pocket of the denim cut-offs she had been wearing. She glanced at it and looked again, not believing the hour. Wow, it was nine; she never slept this late.

There was no time for a run, but a few laps in the cool pool water would feel refreshing right now. Lola walked into the bathroom and put on the yellow bikini still hanging on the bathtub taps from the other night. She grabbed a short towelling robe from the back of the door and walked toward the kitchen. Coffee was what she needed. The living area looked so tranquil in the morning light. She noticed Claudette was outside watering the lavender in a pretty porcelain jardinière. Claudette looked up and waved at Lola through the large window. She stepped outside and waved good morning.

"Good morning, Lola. I made some coffee and decided to start watering outside first. Hope I didn't disturb you."

"No, not at all. Thank you for making coffee. It's just what I need; then I'm going to take a swim."

Claudette smiled. "I'm about to go to the Hypermarché before they get too busy. Are there any other things you need? More wine perhaps?" she said, laughing.

"Very funny, Claudette. I guess I can't fool you after all these years."

"You are very much like your grandmother. You know she was the life and soul of a party. Well, I'm going to get going." She walked toward the side gate, putting the watering can down next to a small herb garden.

Lola wandered back in and poured a large cup of coffee. She stared at the closed laptop. Ingrid's message came back to her as much as she tried to squeeze it out of her head. She decided that since it was Saturday, she didn't need to open it at all. Jill would call her if anything needed immediate attention. Walking back out to the pool, she put the coffee down, shrugged out of the robe, and dove in. The cold morning water was the best medicine right now, and after swimming a few laps, she felt much more clarity.

After the swim and a quick breakfast, Lola stepped out of the shower, drying herself as she walked into the closet to select her ensemble for the day. She decided on a short abstract-print Pucci dress. It would be perfect for the daytime wedding, and she planned on bringing her oversized YSL Le Smoking tuxedo jacket for the evening reception. The look was finished off with a pair of gold strappy sandals and a small gold clutch bag.

It was close to midday and time to leave. Traffic could be heavy on a Saturday afternoon, and she didn't want to feel rushed. Lola locked the door to Bonne Chance, jumped into her Porsche, drove slowly down the driveway, and floored it as she took a right onto the street. She enjoyed the drive, singing along to the Barenaked Ladies' new album, *Detour de Force*, the whole way.

She arrived at La Colombe d'Or just after one. The valet parking attendant greeted her and took her keys. Lola walked through the luscious garden terrace filled with people enjoying lunch and made a left into the bar area. Chase was sitting in the window at the far end of the bar. There was an ice bucket with a bottle of Champagne and two glasses sitting on the table. When she walked in, he immediately stood up and gave her a warm embrace.

"Hi, great to see you. You look beautiful."

Lola smiled at him, remembering how good-looking he was. What is wrong with me, she thought, this man is hot!

"Thank you." She stood back to look at him. "Looking pretty good yourself, Chase."

"Champagne?"

"Yes, that would be lovely." Chase poured two glasses, and they toasted before taking a sip.

"So, have you met a lot of the other guests yet?"

"There was a dinner last night, and I met some friends and family of Riggs and Scarlet from Houston and a couple who live in Paris. And Riggs's son Bentley, who runs an art gallery there."

Lola nodded. The bar area was filling up, and they chatted until Chase suddenly said, "Oh look, there's the couple I told you about. They live in Paris, and she's a top fashion model." Chase waved at them across the crowded room; Lola's view was blocked by two men standing just beyond the small wooden bar table.

It took a minute for them to make their way through the crowd, stopping to greet a few people on the way. Finally, the two men blocking Lola's view moved to the end of the bar. Chase stood up to greet the couple, not noticing that he had knocked Lola's gold clutch bag on the floor. She leaned down to pick it up quickly and noticed a pair of suede driving shoes on the other side of the small wooden table. She came up quickly as Chase was introducing her.

"Fabian, Anais, this is Lola Delphine." Lola was completely gobsmacked. What was Fabian doing here? She was frozen, not knowing what to say. Thankfully, Fabian spoke first.

"Lola, what are you doing here?"

Chase turned to her, waiting for her reply. "I'm here with my friend Chase. I knew the name Riggs sounded familiar; it's because you mentioned him when you came to my parents' house for dinner, remember?" Anais looked slightly bored with the conversation. Lola wondered if he had told her anything about their history. She quickly reached her hand out to Anais. "Nice to meet you; Fabian has spoken very highly of you."

Chase was looking a bit confused but said, "Why don't you join us? You can help us finish the Champagne." He gestured to the bartender for a couple more glasses.

Lola glanced at Anais, who looked different in person from her pictures. She could see why Anais photographed so well. Rail thin, she had the most intriguing face and amazing bone structure, almost severe. She wore a skin-tight red-leather dress, an interesting choice for the occasion, Lola thought. She seemed like a strange match for Fabian, who was outdoorsy and athletic; Lola wondered what the attraction was.

Chase interrupted her thoughts. "How do you two know each other?"

"Fabian's family and mine have been friends for years, and Fabian and I used to ride horses together when we were kids." Lola could feel Fabian staring at her, and she didn't dare look at him. The surprise meeting was slightly uncomfortable, considering the deeply intimate moments they had shared the last time they had seen each other.

As the bar started to clear, Chase finished his Champagne and stood up. "Well, we better get going; the ceremony starts in fifteen minutes." They made their way to a private room and were greeted by an American woman whom Lola assumed was Scarlet and Riggs's wedding planner. She was holding a list with the seating plan on it. Lola looked around the room as the woman found their names, noticing there were five tables of six, all with the most beautiful peach-coloured floral arrangements on them. Around the outside of the room, at various intervals, stood tall pedestals with long-stemmed ivory roses. It looked so elegant. A pianist in the corner was softly playing old jazz standards.

"Well, it looks like you guys are all sitting together." The wedding planner directed them to the middle table on the left. Pointing to an area between two of the tall pedestals, she said, "The short ceremony will start in about fifteen minutes and will take place over there. Feel free to turn your chair if needed. The bride and groom wanted this to be more of an intimate affair; that's why they are doing it like this. They are being married by a friend of theirs from Houston, who is an ordained minister." She smiled and walked away to help other guests.

Lola was seated between Chase and Fabian. It was slightly awkward. She looked over at Anais, who sat looking at her phone, texting with a smile on her face. Lola was intrigued by her and how aloof she seemed; she could tell Fabian was getting frustrated with it. All the guests were now seated, and the minister stood at the front of the room.

"Good afternoon. My name is David Talbert, and I'm a childhood friend of Riggs who persuaded me to become an ordained minister so I could marry him to the lovely Scarlett. This is my first wedding, so hopefully, I won't mess it up." There was light laughter around the room. The pianist started playing "It Had to be You" as Riggs and a young man, whom Lola assumed was his son Bentley, both wearing tuxedos, walked to the centre of the room and stood at the front next to David.

All the guests turned as Scarlet entered the room on the arm of her father. She wore the most beautiful ivory-lace column gown that was extremely figure-hugging; her blonde hair was swept up into a classic chignon. The only jewellery she wore were beautiful, large, pearl stud earrings. The whole effect was pure and simple elegance. She progressed to the centre of the room toward the minister and her future husband. Her father kissed her sweetly before taking his seat at the front table. Lola couldn't help noticing Anais roll her eyes as Scarlet passed them. It was a strange reaction to a beautiful bride.

The ceremony was short and sweet. Everyone clapped at the end of it, and the waiters poured Champagne and served *canapés* while the bride and groom posed for a series of photos.

Lola stood up. "Will you excuse me? I'm going to the restroom before the speeches."

"I'll join you," Fabian said. As they walked away, Lola noticed the sour look on Anais's face while she watched the bride and groom pose for photographs. They left the room and walked side by side to the restrooms. Lola felt the energy between them, especially when Fabian's hand touched hers slightly as they navigated a narrow hallway. He turned to her, and they both stopped. "It really is a big surprise seeing you here, such an amazing coincidence. How do you know Chase?"

Lola looked at Fabian. He was so familiar to her; after all these years, it was hard to get her feelings in order. "Weirdly, I met him in the BA club lounge at Heathrow. It was a pure coincidence that we were both on the same flight and ended up sitting together on the plane. He needed a tour guide, and I showed him St. Tropez on Wednesday."

Fabian could sense that Lola had left out some details but didn't press her. They stood facing each other, both remembering what had happened in London. Lola leaned against the stone wall as Fabian took her hand and moved closer; she could feel the heat between them, the sexual tension undeniable. They took a moment to embrace the connection that had been an underlying current for years. Gazing up at him, Lola said, "Fabian, we just can't. You know that, especially right now, of course. I'm in the middle of sorting out some unresolved issues, and I need to get my heart and head together."

Fabian nodded in agreement. "I understand. I'm not sure what's going on with my situation at the moment. Anais has been different lately, and we seem to be drifting apart or something." He looked sad as he said it.

"I hope it works out for you, Fabian, I really do. You deserve to be with someone who's really crazy about you." They walked a few more steps and disappeared into the restrooms, returning to the wedding separately.

The reception was now in full swing. Riggs and Scarlet were making their way around to the tables. Lola got back just in time for them to be introduced. Fabian was already seated but stood up again to greet Riggs and congratulate them. Scarlet shook both of their hands, and Chase gave Riggs a friendly hug.

Weirdly, Anais sat coldly in her seat until Fabian turned and touched her shoulder. She finally stood up, towering above them in six-inch heels. "Congratulations, Scarlet, it's nice to finally meet you. I have heard so much about you." She had little emotion in her voice. Lola thought she was strange and again couldn't see what Fabian saw in her. Anais released Scarlet's hand and turned to Riggs. "Good to see you, Riggs. It's been a while since we've been able to come to the gallery, but I can imagine you have been a little 'tied up' lately, anyway." Riggs coughed, and Lola could have sworn that a few beads of sweat dripped down his brow.

"Yes, yes, very busy. Well, darling, we should go and say hi to the next table." Riggs hurriedly moved them on, and the group sat down again. There were a few short speeches, and the waiters started to pour wine and bring out the first course, a choice of Provençal stuffed squid or *tartare de filet de boeuf.*

Lola was having fun talking to the other couple at the table who were from Houston and owned the Koelsch Haus art gallery and a fashion line called Ears of Buddha. They had met Riggs and Bentley through their art connections a few years ago. Fabian and Chase were getting on well, and Chase had Fabian laughing constantly with his Hollywood stories. Every now and again, Lola noticed Fabian turning to Anais, who was constantly checking her phone. She couldn't help overhearing Anais tell Fabian it was her girlfriend Nadine who had man problems and needed advice.

The room was in full swing as Riggs walked past them and waved as he made his way out of the room, probably to smoke or something. A few minutes passed, and Anais stood up and turned to Fabian. "I really need to call Nadine; she is so upset. I won't be long, I promise." Fabian stood up as well and gave her a quick kiss before she turned and strutted out of the room. Lola looked at him, but he just shrugged and carried on talking to Chase.

After about twenty minutes, Fabian looked toward the door, expecting Anais to be back by now, but instead he noticed Scarlet disappear from the reception. He carried on talking for a few minutes and stood up. "I think I'll go and see if everything is okay." Lola could tell he was concerned. Fabian made his way to the bar to see if Anais was sitting in there on the phone, but she wasn't, so he stepped outside to have a quick look around the garden terrace. It was empty except for waiters getting the tables ready for the evening dinner service.

Walking back, he checked the pool area, admiring the Calder sculpture moving slightly in the breeze. There was no sign of Anais. Fabian thought for a minute; she must have gone back to the room. As he walked back inside, he noticed Scarlet looking around the terrace, and he wondered what she was doing.

Fabian made the short stroll to his room. He could hear a muffled voice through the door, so he paused for a moment. When he turned, he saw Scarlet down the hallway going into her room. Fabian noticed the door was not closed all the way, so he was able to push it open softly without making a noise. It swung open, and what he witnessed took his breath away.

Riggs was standing, his hands handcuffed together above his head, and he had what looked like a black silk tie blindfolding him and another one preventing him from talking. Anais was kneeling in front of him, still in her red leather dress, bobbing her head back and forth as she took his cock in and out of her mouth. They had no idea Fabian was standing there. He was transfixed by what was going on and couldn't say or do anything.

Anais pulled back suddenly. "Do you want more?" Riggs let out a muffled sound. "Louder, do you want more? You need to beg for it." Riggs continued to beg. Fabian stood there still, silenced by the shock. Anais took his cock in her mouth again, and Fabian could tell Riggs was not going to last much longer. A noise behind him brought him out of his shock, and he turned to see Scarlet coming down the hallway toward him.

"Have you seen Riggs? He said he was going outside to smoke, and I couldn't find him anywhere. It's time to cut the cake." She was now just a couple feet from where Fabian stood, the door still open to the horror inside.

Fabian thought quickly and let the door close quietly as he spoke in a hushed tone. "Scarlet, I'm not sure."

He was tongue-tied, and she sensed something was going on. "Are you okay, Fabian?"

Suddenly, there was a loud crash. Scarlet pushed past him and shoved the door, which swung open. She screamed the most guttural scream. Riggs was naked, lying on the floor next to a smashed lamp, while Anais stood over him with a shiny black switch. As he squirmed and writhed around in his handcuffs, still muzzled by the gag, the blindfold had slipped, allowing him to see his wife and Fabian standing in the doorway.

Fabian put his arm around Scarlet and led her out of the room, slamming the door behind them. She was shaking, and he could hear the smallest of sobs coming from her. He led Scarlet back to her room at the end of the hallway and took her key. Her hands were shaking too much to open the door. They sat down on the bed, and she cried uncontrollably. Fabian tried to comfort her, putting his own emotions aside as he let her sob in his arms.

"Why, why did he do this to me on our wedding day? I can't believe what a mug I've been. People warned me of his reputation, but I thought it was all gossip."

Fabian felt sorry for her; she was so young and had such a sweet innocent quality. He was disgusted and sick with anger that both Riggs and Anais would do something like this to her. He knew he would get over it. Over the last few weeks, he had started to see that Anais might not be his dream girl after all, and now he knew why. Wondering how long it had been going on, he thought back to all those times when she had claimed her friend Nadine needed her. He realised now that it was probably all a lie. What she really was doing was shagging Riggs. Fabian sat quietly with Scarlet, both of them distressed by what they had witnessed. He couldn't help but wonder what was going on down the hallway.

* * *

Anais went into action mode and frantically started throwing all her stuff into her suitcase. Riggs sat slumped against the wall, still gagged, begging with her in muffled tones to please unlock the handcuffs. Ignoring him, she threw her clothes that dotted the room in the direction of the case. She needed to come up with a plan and quickly. She wasn't ready to go back to Paris just yet, and she could hardly go back to their apartment. Riggs's whining was becoming tiresome, so she went into the bathroom to think for a moment, slamming the door behind her.

Anais picked up her phone, which was sitting on a tall decorative washstand, and started scrolling through her contacts to come up with an idea. Suddenly she remembered someone who may be close by—her ex-boyfriend, Stefan van Carson. He used to spend August and September on his yacht in the Côte d'Azur. Praying he would answer, she dialed his number. The phone rang several times, and just when Anais expected to get his voicemail, he picked up.

"Hello, Stefan here."

"Stefan, it's Anais. How are you?"

"Hi, baby, how are you? It's been a long time. To what do I owe this pleasure? I can tell from your voice this is more than just a catch-up call." He knew her well, she thought.

"You're right, Stefan. I just wondered if by some sheer fluke you are on the Riviera right now."

"As a matter of fact, I am. I'm on my yacht, *Lekker Kontje*." Anais smiled at the name Stefan had selected for his yacht; he certainly had a sense of humour. "We are docked close to St. Tropez. What do you need, Anais?"

She hesitated for a moment. "Well, I'm at La Colombe d'Or in Saint-Paul de Vence at a very boring wedding, and I was wondering if you wanted to have a little fun." She could almost hear Stefan's wheels spinning, remembering what she meant by "fun."

"I tell you what. I can send the helicopter to pick you up. There just happens to be a helipad a couple of miles from you at the Mas d'Artigny Hotel. It will probably take Felix about thirty to forty-five minutes to get there. How does that sound?"

"I will be there, Stefan. Thank you."

"I look forward to seeing you. Another good friend of mine, Annika Barinov, is on *Lekker Kontje* this weekend, and I have a feeling you two are going to get on well, yes, very well indeed."

They hung up, and Anais hurriedly put all her cosmetics in the washbag and opened the door. She ignored Riggs as she stuffed the few remaining items in the suitcase and was about to leave when she remembered something. She went back into the bathroom and took the small handcuff key that she had left on the counter by the sink. Without looking back, she turned and wheeled the case out of the room, the door closing behind her. She had made it halfway down the hall when Fabian appeared from another room. He stopped dead in his tracks as she continued to wheel the suitcase as if he wasn't there. He was so utterly repulsed that all he could do was shake his head.

As Anais passed him, he managed to say, "Let me know where to send your things; you have one month. After that, I will donate your stuff to charity. And Anais, I never want to see you again. You disgust me." She said nothing and carried on and out of his life forever.

*　*　*

Anais walked out onto the garden terrace, and the cool early evening air felt good. She began to walk toward the valet when she decided to make a quick detour. She walked back to the pool area, which was now illuminated for the evening. She unclenched her hand, which still held the silver handcuff key. Laughing as she threw it high in the air, she watched as it took its resting place on the bottom of the pool, looking like a lucky penny in a fountain.

As she turned and walked out of La Colombe d'Or, Anais did not know yet how she would get to the helicopter at Mas d'Artigny. There was a valet parker standing outside, and she asked him if there was taxi service in Saint-Paul de Vence. He explained where she needed to go, but then he paused and shook his head. "I am about to get off work. I can give you a lift. It's ten minutes down the road."

"Thank you so much. That would be so helpful." She gave him her best supermodel smile, and he ran off to get his car. He returned in less than a minute and asked if Anais was staying at the Mas d'Artigny. She just nodded because she wasn't in the mood for small talk.

They arrived at the resort in under fifteen minutes, and he dropped her off at the front entrance. She dug €50 out of her bag and handed it to him. His face lit up like it was Christmas and New Year's Eve rolled into one. Retrieving her suitcase, she pulled it into the foyer and walked up to the concierge to ask where the helipad was located.

"Ah yes, *madame*, they called ahead and told us you were coming. Please follow me." Anais followed the man through a series of hallways out to the back of the property. They could hear the whirl of the helicopter blades. She looked up to see the lights approaching. They both automatically shielded themselves from the wind turbine as the helicopter approached. Anais turned to the concierge and thanked him over the loud engine noise. She crouched down as she approached the aircraft. The small door opened, and she climbed in, lifting the suitcase in behind her.

"Good evening, *Madame* Anais, please buckle up. We should be arriving at *Lekker Kontje* at approximately 21.00 hours." Anais looked out the window as they hovered up and away. Goodbye, Riggs and Fabian, she whispered to herself as she washed their memory out of her mind.

*   *   *

Fabian was unsure what to do. He sat in the hallway for a moment, reflecting on everything that had just happened. He had told Scarlet he would handle the guests downstairs, but what about Riggs, who was still handcuffed in his room? It would be like re-entering a crime scene, and he just couldn't face it right now.

Fabian stood up in time to see Scarlet's parents' worried faces as they entered her room. He waved sadly at them, glad they were here to comfort their daughter. He came up with an idea and went downstairs back to the reception, feeling sorrowful as he glanced at the extravagant uncut five-tiered wedding cake that was now the centrepiece of the room.

Lola looked up, knowing instantly something was wrong. Fabian's face said it all. He signalled for them to step out of the room with him. Thankfully, the guests didn't seem to notice the missing bride and groom.

Lola and Chase followed him to the bar area, which was empty except for the bartender cleaning glasses. Fabian ordered a double whisky on the rocks and asked if they needed anything. They both said no. Waiting for Fabian to speak first, they sat in the corner watching as he downed the drink in two gulps and waved at the bartender for another one.

"I just caught Anais and Riggs in a very uncompromising position, shall we say." Lola put her arm around Fabian while he explained what had happened, including the fact that Riggs was still handcuffed in his room upstairs. Lola and Chase were silent as they listened.

Chase spoke next. "Why don't you let me handle Riggs? He can stay in my room tonight, and we can sort out the rest tomorrow. We can let the wedding planner handle the guests tonight, and Riggs will have to face the music himself in the morning."

"I will go and find her now and meet you back here in a few," Lola said. She stood up just as Scarlet and her parents, with all their luggage, walked out to the garden terrace. Fabian put his whisky on the table and hurried over to her. She stopped for a second, telling her parents to continue out to the valet.

Fabian looked into her sad face; all he could do was give her a tight hug.

"We are going to spend the night in Nice. My parents were able to change our flights back to Houston. We leave first thing in the morning."

"Good luck, Scarlet."

"I'm not the one who's going to need good luck. It's Riggs. I'm going to take him for everything he's got. My dad is the top divorce attorney in Texas."

Fabian smiled slightly at her moxie. As he looked at her one last time, he thought how strange it was that they would always be bonded somehow by this deplorable event. Then he noticed something. "You are missing one of your pearl earrings."

She touched her ear. "That's upsetting. They were a gift from my grandmother, but I'm not going back in there, that's for sure." She reached in her bag, pulled out a business card, and handed it to him. "If anyone does find it, here's my contact info." Fabian put the card in his pocket as she turned and climbed into the car that waited outside. He waved at her as they drove off.

Fabian turned and walked back into the bar. Lola and Chase were not back yet. He sat sipping his whiskey when something under the small bar table caught his eye. Reaching down, he picked it up and held it in his hand. It was Scarlet's pearl earring; the back was missing, but otherwise, it was in good shape. Digging her card out of his back pocket, he dialed the number, but it went straight to voicemail, so he left a message. Fabian pulled out his pocket square and wrapped the precious pearl in it for safekeeping. He put it in his breast pocket, along with her card, and sat back down to finish the whisky. A few minutes passed, and Lola appeared and sat down.

"I'm really sorry you had to go through all this," she said, giving Fabian a quick hug. What a day. I'm exhausted. I talked to Carly, the wedding planner, and she is taking care of everything."

"Great. As soon as Chase gets back, I'm going to bed. I think I'll try to change my flight. Originally, we were set to stay the week, but quite frankly, I just want to go home."

A few wedding guests were starting to disperse into the bar area, talking in hushed voices. Lola wondered how much Carly had told them. They sat in silence for a while, both lost in their own thoughts, watching as more of the wedding party came into the bar.

Chase came back and sat down. "Well, I took care of Riggs. It turns out that Anais took the key to the handcuffs." He couldn't help but smile when he said it. "Luckily for Riggs, they were very similar to the handcuffs we use on set. There is a safety catch that unlocks them just in case someone loses the key. He was a mess, I can tell you. He was very drunk, so I made him shower and put him to bed on the sofa in my room. When I left, he was passed out, snoring. As much as he is an old friend of mine, I'm completely shocked that he would do something like this."

They both just nodded; there wasn't much to say. Lola stood up. "Well, gentleman, I'm going to leave."

Chase stood as well. "Are you okay to drive?" he said softly, putting his arm around her.

"Yes, I didn't drink that much today, knowing I was going to drive home." She could sense Chase was a little disappointed.

Fabian stood up. "Thank you, Lola, for all your help. I'm off to bed; let's talk tomorrow." They watched as Fabian walked away.

"Let me walk you out." They walked out and through the pretty terrace and waited while the valet brought Lola's car around. Chase turned to her. "I'm crazy about you, Lola. It's weird since I barely know you, but I haven't felt like this about anyone in a long time."

Lola looked at his handsome face and kissed him gently. "Let's talk in the morning. You leave on Wednesday, right?"

"Yes. Originally, there was a brunch tomorrow for the wedding party, but I'm sure my day will be spent helping Riggs sort out this mess."

"You're a good friend, Chase."

The valet pulled up in her car, handed her the keys, and said, "*Madame,* is this yours? I found it on the floor in the room where we keep the keys, and I thought it might have fallen off your keychain." Lola looked at his open palm. There was a brass keychain with a miniature horseshoe attached to it. She stared at it for a moment, not knowing why it seemed so familiar.

"*Madame?*"

"No, it's not mine. Sorry." She turned to Chase. "Goodbye." She looked at him one last time before getting in the car. Chase watched as she drove off with a small piece of his heart. He turned and walked back inside.

CHAPTER SEVENTEEN

I ngrid lay in bed staring at the ceiling. She couldn't sleep. Again, her mind was racing after the dinner with Max. Looking at the time on her phone, she saw that it was four-thirty. She got up and went into the kitchen, pausing on the way to look out the window. The River Thames looked dark and slightly ominous at this hour, or maybe it was just her mood. The river path was lit and quiet; she almost felt like taking a walk. She liked London in the early hours before the city woke up. She made herself a cup of tea, sat down at the kitchen island, and flipped open the laptop. There was still no response from her Friday evening email to Lola. She was unsure how to proceed.

Max had not given her much information. Even though it was a real surprise to find out that he and Francis Williams had a history with Lola's mum from many years ago, she just didn't understand why Lola was so upset about it all. Max had just said that the three of them had become friends after meeting Roberta at the Eden-Roc Hotel. She was very upset because her boyfriend Ollie had proposed to her that night. She had turned him down, saying she was too young. He had ended the relationship on the spot and left her crying in the Champagne Lounge.

Arriving at the lounge after the show, the two men noticed the beautiful blonde sobbing quietly to herself. They had invited her to sit with them and managed to turn her tears into laughter with all their funny tales. It was a fun friendship, and they enjoyed spending time together. Max even remembered visiting Villa Bonne Chance when Lola's grandmother, Delilah, was in London. They had spent the day swimming and drinking wine. He had smiled when he said it because Francis had started playing his guitar, and he and Roberta sang and danced the night away. It was amusing to think of Lola's mum at twenty-one being wild and carefree. Ingrid wondered when Roberta had reunited with Ollie.

Ingrid stood up and looked at a framed photo that faced her from a small built-in shelving unit that mostly contained cookbooks. It had been taken right after Ingrid had been born, her parents proudly holding their new baby girl. Ingrid wished that she had known her dad. Sadly, he had been killed in a tragic car accident shortly after the picture was taken. He was so handsome; her mum always said that Ingrid had his smile. Her parents met when her father moved from his home in Jamaica after securing a teaching job at the Universidad Complutense de Madrid. He met his wife Paloma, also a professor, and they fell madly in love. Her mother always joked that it was their love of food. They regularly cooked together, blending Jamaican with Spanish cuisine. She often said cheekily, "There was certainly a lot of spice around."

He proposed on Paloma's thirtieth birthday, and she got pregnant soon after. Ingrid felt sad when she thought how much she would like to ask her dad for advice right now. She decided she would definitely call her mum this afternoon. Maybe she could plan a visit. The thought of that calmed Ingrid's mind. Everything would be okay, she told herself. Lola would have to come around at some point. They had too much history together and had always felt more like sisters; they were that close.

She picked up the cup of tea and walked back to her bedroom, pausing again to look at the dark river. A tugboat was making its way, slowly heading east. Ingrid climbed back into bed and put the tea on the nightstand, focusing on planning a trip to Madrid. She dozed off and fell back into a much more peaceful sleep.

CHAPTER EIGHTEEN

Jack's phone buzzing woke him from a restless night; he felt like he was writing letters to Lola in his sleep. Constant conversations and things he couldn't wait to share with her replayed over and over. Now that he had cracked open the door in his heart, it all seemed to be flooding out in a mad torrent. He looked at the phone. There was a new pop-up that amused him. It was a story of an old fisherman from Cornwall who had caught an oyster thought to be one of the biggest ever recorded. Jack looked at the salty old man holding the immense mollusc and wondered if he was tempted to crack open the beast to see what was inside. The thought made him happy.

Jack put down the phone and picked up the hotel phone to call room service for a pot of coffee and fresh croissants. He got up and opened the terrace door. The sun was just coming up. It was such a glorious morning that he brought his laptop outside. He had spent all day yesterday researching both Annika Barinov and Augustin and Marceau Art Installation Services. Unfortunately, he kept coming up with dead ends. He discovered pretty quickly that Augustin and Marceau were still in business, but the company had been sold in 2000, and the new owners didn't have records of the installations as far back as Jack needed.

There was a loud knock on the door. Jack greeted the room service waiter, who carried a tray with a steaming coffee pot and a basket of warm croissants. He followed Jack out to the terrace, set them on the table, and retrieved the tray. Jack thanked and tipped him as he swiftly exited. Jack sat down again, poured himself a cup with steamed milk, and took a bite of the warm croissant. It was flaky and delicious. He wondered if Annika had received his letter. Hopefully, Jimmy had given it to her executive assistant as promised. Jack would just have to wait and see.

The fact that Claude had been in Italy the last few days due to a death in the family had bought Jack more time. His phone started to ring. It was Fiona. "Good morning, Fiona. How's everything going?"

"Good, good. I've been trying to find out as much about Miss Barinov as possible. The thing that keeps coming up is she seems to have the most unbelievable connections. There are photos of her with everyone, from supermodels to presidents. She's also a real philanthropist and has given millions to various charities, along with being a mega supporter of the arts. I'm looking at a picture of her at the Met Gala last year draped on another gorgeous man. The lady loves a party, that's for sure!"

Jack laughed. "Yep, I came up with the same stuff. I guess I'm going to have to wait and see if she's intrigued enough to reach out to me."

"Be careful Jack, she looks dangerous!" Fiona then filled him in on other clients and what was going on. He thanked her for checking in on a Sunday. It was the nature of their business; it was never just nine to five.

He put the coffee on the table, stood up, stretched, and walked inside. He stopped in front of Delilah's painting, studying it for a while, desperately searching for a sign. For some reason, he noticed that it was slightly wonky. Maybe it had shifted when the waiter had shut the door. Jack moved it this way and that and stood back to see if it was straight. Standing back and looking at it, he suddenly thought of something. He lifted the piece off the wall and laid it on a small desk in the corner. Turning it over, he saw that there was a paper receipt taped to the back. It had Augustin and Marceau's names on it and some kind of delivery information. He looked at the small print and there it was, a name. Jack read the two lines aloud: "Delivery driver Leon Martin, pick up seven paintings at Villa Bonne Chance. Drop off at Eden-Roc." The seven pieces were listed, and there was a faded signature from Delilah Cornel. Unfortunately, the rest of the text underneath her signature was illegible, probably due to age. Jack assumed that, sadly, it had included her address. He took a photo of the receipt and hung the painting back on the wall, this time making sure it was straight. He wondered if Leon Martin still worked for the company. It was a long shot, but he would definitely call them first thing Monday morning.

Jack sat down on the terrace. The morning sun was warming up, and he thought how nice it would be to take a swim. He leaned back, reflecting on what a strange coincidence it was that he was on the Riviera searching for the Kandinsky and its owner, and then on the flip side, searching for Lola through her grandmother's painting. He hoped and prayed it would all come together.

Jack got up and walked inside to change into swimwear and noticed the time was nine. He yawned and started throwing some things in a beach bag to take to the pool. When he was just about to leave the room, his mobile phone started ringing; the number came up as "unknown." Jack decided he better pick it up in case it was Claude calling from Italy on a different number.

"Hello?"

There was a short silence and then, "Good morning, I'd like to speak to Jack Alistair, please." The woman had a very clipped unusual accent, one he couldn't put his finger on.

"This is Jack Alistair. Who is this, please?" Jack waited, not knowing what to expect.

"My name is Lara Lenkov, and I am Annika Barinov's executive assistant. I want to inform you that Miss Barinov has decided she will meet you this afternoon at noon sharp on Stefan van Carson's yacht, *Lekker Kontje*. You are to come to the dock at your hotel, and you will be met by a tender that will transport you there."

Jack was so surprised it took him a minute to answer. She spoke before he had time to respond. "Do you agree to this meeting?" She obviously was not one for idle chit-chat.

"Yes, I will be there at twelve noon," he confirmed.

"Oh, and Mr. Alistair, absolutely no weapons, no photos, no social media. Is that understood?"

Jack was taken back but answered quickly, "You have my word." She hung up instantly, almost before he had finished the sentence. He couldn't believe Annika had agreed to see him. He immediately dialed Fiona in London, and she picked up on the first ring. "You are not going to believe this. Annika's assistant, Lara Lenkov, just called and set up a meeting with Miss Barinov at noon today!"

"Really? That's shocking; according to everything I've read, she is extremely particular about who she lets on *Miroslava*."

"Well, that's another thing. I'm meeting her on Stefan van Carson's yacht."

Fiona whistled. "Not bad going, Jack." She laughed.

"They also told me not to bring any weapons on board! Who do they think I am?" He couldn't help but be a bit excited and a little nervous, all wrapped up in one.

"It's all very James Bond and intriguing. Have you figured out yet how you are going to approach her about the Kandinsky?"

"Well, she already knows my interest because I put it in the letter. Why else would she want to meet me if it wasn't to discuss the painting?"

"I don't want to jump to conclusions, but Annika Barinov is known as quite the man-eater. Do you think she checked you out online and decided you may make a tasty treat?" Fiona was cracking up. It was such a role reversal for a woman to play that card.

Jack burst out laughing. "What do you think I am, a chew toy or something? I can handle myself just fine, thank you. Besides, I'm completely focused on getting her to sell the Kandinsky; this might be my only chance."

"Take care of yourself. I can't wait for the next instalment." They hung up, and Jack looked at the time; it was close to ten. He decided to forgo the pool. Instead, he opened the laptop. He wanted to double-check that he hadn't missed any details and knew everything possible about the painting, including past auction results, increases in value, when it was last appraised, and for what value. It was hard to plan for this meeting because he was completely unsure of what he was about to walk into. He wondered if he would even meet the film director. Also, it would be hard to bring up business if he were present. Jack decided the best plan was to be as prepared as possible. He made sure he had all his research paperwork in order; he wanted to be completely organised.

After Jack collected the papers and put them in his bag, he walked into the bedroom, undressed, stepped into the bathroom, and turned on the shower. He looked at himself in the mirror. Due to his strict workout routine and his love of tennis, which he played regularly, he looked very fit at forty-five. His body looked like a pro. His wavy, unruly, light brunette hair gave him a slightly mischievous allure, but it was his sparkling blue eyes that always drew comments from women.

The shower was beginning to steam up the mirror, so he stepped in and stood enjoying the sensation of the hot water hitting his sore muscles. As usual, when he let his mind wander, it always went back to Lola. He wished she was standing here with him in the steaming shower. Envisioning her hands on him, he could feel his cock waking up. The power she had over him was amazing. He savoured the sensation for a few minutes before stepping out of the shower and quickly drying off and dressing. He decided on some relaxed blue chino trousers and a cream Burberry polo shirt. Knowing it could be breezy on the water this time of year, he grabbed a sweater to bring along. Jack walked into the other room and checked one last time to ensure that he had all the papers in order. He looked at the time on his phone; it was eleven-forty. Slinging the bag over his shoulder, he headed down to the boat dock; he wanted to be there when the tender arrived.

Surprisingly, when Jack arrived at the dock, he spotted a Sea Ray powerboat waiting for him. As he got a little closer, he saw a woman behind the wheel wearing a striped one-piece swimsuit and a white baseball cap, both with a crest on the front with the initials L.K. As he got nearer, a husky woman wearing what looked like a grey military jumpsuit stepped off the boat and stood in front of Jack with her arms crossed. He greeted both of them. "Hello there, I'm Jack Alistair. Thanks for coming to pick me up."

The woman in the boat nodded as the other one spoke in a very thick Romanian accent. "I am Helga Petrov, Miss Barinov's head of security. First, I will need to see some form of identification, then I will check you for weapons, and last you will give me your cellular phone, which I will be looking after during your visit with Miss Barinov."

Jack looked up at her; she must be six-foot-four with arms that could give Arnold a run for his money. She wasn't the type of woman you said no to. He pulled out his wallet and handed her his driving licence, which she scrutinised before handing it back to him. Next, she had him put his arms out to the side as she frisked him roughly. She pulled a small shiny bag out of her pocket; it looked like it was made of aluminium foil. "Your cellular phone, please." Jack hated giving up his phone, but he knew he didn't have a choice. He handed it to her, and she powered it off before placing it in the bag, which she returned to a pocket on the side of her muscular thigh. Lastly, she pulled the paperwork out of his bag and flicked through it. Satisfied, she returned it to the bag.

"Follow me, please." As Jack followed her onto the boat, she pointed for him to sit on the wide leather bench at the back. She sat next to the driver in one of the captain's chairs. Helga turned to the woman. "Miss De Vries, we are ready to depart." The driver quickly untied the two lines holding them to the dock and eased the boat slowly away through a short no-wake zone before accelerating at such pace Jack almost flew off the bench.

Helga turned and yelled at him over the engine noise. "We should be arriving at *Lekker Kontje* in fifteen minutes." Jack nodded as he held on, as the boat sped along at what most people would consider a dangerous speed.

Neither of the two women said anything as they approached the superyacht, which looked about half the size of *Miroslava* but was still incredibly impressive. He could see a helicopter at the stern above board. Miss De Vries slowed the boat way down, and they pulled up to the starboard side where a sunbathing deck extended over the water. Jack assumed that when the boat was moving, the sun deck closed up like a large door. Above that was a davit crane that could lift the tender out of the water. Two crew hands appeared immediately and began to tie the lines to the dock cleats, securing the boat to the side of the deck. Jack thanked Miss De Vries as she barked orders to them in Dutch.

Helga stepped out of the boat and turned to Jack. "Follow me, please." They made a sharp left, then came around to another sunbathing deck at the stern. He followed her up a flight of stairs and was met by an infinity pool next to an outdoor lounge area with a large white curved sofa with red-and-white striped throw cushions on it, all embroidered with the initials L.K.

"Wait here." Helga pointed to the nearest armchair. Jack sat down, and within thirty seconds, a young woman wearing a uniform of white shorts and a red polo shirt came over to him. "Good afternoon. My name is Nova. Can I get you a drink while you wait, sir?" She handed him a drinks menu and told him she would return to take his order in a minute. Jack noticed her Dutch accent; he wondered if all the staff were Dutch. He scrolled down the list, noticing some of the finest wines and Champagnes in the world, along with several mixed cocktails. Nova appeared again and asked him if he had decided. At that moment, a man walked up whom Jack instantly recognised as the film director Stefan van Carson. He stood up to meet him.

"Welcome to *Lekker Kontje*. My name is Stefan van Carson. I'm glad you are joining us today. We will be having lunch in about half an hour; the ladies said they would join us then. Why don't you and I have a drink first?" He signalled to Nova, who had stood back for a moment. "Do you like Champagne?"

"Yes, that would be lovely, thank you."

"We will take the '96 *Dom Perignon*."

"Right away, sir." Nova walked away swiftly.

Jack turned to Stefan. "Let me introduce myself. I'm Jack Alistair." The two men shook hands. "Thank you so much for having me aboard your stunning yacht." They both turned their heads as two beautiful tall blonde women wearing robes came down a stairway and stopped at the head of the pool. They waved at Jack and Stefan, giggling.

"Why don't you two come over and meet our new guest, Jack Alistair."

The ladies sauntered over and stopped right in front of them, reaching out their hands. Almost in unison, they said, "Nice to meet you, Jack." Jack smiled at them. "I'm Kitty, and this is Giselle." Kitty sounded American and stood staring into Jack's eyes, beaming with some of the whitest teeth he had ever seen.

Stefan said, "Aren't you two hot in those towelling robes?"

"We are Stefan; we're sweltering." The two beauties stood, undid their knotted belts, and let their robes fall to the floor. They were both completely naked, and Jack couldn't help noticing they had a matching peroxide blonde strip of fine hair, which was the only thing hiding the jewels beneath.

"Off you go! Let me catch up with Mr. Alistair." They turned and took a quick run before diving into the pool. Jack quickly composed himself as he watched them frolic around in the water, splashing each other and thoroughly enjoying the audience. "Fun girls. I met them in St. Tropez last week. They came on the yacht with a mutual friend, and they haven't left. I guess they are enjoying themselves."

Nova returned with the *Dom Perignon* and showed Stefan the bottle before opening it and pouring two glasses. Jack couldn't help but wonder what she thought of the naked blondes in the pool. She was probably used to it by now.

"So, how do you know Annika? She just told me you were someone she'd like to get to know better."

What an interesting thing to say, Jack thought. "Funnily enough, I've never met Annika. I delivered a letter to her on Friday regarding a business proposition. Her executive assistant called me this morning to let me know Annika wanted to meet."

"May I ask what kind of business?"

Jack didn't really want to tell him, but he felt that he didn't have a choice. "I'm an art dealer, and my client is interested in buying a painting in Miss Barinov's collection."

Stefan scratched his chin. "Exciting indeed. Good luck with that."

Nova came back to the table. "Gentlemen, lunch is served. You will be dining on the aft deck." They stood, and Jack followed Stefan up to the next deck. There was a rectangular table set for lunch and shaded by a sun umbrella and to the right of that, a bar with a large aquarium running its length. Next to that was another lounge area. It was all incredibly luxurious.

"I hope you like lobster. We're having surf and turf."

Jack smiled, looking at the table set for four, wondering who else was joining them. "That sounds delicious!"

"Why don't you sit right there," he said, pointing to one of the chairs. They sat down and sipped on the Champagne that Nova had brought from the lower deck. Jack was just about to ask Stefan about his latest film when he saw two women approaching the table. One of them he recognised instantly as Annika Barinov. They were both tall and very slender. The other woman was exceptionally tall and had blonde, almost white hair cut into a sixties-style pixie cut. She was wearing an emerald-green floor-length caftan; it looked vintage, the sort of thing Elizabeth Taylor would wear on a yacht.

As they approached, he looked at Annika, who was softer looking than her pictures despite the almost wolf-like eyes and razor-sharp cheekbones. She was wearing a very low-cut bronze silk slip dress, and quite obviously from the way it hugged her figure, nothing underneath. He noticed she was barefoot, which added to the confidence she exuded. Both men stood up to greet the women, and Stefan introduced them.

"Jack Alistair, I'd like to introduce you to Miss Annika Barinov and Miss Anais."

Jack reached out his hand to Annika. She took it and held his gaze as if she were trying to read his mind. "It's very nice to meet you; I appreciate your invitation." The intensity of her eyes made him a little nervous; she was difficult to gauge. He released her hand and turned to Anais. "Very nice to meet you, Anais." She had little emotion on her face, but she managed a thin smile. She looked vaguely familiar, and then he remembered she had been on the cover of French *Vogue*. The cover had created a lot of press due to the fact that Anais was fifty-five. It had been celebrated by many people, particularly women who were tired of the ongoing conversation about aging and beauty standards for women past a certain age, especially in the media.

"Well, let's all sit down," Stefan said. We have Champagne to drink!" Both men pulled the chairs back for the women. Annika made a point of sitting next to Jack; he could smell her spicy and fruity perfume, and her aura was quite enticing.

Nova opened another bottle of the *Dom* and poured fresh glasses for everyone. They raised them, and Annika made the toast. She turned to Jack. "Here's to new friends," once more holding his gaze for longer than normally expected. She had only a trace of a Romanian accent, and he remembered from during his research on her that she had been educated in the U.K. Jack didn't know what to make of all this. It was almost surreal being on this beautiful yacht. He was wondering how to approach Annika about the painting when she turned to him and said, "So Jack, you want to buy my Kandinsky?"

Jack was taken back. Thankfully, Nova interrupted the conversation for a minute as she placed a dozen oysters on the table, giving Jack a moment to think. Everyone seemed interested in his response. "Yes, as I said in the letter, I'm an art dealer, and my client wants to buy your painting for his wife as an anniversary gift."

Stefan laughed. "He must have been caught with his pants down or something." Jack couldn't help but nod in agreement because he also guessed that to be the truth of the matter.

Annika smiled. "And for a second, I thought what a nice romantic gesture that was. Who is your client who can't keep his trousers on? Maybe I know him."

"Unfortunately, I can't give divulge that information. He asked to be kept anonymous. What I can say is that he is a wealthy French businessman from Monte Carlo."

Annika looked intrigued. She picked up an oyster and squeezed some lemon on it before letting it slide into her mouth. She turned to Jack as she licked her lips in a very seductive way. "Interestingly, that painting is hanging in my place in Monte Carlo, and I'm sure I'd miss it if I sold it." She picked up another oyster and popped it into her mouth.

Jack wanted to keep the conversation going. "My client is willing to pay well above market value if that might change your mind."

Stefan and Anais were amused to be part of the banter as they sat eating the oysters. Jack watched as Anais loaded an oyster with some of the spicy cocktail sauce that accompanied them. She tilted her head back slightly as the oyster slipped from its shell into her mouth, and unfortunately, some of the red sauce was left accidentally on the corner of her lip. Annika turned to her. "Here, darling, let me." She leaned forward, moved slowly toward Anais's lips, and licked off the sauce. Anais brought her hand up and touched Annika's face. The two women's mouths met in the most sensual way as they kissed, not caring who was watching.

Jack sat back, mesmerised. The moment was so tantalising that he felt himself getting aroused. He didn't dare look at Stefan, who said, "Now, ladies, let's save some fun for later." They both smiled, knowing the effect they had on the two men.

Annika turned to Jack. "I tell you what, Jack, let me think about it. I rarely sell paintings from my collection, but for some unknown reason, I feel that I want to help you with this." Jack was flabbergasted that she would entertain it; at least there would be something to tell Claude. Jack noticed that Anais had her hand on Annika's leg, and she was lightly running her long sanguine-red nail up and down Annika's inner thigh. He was distracted as he watched.

"I knew you two would get on well," Stefan said to the women. "It was all such good timing that you called when you did, Anais."

"I'm so glad I called you, Stefan. I was at the dullest wedding with the most boring man. This is so much more amusing," Anais said as she turned to Annika.

Jack couldn't help but ask. "So, what happened to the boring man?"

"Well, actually, there were two boring men, one that I was living with and one that I was having an affair with."

Jack was surprised at her candour. She carried on with the story, obviously enjoying the shock value. "You see, the man I was having an affair with was actually the groom, and we got caught by his new wife and my boyfriend when we were in the middle of something."

Stefan interrupted. "She called me from the Colombe d'Or, and I had Felix pick her up last night in the helicopter."

Jack couldn't help but be a little cheeky. "But why was it boring?"

"The thing is, Fabian and I were at the table with this annoying woman named Lola and her film-star boyfriend, whose name I can't remember, and to be honest, I'm pretty sure she and Fabian had something going on. I could tell he was flustered when he saw her. Apparently, they had been childhood friends or something."

Jack was utterly dumbfounded. This was the most amazing coincidence, and he had to find out more. "Her name wasn't Lola Delphine and your boyfriend, Fabian Whitecliff?" He waited with bated breath.

"Yes, that's it. She's British with a French last name. I remember now. Do you know them?"

Jack felt butterflies in his gut. "Yes, I do from a long time ago, but we lost contact some years back. I don't suppose you could give me Fabian's number?"

"Well, I would have, but I lost my phone in transit from the Colombe d'Or to the resort where the helicopter picked me up. Unfortunately, my memory is such that I don't remember anybody's telephone number. You don't really have to since mobile phones."

Jack nodded. He didn't remember phone numbers either.

"I tell you what, though, the guy I was having an affair with is called Riggs Howard. His art gallery in Paris is called Galerie Raphael, and his friend was the film star who was Lola's date. Maybe if you give him a call at the gallery, he will be able to help."

Anais wasn't usually so nice, but for whatever reason, she saw something in Jack when he mentioned Lola's name. There was a tenderness to his voice, and Anais could tell he was madly in love with her, and it had temporarily broken down her hard exterior.

"Thank you, Anais, I will do that. And by the way, that wedding sounds anything but boring," he said, trying to lighten the mood a little.

They all turned as a young male crew member wheeled over a table with two immense coral pink lobsters on it and proceeded to crack open the shells, exposing the succulent meat. Nova came over and asked if they wanted to keep the oysters on the table. Stefan looked at his guests, and they agreed that they were ready for the lobster. She took the chilled plate away, replaced it with the platter of lobster, and quickly returned with a large tray carrying four filet mignon steaks, each with a side of grilled asparagus. Nova topped up their Champagne glasses and asked Stefan if there was anything else. He shook his head, smiling.

Jack wondered what time it was and felt as though he had been transported into another bizarre world with these people he didn't know, with no idea when he was leaving and what would happen next. He was actually enjoying the weirdness of it all. Having been around many very wealthy people, he knew it could often get out of control at any moment, so he decided to relax and enjoy the experience. Maybe he would end up with the Kandinsky at the end of the day.

Stefan chatted away about his new movie, a horror film about a group of children living on a haunted farm. The inspiration had come from some scary British public information films from the 1970s. It turns out that he had been sent to boarding school in the U.K. when he was a child, as his parents travelled so much for their business. In his next project coming up next month, he was stepping away from the horror genre to film a new romantic comedy set in London and Venice. He was especially excited because James Pearson was on board to compose the film's score.

They were finishing lunch when Annika turned to Jack, placed her hand on his, and looked into his eyes. "Would you like to come with me after lunch? I'd like to show you a new catalogue of my entire collection." He felt the intensity of her eyes, and he couldn't help but notice her pert nipples straining through the delicate fabric of her dress. She was a mixture of incredibly sexy and incredibly dangerous, especially after the Champagne they had consumed at lunch.

"Yes, I would like to see it, thank you. I have read a lot about your important art collection." He tried to sound as business-like as possible.

She smiled at him. "Follow me, then. Stefan, Anais, are you joining?"

Stefan shook his head. "I'm going to take a swim. I can hear Giselle and Kitty down there still; I'm sure they need some company." He turned to Jack. "Well, if I don't see you before you leave, it's been a pleasure meeting you. Why don't you give me your card? Maybe we can do some business in the future."

Jack pulled a card out of his pocket and handed it to Stefan. Shaking his hand, he said, "Thank you very much for your kind hospitality, Stefan." They all stood up, and Stefan waved as he made his way down to the pool. Jack had a quick flashback of the two naked women from earlier. From the sound of the music drifting up the stairs, it sounded like they were having fun.

Anais and Annika linked an arm through each of Jack's and guided him in the direction of a private lounge that Annika used on her annual visits to *Lekker Kontje*. It was a luxurious room with a huge picture window and various seating areas. The large, colourful abstract paintings that lined the walls worked very well with the neutral tones of the furnishings. Annika flipped on some music and pressed a button on the wall. Almost immediately, Nova opened the door. "Can we have another bottle of the *Dom Perignon*, please?" Nova returned moments later with the Champagne in an ice bucket and three glasses, which she promptly filled.

"Thank you; we would like not to be disturbed again." Nova nodded and shut the door behind her. Jack couldn't help but wonder again what it must be like to work in this environment all the time. He was pretty sure Nova must have some good stories to tell. Annika sat down next to Anais on one of the large sofas and signalled Jack to have a seat on the opposite sofa. On the coffee table there was a hardbound book, which she moved in his direction. "This is my European collection. I still have some pieces in Romania which are not in the catalogue."

Jack started flipping the pages in awe of the amazing paintings she owned. He was so engrossed in the art that he hadn't yet noticed what was happening with Anais and Annika. Looking up to ask a question about an individual piece, he remained silent. The two women were kissing each other again, and he could see Anais was lightly touching Annika's breast. He watched in a trance; it was so tantalising to watch these two stunning women act so sensually with each other. Anais let the strap of Annika's dress fall off one shoulder. Jack could see her hardened nipple. He sat motionless, unable to turn away from the erotic show. Anais was making her way down Annika's neck, circling the dark fuchsia nipple with her tongue. He could hear Annika starting to make muffled noises of desire.

Jack could feel himself getting very hard. Lost in fantasies of his own, he watched Annika slip out of the bronze silk dress; it lay on the floor in a crumpled heap. As he suspected earlier, she was completely naked under the dress. Anais slipped out of her emerald caftan. She made her way to the other nipple while lifting Annika's leg. Jack could see she was inserting one finger in and out of Annika, who was now groaning in pleasure and lifting her hips in time with Anais's finger.

Through the moans of pleasure, Annika turned to Jack. "Why don't you come over here and join us," her Romanian accent now suddenly more noticeable. He was so perplexed. He wanted nothing more than to join their party, but he knew he would regret it later. He couldn't find the words, but thankfully Annika did. "Don't worry, darling; you can just sit and watch if you like." He just nodded, not moving, unable to turn away.

Anais pulled back for a second, and Annika asked her not to stop. "Shh, you will come when I say so." She reached over to a small red-velvet drawstring bag on the side table, opened it, and pulled out what looked like a large dildo with something attached to it. There was also a red-silk rope and a red eye mask. Annika watched as Anais swiftly tied her hands behind her back with the silk rope. Annika begged her to hurry. Jack could tell that Anais was entirely in control. She stood up, and Jack saw that the dildo had two leather leg holes and a belt. She slipped it on and fastened the belt, the strap-on now in place. Taking the eye mask, she covered Annika's eyes and turned to Jack.

"Are you sure you don't want to go first? Introducing the 'Lord Guvnor,'" she said, pointing at the large strap-on. Jack shook his head, still unable to speak. She opened Annika's legs and lightly licked just below her fine landing strip of hair. Gently licking back and forth, she made her way to Annika's dripping pearl. Jack could tell she was very close to reaching the final waves of climax, but right at that moment, Anais would pull back, causing Annika to scream in pain and pleasure. It was everything he could do not to join them, his excitement hard to contain, but he still sat glued to the sofa.

Anais lifted herself and kneeled back on the sofa. She opened Annika's legs as wide as possible. Using her hands to lift Annika slightly, she thrust the strap-on into Annika, sliding it in and out, her own pleasure mounting as the leather leg straps were just high enough to cause friction to her sopping jewel. Both women were moving in complete rhythm with each other, both now about to reach the final waves of pleasure. Annika was the first to scream out as she was finally allowed to fully surrender to Anais, who was a second behind her, throwing back her head and gasping in pure ecstasy. The two women were still and lay entwined for a moment with their eyes closed. They almost looked like a Helmut Newton photograph.

Not quite sure what to do, Jack decided to go the bathroom, getting up quietly so as not to disturb them. The bathroom was just off the lounge and equally luxurious. He shut the door, went to the sink, and splashed cold water on his face. He really couldn't believe what he had just witnessed. The cold water felt good and helped bring him back a little to reality. He decided it was time to leave and get back to the hotel. Jack stepped out of the bathroom and resumed his seat on the sofa, not knowing what to expect.

"Oh, there you are." Annika was dressed and sitting on the sofa drinking Champagne next to Anais, who was wearing the emerald caftan again. The toys had been put away, and it was as if nothing had happened at all. "So, what did you think?" Jack didn't know what to say but decided quickly to act like he hadn't just watched the two women in front of him enjoy extremely erotic sex. "About my collection, Jack. You looked through the book, no? I tell you what, why don't you take it with you, and you can have a better look."

Jack stood up. "Thank you. I'd like that." He picked up the book and put it in his bag, pulling out the paperwork he had brought with him. "May I leave these papers with you to review at your leisure?"

Annika took them and glanced at the front page that had the offered amount on it. She put them down on the coffee table. "Let me look over them, and I will be in touch." She stood up, walked over to the wall, and pressed the service button. Almost immediately, Nova arrived.

"Our guest is ready to leave. Please call Helga so she can bring Mr. Alistair his phone and take him down to the tender." Nova left, and Annika walked over to Jack and faced him. "It has been fascinating meeting you, Jack, and I have a feeling this is not going to be the last time." He was about to say something when she leaned forward and put her mouth on his. He automatically parted his lips, and their tongues met. He could feel his excitement growing again. She pulled back suddenly, knowing very well the effect she was having on him.

"It was very nice meeting you also, Miss Barinov, and I thank you for considering my business proposition." He turned to Anais who was now standing next to Annika, took her hand and kissed it, smelling Annika's scent on her fingers.

Anais looked up at him from beneath her eyelashes. "It was a pleasure to meet you, Jack. When you come to Paris, give me a call. I'm sure we could find a way to tie each other up for a couple of hours." She handed him a calling card, which he put in the outside pocket of his bag. The door opened. Helga stood there holding the aluminium bag containing his mobile phone, which she took out and handed to him. Jack turned to face the two women one last time before following Helga out of the lounge and through a long hallway and down a staircase.

They were soon back on the sundeck, the Sea Ray waiting, with Miss De Vries holding it steady. As Jack jumped on board, Helga yelled at him above the engine noise. "Good luck, Mr. Alistair." It was a strange thing to say, and he wasn't quite sure what she meant. He turned to say goodbye, but she was already gone. Remembering Miss De Vries' speedy ride last time, Jack sat in the captain's chair next to her and held on as she sped off in the direction of the Eden-Roc. Neither one of them spoke on the fifteen-minute journey. Jack realised how exhausted he was. It was nearly dark by the time they arrived back at the hotel dock. He thanked her and stepped off the boat. She waved as she turned the Sea Ray and headed back to *Lekker Kontje*.

CHAPTER NINETEEN

Jack still hadn't had a chance to look at his phone. He guessed it must be close to eight. Making his way back to the suite, he looked forward to a hot shower and room service. He unlocked the door, put his bag down on the chair, and turned on some of the table lamps before digging out his phone and turning it back on. It was just after eight. He scrolled through his messages and found two from Fiona and one from Claude. After the shower, he would call Fiona. Claude would have to wait until Monday morning. He was just too tired to deal with him tonight.

Walking to the bathroom, he noticed on the floor an envelope he hadn't seen when he entered the dark room. Thinking it was probably just an updated hotel bill, he picked it up and put it on the coffee table to open after his shower. Jack undressed quickly, laying his clothes on the back of a chair, and wandered into the bathroom. Turning on the shower, he waited a minute for the water to be extra hot before stepping in. Standing with the steamy water hitting his chest, he reflected on the day.

It was probably one of the most bizarre meetings he'd ever had and, of course, totally unexpected from start to finish. He was confused because it seemed that Annika had wanted to seduce him from the minute they met, and he wondered if that was her intention all along. She seemed like the type of woman who had a plan for everything. Of course, he thought back to the incredibly raunchy show they had performed, and even though he had been invited to join in, he knew that the real turn-on for them was his being a voyeur. There had been something extra carnal about the way Anais had been so dominant with the Romanian billionaire, who was usually the one with all the power and control.

Jack wondered what would happen next and if Annika would stay true to her word and think about selling the Kandinsky. He knew it had nothing to do with money, so what did it concern? Maybe she enjoyed the game? Before he left, her sensual kiss had also caught him entirely off guard, and he felt slightly guilty because he couldn't help but enjoy it. Anyway, he would just have to wait and see. One thing for sure, he knew Annika Barinov was going to do exactly what she wanted to do and could not be persuaded to do otherwise.

Anais's confession about the wedding was another part of the day that had totally shocked him, and he was only just processing it. He couldn't believe that she was Fabian Whitecliff's girlfriend and had met Lola. It was all the most incredible coincidence. He had made a note to look up Galerie Raphael tomorrow and see if Anais' friend Riggs Howard could help him at all. Jack felt a little sad. He hadn't wanted to think of the possibility that Lola had someone special in her life, let alone an American film star. He would just have to hold faith in the universe that she still had a prominent place for him in her heart. Everything that had happened lately, and how strongly he felt, certainly made him think that it was all meant to be. All he knew was that he had to be true to himself and finally be honest and transparent with his feelings for her.

Jack turned the water off and towelled off. He slipped on a terrycloth robe that was on the back of the door and walked into the lounge area to call room service. He just wanted something simple for dinner. He picked up the phone. "Good evening. I'd like to order some dinner, please."

"Yes, *Monsieur* Alistair, what can I get you this evening?"

"I want something very simple; is there anything you can recommend?"

"Yes, of course, sir. May I suggest linguine with parmesan and shaved black truffle?

"That sounds perfect, and I'd also like a bottle of red wine to go with that. Whatever you think would pair well with the pasta."

"Certainly, *monsieur*, it will be about thirty minutes." Jack hung up the phone.

Forgetting about the envelope sitting on the table, he picked up his mobile phone to call Fiona. He had already decided that he was only going to tell Fiona the business details of the day; the rest was obviously private. "Hi Fiona, I'm back. I survived," he joked.

"How did it go? Good news, I hope!"

"Well, as a matter of fact, she did entertain the idea of the sale of the painting."

Fiona could tell he was being vague for some reason. "Tell me more. What did you do, and did you also meet Stefan van Carson?"

"I did. We all had lunch together along with that famous model Anais. You know, the one that is on the cover of French *Vogue* this month. I only know about her because of all the positive press she's been getting for it."

"Oh yes, I love her. What was she like? And what was Annika like?" Jack was silent for a second as he remembered exactly what they were like. He found himself blushing down the phone. "They are both brilliant, strong women."

Fiona squawked. "Come on, Jack, there's more gossip than that. I just know it!" After knowing him so long, she knew when he was not telling the whole story. As much as he liked her and had a great working relationship, he didn't feel it was appropriate or necessary to tell her everything. To give her something to gnaw on and to throw her off the trail a little, he decided to tell her about Giselle and Kitty.

"Okay, here's something you don't see every Sunday afternoon. After Annika's bodyguard searched me and took my phone away, she brought me to the pool area. Stefan came to introduce himself. Well, at that moment, two beautiful blonde women appeared wearing robes. Stefan called them over, and they both took off their robes and stood there completely naked before diving in the pool."

Fiona laughed. "And I'm sure you covered your eyes, didn't you, Jack?"

"Of course I did," he said jokingly. "But the important thing here is I think I can close this deal and get Claude his Kandinsky."

"Fantastic. I'm glad it was a successful meeting." Fiona knew there was more to it than that, but Jack was her boss, and if he chose not to tell her the whole story, that was his prerogative. So, she didn't ask any more questions, even though she would have loved to hear some juicy gossip.

"Thank you for all your help, Fiona. Let's talk tomorrow." Jack yawned as he put the phone down. He was looking forward to his dinner, which should be arriving at any moment. He glanced down at the table, suddenly remembering the letter that had been put under his door. Picking it up, he noticed that his name was handwritten on the envelope in magnificent calligraphy. He opened it carefully and took out the thick, almost watercolour-paper note. On the top in embossed gold lettering were the initials A.B. He couldn't resist sliding his fingers over the raised lettering. Inside was a message written in the same stylish calligraphy. It read:

> *Mr. Alistair,*
>
> *It was a pleasure meeting you today. I will be at Hotel du Cap-Eden-Roc on Thursday the 20th for a private early-evening soirée. Let's have dinner after. Miss Lenkov will call you to discuss the details.*

Jack read the note over. He couldn't believe it. She must have had someone deliver it when he was still on the yacht. The twentieth was this coming Thursday, so at least he had a little time to think about it. He remembered that Charlie had said that *Miroslava* was heading to the Italian Riviera next. She must have changed her mind, Jack thought. He felt conflicted; he didn't want to risk upsetting her and losing the sale of the painting, but he also had no interest in getting involved with her, even though he found her incredibly breathtaking and intriguing. His heart was Lola's and putting things right with her was his top priority. A knock on the door interrupted his muddled mind. He got off the sofa and opened it.

"Good evening, *Monsieur* Alistair." Alberto stood outside with his dinner and a bottle of wine.

"Good to see you, Alberto. Please come in." Alberto wheeled the service table into the room, asking Jack where he would like it. Jack pointed to where he had been sitting. "I didn't think you normally worked in room service."

"I don't, *monsieur*, but I asked Oscar, the usual waiter, if I could bring your dinner up to you because I have some information for you regarding Leon Martin, the delivery driver for Augustin and Morceau."

Jack waited as Alberto continued. "It turns out that Leon Martin's daughter, Marie Allard, works in housekeeping at the hotel. I didn't put it together before since she is married, so her last name is no longer Martin."

"Can I talk to her?" Jack was suddenly excited.

"She is on holiday this week, and I think we should wait until she returns. I've never spoken to her personally, but when I asked the staff, they all said the same thing. She is difficult to get along with. The only reason she still works here is that she is so good at her job and works twice as hard as the other housekeepers." Jack nodded in agreement. It was not a good idea for a stranger to call her, especially when she was on holiday. Alberto spoke again as he opened the wine and poured Jack a glass. "When she returns, I will let you know. In the meantime, I will have a think about the best way to approach her."

Jack felt that he was getting closer to Lola, and he was grateful to Alberto for his help. "Thank you, Alberto. I really, really appreciate everything you are doing to help me." He reached in his pocket for his wallet.

Alberto shook his head. "Thank you, *monsieur*, but that is not necessary."

Jack could tell Alberto looked downcast. "I hope I didn't offend you."

When Alberto looked up, Jack could detect that his eyes looked sad. He spoke quietly. "Many years ago, when I was a young man, I fell in love with a Parisian poet. She was from a wealthy family, and I was not. That was the problem. We met one summer in Paris when I worked as a waiter in a *café* called *Café Chopin*, which is very close to Père Lachaise cemetery. She would come in there, drink coffee, and write after walking around looking at the graveyard, saying she gained inspiration from such famous tombs as those of Oscar Wilde and Frédéric Chopin." Jack listened. He could hear the heartbreak in Alberto's voice as he continued. "Her parents had wanted her to be a lawyer, not a poet, and they thought I was a bad influence because I always encouraged her to write, not to mention I was as poor as a church mouse. We carried on in secret for a while, but I got scared of my intense love for her. One day, without telling her, I quit my job at the *café* and soon after that, I moved down here to get away from all the painful memories. I live with regret every day and wish to God I could turn back the clock."

As Jack put his arm around Alberto, he felt a special bond forming and knew they had made a unique connection. "What's her name?"

Alberto looked at Jack with sorrow in his eyes. "Her name is Claudette."

CHAPTER TWENTY

Lola was dozing off on the sofa with James Pearson playing softly in the background. After all the drama of yesterday's wedding, she felt relaxed and had not left the villa today except to take her morning run. She spent the rest of the day lying in the sun by the pool and chatting on the phone with friends and family in London. Thinking about Ingrid still upset her. She missed her terribly but couldn't get over the feeling of betrayal. Logically, Lola knew that she was completely shutting down the actual reason she was so upset and, in a way, Ingrid had become the scapegoat for the real issue that lay buried deep in her bruised heart. She wasn't ready to go there yet; it was just too painful.

Domino and Solitaire were lying stretched out sleeping next to her. They looked so cute and sweet that she took out her mobile phone to take a picture of them. After she snapped a couple of photos, a pop-up from a celebrity rag appeared on the screen. The headline said, "Stefan van Carson, a Romanian billionaire, supermodel Anais, and a mystery man frolicked with naked blondes on Van Carson's yacht, *Lekker Kontje*." Lola couldn't believe what she was reading.

First, she remembered that Chase had said he was friends with Stefan, but how did Anais end up on the yacht? Fabian had

said she packed and left very quickly. He assumed she had gone
back to Paris and was staying with friends. She definitely didn't
waste any time, and Lola had to admit it was amazing that she
had parlayed one very controversial situation into hanging out
on a famous director's megayacht. She opened the article to
read it in full and saw several more photos. The first one was
Stefan and the "mystery man," whose face was hidden by one
of the two naked women standing in front of him. In the next
photo, the blondes were diving into the pool as the two men
watched. The picture was pretty grainy and had obviously been
taken at a distance from another boat with a long-lens camera.
The other two images were a lot clearer. The two men were
having lunch with the Romanian billionaire Annika Barinov
and Anais. Lola had read about Annika several times and had
seen her photographed at charity events, society galas, and New
York Fashion Week, which she attended annually. She studied
the photo for a moment, wondering again how Anais had managed to get herself from the Colombe d'Or on Saturday night
to have what looked like a lobster lunch on the superyacht in
less than twenty-four hours. She must be very well connected,
Lola thought.

Stefan, whom she had often seen in celebrity magazines,
appeared to be about sixty-five. Lola studied his image for a
minute. It was strange; he seemed somehow familiar to her, and
she couldn't understand why. She looked a bit longer and oddly
felt a strong connection to this man. Lola switched her attention
to the other man, whom the press didn't seem to know. Lola
looked at the man seated next to Annika, who was gazing at him
intensely. He was smiling, and as Lola stared at the photo, she
knew without a doubt that the man was Jack. She pulled her eyes

away for a moment to look at the last picture, which depicted Jack with Annika and Anais, who had their arms linked through his as they walked away from the lunch table. Annika's leaning into him slightly indicated that they were more than just friends. She couldn't help but feel jealous even though she knew her feelings were not justified.

Lola's mind wandered back to that evening at the casino in Monte Carlo, and she wondered if he had been there to meet Annika, whose Monte Carlo penthouse had been featured in *Maison Française* magazine last year. Not wanting to look at the pictures any longer, she put the phone down. She felt like the wind had been knocked out of her. Lola eased herself off the sofa so as not to disturb the sleeping cats and made her way to the bedroom. After undressing quickly, she climbed naked into the cool sheets, trying to put the photos of Jack out of her mind. Finally, she fell into a restless sleep.

* * *

The early morning sun streamed into Lola's bedroom and woke her. She felt like she had tossed and turned all night. A morning run and getting to work would probably take her mind off last night's discovery. Putting on running shorts and a tee-shirt, she headed into the kitchen to make coffee. The cats were still fast asleep and snuggled together on the sofa.

While waiting for the coffee to brew, she opened the laptop and went through her emails. One from Deux Margaux's buyer, Clemence Dubois, reminded her of the Eden-Roc event on Thursday. She said that she was looking forward to meeting Lola, and that Jetset Delilah had arrived in all their stores. Over the weekend, the line had been a big hit with their best customers.

The email lifted Lola's mood; she sent a quick reply saying she eagerly anticipated attending the party and meeting Clemence.

Time for her run. Claudette was pulling in the driveway, and Lola waved at her. She could see a baguette on the front seat and a small bag of groceries. Jogging at a steady pace along the tree-lined street, Lola enjoyed the odd glimpse of the Mediterranean between the villas and umbrella pines. Once again, she felt grateful that she lived in such a beautiful and inspiring place. As she turned and jogged toward home, she recalled that she needed to call Saks Fifth Avenue's buyer in New York first thing. Ingrid had done most of the groundwork, but Lola always liked to hear the details for herself and build a relationship with the stores.

Entering her driveway, she looked at the weathered old Villa Bonne Chance sign. Perhaps a new one would be in order or at least she should restore this one. But for some reason, the sign contained a lot of nostalgic emotions. Since it reminded her of her grandmother, the old sign would stay for the time being. She paused for a minute and traced the outline of the rusted metal with her finger. Delilah had told her she often touched it for extra good luck when she needed it. Her mind went back to Jack and the photo she had sent him with the sexy message over twenty years ago. She knew how much he had liked her sunbathing here by the pool in the white bikini. Trying to push the thought out of her mind, she continued up the driveway and into the villa.

Claudette was putting away the last of the groceries and greeted Lola warmly as she came into the kitchen. "Good morning! How are you today?" Claudette looked at Lola, seeing she looked a little lost or something.

"I'm okay, thank you."

Claudette put her hand on Lola's arm. "I see something going on behind your eyes, *chérie.*" Claudette had known Lola since she was three months old, and even though they didn't share a vast amount of personal details, Lola considered Claudette to be family.

Lola turned to Claudette. "I'm just confronting some things from my past, things I've buried for a long time. It's almost like I have no choice, like a greater force is steering my heart."

Claudette listened to Lola's soulful admission. Her voice sounded tender as she looked at Lola, deep in thought. "Many years ago, when I lived in Paris, I met a waiter named Alberto at *Café Chopin*, where I would sit and write my poetry. We fell madly in love, but there were many problems with my family. They didn't think he was good for me. You see, he encouraged me to follow my passion for writing. All they wanted was for me to go to law school. I think Alberto got scared because when I went to the *Café Chopin* one day, he no longer worked there. His friend, who shared an apartment with him in Ménilmontant, was also a waiter at the *café*. He told me Alberto had packed his bags and left with no forwarding address. I was devastated and heartbroken for months. I decided to leave Paris and move here to follow my dream. For some reason, it made me feel closer to Alberto." She looked crestfallen as she spoke.

"Do you know where he is today?" Lola asked softly.

Claudette shook her head. "The reason I'm telling you this is because I wish I could go back and do things differently. I didn't follow my heart at the time, and I think I gave up way too soon. I suppose I was so terrified of being hurt again that I gave up searching for him out of fear and heartbreak." Lola said nothing; she could see that Claudette still loved Alberto. Her eyes said it all. She spoke again. "What I do know, Lola, is true love is a rare and special thing, and when you are on the right path, it feels like magic."

Lola embraced Claudette in a tight hug. Words were unnecessary; they stayed like that for a moment, each lost in her own thoughts. "Why don't you sit for a minute and have a coffee with me?" Lola said.

Claudette straightened up and smiled, composing herself. Maybe talking about Alberto had lifted some of the burdens from her heavy heart. "Thank you, Lola, but I have a new olive tree sapling I want to plant on the side of the house where it will get just the right amount of sun. In a couple of years, you may have some fresh olive tapenade."

Lola smiled. Claudette knew how much she loved tapenade on thin slices of toasted baguette. As Claudette opened the wide glass door to the pool area, Lola walked a few steps and put her hand gently on her back. "If you ever want to talk about Alberto or anything else for that matter, you know you can."

"Thank you, I appreciate that. The way I've dealt with it all these years is by pouring my heart and soul into my poetry. It's as if they are love letters in a way. I kept the intimate notes we shared that have hidden meanings that inspire me. If he read my poetry, he would know how I still feel."

Nodding again, Lola completely understood as she watched Claudette walk outside to plant the olive tree. As she turned back to her emails, Domino started weaving her way around Lola's legs. When she bent down to pet the cat, something caught her eye on the bottom shelf of a small vitrine. Next to the collection of her childhood Beatrix Potter books, which Lola read from time to time, especially *The Tale of Squirrel*

Nutkin, were Claudette's three poetry books. Opening the door of the vitrine, she took out the first edition. It was simply called *Une Perle Dans L'huître*. Lola read the title to Domino as she continued petting her, "*A Pearl in the Oyster*." She picked up the book and flicked through the pages. After Claudette's soulful admission, Lola was moved to reread the poetry. She put it on the island to read thoroughly this evening. Pouring another coffee, Lola walked outside to her office to call the Saks buyer in New York. As she was about to dial the U.S., her phone rang. It was Chase.

"Hi, Chase. How are you?"

"I'm doing well. I've just been trying to help sort out Riggs's mess. It turns out that Scarlet's father is one of the top divorce attorneys in Texas. That makes Riggs very nervous. Since there was no prenuptial agreement in place, I almost feel sorry for him."

"I don't! He deserves everything he has coming."

There was a short silence, which Chase interrupted. "Would you like to have dinner with me tonight or tomorrow night? I'd love to see you before I go."

Lola thought back to the pictures of Jack and Annika on the yacht. The way they had looked at each other jumped out of the photograph; they definitely appeared to be an item. This image steered her decision. Dinner with Chase might take her mind off it. She decided not to mention the article to him right now, even though Stefan was his friend.

"How about tonight? Why don't you come here? I will make us something." She could tell he was surprised and happy that she had agreed.

"That sounds perfect."

"How about seven? We can have drinks first."

"See you then," Chase said excitedly as he hung up. Lola knew she partly agreed to the date to put her on an even playing field with Jack, even though Chase had no idea. Then suddenly, something struck her. She wondered if Anais had divulged information about what had transpired at the wedding. Anais had been so aloof and disinterested; it was possible that she wouldn't even remember Lola's name. Since it was totally out of her control, it wasn't worth worrying about.

Lola scanned her emails, searched for one from Saks, and immediately dialed the number before she had any other distractions. The rest of the day flew by and at about five, Claudette tapped on the door; Lola waved her in. "I think I'm going to head out for the day; I'll see you tomorrow, late morning."

"Thank you, Claudette. I really enjoyed our conversation this morning; thank you for sharing your story with me."

"Well, I would hate for you to make the same mistakes I made."

Lola stood, turned off the computer, and stretched. "I'll walk that way with you. I'm done for today and ready for a glass of wine!" The two women walked into the villa together, and Lola closed the front door behind Claudette. Returning to the kitchen, Lola opened the wine fridge and pulled out a bottle of *Dagueneau Pouilly-Fumé*. She liked the label on this bottle; it displayed musical notes of an interpretation of a George Brassens song. Opening the cellarette door, she selected a crystal glass, opened the wine, and poured a healthy portion. Thinking it would be nice to have company tonight, she opened the fridge to ponder what to make for dinner. It was lucky that Claudette had stocked the pantry this morning. Deciding to roast a chicken and some potatoes, she could serve it with *haricots vert*, which could be prepared ahead of time. Contemplating the music choice for getting ready, she went with Morphine; she loved the sultry sound of the two saxophones and recalled seeing the band play at the Montreux Jazz Festival in the nineties.

Lola took a long sip of the cool wine and looked down at Claudette's book of poetry. She flicked through the pages, randomly stopped at one, and read the first couple lines. The title was "*La Demoiselle.*"

A moment of hope with your visit,

A moment of love with your notes,

A moment of desire in your voice,

A moment of craving for your touch,

A moment of sorrow in your choice.

Lola swallowed her tears as she read the poem. She could feel Claudette's pain, transparent through the words. Closing the book for now, she walked back to the bedroom to decide what to wear. Quick decision. It would be a white silk charmeuse camisole and a pair of denim cut-offs. It was a lovely balmy evening, and she felt like being casual and relaxed tonight. Slipping into the shorts and cami, she glanced at her reflection in the large antique mirror that hung in the closet. Happy with the look, she danced her way into the bathroom and ran some amber oil through her hair, applied some lip gloss, and she was ready.

Chase would be here in just over an hour. It was time to get the chicken and potatoes in the oven, so she made her way back into the kitchen and began to get everything prepared. Deciding they would dine inside, she laid the table and lit the various candles that dotted the room. With the meal nearly prepared, Lola sat on the arm of the sofa and stroked Domino, who was rolled up in a fury ball and purring softly. The room looked inviting in the blush evening light of the sunset. The candles flickered softly, casting shadows on the walls. Time check. Chase would be here any minute. As if on cue, she could hear car tires on the gravel driveway. She stood up and checked on the dinner. Everything was ticking along nicely and would be ready to eat whenever they were. She waited for the knock, which came a second later, and opened the front door.

"Hi, Chase, please come in."

"Great to see you, Lola." He wore the biggest smile. Noticing his hands were full, she waved him into the kitchen. Turning to her, he said, "These are for you," as he handed her two dozen white roses.

They were absolutely perfect. "Wow, these are gorgeous. Thank you." She could smell their sweet fragrance.

"I noticed last time I was here you had white roses on your coffee table. I also have this. I hope you like it." He handed her an olive-green velvet wine bag, which she placed on the island. Inside was a bottle of *Louis Roederer Cristal Rosé* Champagne. Looking at his generous gifts, she smiled at him, but he could tell something was wrong.

"What is it, Lola?" It was amazing that he could read her that well.

"First, thank you for these lovely gifts; they are very thoughtful." She gave him a light kiss on the cheek. "I think we should open the Champagne now."

"Well, let me; where are your glasses?"

She pointed to the cellarette on the side of the dining area. He picked out two flutes, set them in front of her, and opened the *Cristal*, pouring each of them a glass. Lola picked up her glass, admiring the pink bubbles.

"Cheers," she said, smiling. They each took a sip. It was so tasty. Lola felt like she owed Chase an explanation for her slightly downcast look earlier. "I'm sorry if I looked strange a minute ago. It's just that the last time I had *Cristal*, I was with my best friend, Ingrid, in London. We were having lunch at a restaurant, and an old family acquaintance sent us a couple of glasses of *Cristal* as a friendly gesture." Chase sat on the barstool, listening and giving her space to talk. "Well, to cut a long story short, very soon after that, Ingrid and I had a massive row and haven't talked since, other than through work emails. She also happens to run my London office."

Chase could tell how distressed Lola was. He knew from growing up with three sisters that women's friendships were intertwined and emotional. He was glad that she had shared her story. "I'm sorry the Champagne jogged a painful memory."

She interrupted him quickly. "Don't be; it's the best thing I've tasted in a long time," she said, smiling.

He put his hand on her arm. "One thing I do know about close friendships is that they can be like a marriage. There will be conflict and hurt sometimes, especially when you pair two very passionate people. With that kind of love comes anger occasionally."

Lola thought about what he said for a minute. "You are right, Chase; I appreciate your advice." He really was the most thoughtful man. Spontaneously, she leaned forward and brushed her lips against his in a very delicate way. He stood up and pulled her to him. She could feel the strength of his arms wrapped around her.

Closing her eyes for a second, she enjoyed the way she felt so safe in his arms. When she opened them, he gazed at her deeply, as if he wanted to say something. Lola smiled at him, trying to figure out where her emotions were going. "I should probably check on the dinner. I hope you like roast chicken." She took another sip of *Cristal* and went to check on the food.

"So, you mentioned you have three sisters." Lola said. "Do they live in L.A. also?"

"Olivia, the youngest one, does; she's also an actress. The other two still live in Santa Barbara, where we all grew up."

"You are lucky to have siblings. I always wanted to have a sister. The closest thing I had was my friendship with Ingrid."

"Well, I hope you two can figure out the problem. Sometimes, it's just a matter of time."

Lola carefully lifted the chicken and roasted potatoes out of the oven and strained the green beans. Spooning the vegetables into a serving dish, she placed the chicken onto a wooden butcher's block and set it all on the table with Chase's help. Lola quickly placed the roses into two vases and put one on each end of the dining table so they could enjoy them while they ate. Chase took on carving duty, serving Lola and then himself.

"Thank you so much for cooking me this lovely dinner. I can't think of anywhere else I'd rather be right now."

They chatted their way through the meal, only stopping once for Lola to open a bottle of *Châteauneuf-du-Pape*. She was feeling a little bit squiffy as she turned to Chase. "Do you like to dance?"

He nodded. "Sure, but I'm not sure how good I am," he said, laughing, as she got up to change the music from the seductive sounds of Ibrahim Maalouf to the Stray Cats. Lola took Chase's hands, encouraging him to get up, and led him to the other side of the table, where there was plenty of space to dance. Lola kicked off her flip-flops and led Chase in her version of a swing dance. He was definitely very modest about his dancing skills, Lola thought, as he took the lead and spun her around on their makeshift dance floor. She was having fun with him as they continued dancing, pausing here and there to sip some wine.

The tempo slowed a little, and Chase brought Lola into his arms, holding her tightly. She could feel the heat of his body through the fine silk of her camisole. Lola closed her eyes as they danced together in a very sensual way. As he started to kiss her neck softly, his hands moved under the silky top and caressed her back. Lola shadowed him. Lifting his shirt slightly, she gently traced the muscles of his lower back. They were consumed by the passionate embrace, enjoying each other's touch. She freed her hand from his back and led him to the bedroom. Picking up one of the crystal votive candles along the way, she set it on the nightstand.

Chase stood in front of her in the flickering light and gently lifted the camisole over her head. Standing back, he admired her beautiful body, her pert nipples hungry for his touch. He reached over and ran his finger lightly over them one by one. Lola let out a small groan of pleasure, her desire mounting by the second. She unbuttoned his shirt, letting it slip to the floor, exposing his chiselled chest. She moved toward him, and their tongues met again, this time with a deep intensity. Lola undid her shorts and stepped out of them.

She was left standing in her white see-through lace panties. He stepped back to take in her beauty as he undid his jeans. Lola eased back on the bed and took a sip of wine. Chase came around to her side and lightly pushed her down as he started kissing her neck. Slowly he made his way down and circled each nipple, gently sucking as each one grew harder and harder.

Lola arched her back with pleasure as he made his way down, licking and kissing until he got to the delicate scrap of lace. When he leaned over her, he could see the outline of a thin sandy strip of hair that barely covered her slightly parted lips. Using his finger to outline the edge of the lace, he teased her slightly, pausing as she almost begged for more. Gently he eased her panties off and started to circle the top of her moist lips. Her legs naturally parted.

Lola whispered to him, "I want to feel you inside me." She leaned over and opened the drawer of her nightstand, feeling around for a condom. Chase carried on kissing her while she fumbled around blindly, trying to find one. It was no good; Lola sat up slightly and used the candle to shine some light in the drawer.

Then she remembered a while ago she had hidden them in the back of *The Tale of Jemima Puddle-Duck*. She pulled out the book and flipped through the pages, and out fluttered the photograph of her in the white bikini. It landed on her naked chest as if it was trying to tell her something. Chase continued to lick and caress her, not noticing the photo. Like a camera flashing in the dark, in an instant Lola's mind was transported into the past as she stared at the photograph. It was as if she had been snapped out of a dream. At that moment, she knew she couldn't go any further with Chase. Lola put her hands on his shoulders. "Chase, wait a moment."

He looked up at her, sensing something was wrong, and shifted his position, moving up until he was half-sitting on the side of the bed. "What is it? Are you okay?" he said, still in a state of arousal.

"Look, I have to be honest with you. I really like you and thoroughly enjoy your company. It's just that I have a lot of things

I need to resolve from my past, which includes an unresolved heartbreak with someone from over twenty years ago."

"What was it that suddenly reminded you of all that right now?"

"Well, it's something that I've been pushing away all these years, and some things have come up lately that have opened up the old wound, forcing me not to ignore the driving force inside me, which is winning over the terrified girl." Lola couldn't believe she had just admitted all that to Chase. She hadn't even admitted it to herself. He sat and listened, not saying a word. He took her in his arms and rocked her gently, feeling the wetness of her tears on the nape of his neck.

"Lola, it's not easy to be vulnerable and face your true self. I could see through your strong, gorgeous, independent exterior from the start. There is a lot more going on behind the scenes; maybe that's one reason I like you so much. I read somewhere once that we often fall in love with people whose darkness and vulnerability we recognise." He poured them another glass of wine and climbed under the duvet beside her. They sat together, not speaking but enjoying the wine and the candlelit room.

Lola picked up the photo to show Chase. "You asked earlier what had triggered the memory. Well, it was this." She picked up the photograph next to her on the bed and showed it to him. He studied it for a while. "It's me here at Bonne Chance when I was about twenty years old. I found the photo in my grandmother's old paintbox. I had two copies made; I gave this one to my grandmother, and the other one I sent to Jack." She hadn't dared speak his name in years, and it felt weird to do so now with this lovely man. Chase still held her; he felt like she just needed him to listen right now. "Chase, I'm sorry I have given you mixed signals.

I've been very confused, and it probably wasn't fair of me to drag you into my mess."

"It's okay, Lola; I was willing to take that chance. I just hope that Jack realises what a lucky guy he is." He looked at his watch. "I should probably head back to the Colombe d'Or."

"I don't think you should drive tonight. Would you like to stay? We can lie in bed and drink some wine and watch a film or something."

"As long as you are sure, I would like that." He kissed her on her forehead.

Lola turned to him. "Chase, I won't ever forget how tender and caring you have been with me. You are truly special, and I hope we can always be friends."

"Lola, I kind of fell in love with you the first time we met. I believe fate brought us together for a reason, and if we are meant to be just good friends, then I'll be there for you.

"And I will be there for you too, Chase. I promise."

CHAPTER TWENTY-ONE

Fabian lay in bed listening to the rain coming down on a wet Tuesday morning. After changing his flight, he had been able to leave the Colombe d'Or in the early morning before Saturday's confusion hit the hungover guests and had arrived in Paris on Sunday afternoon. Surveying his bedroom in the dim early-morning light, he saw in the corner five or six boxes and a couple of Louis Vuitton cases filled with Anais's things. Soon after setting foot in the apartment, he had packed everything of hers he could find. After what she had done to him, he wanted every memory of Anais out of his life.

Then he remembered something. Switching on the bedside lamp, he rolled over to her side of the bed, opened the nightstand's top drawer, and pulled out a zippered leather pouch. Anais had always kept the pouch very private. Once, when he had come home from work early, he had caught her sitting on the bed looking through photos and letters. He had thought it was sweet for a moment; she had looked up with tears in her eyes, surprised to see him. While he wondered what the problem was, she quickly stuffed the photos and letters back into the pouch, zipped it shut, returned it to the drawer, and closed it quickly. Claiming nothing was wrong, she wiped away the tears with the back of her sleeve.

It was clear to Fabian that the contents were personal, so he had respected that and never considered looking at it. But now, something drove him to inspect what was inside.

He tipped the contents onto the bed. It was mostly what it looked like—old modelling photos that he looked through quickly. But then he spotted some old Polaroids of Anais wearing what looked like sheer black lingerie. He studied them closely, holding them up to the light. She appeared to be only fifteen or sixteen, much too young to be photographed like this. She was all gangly arms and legs, and her hair was long. Her heavy black eye makeup almost hid the vacant look in her eyes.

Something about the Polaroids made Fabian very uncomfortable; these were not like her other early model shots. He flipped the photo over, and in fine black marker, it said, "No. 16 Brewer Street." In the corner was a date. It was faded, but he could make it out: 1980. Fabian picked up his phone and quickly did a search on No. 16 Brewer Street. Funnily enough, what came up was a seafood restaurant in London's Soho district called Randall & Aubin.

Coincidentally, before his job had taken him to Paris, Fabian had eaten there many times when he lived in London. He looked at their website, and it revealed that the restaurant had been launched in 1996. He wondered what business had occupied the space before, especially in 1980. The other Polaroids looked very similar, except for the last one. This time Anais was topless, posing on a bed with another very young girl, also topless. Anais was crouching over the other girl, who was lying on the bed and had the same long blonde hair and skinny limbs. Her hand was cupping Anais's breast as both of them gazed listlessly at the camera. Fabian felt sickened by the image, especially when he flipped it over to read two names, Clara and Esmee, written beside the same address on Brewer Street. The date was 1980, making Anais only fifteen years old.

The question was, why had she changed her name? He sat for a moment, saddened by what he had discovered. When they talked about their upbringing, she always said she was a single child. Her family story was boring, and she always changed the conversation to Fabian's somewhat wholesome family background. He now understood why he felt that he could not get inside her heart. She was protecting herself from exposing too much; all of it was probably just too painful. As much as she had utterly betrayed him, he sincerely hoped for her sake she could one day reveal her true self to someone; maybe then she would stop running.

Fabian started to put the contents back into the leather pouch when he noticed a small envelope he hadn't seen before. He took it out and opened it. Inside was a tarnished gold heart-shaped locket on a chain. Easing it open, he held it under the lamp for a closer look. There was a tiny double photograph of two young girls who appeared to be around twelve or thirteen years old. One was definitely Anais; he moved onto the other girl's picture. Strangely, it also seemed to be a picture of Anais. Suddenly, Fabian froze. He picked up the photo of the two girls on the bed and compared it to the locket. As grainy as the pictures were, there was not a question in his mind. The other girl was Anais's twin, a twin she had never mentioned.

Wishing that he hadn't snooped now, he put the locket back in the small envelope and returned all the photos to the pouch, pausing at the one of Anais and her sister on the bed. For some unknown reason, he felt compelled to take a photograph of the reverse side of the Polaroid. Turning the image over, he saw something that had gone unnoticed before. A mirror on the wall behind the bed had captured a reflection of a man holding a camera. There was something written on the front of his tee-shirt, but he couldn't figure out what it said.

Getting out of bed, Fabian walked quickly into his small study and retrieved an antique magnifying glass that had been his grandfather's. It mainly sat on his desk as a fascinating curio because of its unique tortoiseshell handle, but it came in handy now. Sitting on the bed, he turned on the flashlight on his mobile phone and illuminated the Polaroid. Picking up the magnifying glass, Fabian held it over the man's tee-shirt; he could just make out what the faint lettering said in reverse: "Reggie's Whitechapel Photo Studio." Fabian made a note of it on his phone and placed the sordid picture back in the pouch.

Not understanding why any of this mattered to him now and why he was bothering to spend any time on it, he took the pouch into the study and sat down at his desk. Questioning again why he cared, he took a small notecard out of the desk drawer and wrote a short note.

If you would like help finding your sister, let me know.—Fabian

Then he slipped the note inside the pouch and zipped it shut. It was mainly for his own peace of mind; it just felt like the right thing to do. Now he understood why she seemed so cold at times. Knowing a bit about psychology, he thought that perhaps her disconnect had led her to the affair with Riggs, not that he was excusing her behaviour. Picking up the pouch, he went back to the stack of boxes, opened the side flap of the Louis Vuitton case, and placed it inside, zipping it up safely. The movers were coming this afternoon. He had decided to put all her stuff in a storage unit that he would pay for one month, and then it was up to her. He expected a call from Anais when she found somewhere to live.

Fabian made a large pot of coffee. He was working from home today to wait for the movers who were scheduled for two. Making some toast while he waited for the coffee to brew, he couldn't help thinking what a complex person Anais had turned out to be. Carrying the steaming Joe back to his study, he turned on the computer and began checking the long list of emails that already faced him by eight a.m.

Scrolling down to one that had come from his company, Banque du NKB in the U.S., Fabian read the email and reclined in his chair, thinking. They wanted him to go to Houston on September 21 to negotiate a major merger with another bank for the U.S. markets. He read the email a couple of times and started writing back to them to confirm that he would be in Houston to handle the merger.

Finishing the email, he suddenly thought of Scarlet. This would be an excellent opportunity to return her pearl earring, as he remembered how much it meant to her. He pulled out his wallet, found her card, and typed in her email address while thinking about what to say. Remembering everything she had gone through, he began to type.

Dear Scarlet,

I hope you are doing well and made it back to Houston okay. I have some good news for you. I found your earring right after you left the hotel. It was under one of the tables in the bar! I have tried calling you, but the mobile phone number keeps telling me your phone is no longer in service.

*I will be in Houston Sept. 21-27 and would be more
than happy to deliver your earring personally. If this is
inconvenient, I could mail it to you.*

Fabian

He read through it one more time and hit send. For an
unwilling moment, he thought back to the horrors of seeing Riggs
and Anais together. It was hard to imagine what kind of impact it
would have on Scarlet in the long term. Fabian thought how tragic
it was that other people's actions could change the fabric of one's
life. Putting this into context with his own history, he realised that
he had never really gotten over Lola and always harboured hope
that they would get back together someday. Without knowing it,
Lola had hijacked his heart in a way that had prevented him from
having a healthy, happy relationship with anyone else. Realistically,
Fabian knew they were never going to be together, and he had
a feeling that even after all these years, she still had feelings for
Jack Alistair. Fabian reflected on when Lola had basically dumped
him when she met Jack. She was his first love, and at the time, it
had shattered his heart into a million pieces. Now it was weirdly
refreshing to be able to see everything more clearly. He finally
realised that it was time for him to move on.

Fabian stood up, thinking how potentially favourably the
twisted turn of events could end. He looked down at his computer
again and saw that Scarlet had already responded:

Dear Fabian,

*That is great news about finding my earring! Thank you
for looking after it. I'm sorry you have had trouble with*

my phone. I actually changed my number as soon as we landed so Riggs couldn't reach me. He kept calling over and over. It would be great to see you when you are in Houston. Let's figure out the details later! Here's my new number: 713-555-7999.

Scarlet

Fabian smiled when he read the email. He was looking forward to seeing her again. Interesting how things turn out sometimes, he thought.

CHAPTER TWENTY-TWO

It was also raining in London as Ingrid scrolled through her computer, looking for flights to Madrid. She wanted to leave on Friday and return either Monday or Tuesday. She half-considered flying from Madrid to Nice to surprise Lola. Maybe that kind of drastic approach would be what it would take to sort out their problems. As Ingrid looked around her office, she saw so many flowers on every available surface that she felt like someone was getting married. Max had sent her roses every day since their dinner at Langan's. Standing up, she walked over to the arrangement he had sent yesterday and looked at the small note card that accompanied it.

Ingrid, come to my place tomorrow night at 7. I'll make us dinner. X

It was impossible not to be impressed by his persistence. There was a knock on the door. Ingrid looked up and waved in Rebecca, who was holding a beautifully gift-wrapped box. Rebecca giggled as she set the large box down on the desk, saying, "At this rate, I'm going to have to hire an assistant just to handle all the gifts and flower deliveries."

"Thank you, Rebecca," Ingrid said, as she shut the door behind her and turned the box around to admire the white glossy gift wrap and black silk bow. There was no accompanying card. She slowly began to open the black bow, placing the silk ribbon to the side.

Using a pair of scissors to cut through the tape on the paper, she eased it off, folded it neatly into a square, and laid it next to the ribbon. It was a large, black lacquered box. Ingrid lifted the lid off and was met by layers of red tissue, which she also pulled out and put to one side. There was another gift-wrapped box under the tissue, this time with natural tan-coloured paper and a red bow. Ingrid lifted it out and pushed everything else to the side, laughing a little as she compared the layers of gift wrap to a Russian doll. Quickly undoing the final wrapping, she looked down at the large box on the desk, reading the white lettering on the front of the tan box: Christian Louboutin! Now Ingrid was excited. Opening the lid, she found more red tissue and a card, which she put down for a second, her anticipation of the present getting the best of her. Inside were the most stunning sky-high black booties, transparent mesh with leather strips running at different intervals through them and, of course, the signature high-gloss red-leather soles. Ingrid picked one up and turned it over; of course, it was the perfect size. He must have looked at her shoes when she spent the night. Hastily, she opened the card and looked at the picture. The card had to be homemade. It was a photo of a luxury speedboat with a man steering and a dark-haired woman lounging in the back in a bikini. They were heading down the River Thames with the Tower Bridge behind them. Ingrid remembered the speedboat comment he had made that night when she mentioned she also lived on the river. Inside, it said:

> *Ingrid,*
>
> *These boots are made for walking (to my place tonight). Actually, a better idea is I'll send a car to your office; why don't you just come straight from work? The car will be waiting at 5.30 at the top of Langley Court on Long Acre.*
>
> *Max*

It was the most thoughtful and generous gift, and she was also impressed that he had made the extra effort with the card. She knew what she wanted to do. If Lola refused to be in her life, why should she sacrifice the possibility of love? Picking up her phone, she decided a text message would be a perfect response.

I think those boots were made for dancing! See you later. X

She hit send and smiled at the message, knowing the undercurrent of innuendo referring to the racy dance show she had performed for him last time. The phone buzzed almost instantly, and she read the message:

The disco ball, lights, and DJ will be here waiting!

She enjoyed Max's sense of humour and was looking forward to the evening. Unable to resist, she sat down on the chair and took off her stilettos, replacing them with the Louboutins. They were so sexy and went well with the red-wine-coloured, skin-tight leather pencil dress she was wearing today.

It was close to four-thirty, and she wanted to lock in her flight to Madrid before leaving the office. Clicking onto the British Airways website, she scrolled through the flights departing on the twenty-first and found the perfect one leaving at 11 a.m. and returning Tuesday at 9.30 a.m. Putting in her credit card details, she secured the flights and made a note of the confirmation details. Knowing how excited her mum would be to see her, Ingrid picked up her phone to text her the schedule.

She was thinking about asking Max's advice about Lola and if he thought it was a good idea to fly to the South of France to surprise her. That would be a decision for later. Picking up her makeup bag, she walked to the restroom.

Jill whistled as she went by. "Those boots are amazing! Is that what was in that humongous box?"

"Yep! They are pretty hot, right?" Ingrid twirled around and carried on to the restroom to check her hair and makeup before leaving. After a quick freshen-up, she walked back to her office, grabbed her ankle-length camel coat and Burberry scarf, and headed out, waving at Jill and Rebecca as she waited for the lift. Checking the time, she thought it would be a nice gesture to nip into Paul Smith opposite and buy Max a pocket square as a little host gift. She found the perfect one very quickly and had them gift wrap it. The time was now five twenty-five, so she took the short walk up to Long Acre, where a black Range Rover with dark windows waited. As she approached, the driver's side door opened, and the driver got out and opened the passenger door for her. She climbed in, thanking him.

"Good evening, *madam*. We should be there in about twenty minutes, depending on traffic."

Ingrid immediately recognised his voice from the other night. "Thank you. I think I met you the other week. Harry, isn't it? Didn't you take us to Ronnie Scott's?"

"Yes, that's right. I always drive for Mr. Francis Williams and Mr. Valentine-Smithe. Have for thirty years."

"Well, nice to see you again, Harry." This was the way to travel, she thought, as they cut through rush-hour traffic. Now and then, she glanced down at her new boots, which added a whole lot of sexy to her outfit tonight. They arrived at St. Katharine Docks right around six, and Ingrid walked the short distance to Ivory

House where Max lived. As she got closer, she could see Max holding the door for her.

"Well, hello there," she said, as she walked through the open door. He held her for a moment, looking into her eyes.

"I've missed you, Ingrid." Taking her hand, he led her to the lift, and they rode up to his penthouse. Opening the front door, he led her in and helped her out of the coat. Quickly hanging it in a closet in the hallway, he returned to ask her what she would like to drink.

"I'd love a glass of Champagne, thank you." Max opened the wine fridge, pulled out a bottle of *Dom Perignon*, swiftly opened it, and poured two glasses.

"*Salute*!" They lightly clinked the flutes, and Max stood back to admire Ingrid in the tight leather dress and new boots.

"You look gorgeous, darling."

"Well, partly thanks to you. These Louboutins are so fabulous. These are the most generous gift." Ingrid spontaneously kissed him full on the mouth, quickly remembering the intense chemistry they had. "Oh, and this is for you," she said, handing him the Paul Smith gift bag.

"Well, I guess I now know what it takes to see you," he joked. "I hope you like steak. Ingrid nodded. "I have some potatoes *Dauphinoise* in the oven, and I thought I'd make a simple Caesar salad. I'll sauté the steaks right before we are ready to eat."

"That all sounds fabulous. Thank you." Ingrid was glad she had accepted his invitation. Max poured more Champagne and placed the bottle in a vintage-looking ice bucket with Club 55 engraved on it.

He rested his hand on her leg. "So, did you sort things out with Lola?"

"No, I tried, but she refuses to have any contact with me."

Max could tell from looking at Ingrid how upset she was. "Listen, there's something I didn't mention to you at Langan's the other night because I wasn't sure if it was relevant, and I don't know a lot of the details, but I'm willing to share what I do know," he said.

Not sure if it annoyed her that he had withheld details, Ingrid didn't say anything while she waited for the story to begin.

"After Roberta married Oliver Delphine, I lost contact with her until many years later when I retired from the music business and bred Hanoverian horses in Hertfordshire. I'm not even sure exactly when it was now because it was so long ago. I went to watch a friend compete at the Stoneleigh Classic Horse Show."

Ingrid nodded, encouraging him to go on.

"Weirdly, I had met Ollie a couple of years before at my brother's birthday hunting trip. Neville and Ollie had some kind of business connection. I never let on that I had once been friends with Roberta because I didn't know what she had told him, and I didn't want to stir things up. Also, when Roberta knew me all those years ago, I went by Max Valentine because fans of Francis would find my phone number and bug me at home. So that day at the horse show, Ollie and his family and some friends were having lunch. He spotted me and waved me over to the table. I hope I'm not losing you here with the story?"

"No, please keep going."

"It was very uncomfortable because Roberta acted like she didn't know me. To cut a long story short, Ollie insisted that Lola, who was probably eighteen at the time, should come to my stables and see some new mares I had just acquired. To be honest, I offered because I was so intrigued to meet Lola and see Roberta again."

Ingrid wasn't sure she liked where this story could be going, but she didn't want to interrupt.

"I only spent a minute at the table because their lunch arrived, but after they finished, everyone left the table except Roberta, so I went over to her and we spoke. I think she was in shock about seeing me again, and I could tell it brought up old memories. Unfortunately, I couldn't talk to her much because Ollie came back looking for her. I figured I would let her contact me if she wanted to."

He refilled their glasses with the *Dom*, finishing off the bottle.

"A couple of weeks later, Ollie called to ask if Lola could come over to the stables. She was horse-mad back then. I agreed, and she showed up the next day. Actually, I was away that weekend, so I had my stable lad, Jack Alistair, show her around. They must have gotten on very well because when he wasn't at university, she was always there helping him with his work or going to her parents' estate, which was nearby. It was sweet young love that went on for a couple of years until a horrible accident at the Delphines' estate severed them, and Jack never heard from her again."

Ingrid felt like she was in a trance. It was a lot to take in all at once, but she finally found her voice. "What kind of accident?" Her speech was a little shaky.

"Well, unfortunately, Jack and Lola must have had a big fight because she took off on her horse, and he jumped on Penny, which was Lola's retired childhood pony, and chased her. Tragically Penny tripped, causing her to go down, and due to her age, she suffered a heart attack. Jack was, of course, thrown off but managed to roll out of the way. Lola heard Jack's cry for help and turned back, but in her frantic haste, she snared her leg on an old section of barbed-wire fence, which ripped right through her jodhpurs. Again, I don't really know all the details because Jack was so devastated and refused to talk about it much. Shortly after that, he got another job closer to the university. I didn't hear from him again until years later when he contacted me to see if I'd had any news from Lola. I hadn't until I ran into you two at Scott's."

Ingrid was silent for a minute and suddenly remembered the crescent-moon-shaped scar on Lola's lower leg. She had asked Lola about the scar years ago, but Lola just said the skin was damaged after spilling a cup of freshly boiled tea down her leg. Quite often she covered it with makeup, and Ingrid didn't notice it anymore. It was like a birthmark or something, which she always thought made someone more unique and exciting. "I still don't understand why she is so upset about you and me…" She paused for a moment, not knowing how to categorize the relationship, but she continued, "…being friends."

Max was opening a bottle of Silver Oak cabernet. "Maybe just hearing my name brings up a lot of painful memories for her."

Ingrid was so confused, she didn't know what to say. It felt like there was a big slice of the story missing, but what could it be? She must go to the Riviera next week after visiting her mother. It was a risk, but it felt like the right thing to do. "Do you mind if I spend a moment on my phone? I just decided to take a little trip to France next week."

"No, of course not; go right ahead. I'm going to start the steaks." Max was pleased she was so distracted because she hadn't noticed the slight nervous twitch he had in his right eye as he talked, nor the hint of anxiety in his voice as he told the story. For a second, he let his mind wander back to that balmy July and the catastrophic secret that bonded Roberta, Francis, and him together, one that he had never told anyone. Max had made that promise years ago and felt bound to honour it. Thankfully, it had been easy to lock it in a vault inside his heart, which he had bolted shut. He would never reveal the events that took place that summer in the Côte d'Azur.

CHAPTER TWENTY-THREE

When the phone rang, Jack thought it was Fiona calling. Since the number said unknown, however, he had a feeling he knew who it was. He hesitated to answer because he had been expecting to get a call since receiving Annika's note. It surprised him that she had waited until Thursday afternoon to contact him. "Hello?"

"Mr. Alistair." He immediately recognised the clipped Romanian accent. "This is Lara Lenkov. I am calling to tell you that Miss Barinov will meet you tonight at Louroc Restaurant at your hotel at eight p.m."

Jack was about to respond when she abruptly hung up. Amusing, but she had not given him room for any questions. If it weren't for the Kandinsky and Claude's daily phone calls, he would have liked to tell Lara Lenkov where to stuff it. Glancing down at Annika's note again, he remembered she said she would be here for a private party. Jack just didn't know what kind of angle to play. Annika was just so unpredictable, and he had a feeling that she probably didn't give anyone a second chance. He had to get it right tonight. Thinking back to that insane afternoon on *Lekker Kontje*, he felt the events had been shocking on so many different levels.

If someone had told him the story, he wouldn't have believed it himself.

Glancing up from the small desk that had turned into his Riviera office in the last week, Delilah's painting caught his eye. He couldn't wait to get the deal done with the Kandinsky so he could focus totally on Lola. Alberto had left a message saying that Marie Allard was returning from her vacation tomorrow, and he was figuring out the best way to approach her about her father, Leon Martin. Jack hoped and prayed that Mr. Martin could help, and it was an unthinkable possibility that he was no longer alive. It was such a long shot that he would remember the location of Villa Bonne Chance anyway. But it was his strongest lead for now, so Jack wanted to stay optimistic that things would unfold in his favour. He had decided not to call Anais's ex, Riggs Bentley, because he knew Riggs wouldn't give a stranger any numbers, especially that of his American film-star friend.

With a few hours to go before his dinner with Annika, Jack turned back to his emails. Leaning back in the chair, he stretched a little, and an involuntary flashback to Annika's naked body lying on the sofa under Anais came flooding back. It was how she kept her eyes on him that was so mysterious and unforgettable as he sat there watching the show unfold. Jack had tried not to think about it too much because, for some unknown reason, he thought it was disloyal to Lola. It was all very confusing, and he knew tonight was not likely to be a simple dinner to discuss a business deal. Annika definitely had a hidden agenda. The question was, what did she want from him?

CHAPTER TWENTY-FOUR

Lola closed down her computer for the day and scooped Solitaire off her lap, returning her to the warm cushioned seat of the office chair. The plan was to meet Clemence Dubois in the hotel's foyer at six-thirty. They wanted to arrive together at the party in the Champagne Lounge. Lola was looking forward to a long-awaited return to the Eden-Roc, and it would also be informative to meet some of her new customers, along with Deux Margaux's top executives.

Passing by the pool on her way inside, Lola thought about Chase for a minute. He had been so very understanding, and after spending the night with her, he had simply given her a hug in the morning and wished her luck on her journey. She had texted him yesterday to say goodbye and wish him a safe flight back to Los Angeles. They had promised to keep in touch. It was so bizarre how one could meet a stranger in an airport and share so much with him in such a short amount of time. Lola knew they would always have that special bond, cementing their friendship forever.

Opening the door to the villa, she went into the kitchen and poured a glass of Champagne. Deux Margaux was sending a car to pick her up at five-thirty, which afforded her the luxury of not having to drive. After turning on the music, she walked to her bedroom and into the closet to get dressed. The attire for the evening had been selected earlier: a short black silk slip dress and the same almost-knee-length YSL Le Smoking tuxedo jacket she had worn to the wedding. She completed the look by pairing it with one of her Jetset Delilah neckties with a large freshwater pearl suspended from it.

Lola smiled as she went through her extensive collection of slip dresses. She paused at the beautiful white knee-length dress with the thigh-high slit. It was the dress she had worn to the Casino in Monte Carlo the night of seeing Jack. When she looked at it, all she could remember was his sparkling blue eyes and the way his arms felt around her all those years ago.

Trying not to linger on that thought now, Lola found the black dress and hung it separately next to the tuxedo jacket. After a long shower, she took her time getting ready and finally, at five-twenty, she fastened the buckle on her Dior black-suede mesh ankle boot, took one last look in the mirror, and picked out a small clutch bag on her way to the kitchen. The driver would be here any minute, so she pulled a paper roadie cup out of the pantry and filled it with Champagne for the hour-long journey. Hearing the car coming up the driveway, she grabbed her bag and locked the door behind her. The chauffeur jumped out of the black Mercedes sedan and opened the back door for Lola.

"*Bonjour, Mademoiselle* Delphine. My name is Jean."

"Thank you, Jean." Lola made herself comfortable, placing the roadie in the cupholder as the car headed to the Hotel du Cap-Eden-Roc. They arrived just after six-thirty, and Lola proceeded to the foyer. Clemence Dubois was already there and greeted her in impeccable English with a warm smile. Her hint of a French accent was incredibly sexy.

"Lola Delphine, lovely to finally meet you. I'm Clemence Dubois," she said, taking Lola's hand and kissing her on each cheek in the traditional French way.

"Very nice to meet you, too."

"Why don't we go up to the party? We can talk over a glass of Champagne." The two women walked upstairs side by side, chatting about how much they loved this historic hotel. Clemence was probably in her early sixties, Lola thought. She was elegant and had a shiny, mahogany, long-bob hairstyle and wore crimson lipstick. To compensate for her petite stature, she wore six-inch classic YSL heels.

The party was in full swing when they arrived. The DJ was playing, and waiters were circulating with trays of *canapés* and Champagne. Clemence introduced Lola to several people, and she enjoyed chatting with them about her accessories line.

"Why don't we sit for a minute?" Clemence sat down on one of the cream-coloured sofas. They took in the breathtaking view of the Mediterranean. After Clemence briefed Lola on what their stores projected for Jetset Delilah, she moved on to a bit of gossip. Lola liked her a lot and found that she was very down-to-earth.

Clemence was actually from a small town in Belgium and had moved to Paris when she was eighteen to pursue her dream of working in fashion. Starting on the shop floor of a small boutique in the Faubourg Saint-Honoré district, she worked her way up the ladder in the fashion business and had worked for Deux Margaux for the last twenty years. Lola was intrigued as she listened to Clemence's stories. It was turning into a perfect evening as the sun went down on the Côte d'Azur.

While Lola was chatting away at the *soirée*, Jack decided to have a quick drink before meeting Annika for dinner. The hotel was buzzing tonight with exquisite people; he assumed it was because of the event she was attending. Even though he knew it was a private party, he was intrigued enough to have a quick look. He made his way to the Champagne Lounge, passing several chic women on the way. He stood back admiring the crowd and smiled as he noticed a couple of people dancing. After scanning the guests, he did not see Annika. However, it was hard not to notice the scary bodyguard, Helga Petrov, who stood guard with her hand resting on the pistol in its holster. He was just about to move on when he spotted Alberto, who was passing around Oysters Rockefeller. Jack waved, but Alberto didn't see him, so he took one more look around before deciding to make his way to Louroc to wait for his dinner date.

* * *

Lola had just finished telling Clemence about the new collection she was working on for the spring when they noticed an air of excitement ripple through the festivities.

"Guess what," Clemence said. "Rumour has it Annika Barinov is coming tonight; apparently, she often shops at our flagship store in Paris." Lola quickly thought back to those celebrity rag photos she had recently seen of Jack on the yacht with Annika. "You know who she is, right?"

Lola was still a bit lost in thought. "Yes, the Romanian billionaire. I've seen her pictures in the papers."

Clemence moved on to another subject, but they were interrupted by the head of advertising, Pierre Blanchet. Lola stood up and excused herself. As she made her way through the crowd of glamourous people, she could see that some of the guests were looking in a particular direction. Their focus was definitely on a specific person. Lola could not avoid looking. It was hard to see what the subtle commotion was all about because there was a very tall, husky, muscular woman in a grey military-style jumpsuit standing guard and blocking the view. Lola was intrigued, so she moved a little to the right as she made her way through the party. The husky woman bent down suddenly to retrieve something, and there, sitting on the sofa, was Annika Barinov. Freezing temporarily, Lola remembered the photos of Annika looking at Jack with adoring eyes. She couldn't deny it; Annika was even more beautiful than her pictures. An involuntary feeling of intense jealousy swept over her. She hurried toward the restroom, not wanting to look anymore. Shaken by what she had seen, she dropped her clutch in her haste. Scrambling to pick up the contents before anyone noticed, an amiable waiter bent down to help her.

"Let me help you, *madame*," he said, as he put down his tray of *canapés*.

"That's very kind of you. Thank you."

Looking at her, he noticed that she seemed distraught. "I don't want to intrude, but are you all right? You look like you've seen a ghost or something."

Lola looked at the waiter and noticed that he had a kind face. "Yes, I'm fine, it's just…" She stumbled on her words, not knowing why she would divulge to a stranger, but she said, "I feel like the past is catching up to me after many years of running." Maybe it was the Champagne that was making her reveal so much.

The waiter looked at her and sweetly took her hand. "My name is Alberto; if you need anything tonight, just let me know."

Lola squeezed his hand. "Thank you, Alberto." She suddenly felt tired from the outburst of emotion.

"May I ask your name, *madame?*" He waited as she lifted her crestfallen face.

"Lola. Lola Delphine." Alberto watched as she hurried away, not knowing the importance of this meeting since Jack had never actually divulged her name. All he knew at that moment was that she was a lovely girl who, in those few words, had revealed herself to him. There had been something very fragile and delicate about her that resonated in his core. It was a connection of matters of the heart that he couldn't put his finger on. The thought stayed with him as he continued to make his way around the guests with a fresh platter of Oysters Rockefeller. Lola made her way out of the party and went to the restroom to compose herself before leaving.

* * *

Jack was greeted by the maître d'. "Mr. Alistair, I have a note for you, sir." Noticing immediately the same perfect calligraphy as the last letter she had sent him, he opened it quickly and read the single straightforward line:

Change of plans. Meet me outside. I will be waiting in the red Bentley Mulsanne.

Thanking the maître d', he turned and made his way to the long line of cars waiting outside.

* * *

After composing herself in the restroom for a few minutes, Lola decided to leave the party. She was ready to get home and would text Clemence from the car. Arriving outside to a long line of chauffeur-driven cars, she couldn't help noticing the large red Bentley that stood out among the primarily black vehicles that were either dropping off or picking up people. Hurrying past a man who looked like he was also searching for his car, she spotted the Mercedes and Jean, who was standing waiting with the back door open. She slid into the air-conditioned back seat.

Jack just happened to turn his head at that moment to see the beautiful woman swing her legs into a black Mercedes. Something about her caught his attention. It took him a second to comprehend what he had seen. When he snapped out of his daze, he saw it—the crescent-moon-shaped scar. This time, he knew it was his Lola. Watching as the car drove off, he could see the profile of her blonde hair cascading over the side of her face, obscuring her view of Jack. Suddenly, as if an electric current had struck him, he darted between the cars only to see her vehicle's taillights making the bend. Without access to transport, there was no way to follow her. To make matters worse, he could now see Helga Petrov making her way toward him. Choking back the heartbreak he felt and the sadness that he hadn't acted quicker, he walked toward Helga and climbed into the red Bentley.

*   *   *

Lola took another deep breath as they made their way out of the hotel grounds to her sanctuary at Villa Bonne Chance. Opening her bag to retrieve her phone, she texted Clemence to thank her for being such a gracious host. She put the phone back in the clutch and checked for her keys; they were there. However, she noticed that her driving licence was not. Searching quickly, she realised that it must have fallen out when she dropped her bag at the party. They were now a good twenty minutes from the Eden-Roc, so she decided to call them in the morning. By then, there would be a good chance that someone would have handed it in, or maybe Alberto had found it after she left.

Thinking back to the kindly waiter for a moment, she felt there had been something very comforting about him, which is probably why she had opened up the way she did. Lola wondered if Alberto was Italian. For some reason, she felt that she had heard that name recently, but she couldn't recall where.

After almost dozing off on the drive, Lola was glad when the car stopped in front of Villa Bonne Chance. Thanking Jean, she handed him a generous tip and waved as she unlocked the door. Thinking that her bed would be the best place for her now, she headed straight for the bedroom, throwing her silk dress on the chair and slipping off the booties. Trying to beat all thoughts of Annika Barinov out of her head, she fell into a restless sleep, not noticing that Domino and Solitaire immediately jumped on the bed and snuggled next to her purring, instinctively knowing she was upset.

* * *

Annika turned to Jack. "So, I hope you don't mind the change in plans. I thought you might want to see the Kandinsky since it's hanging in my penthouse in Monte Carlo. I'm having my chef prepare dinner tonight." Smiling coyly, she added, "I hope you like a nice duck now and again."

Jack was so distracted after another chance encounter with Lola that he didn't answer for a moment. "Yes, that sounds lovely, thank you, and I'm looking forward to seeing the Kandinsky."

Helga sat in the front seat next to the driver, who, he observed, was also armed. She opened the console, which served as an ice bucket, and pulled out a chilled bottle of vodka. A smaller console was in front of that. Helga opened it and pulled out two large crystal shot glasses. Opening the vodka, she poured two shots and handed them to Annika and Jack. Annika turned to Jack and raised her glass. He followed suit.

"*Here's to a delicious duck.*"

They both tipped back the vodka, and Helga swiftly poured them another round. This time Annika simply said, "*Noroc.*" Jack enjoyed the buzz. It almost muted his shattered heartbreak temporarily. Putting down the empty shot glass, he asked her to translate her toast.

"*Noroc* is the Romanian word for 'cheers,'" she said.

As Annika sat with her legs crossed, Jack took in her fuchsia floor-length dress with a slit almost to the top of her hip; she was frighteningly sexy and provocative. After about an hour's drive, they were making their way through the streets of Monte Carlo. Surprisingly, he found her very easy to talk to, as they swapped tales of their upbringing in the U.K. The car slowed to a stop. Helga got out and opened their doors.

Annika's penthouse was in the Tour Odeon, a skyscraper in the principality of Monaco. The three of them entered the building and rode the elevator up to the forty-fourth floor. The doors opened directly into Annika's five-floor sky penthouse. Jack noticed a Will Martyr painting from the "You Gave Me Paradise" collection. It was even more breathtaking than he remembered from seeing the exhibit in Mayfair.

Helga motioned for them to stop while she did a routine security check of the place. She returned in a few minutes and checked the security cameras to ensure there hadn't been a breach. Satisfied, she settled into a chair on the right of the lift door. Annika took Jack's hand and led him up a short flight of stairs to the main floor, which of course had floor-to-ceiling windows with views of the sparkling lights of Monaco's Sainte-Roman district below. There was a very open-plan modern kitchen, and just beyond that, in front of the window, a long table set for dinner. While they watched, the chef chopped and julienned vegetables. A young woman approached and asked them what they would like to drink.

"How about a dirty martini with blue-cheese olives?" Annika suggested. Jack nodded in agreement; he was beginning to enjoy the mind-numbing effect of the vodka, although he was well aware that he still needed to be *compos mentis* to do business. The young woman came back from behind the curved glass bar on the other side of the room carrying a tray with the two martinis and served them.

"We would like to eat in thirty minutes, please."

"Very well, *madame*." The chef carried on julienning the vegetables before placing them in a large wok. Annika turned to Jack, who was slightly awestruck by the world-class paintings she had on the walls, not to mention a Rodin sculpture in the corner. In the course of his business, he had, of course, experienced many fine collections, but this was something else. He began to imagine what surprises the rest of the penthouse might hold.

"Shall we sit for a moment?" Annika sat on one of the large contemporary sofas, which was almost the same colour as her fuchsia-pink dress. Her taste was undoubtedly eclectic, Jack thought. As he surveyed the room, he noticed an ONYX sofa by Peugeot that lined the other wall and a couple of white Eames chairs that faced a Carrara marble fireplace with a chrome flute.

While they sipped their martinis, he watched Annika lift the cocktail stick that speared the three blue-cheese olives out of the martini. She brought it up to her lips, and using her tongue provocatively, circled the first one before popping it into her mouth.

Jack couldn't turn away as she continued with the second olive, slowly circling it with her tongue and then slipping it between her rosebud lips. Pulling the last olive from the thin wooden stick, she brought it up to Jack's mouth. Encouraging him to part his lips, she let the olive sit there for a moment before pushing it lightly into Jack's slightly open mouth, not letting go of the olive as her fingers caressed his tongue slightly. He could feel himself becoming aroused as she took her moist finger and traced the outline of his lip. He swallowed the olive as she lowered her hand and continued to drink her martini, fully aware of the effect she was having on him.

"Are you hungry for a little duck, Jack? I think it's ready," she said in an almost raspy voice. As her eyes looked deeply into his, he thought at that moment that it would be very easy to become hypnotised by her carnal seduction, especially after so many vodkas.

"Yes, I am, thank you." It was not often that Jack felt so out of control and slightly intimidated. He thought it might be better to switch from vodka to water during dinner if he was going to be able to convince Annika to sell the Kandinsky. As they walked across the room together, Annika slipped her arm through Jack's. The heat of her body permeated the silky dress, and he couldn't help glancing at her erect nipples that were barely covered by the luxurious fabric. Reaching the table, Jack pulled out her seat for her and then seated himself as the first course of caviar with small blinis was being served.

"So, this caviar is the rarest in the world and comes from the Beluga sturgeon that swim in the Caspian Sea." Spooning some onto a blini, she savoured it for a moment. "It has the most delicate flavour, don't you think?"

Jack followed suit and spooned a little Beluga onto the tiny Russian pancake; it really was delicious. "So, do you spend a lot of time in Monte Carlo?"

"It depends. I attend a lot of charity events around the world so that somewhat dictates my schedule. Usually, at this time of year, we sail down to Portofino, but I changed my mind after meeting you and decided to stay."

Jack was unsure how to answer. Against his better judgment, he polished off the martini. Almost simultaneously, the server brought two more fresh martinis, this time with a twist of lemon.

Annika didn't seem to mind that he didn't comment and followed with something that surprised him even more. "I didn't grow up with money. You know, all of this comes from a lot of hard work." She gestured around the room. Jack remembered his humble background. Although he was exceedingly wealthy, it was nothing compared to this. For some reason, he had assumed hers was inherited family wealth. His research on her hadn't revealed anything about her family background. He wondered now if she had paid a large sum to keep her true identity private and out of the press. Her admission made her seem more approachable, so he thought she wouldn't mind if he asked her about it.

"I thought that since you said you went to boarding school in England that you must have come from a wealthy background. I hope it's okay to ask."

Laying her hand on top of his, she traced the outline of his large hand with her vermillion fingernail. As she spoke, the sensation started to cloud his judgment again. "No, it was not an expensive boarding school, as I led the press to believe. With enough money, one can silence a lot of people. That 'boarding school' was actually an orphanage. I was dumped on the doorstep when I was three months old. The only information I came with was around my neck on a tattered string. Attached to it was a scrap of paper with my birthplace and date, which happens to be 7/7/70. Maybe the lucky sevens helped push me to where I am today," she said, smiling slightly.

Jack felt a little saddened by her story. Now he could see why she was so hard-edged. Looking up as her fingers started to circle his forearm, he queried, "You mentioned there was also a birthplace written on the paper?"

"Yes, it simply said Romania."

Jack could tell that the subject was painful for her. For those few moments, the unbreakable exterior cracked, and he could see the young girl who was abandoned at such a young age. Thinking back to the events of last Sunday on the yacht, he could understand now how she could behave with such a lack of conscience. As if she could read his mind, she carried on with the story. "This is the first time I've talked about this in years, especially with a man. In the past, when I got close to people and opened up, they couldn't handle the vulnerable Annika. I think many men are attracted to my lifestyle and my ability to remain unflappable; I suppose we all have many dimensions."

Jack took both her hands, not knowing how to answer, so he simply said, "Listen, I understand." Looking up at her, he could see the hurt in her eyes.

"One of the reasons I'm telling you this is because my past reared its ugly head last Sunday on *Lekker Kontje*. It turns out Anais and I knew each other years ago. It didn't click at first because back then, she called herself Esmee. One day I was sitting in Bar Bruno on Wardour Street."

Jack nodded; he knew the place well.

"I was fifteen and renting a room just down the street. It was pouring rain when Anais and her twin sister Clara ducked into the *café* to shelter from the storm. I had been sipping on the same cup of tea for thirty minutes, not knowing what to do next. I had just lost my job working in a bar when the lecherous landlord found out how young I was. To add to the worry, I only had one week of rent money left. I don't know if the twins felt sorry for me or what, but I could see them whispering to each other as they waited in line to order. They joined me at the table and bought me another cup of tea and some toast. It was nice to have some company, and I ended up telling them my dilemma, and that's how I ended up at the photo studio on Brewer Street."

Waiting for her to continue, he remained silent as he watched her finish the last sip of her martini. Noticing a break in the conversation, the server appeared with a bottle of *Château Mouton Rothschild* and poured each of them a glass. "*Madame*, are you ready for the second course?"

"Yes, bring it, please." Jack could already tell from her tone that she had switched back to bodacious Annika and had finished telling her story for the time being.

"Annika, thank you for sharing a piece of your life with me. I want you to know you can trust that I will never take advantage of your honesty."

"There is a lot more to it, things that I am not proud of, but I needed to survive, and sometimes that overrides good decisions, especially at fifteen. Thankfully, I came up with an idea for a business when I was twenty. It turned my luck around in ways beyond my wildest dreams."

She looked around the room for a moment as if it suddenly registered how enormous her wealth was. "I decided to start my business under a different name. At the time, I was trying to re-create myself and become a shining new Annika. That is why one must search hard to find anything about my earlier life. For now, I don't want to talk about it anymore. Maybe one day, I will tell you the whole story."

Jack thought back to when he had done his research. He had not found anything about her business ventures. It certainly was intriguing. He looked at her fondly and said with a gentle tone, "If you ever want to share more of your story with me, I would love to hear it. From everything you have said, it appears you are a very courageous person who has battled through some hardships. I admire that in you."

She smiled at him, nodding but not saying anything. He knew from the intensity of her eyes, however, that she appreciated his understanding words.

The server returned carrying a platter of seared duck breast. Jack noticed Annika barely ate anything, and he had to admit he wasn't very hungry either. She must have sensed this because she said, "Why don't I show you the Kandinsky?"

Leading him by the hand, Annika took him up a short flight of stairs and into her expansive bedroom. Everything in the room was white except for the paintings that lined the walls. There was a reclining Henri Moore sculpture by the window. Once again, Jack was amazed by her collection. Following Annika to the middle of the room, she faced the wall opposite the bed, and there it was, Wassily Kandinsky's *Piano Notes*. The painting was breathtaking, and they admired it silently.

"So, do you know what inspired Kandinsky to create this piece?" Annika said.

Jack had done so much research on it that he did know. "A concert he attended in 1911 here in Monaco by Austrian visionary artist and composer Arnold Schöenberg. What impressed Kandinsky the most was the *Three Piano Pieces, Opus 11*. It is said that he saw the notes of that concert, and that is when his abstract phase began."

Annika looked pleased with herself as she spoke. "Yes, all of that is true, but there is more to the story than that if you'd like to hear it."

"Yes, absolutely. I'd love to hear it."

"The 1911 concert was definitely a significant influence. Kandinsky was said to possess synaesthesia, which is hearing the sound of colours, feeling the smell of words, and perceiving the taste of forms. But the real inspiration behind this particular painting comes from a story his close American friend, Herb Gomes, told him in confidence. Herb was the pianist at the Ritz Hotel in London during the 1940s. Kandinsky would often go to the Palm Court and listen to his friend play the beautiful Pleyel grand piano. Well, I was so intrigued by the painting and the history that I tracked down Herb's son. Another benefit of having all this money is when you are trying to find people. I explained I owned the painting, and this is what he told me."

"During the Second World War, Herb formed some kind of secret code using music notes that were sent back and forth between England and the Resistance in France. There was a music shop in Paris that became the headquarters. Unfortunately, Herb never got a lot of recognition for his brilliant code, as he was still very uncomfortable talking about it. Apparently, he and Kandinsky became close friends and their friendship continued until Herb died in 1944. Kandinsky was so devastated about losing his friend he painted *Piano Notes* in his honour. Sadly, he passed away himself at the end of that year."

"That is a fascinating story, and if I'm being honest, it makes the painting even more valuable. What an amazing piece of history. So, I have to ask, are you still willing to part with this beautiful treasure?" It was strange; he almost felt guilty trying to persuade her, especially after what she had just told him.

Annika was just about to answer when they heard Bang! Bang! Bang! She went into action, immediately grabbing Jack's arm and pulling him into her expansive closet and then into a safe room that lay just beyond that, slamming the bulletproof door shut.

"What's going on?" It happened quickly, but those were definitely gunshots. There was no question about it.

"I don't know, but we are safe in here. It's bombproof." There was a landline phone on the wall, and Jack quickly called the Monaco Police. As soon as he hung up the phone, it rang, and he picked it up. It was Helga; Jack handed the phone to Annika.

"You can come out; everything is clear. We had a female intruder. I shot her when she stepped out of the elevator and ran in the direction of your bedroom; unfortunately, she is deceased."

Jack looked at Annika to see how she was handling the situation. Remarkably, she was very calm. "Are you okay? Are you ready to go out there and face all of this?" he said.

"Yes, I'm fine. This is not the first time something like this has happened. That's why I have Helga with me all the time." They opened the door slowly and stepped back into the closet and then through her bedroom. Jack took one last look at the Kandinsky; he certainly would not be doing a deal tonight. Helga met them at the bedroom door, and they walked together down the stairs. The woman lay face down on the white marble floor; a small puddle of blood was forming beside her right shoulder.

"Do you recognise this woman?" Helga asked them. They both shook their heads. Jack looked at his watch; the police should be here any minute. Helga pulled a pair of disposable gloves out of her back pocket and put them on. She bent down and gently rolled the woman over. What happened next was shocking.

As the woman's body turned, the long chestnut wig and glasses came off to expose not a woman at all but a man in female disguise. It was as if time stood still for a second; then everything happened at once.

Annika screamed, "CLAUDE, no, not CLAUDE!" Instantaneously Jack yelled, "Claude Laurent?" He turned to the women. "What is going on? I don't understand. You know Claude?"

Jack spoke quickly in an elevated voice. "He is my client who wanted to buy *Piano Notes* for his wife. I suspected that his wife had caught him with another woman." As soon as he said it, he knew the other woman was not Violetta Martini. It was Annika.

Annika got right to the point without his having to ask. "We had a brief affair, but he got obsessed with me and was calling incessantly and acting irrationally, so I cut it off a month or so ago. I told the downstairs security never to let him in. That's probably why he used a disguise. He must have stolen an elevator key from me and had a personal one cut. I can't believe he hired you to try and play some kind of power game. I guess he knew how much I loved the Kandinsky."

Jack was flabbergasted that Annika had been involved with him. It was all so crazy; he couldn't believe Claude was so deranged. Now he understood why she needed a bodyguard. Jack was baffled

by the fact that Claude would send him on such a wild goose
chase, especially when he knew where the painting was all the
time. Looking down at the body, Jack thought it was a tragic way
to go. He also felt very sorry for Claude's wife, Helena, whom he
had met a couple of times over the years.

There was a buzz coming from the small screen by the elevator.
"That must be the police," Helga said as she walked over and
pressed a release button on the elevator door. Three policemen and
two paramedics with a gurney entered the penthouse and quickly
came to inspect the body. After a final check for any vital signs,
the paramedics put the body on the stretcher and took it away.
Jack was surprised that the police didn't require a more thorough
investigation. All they had done was pull Claude's driving licence
out from the woman's handbag he carried, which also contained a
pistol and some handcuffs.

As the police were departing, one officer said, "Miss Barinov,
we suggest you beef up your security measures to ensure this
doesn't happen again. Good evening."

"I think I'm in good hands with Captain Petrov; she saved my
life again tonight."

Jack could tell Helga's iron-clad curtain fell for a split second
as she enjoyed the compliment. "Thank you, officers, and good
evening to you." The policemen turned and got back in the
elevator. Helga was already cleaning up the puddle of blood.

"I can't believe they didn't want to question us."

"I donate around ten million euros to the Monaco Police
every year; it helps at a time like this."

Ah, now Jack understood. Money really could buy you
everything. Well, almost everything, except for the thing
everyone wants—love, of course. His mind immediately went

back to earlier in the evening when, as fate would have it, he had just missed Lola again. He would talk to Alberto tomorrow to see if he had spoken to Marie Allard yet. Feeling inspired that he was getting closer lifted his spirits a bit after the horrendous twist of events tonight. As much as Claude had been a difficult and demanding client over the years, it was still unfortunate that he had not reached out for help with his apparent mental issues. Suddenly feeling completely exhausted, Jack suppressed a yawn. "I need to get going if you don't mind; this is all a lot to take in."

"Of course. I'll have my driver take you." She turned to him. "I really like you, Jack. There is something very honest about you that I appreciate and trust; this is very rare for me. I have a feeling, though, that there is already someone special in your life. I'm guessing it's the woman you asked Anais about at lunch on *Lekker Kontje*. Maybe it's just woman's intuition. Am I right?"

"Yes, you are." He kissed her on the cheek and stepped into the waiting elevator. As the doors closed, he could have sworn he saw a tear roll down Annika's cheek.

CHAPTER TWENTY-FIVE

Lola dove into the pool to cool off. After her morning run, she swam a few laps and then sat on the step, drinking coffee and planning out the week. First, she needed to call Eden-Roc to see if anybody had handed in her driving licence. She hoped it would be possible to talk to that kind waiter, Alberto, as he knew precisely where the bag had fallen. Thinking back to the party, she remembered how flustered she had felt after seeing Annika. The idea that Jack could be in a serious relationship with someone like Annika bothered her. It was because the thought that he had finally moved on brought out some deep-seated emotion that was confusing. Logically, of course, she knew this was exceedingly selfish, especially since she had turned him away all these years.

Lola gazed out to the Mediterranean, lost in the beautiful shades of turquoise and cobalt blue. She could see a superyacht with a helicopter on the stern anchored in the Bay of St. Tropez and smaller craft enjoying the morning sun. She wished she could ask Grandmother Delilah for advice. Delilah had always been so good at sorting out matters of the heart and putting things into perspective. Silently, Lola asked her grandmother for help, which somehow settled her nomadic heart. Picking up her empty coffee cup, she walked back into the villa. She noticed that it was nine and thought it would be a good time to ring the hotel. Scrolling through her phone, she found the number and called. Reception answered promptly.

"*Bonjour*, my name is Lola Delphine. I was at the party last night for Deux Margaux in the Champagne Lounge, and I seem to have lost my driving licence. A very nice member of your staff named Alberto helped me after I dropped my bag. Would it be possible to speak to him?"

"Can I get your contact details, *madame*? I will check with lost and found and also leave a message with Alberto. He starts his shift in thirty minutes." Lola gave the woman her details and thanked her before hanging up.

Opening her laptop on the kitchen island, Lola responded to a couple of questions from Jill about the shipment to Saks Fifth Avenue in New York. Then she sent a quick email to Clemence to thank her again for her gracious hospitality and to say she was sorry she had left in a hurry, blaming it on a made-up stomach upset. She would send flowers to the Paris office later today.

Claudette's poetry book, *Une Perle Dans L'huître*, sat next to her computer. She picked it up, randomly flicking through the pages until it stopped on one that was marked with a bent corner and a dried paper-thin gossamer rose.

"*Derniere visite au Café Chopin*" ("Final visit to the Chopin *Café*")

Woven memories,

nostalgic heart,

two paths crossed,

secret code,

everything lost.

It was amazing to Lola how so few words could encapsulate just what she was feeling. There was such a rawness to the words, especially knowing Claudette's backstory. Rereading it, she felt that Grandmother Delilah had just sent her a sign.

Directing her thoughts back to work, she saw another email from Jill, who was handling an expanded workload while Ingrid was away. Jill wrote that Ingrid had requested a few more days off; Lola responded that it was fine. That day at her parents' house in London seemed so long ago. Was she punishing Ingrid unfairly? After all, Ingrid did not know the whole story unless Max had told her, and she was sure he hadn't. The fact was she didn't even know herself, but every day, it seemed that she was inching closer to wanting to unravel the truth. Lola shivered, remembering she was still sitting in her damp bikini. She went into the bedroom to change. When she emerged from a quick shower, her phone was ringing. Grabbing a robe, she dashed back into the kitchen just in time to answer.

"Hello, this is Lola."

"Hello, *Mademoiselle* Delphine. This is Alberto calling from the Hotel du Cap. I wanted you to know that unfortunately, your driving licence was not handed in. I just did another check around the area and didn't find it. I'm sorry."

"Hello, Alberto. Thank you for looking and for being so gracious and kind to me last night. I appreciate your efforts."

"No problem at all. If it turns up, I will, of course, call you immediately," he said as he clicked off.

In case they found it, she decided to wait a few more days before applying for another one. Pouring another coffee, she went back to her emails.

CHAPTER TWENTY-SIX

Jack rolled over and glanced at his phone. It was ten a.m. He was surprised how late it was. The night had been fitful to say the least, with turbulent dreams as he tossed and turned to a combination of Lola's profile as she left the hotel and having her out of his life again. There was also Claude's deathly face as Helga rolled him over—two visions he would rather not ever mix again. Then there was Annika's sorrowful tale of her childhood; it gave him a whole new perspective on her. And yet again, it made him realise how many people carry around concealed truths and old wounds, and wear armour of different styles to camouflage their pain. He liked her more now that she had given him a glimpse into her vulnerable side.

After ordering his usual breakfast of coffee with steamed milk and a croissant, he checked through his emails. Fiona had sent a couple and called twice. He knew he would have to call soon and tell her what happened last night. As much as he hated having to give her the grim details, there was no way around it. She knew how desperate Claude had been to obtain the Kandinsky, and she wouldn't believe it if Jack just told her he had given up. Besides that, Claude had been a constant client over the last few years.

There was a knock on the door. Jack quickly opened it and found Alberto standing there with his breakfast tray. "Please come in, Alberto. How are you doing?"

"Very well, *monsieur*." Getting straight to the point, he said, "Except unfortunately, I talked to Marie Allard, and her father Leon Martin passed away some years ago. As it was, she and her father had a fractured relationship, and she hadn't talked to him for years before that, so our trail may have gone dead." Alberto could see the news saddened Jack.

"Well, I guess I'm going to have to think of something else. Thank you again for all your help; I hope one day I can repay you." He didn't even think to mention he had seen Lola at the hotel last night, and anyway, he had never actually given Alberto her name. Maybe his mind was cluttered from the dire evening, but Jack felt the need to keep it private so he could process the layers of emotion that the sighting had caused.

"As I said before, I'm happy to help, and if you need help with anything, please let me know," Alberto said as he exited. Jack sat down, poured the coffee, and took a bite of the flaky warm croissant.

Fiona's call interrupted his next bite. She was probably concerned that he hadn't returned any of her calls or emails. He picked up. "Hi, Fiona. How are you?"

"There you are. I was beginning to think Annika Barinov had eaten you for dinner." Jack had to laugh at that comment. Little did she know, and she would never know the entirety of what had transpired between him and the Romanian on his way out.

"No, but I do have something to tell you regarding Claude. Why don't you tell me your updates first?"

"Okay, well, you are never going to believe this, but the supermodel Anais that was on the yacht with you reached out to

me. She said she got the office number from Stefan van Carson."
Jack remembered he had given a card to Stefan. "Well, she's looking
for a particular Tamara de Lempicka painting called *Rhythm No.
5*. Do you know it?"

"Yes, I do, from 1924. It's a group of nudes featuring a cello
but no percussion instruments as the title would suggest. The title
is defined in more of a metaphoric sense. The charismatic Italian
writer, Gabriele D'Annunzio, even wrote about it. Do you know
D'Annunzio?"

"No, sorry, I don't."

"No problem, most people don't. He was a sex-obsessed Italian
poet, libertine, and war hero who essentially invented fascism as
an art project. One of his favourite quotes was 'You must create
your life as you'd create a work of art.'"

"He sounds like a thought-provoking man, and that makes
the painting even more intriguing," Fiona said as she listened to
Jack type away on his laptop.

"Well, it looks like we are in luck. That painting is privately
owned, possibly in Switzerland. Here we go again, Fiona." Jack
thought it was curious that Anais had reached out to him. After
all, there were plenty of art dealers out there. He hoped she didn't
have ulterior motives, and he didn't need another wild goose chase
ending in exhaustive drama. Jack decided he would have Fiona
contact her tomorrow to go over the contract. His research would
begin when he returned to London. Lola was his priority now, and
he didn't need any more distractions to divert him from his search.

"So, what was it you wanted to tell me about the Kandinsky?"
Taking a long sip of coffee, he filled Fiona in on the details of last
night, of course leaving out some of the more intimate moments
of the evening. Choosing not to tell Fiona the real back story of

Piano Notes seemed like the right thing to do. He felt like he wanted to honour and respect Herb Gomes' secret. Of course, Fiona was shocked by Claude's death and his connection to Annika, and she had a lot of questions.

"He was dressed as a woman and had turned crazy after having an affair with her? Thank God you were not hurt."

"It will probably go down as one of the most unforgettable nights of my life, that's for sure." He filled her in on a few more details, and they agreed it was a tragic waste of life and felt sympathy for Claude's family. Finishing the conversation, Fiona said she would send flowers and a bereavement card from the company to Claude's widow, Helena.

Jack worked for a few hours and felt like he needed a break, so he shut down his laptop and decided to get a late lunch at the Eden-Roc Grill. He was seated at a table overlooking the Mediterranean. One couldn't ask for a better view; it was stunning. A waiter appeared to take his order. For some reason, Jack got a wild hair and ordered a bottle of *Sancerre* instead of a glass. He could always take the rest back to his room.

"Will someone be joining you, sir?"

"No, it's just me today." He quickly looked over the menu and ordered the crab salad and a side of *pommes frites*. It seemed fun and decadent, and after the last couple of days, he needed that. The waiter brought the wine and gave Jack a taste; he nodded. It was crisp and delicious, just as it should be.

Sitting back in his chair, he watched the yachts pass by. A beautiful sailboat was anchored, and he could barely make out the name—The Golden Horseshoe. The irony of the name struck him as he thought back to the lovely photo of Lola in the white bikini at Villa Bonne Chance. Ah, Lola, his heart ached for her. It was so strange to be missing someone you had only seen twice for a split second, and before that, over twenty years ago. He tried to make sense of it, but as much as he went round and round and tried to be logical, he always came back to the fact that he was still deeply in love with her. All reasoning and logic didn't matter.

The crab salad and fries arrived, and the waiter filled up Jack's empty glass. The wine was undoubtedly relaxing his mind a little, which was just what he needed today. The restaurant was thinning out, and there were just a couple of diners left finishing off *digestifs* after a lazy lunch. It was quite hypnotic watching the white-tipped waves dance in the sunlight, and he barely noticed that the waiter topped off his glass again. It felt good to not worry for a change, and he enjoyed the effect the *Sancerre* was having as the waiter poured out the last of the wine and interrupted his haze.

"Would you care for another bottle, *Monsieur* Alistair?" Jack chuckled.

"No, thank you, I better not." He signed the bill that had been discreetly left on the table, got up, and strolled out of the restaurant. On the way back to his suite, he decided to stop in the hotel boutique. Facing him as he walked in was a display of Jetset Delilah pendant scarves. Now it made sense why she had been at the party last night. He looked at them for a minute, lost in thought. He moved on to a small jewellery case where he found what he was seeking. The sales assistant stood waiting while he looked. "Can I help you, *monsieur?*"

"Yes, I would like that fine gold chain, please." She took it out of the case and placed it in a navy-blue box, asking if he would like it gift-wrapped. "No, thank you, I have a pendant I want to add to it first." He paid, and she handed him the bag.

On his way out, he passed a book display, where an enticing image caught his eye. When he looked more closely, he instantly recognised that the front cover featured a beautiful painting by the renowned artist Will Martyr. What a coincidence, Jack thought; he had just seen a Martyr painting last night at Annika's penthouse. The title of the book was *The Golden Elephant*, and it was on the Sunday *Times* and the New York *Times* bestseller lists.

Intrigued, he flipped it over and read the synopsis: "A captivating story about people finding their inner truths, who they really are, and what they really want. Set against the glamorous backdrop of the Côte d'Azur and London's hotspots, the story follows the journeys of Fleur Tavistock and an old friend from her childhood past. Both are running from broken hearts, but signs and symbols from the universe guide them back together." After finishing the synopsis, he felt a connection to the story and decided he could read it on the plane. Waving to the shop assistant, he asked, "Would you charge this to my room, please?"

"*Bien sûr, Monsieur* Alistair"

"*Merci.*"

Upon returning to his suite, Jack took the horseshoe pendant out of the nightstand drawer where he had placed it for safekeeping. He took it off the broken chain, replacing it with the new one he had just purchased. Holding it in his hand for a minute, he visualized returning it to her one day. He placed the pendant next to her photo, which he kept propped up against the lamp, climbed into bed, and immediately fell into a much-needed sleep.

CHAPTER TWENTY-SEVEN

Annika picked up her phone and dialed the number on the cream-coloured calling card.

"*Bonjour.*"

"*Bonjour*, Anais, this is Annika." She got straight to the point. "Listen, can you give me that woman's name that you met at that wedding. It was Lola something."

There was a short silence while Anais thought. "Her name is Lola Delphine. May I ask why?"

"I'm just trying to help a friend. Are you still with Stefan?"

"No, I'm back in Paris looking for a new apartment."

Annika thought for a moment; she wasn't typically as generous as she was about to be. "Listen, I have a townhouse in the Trocadero. I only use it a couple of times a year. Why don't you stay there until you find a place?"

Anais was touched by her kindness, especially after what had happened many years ago. "That is very generous of you. Thank you."

"I will have my assistant, Lara Lenkov, contact you, and she will give you all the details." Anais thanked her again and was just about to hang up when Annika said, "Listen, Anais, I think it's time we talked about our past and the modelling days in London." She could almost feel the discomfort over the phone.

Anais's voice sounded weary all of a sudden. "To be honest with you, it's something I try not to think about, but maybe it's the right time. I still wonder where Clara is every day." She also felt horrible guilt at taking the fifteen-year-old Annika from Bar Bruno to meet Reggie at No. 16 Brewer Street.

Annika switched back into business mode. "Good, it's settled; expect a call from Miss Lenkov." She hung up before Anais could answer. Feeling pleased that she had finally decided to face some demons, she walked into the main hallway where Helga sat in her normal on-guard position by the side of the elevator. Helga stood up immediately when she saw Annika.

"Helga, I need you to call Dimitri Orlov. Tell him I need him to find a Miss Lola Delphine as soon as possible."

"Of course, Miss Barinov. I will take care of that immediately."

Dimitri Orlov was the best there was at finding people; Annika expected a call within a few hours. While she waited to hear back from retired Romanian General Orlov, she walked into the living room, stepped behind the long, curved bar, and poured herself a double shot of vodka. Picking up the chilled elixir, she walked up the stairs and into her opulent bathroom, deciding to take a bath while she waited to hear back from General Orlov.

Annika slipped into the hot water. She had added some gold-flake-infused sandalwood bath salts that were reputed to possess the most amazing healing properties. Mainly she just liked the way it made the water sparkle slightly. Thinking back over the last twenty-four hours, it was just what she needed. There was something very arousing about the combination of the icy-cold vodka and the steamy aromatic water. Taking the chilled shot glass, she lightly rubbed it on her nipple, which immediately hardened. The sensation sent a quiver of excitement through her lithe body; automatically, she started to caress and play with the other nipple. Putting the glass down, she let her hand travel to her newly Brazilian-waxed *pussoir*. Entirely hairless, she was able to trace every outline, her pleasure growing by the minute. Using both hands now, she continued to circle the pearl inside delicately while lightly inserting the other finger between her lips, slowly moving it in and out in a rhythmic motion. Waves of pleasure were coming faster and faster as she let her finger go deeper and deeper all the time, keeping the tempo the same.

Annika held on for as long as she could, but suddenly she lost control, and with a mind-blowing crescendo of ecstasy, she came so hard it was almost painful. Slowly, her quivering body relaxed back into a blissful state of contentment. Picking up the vodka, she tilted the rest of it down in one gulp. A knock on the door brought her quickly out of her euphoric state.

"Yes?"

"Miss Barinov, a letter has just arrived for you; the downstairs concierge just brought it up. I believe it may be from General Orlov."

"Thank you, Helga. Please place it on my bed. I will attend to it when I'm finished here." Well, well, Dimitri certainly had beaten his record this time. She glanced at the clock; it had taken him precisely fifty-five minutes to find Lola Delphine. Annika stepped from the bath to the shower and washed off the golden bath salts. She dried off, slipped into a leopard-print floor-length silk robe, and padded into the bedroom to find the large, crisp white envelope on the bed. Sitting down, she opened it and took out two pieces of paper. The first sheet was a short letter from General Orlov. The contents surprised her a little.

Dear Miss Barinov,

It turns out Lola Delphine was a bit more of a challenge to find, as she had done a fairly good job of keeping her personal details secure. It would have been impossible for a mere civilian to crack through the layers she had set up to hide her address, et cetera. However, I talked to some friends who have unique resources, and they found her in no time. If you need anything else, please let me know. I am at your service.

General Dimitri Orlov

The next sheet of paper had a printed photo of a blonde woman in a Porsche convertible. She was turned toward the lens and wore sunglasses. Annika wondered if it had been pulled from a speed camera. Underneath that were basic details such as name, age, and family members. Then she came across what she was seeking— Miss Delphine's address. She smiled when she read the top line: "Villa Bonne Chance." Gathering the papers, she went down the stairs and into the hallway to talk to Helga, who stood quickly.

"Helga, can you please send General Orlov five cases of Stolichnaya, and since he found her so quickly this time, why don't we match that with five kilograms of Beluga caviar?"

"Of course, right away, Miss Barinov." Helga pulled out her phone to start the transaction.

Annika liked to keep the general happy; he had been very useful over the years. She walked into the kitchen, thinking about the information she now had. There was a time when the old Annika would have used it to play power games with a man. But lately, for some reason, she was tired of all the manipulation.

Deep down, she knew Jack certainly didn't deserve it after he had been so honest with her. Departing from her usual mode of Lara making her calls, she decided to give Jack the news herself and dialed his phone.

*   *   *

Jack rolled over in his semi-hungover state. He thought he heard his phone ringing, but he had left it in the other room. He had no clue of the time, but the room was dark. Thirsty, he gulped down some water from a bottle by the side of the bed. Fully intending to see who called, he rolled over and fell back to sleep.

Annika grew impatient when he didn't pick up, so she quickly hung up without leaving a message and called back. The phone rang and rang. Still no answer. She was about to hang up again when she heard his voice on the message. Something in his tone softened her irritation, so she simply said, "This is Annika; please call me as soon as possible. I have found what you are looking for."

CHAPTER TWENTY-EIGHT

Alberto did another round of the Champagne Lounge to confirm all the guests were happy. It was a quiet night tonight, which suited him just fine. He walked back to the bar to ask the bartender a question about a specific wine when he noticed that one of the small sofas was slightly out of position. It had probably happened at last night's party. He thanked the bartender and walked the few steps to straighten out the sofa. As he gently pushed it into place, he could see that something was wedged under one of the feet. Bending down, he lifted the sofa, picked up the pink card, and rubbed it on his sleeve to clean it off a bit. There it was—Miss Delphine's driving licence.

Unfortunately, it was quite damaged, but he could definitely make out her name and the bottom line of the address. Coincidentally, he lived about twenty minutes from her in Les Issambres. Alberto thought for a minute. He could easily drop off the licence at her house in the morning before work. Moving to a more private area, he took out his mobile phone, found her contact details, and began texting.

Miss Delphine, this is Alberto from the Hotel du Cap. I have found your driving licence, and it turns out I live very close to you. I would be more than happy to drop it off in the morning before my shift.

He hit send and put the licence in his pocket for safekeeping. Lola was just returning home from meeting a friend for dinner in Sainte-Maxime when she heard her phone buzz. She put her bag on the kitchen counter and dug out her phone. Not recognising the number at first, she opened it and smiled. Alberto had found her licence. How sweet of him to offer to bring it by. She typed back:

"That's great you found my licence and very kind of you to offer to bring it by so long as you're absolutely sure it's no trouble. Thank you so much!

Alberto responded quickly, saying it was no problem and he would be there around eight forty-five in the morning. She was glad that she would be here all day tomorrow to meet him, especially since Claudette would be taking the whole day off. Turning off the lights except the one next to the piano that she always left on at night, Lola walked into her bedroom. After doing her nightly routine, she undressed quickly and climbed into bed, tired after a busy day. As usual, Domino and Solitaire jumped on the bed and snuggled up to her as she dozed off.

CHAPTER TWENTY-NINE

Fabian's plane had just landed at Houston's George Bush Intercontinental Airport. As it was making its way to the gate, he checked his phone messages and saw one from Scarlet.

"Hi, text me when you land!"

Fabian smiled and texted back:

"I'm officially in Houston, on the runway still. How are you?"

A few minutes passed. The flight crew was going through the deboarding process when Scarlet texted back:

"Great! Are you free tonight? Let's do dinner."

Fabian wondered for a moment if he should leave the evening open in case his client wanted to take him out, but of course, he wasn't about to turn Scarlet down.

"Perfect. I'm staying at the Post Oak Hotel in Uptown."

There was a return message in a few seconds.

"How about I come to the hotel at 7, and we can have dinner at Brasserie 19? It's going to be a perfect evening to dine alfresco. They have the most outrageous appetizer of caviar and chips. We also have to go to Bludorn before you leave. Their signature dish is lobster pot pie, which is decadent, delicious, and perfect to share."

Fabian responded:

"Smashing! I look forward to all of that tasty Texas cuisine and returning your pearl earring."

Scarlet's enthusiasm kept him smiling as he made his way off the plane and toward immigration.

CHAPTER THIRTY

The following morning, Lola stood in her kitchen making some toast. It was just after eight, and she had already finished her daily run and showered. Alberto had just texted to say he was called into work earlier than expected and would be working late. Since tomorrow was his day off, they agreed that he would come tomorrow in the early afternoon.

Seated at the counter to eat her breakfast, Lola opened Claudette's poetry book again. She stopped at a page marked by another pressed red rose. She picked up the delicate paper-thin flower gently and turned it around in her fingers; it almost felt like a bird's feather. Lola wondered when her grandmother had put it in the book. The poem seemed to contain a lot more hope than the other two she had read recently. It was called "*Quatre-Vingt-Huit Touches*" (Eighty-Eight Keys).

> I have many keys
> some I like, some I don't
> some are high, some are low.
> You showed me the key that opened my heart;
> this is where the journey starts.

Lola read it a couple more times before carefully replacing the rose between the pages. She wondered about the roses and who had given them to Delilah. Her grandmother had never mentioned any other men in her life after Grandfather Harold passed away. Lola thought there must have been some, especially when she envisioned the resplendent and passionate Delilah. Maybe she would ask Claudette about it someday.

Lola finished breakfast and decided to work at the kitchen island. There was a slight chill in the air of the late September morning, and her office tended to be a little cold. She would light the first fire of the season in the beautiful marble fireplace. When Lola opened her laptop, she noticed a couple of emails from Ingrid that appeared to be personal rather than business. One subject line read "Madrid thoughts" and the other read "Change of plans." Deciding that Ingrid could wait until the end of the day, she responded to Jill's emails.

CHAPTER THIRTY-ONE

Jack woke up abruptly in his dark room. Fumbling around for his phone, he suddenly remembered it was in the other room. When he got up and opened the drapes, a beam of sunlight brightened the space. Jack picked up the hotel phone and dialed room service for some coffee. He walked into the other room and found his phone plugged into its charger. Noticing it was eight forty-five, he scrolled through the calls. There were two from a number he didn't recognise with one message and a couple of voicemails from Fiona, who wanted to know if she should start researching the De Lempicka painting *Rhythm No. 5*. He was about to text Fiona back when there was a knock on the door. Ah, much-needed coffee. Opening the door, he half expected to see Alberto standing there, as he often handled the morning room service.

"*Bonjour, Monsieur* Alistair. Where would you like me to put this?"

"Right over there, please." Jack pointed to the coffee table, and the server put the tray down. He noticed that they had included his usual croissants with the order.

"Is Alberto working today?"

"Yes, he is training a new staff member, so I took over the morning room service."

"Okay, thank you." As he left, Jack handed him a generous tip. Next, he retrieved his phone and sat down on the sofa to pour some coffee. After a few sips, he remembered the voicemail from the unknown number, so he picked up the phone and listened.

"This is Annika. Please return this call as soon as possible; I have found what you are looking for."

The message puzzled Jack, who wasn't expecting her call and wondered what she meant. Quickly calling her back, he listened as the phone rang. He half expected to have to leave a message when she picked up.

"You are fortunate I like you so much because normally I don't have this much patience. However, I have some information that I think will probably make your day."

"Hello, Annika, I'm sorry I didn't get back to you sooner, and I'm intrigued to know what you have found."

"I just sent you an email that should explain everything."

Jack walked over to his laptop and turned it on, waiting for it to reboot. Annika grew impatient as she waited. "Jack, I have a busy day; I hope what you receive will be of some help." The computer was slow today, and the anticipation of what she had sent was growing.

"Annika, my computer is taking its time. I will let you know when I receive it."

"No need, Jack." He thought she had hung up, and as he was about to put the phone down, she simply said, *"Bonne chance."* With that, the phone clicked, and she was gone.

At that moment, his emails popped up. He found the one she had sent and clicked on it. There was no introduction, just an attachment that he opened swiftly. He stared at it in disbelief; there was a picture of Lola in her car. It looked like the same white Porsche he had seen outside the casino. Below were personal details. Then he came to what he had been searching for, the location of Villa Bonne Chance.

Jack sat back for a minute. The enormity of it all was a lot to take in. He thought back to when Annika had basically paid for the police officers' silence. He had felt at that moment that money could buy you everything except love; maybe in this case, he was wrong. Looking at the document and how it was worded, it was apparent that she had friends in the military.

Printing out the sheet and reading it again, Jack realised how close he had been the whole time. She lived just over an hour away. He started to put together a plan that seemed years in the making. It turned out, however, that it was the longest decision that he made very quickly.

Standing up, Jack went back into the bathroom and took a long shower. A calmness came over him. Finally, he would be able to face Lola after all these years of searching. There were so many things he wanted to say to her, and as the water hit his body, he tried to get them all in order. It was so incredible that Annika Barinov had helped him like this. He would never forget her generosity and hoped he could do something meaningful for her one day for the life-changing gift she had just given him.

Jack towelled off and picked out his clothes thoughtfully. He wanted to look as good as possible, of course. It was strange to feel so relaxed and not in a hurry; maybe it was the knowledge that she was so close that was comforting. He finished getting ready and picked up the horseshoe pendant and put it in the velvet pouch, which he put into his breast pocket along with the photo of Lola in the white bikini.

Checking that he had everything, he was just about to leave when Delilah's painting grabbed his attention. He stood in front of it, hardly believing he would soon be outside the real Villa Bonne Chance. Lost in thought for a few seconds, he spotted something that he hadn't noticed before. Having been so focused on the Bonne Chance sign, he hadn't paid much attention to the other stone gate post. There it was, a horseshoe nailed to the post. Yet again, it felt like Grandmother Delilah was sending him the final sign, wishing him good luck. Jack folded the printout in two, put it in his pocket, and left the room.

The *voiturier* brought his car around. He had already typed Lola's address into his phone map, so he hit start and made his way out of the hotel grounds. He had thought about letting Alberto know, but he didn't want to bother him while he was working, plus it would be more fun to give him the good news after he talked to Lola. The drive was easy. Finally, the navigation told him he was now just ten minutes away. She certainly did live in a beautiful area, he thought, as he climbed the hills by Sainte-Maxime.

CHAPTER THIRTY-TWO

After working solidly since early morning, Lola stood up to take a quick break. Turning to look at the fire, she noticed that the cats were curled up in front of it on the rug, fast asleep. It was an unusually grey, chilly day today, but it felt cosy in her living area. She decided to light some candles and change out of the tight jeans into a short cream-coloured cashmere sweater dress and Ugg boots.

Lola switched the sound to legendary pianist James Pearson, whose transportive seductive music seemed perfect for the afternoon. Looking around, she felt content in the warm room. For some reason, even though it was the middle of a workday, she fancied a glass of red wine. Opening the cellarette door, she discovered the last two bottles of vintage *Château La Nerthe* her mum had given her one year. It felt like the right time to open one, even though she had saved them all these years for a special occasion.

Lola opened the bottle, poured it into one of her favourite crystal wine glasses, and took it outside. The brisk air hitting the thin cashmere dress felt refreshing as she walked to the end of the pool and gazed out to the Mediterranean. It looked almost cerulean blue today against the cloudy sky.

*   *   *

Jack sat in his car outside Villa Bonne Chance and was suddenly very emotional. He wanted to compose himself before knocking on her door. He had waited for this moment for more than twenty years. It was all he could do to stop himself from breaking down into a sobbing wreck. Giving himself a little pep talk, he turned into the open gate, pausing again to look at the rusted Bonne Chance sign. Glancing to the other gate post, he couldn't see the horseshoe because there was so much ivy covering the stone column; he wondered if it still hung there after all these years. The car crunched down the gravel driveway; he could see her white Porsche parked under the awning to the left of the one-story villa. There were large ornate tubs of lavender and rosemary placed on either side of the front door. It looked very inviting.

Coming to a stop, Jack parked on the right side of the house, stepped out of the car, and stood for a minute, taking in everything. The powerful emotions that surged through his body were intense. He went from deep anxiety to pure excitement. It was like someone was pressing a remote control in his brain. His body felt like it was vibrating from head to toe, which caused him to freeze for a moment as he talked himself down from the heightened state of intense passion combined with nerves and joy that he was about to see Lola again. Pulling himself together, Jack walked up to the front door. He stared at the brass dolphin-shaped door knocker and lifted his hand to knock.

Lola took a stroll around her pool, stopping here and there to smell various herbs, including the lavender. As she was about to head in, she looked over at the inviting outdoor sofa, where she had added a cosy lamb's wool throw now that autumn was nearing. Deciding instead to sit for a minute and finish the last few sips of wine in the cool air, she settled on the sofa and covered her legs with the soft blanket.

* * *

Jack knocked twice and waited. Due to his heightened senses, the knock sounded extra loud. He stood back, expecting the door to open any second. While he shifted nervously from one foot to another, the door stayed firmly shut, like a warden guarding the crown jewels. After a few minutes, he knocked again. He tried not to think that she might be out or out of the country or worse than that, with the American film star.

Jack brought up his hand to the dolphin once again, then stopped. For some weird reason, he remembered a game he and Lola had invented all those years ago called 333. Basically, one person had to count to 333 while the other tried to make them laugh. It was such a silly game, but they got so much joy out of it. Thinking about it made Jack smile, and he decided to count to 333. If she didn't come then after he knocked, he would leave and come up with another plan. Closing his eyes, he started to count very quietly: 1, 2,3, and so on. The seconds ticked away.

Lola finished the last sip of wine, put the glass down, and returned the throw blanket to the back of the sofa. She glanced over at one of the planters and noticed it was a bit dry. Not seeing the rain clouds forming, she decided to give it a quick water before going inside. Claudette could do it tomorrow, but she wasn't getting here till the late morning. Walking over to the herb garden on the pool's right, she began to fill the watering can.

Jack carried on counting. "245, 246, 247…."

Lola turned off the tap and carried the can over to the lavender planter; as the water hit the plant, the beautiful scent wafted up. Letting the last of the water drip out, she thought it could probably do with one more. Besides, she enjoyed watering plants; it was very relaxing.

Jack was slowing his count down, which was not allowed in the original game, but since the dolphin door knocker and the wooden warden were his only witnesses, he felt like he could cheat a little. "300…..301……302…………303………"

Lola filled up the can a second time and returned to finish watering the lavender. She was enjoying herself so much she decided to carry on with some of the other plants.

"320……………..321………………..322…"

What she hadn't noticed was that the clouds were growing darker, and the wind had picked up. Almost out of nowhere, a large raindrop fell on the paving, starting slowly at first, then rapidly the drops came faster and faster. Lola quickly put the watering can down and ran the short distance to the covered seating area to retrieve her wine glass before going inside. She was temporarily mesmerised by the rhythm of the rain hitting the pool; it almost sounded like someone counting.

"330……………..331……………..332…"

Lola quickly picked up the wine glass and hurried toward the door. As it swung open in the wind, she struggled to pull it to. Finally securing the door, she stood for a second, amazed at how the storm had caught her so off guard.

"……….333." Jack brought his hand up to the dolphin for the last time and gave it the loudest knock of all.

Lola nearly jumped out of her skin when she heard the knock and almost dropped the crystal wine glass, which she placed on the island while thinking her mind was playing tricks on her. Maybe it was just a crack of thunder. Then she remembered Alberto and thought that his schedule might have changed, and he had decided to bring her driving licence today after all. Not wanting to keep him waiting outside in the rain, she hurriedly opened the front door and was so shocked, she was unable to speak. They stood there looking at each other in complete silence until she whispered, "Jack."

* * *

Time seemed to stand still as years of denial suddenly came to a halt. They faced each other, frozen in shock at the intensity of the moment. Jack inched forward as the rain picked up and began to penetrate the small porch area where he stood. He ran his hand through his thick mop of hair, and tiny droplets of water fell to the ground.

Lola shivered in the delicate cashmere dress. She finally found her voice, which came out in a whisper against the rumble of thunder. "How did you find me?"

Jack smiled, causing his blue eyes to twinkle under his wet lashes as he took half a step closer to her, taking her hand. She held it tightly and gently pulled him forward out of the rain. Jack closed the door, shutting out the noise of the tempest. Taking her other hand, he said, "Lola, without really realising it until that moment I saw you at the casino, I have been searching for you all my life. When you stepped out of the car, I spotted the crescent-moon-shaped scar on your leg. I knew that to have true peace in my heart and soul, I had to find you again."

Lola nodded, and a tear rolled down her cheek as she listened to his emotional story, realising that she too had silenced her own truth and had run from the love of her life out of fear. Jack wiped the tear away as he glanced beyond her to a large painting hanging behind the Steinway piano, immediately recognising its style, which was so like the painting in his suite. Noticing his eyes shift slightly, Lola turned to see what had distracted him.

"Grandma Delilah," he said, smiling. He turned back to Lola again as he spoke. "There is a painting by your grandmother in my suite at the Eden-Roc."

Lola looked surprised, although she did know that Delilah had sold several paintings to the hotel many years ago. Finding her voice, she asked, "Which one is it?"

"Villa Bonne Chance."

Suddenly everything became clear. In unison, they thought back to all the lucky signs the universe had presented to them. It was as if a powerful force had brought them back together. Jack took the last small step toward Lola, kissing her lips softly as they gazed into one another's eyes. She held on to him tightly, lost in an embrace that was so heated it took Lola's breath away. After a few minutes, Jack pulled back and looked deeply into her eyes before taking her in his arms again. They stayed that way, not moving or talking, enjoying the moment both had dreamed of secretly for years. Releasing Lola gently, he bent to kiss the nape of her neck, taking in the amber-oil scent he remembered from twenty years ago.

Lola groaned slightly as he made his way down, delicately pulling the neck of the cashmere dress to the side, exposing her shoulder. The intensity growing with every kiss, she could feel the strong connection between them. Lola bent down to kiss him below his ear.

"Hello, Mr. Alistair."

Pausing, he grinned at her cheeky tone. "Lady Delphine."

Jack sat on the piano stool and eased Lola down next to him. She leaned her head into the crook of his neck as he began to play her favourite piece, *Lofty Roads*. The moment was incredibly sensual as an electric current surged between them.

"You remembered," she whispered in his ear.

"Of course, I remember." At that moment, he stopped playing and turned to face her. Their lips met again. This time, she could feel his tongue encircling hers. The kisses and deep underlying connection were things they hadn't felt with anyone else. Standing up, Jack took Lola's hand and looked around the room slowly, knowing that he was desperate to be inside this woman completely. Beyond the linen sofas, he could see the double doors that opened into her bedroom. Taking her hand, he led her into the room, pausing to pick up one of the candles she had lit earlier. Jack put the flickering candle on the nightstand, and it cast an atmospheric glow in the half-light of the tempestuous afternoon. He pulled the duvet back and turned to Lola, easing the dress over her head.

Lola stood there in sea-green lace Coco de Mer French knickers, unable to conceal her lust. Mirroring him, she lifted his shirt over his head; Jack simultaneously undid his jeans. Lying on the crisp white Egyptian-cotton sheets, she reached up for Jack, pulling him closer, their tongues meeting again. The weight of his body on hers was intense; she had been craving it unconsciously for years.

Now he was kissing her neck and making his way down. In turn, she arched her back slightly, hungry for his touch. A small groan left her moistened lips as he began to circle her hardened nipple. Jack paused for a second and quickly eased her lacy knickers off before removing his boxer shorts. Positioning himself over her quivering body, he resumed kissing her nipple as she said in a throaty voice, "Jack, I want to feel you inside me."

"Oh, Lola, you are so beautiful, and your skin is unbelievably soft." His voice was deeper now and a lot raspier. They looked at each other, the invisible force so strong it was as if their souls had become one. His kisses moved down to her fine landing strip bleached blonde from the sun. Parting her legs, she waited, longing for what would come next. Jack lifted himself and looked at Lola as she watched him intently. "You turn me on so much; feel how wet I am," she said.

Sliding a finger between her dripping lips, he moaned with desire. Circling the delicate, precious *bijou*, he teased her, now aware that his cock was so hard, it was getting impossible not to thrust himself into her. Lola was getting close to reaching her peak, so she shifted slightly. "Jack, now please, I need you inside me." He changed his position and hovered over her, their tongues meeting again as they explored each other's mouths with intense passion. He entered her slowly, going deeper and deeper, their mouths never parting. She lifted her hips to change the angle, so his cock would hit her in a way that started waves of pleasure so intense it was euphoric. They were in perfect rhythm with each other, lost in a state of pure ecstasy that was utterly intoxicating.

"Oh, Jack, I'm going to come." He could feel her body quivering under him, vibrating from the inside. "Oh yes, Lola, me too." They realised they had been transported to another world—a fantasy paradise so beautiful and alluring, a place so tantalising that the secret key belonged only to them. Jack's cock thrust harder and harder as they moved together in a tantric state so entwined in their hearts, it was as if a magic spell had been cast upon them. Jack's voice was gravelly. "Yes, yes, oh Lola, Lola!"

Her body was trembling, and the feeling was so intense she could barely speak. All she could manage in a breathy voice was "Jack." At that moment, the waves of pure bliss reached such a heightened state they came together with intoxicating intimacy. Even though the moment was incredibly intense, there was a fragility to it. They both knew how rare and beautiful their connection was and that they would never lose it again. She looked deeply into his eyes, and they both started crying uncontrollably.

Rolling over, Jack scooped her up, kissing her tears away as his mixed with hers. Their lovemaking had been so powerful, it was obvious that their connection had grown stronger over time. Entwined, they listened to the rain.

Jack was the first to speak. "Lola, Lola, I love you so much. It's always been you, even though I've tried to suppress this emotion because I never knew if you would forgive me. I should never have pushed you to confront your mother about the conversation I overheard."

Lola lay with her head on his chest; she felt as if she had finally come home. Propping herself up, she said, "I love you, too, Jack, with all my heart, and all the stuff that happened back then was not really your fault. I just couldn't face the truth."

"Lola, I think we need to talk about all of this in detail later. It's been so amazing since I saw you at the casino. So many things have happened that have led me back to you."

"It happened to me also. I could feel the universe pushing me in the right direction. There have been some unbelievable coincidences and lucky talismans that have been placed in front of me, and this is one of them." He watched as she pulled Beatrix Potter's *The Tale of Jemima Puddle-Duck* from the nightstand. She opened it halfway and pulled out the photo of her sunbathing in the white bikini at the villa. "Do you remember this?"

Jack nodded as he climbed out of bed and bent down to the messy piles of clothes that were strewn everywhere. Picking up his jacket, he placed it beside him. He pulled the matching photo from the breast pocket and put it next to Lola's like they were playing a game of cards. He turned it over and read, "Sexy in Sainte-Maxime."

For a second, his voice sounded a little more concerned. "Listen, Lola, I know we have a lot to talk about; I want to explain everything to you." He decided to wait to give her the horseshoe pendant. They were both in such a heightened state of emotion that it seemed better to hold off for the perfect moment.

"Shhh. It's okay, we have time. For a little while, I just want to lie here with you. Do you fancy a glass of wine?"

"Yes, that would be great. Do you want me to get it?"

"No, I will. There is already a bottle open, and I also need to feed my cats, Domino and Solitaire."

Jack smiled at the names, remembering what a huge Bond fan she was. As he watched her get up and walk to the kitchen, he knew he couldn't possibly love anyone as much as he loved Lola. Knowing they had so much to sort out from the past, he hoped and prayed that she would accept his explanation of the events that took place that fateful summer.

Lola returned with a bottle of wine and two glasses, set them down on the nightstand, and poured each of them a generous serving. Before climbing back into bed, she rearranged the pillows so she could half sit up and face him. She had lost all sense of time, especially since the stormy skies had made it darker than usual, and she hadn't looked at her phone for ages. There was so much to say, and she didn't know where to start. There were twenty-three years of catching up to do, which also meant going down a painful road that had been closed off all these years. Their hands were entwined as they sipped on the wine. For now, content to be in each other's company, it was Lola who spoke first. "I have to ask; how did you find me? It can't have been easy."

Jack had been thinking about the question for a while because he knew she would ask, and there was no way around the answer, only the truth. "A friend of mine, Annika Barinov, found you as a favour to me." He could tell from her face that this was not the answer she wanted to hear.

"I saw a picture of the two of you on Stefan van Carson's yacht. Were you a couple?"

Jack knew some of his answers probably would not please her, but he wanted to be completely transparent and honest, not leaving anything out for her to discover later. "I met her because an old client of mine wanted to purchase a Kandinsky painting that she owns. I was invited on the yacht for what I considered a business meeting. There was just one other evening, last Thursday when she invited me to her home in Monte Carlo for dinner after a party at the Hotel du Cap-Eden-Roc, which is where I am staying. In fact, you are not going to believe it, but I saw you getting into a car there that night. It was just a glimpse, and you were gone, just like the first time I saw you at the Casino de Monte-Carlo."

It was all a lot to decipher, and they both understood that the intricate woven webs of their lives would take a long time to understand. "To answer your question, we did have a dance with the idea, but I just couldn't go there with her because my heart was always yours. As it turns out, she gave me the most valuable gift of all—finding you."

"You know, I saw you that evening outside the casino, too. Of course, I pretended I didn't see you because it took me some time to face the demons I've been fighting all these years. Last Thursday at the Eden-Roc, I left in a hurry because I saw Annika at the party for Deux Margaux. After seeing those pictures of you with her, it really upset me."

Jack held her hand tightly. "We have a lot to talk about, and I want to make sure we sort out the hard stuff sooner rather than later because I think that's the first step to moving forward together." Lola nodded. "But first of all, I'm starving," Jack said. "How about we get up and eat something?"

She was glad he had lightened the mood slightly. "That sounds like a great idea; follow me." They got up, and Jack put on his boxer shorts and tee-shirt. Lola slipped back into the comfy cashmere sweater dress, and they walked hand in hand into the kitchen.

"This is a beautiful place," he said, looking around, taking in all the amazing artwork that lined the walls.

"Wait till you see the view in the morning. It really is special." She blushed a little as she said, "That's if you want to stay, of course." Coming around the other side of the island, he took her in his arms and held her tightly.

"Of course, silly, I never want to leave you."

CHAPTER THIRTY-THREE

After possibly the best night's sleep either one of them had ever had, Jack woke to find he had a furry hat on his head purring. Opening her eyes, Lola smiled as she watched Jack pet Domino; Solitaire, also purring, was stretched out next to her. The evening had been wonderful after a put-together meal of toasted French bread, various cheeses, and charcuterie. They had danced a lot, sat by the fire, and Jack had even played a couple of pieces on the piano, including some Dudley Moore compositions and an eighties favourite of hers, *That's Just the Way It Is* by Bruce Hornsby and the Range. They stumbled into bed late and feasted on each other's bodies again until they fell into a deep sleep entwined in each other's arms. Both of them had turned off their phones, enjoying the luxury of not being interrupted.

Lola got up to make some coffee, and Jack followed. He felt like it was time to have the conversation, the one they were both dreading. Putting two cups of steaming coffee and some warm croissants on the island, Lola came around to join him on one of the comfy barstools. Jack looked at Lola in her white silk robe, elflock hair, and no makeup, and he thought she was absolutely stunning, a natural beauty. He was almost tempted to carry her back to the bedroom, but instead he said, "I know this is very difficult to talk about, but we need to." She nodded, letting him continue. "I'm going to start from the beginning because I know that's what led to everything else that happened. I was mucking out one of the stables on that unspeakable day. Max and your mum probably assumed I was with you at your house because we typically spent the weekends together. I had stopped sweeping when I heard them coming because I was trying to dig a splinter out of my hand. They didn't know I was sitting on an upturned bucket hidden from view in the back of the stable. I suppose I should have let them know I was there, but it all happened so fast, and I just kind of froze."

"Max started by asking if she had told your dad yet. I remember Roberta saying that she thought he probably had some suspicions over the years, and she was planning on telling him. She sounded distraught. He then asked her if she had spoken to Francis Williams about it. Your mother said she hadn't because it was all just too painful. The last thing I heard was Max told her that you, Lola, deserved to know who her biological father is."

Lola just sat staring at him. She didn't know how to react or what to say, but the tragic memory of that day came back in a flash. She was reminded once again that it was not really Jack's fault, and he was just trying to protect her and be honest about what he heard. She took his hands to reassure him it was all going to be okay.

"As soon as they left the stable yard, and I heard Roberta's car drive away, I snuck out of the stall, jumped in my car, and raced to tell you. I'm so sorry about all of it. Had I been older and more mature, I think I would have handled it very differently. I certainly would not have jumped on Penny and chased you in a mad gallop."

Lola still held his hands, saying, "I think I just needed someone to blame. I lashed out at you because I was so hurt and shocked by the news. As a result, poor Penny had a heart attack, which was not your fault. When the vet did a thorough examination, he said she probably would not have lived much longer anyway. So perhaps the best way for her to finish out her life was with a wild gallop." Jack shifted off the stool and kneeled. He lifted the silk robe and lightly kissed the crescent-moon-shaped scar and just simply said, "I'm sorry."

"I know now that I have to go to London and talk to my mother and get the truth," Lola said. "It's time."

Jack agreed. "I will go with you."

They heard a car coming to a stop on the gravel outside. "That must be Claudette, my housekeeper. I will ask her to start outside so we can have our privacy a bit longer." Lola got up and walked out of the front door to talk to Claudette. Jack headed for the shower, admiring the spectacular view on the way. He felt relieved that they had started to sort out the past, but there was still a long way to go. A lot more would be resolved when Lola talked to her mother.

Jack was enjoying the hot water hitting his chest when the glass door opened. Lola stepped into the steamy shower. Making her hands really soapy, she began to rub them up and down his chest. Mirroring her, he gently circled her nipples. Lola's body responded quickly to his touch as she started to caress Jack's already rock-hard cock. The momentum was increasing as they explored each other's bodies, making up for years of absence. Turning around and bending down slightly, she put her hands on the wet marble wall. Jack positioned himself behind her and entered her slowly at first.

"Oh, Jack, that feels so good." Lola's voice was muted in the torrent of steamy water. Speeding up the pace, he steadied himself by placing his hands over Lola's as he continued thrusting his cock in and out, both of them lost in intense ecstasy. He could tell she was very close, and it was all he could do not to explode. He waited, wanting the final moment to be shared.

"Jack, oh….yes….yes….yes!" He gave one final deep thrust as they came together, their hands glued to the wall, unable to move.

Jack eased himself out of her and turned the shower off. Opening the fogged-up door, he grabbed the towels that were on the nearest rack. They dried off, and Lola threw denim shorts and a tee-shirt on her damp naked body. Turning to Jack and smiling, she gave him another quick kiss and said, "Why don't you take your time? I'm going to see if Claudette needs anything, and I should probably turn my phone back on, as much as I'd like to hide away with you forever." Jack still stood naked; she admired his body and couldn't resist kissing his chest one more time before leaving him to get ready.

As she was walking into the bedroom, he called her back. "Miss Delphine." Lola turned, smiling at his tone. "I am bedazzled by you." Blowing him a kiss, she walked out of the room.

CHAPTER THIRTY-FOUR

Claudette was outside scooping leaves from the pool, so Lola went into the kitchen, where her phone was charging. Waiting while the screen came back on, it buzzed, and she saw that she had a variety of messages. Checking the text messages first, she noticed that Alberto from the hotel had texted to say he would drop off her licence at twelve-thirty today. Lola looked at the time. It was twelve twenty-five. Thankfully, she hadn't missed him.

* * *

Alberto was so busy listening to the directions on his phone that he didn't notice the Villa Bonne Chance sign as he drove his turquoise Citroën 2CV down the gravel drive. He thought it was amusing that another 2CV was parked outside the house, so he parked next to it and walked to the front door, picked up the brass dolphin, and knocked.

Lola jumped when she heard the knock, even though she was expecting it. She walked over and opened the door. "Alberto, please come in. I'm sorry I didn't respond to your message, but I'm so glad you came by anyway." She motioned him to come into the kitchen. "Would you like something to drink?"

"No, *madame*, thank you. What a beautiful view you have here."

"Yes, I feel fortunate to enjoy this every day."

Alberto reached in his pocket and placed her driving licence down on the island. "It's a bit damaged but still legible; it was wedged under a sofa leg when I found it. By the looks of it, it's just the top line of your address that's missing."

"I really appreciate your bringing it to me." She opened one of the kitchen drawers where she always kept some spare cash, pulled out a couple of hundred euros, and began to hand it to him.

Alberto stood back on the other side of the island, shaking his head. Refusing to take it, he said, "That is very generous. Thank you, but it is not necessary."

Lola could tell that he would not be persuaded. "Well, at least let me give you a bottle of wine. I'm not taking no for an answer. You could share it with your wife. Red or white?"

"There is no wife, just me. But okay, if you insist, a bottle of red wine would be lovely." Alberto perched on the edge of one of the barstools while she opened the cellarette to select the perfect bottle. Looking around the large bright room, he looked at the artwork and noticed something very familiar about some of the paintings; he just could not put his finger on what it was. As he turned to look at the other wall, a small book on the end of the island caught his attention, and he couldn't help reaching over to have a look at *Une Perle Dans L'huître*. Not noticing the author, he was compelled to open the book and turn to a page that had been marked with something. The paper-thin red rose fluttered out like a butterfly as he picked up the book, mesmerised by what he read.

"Derrière Visite au Café Chopin" ("Last Visit to the Chopin *Café*")

Woven memories

Nostalgic heart

Two paths crossed

Secret code

Everything lost.

Alberto sat back on the barstool. He closed the book, already knowing what he would see as he whispered her name. "Claudette." Putting his head in his hands, he sobbed gently.

Lola finally found just what she was looking for. She knew she had one last bottle of *Château le Nerthe*. Reaching to the back of the shelf, she picked it up and turned toward Alberto, immediately seeing something was wrong.

"Alberto, what is it?" Hurriedly, she put the bottle down and came around and put an arm around him, noticing the poetry book in front of him. He could barely speak and was shaking a little. She tried to calm him down by rubbing his back.

"Miss Delphine, how do you have this book? It's just that the author is someone I knew a long, long time ago."

"You know Claudette?" Suddenly, it all made sense, but surely it couldn't be true. This would be the most incredible twist of good luck, timing, and coincidence. At that moment, Jack walked into the room and saw a man bent over the island sobbing. He quickened his pace.

"Lola, is everything okay?"

Recognising his voice, Alberto turned, his distraught tone muffled. "*Monsieur* Alistair, what are you doing here?"

"Alberto! What a surprise!" Lola just stood looking at the two of them, not knowing what to say; it was all so confusing. Jack gave Alberto a big hug while Lola went to the fridge and poured him a large glass of water out of the pitcher she always kept filled.

Taking a long gulp, Alberto looked up at them and picked up the book. "This book was written by the love of my life, Claudette." Jack nodded, remembering the sweet sorrowful story Alberto had told him. "I would give anything to see her again." Lola looked outside at Claudette, who was sweeping some leaves that had fallen in yesterday's storm. Taking the book from him and placing it on the island, Lola took his hands and held them tightly. Jack looked at them; he could tell from Lola's expression and the crack in her voice that this was an emotional moment for her.

"The other day, I heard a story from someone I've known most of my life. She told me that years ago, when she lived in Paris, she had fallen in love with a waiter who worked at the *Café Chopin*." Alberto stared into Lola's teary eyes as she spoke. "One day she went to the *café* and found that the waiter had quit his job and left Paris."

As the tears began to roll down Alberto's face, he pulled a handkerchief from his pocket and wiped them away. "She was, of course, heartbroken, and shortly after, she left Paris herself to pursue her dreams of becoming a poet. Moving to the Riviera made perfect sense, especially due to its history and connections to many famous artists and writers." Lola's story transfixed both men as she continued. "To support herself, she got a job working for my grandmother, Delilah, here at Villa Bonne Chance." Not wanting to keep Alberto waiting any longer, she released one of his hands and pointed outside. "And there she is." They all looked out the window.

Alberto stood up. All he could manage to say in his emotional state was "Claudette." Lola and Jack watched as he walked toward the door. Pausing before opening it, he turned around. "I don't know how any of this is possible. It's the most magical thing that's ever happened to me, and I'm still confused about this amazing series of coincidences that have woven us together." They walked over to him and gave him one last big hug before he opened the door.

* * *

Claudette took a break from her sweeping. Lost in thought, she didn't hear the door open as she stood looking out over the Bay of St. Tropez, oblivious as to what was about to happen. Alberto didn't want to startle her, so he walked to the side of the pool and stood by one of the sun loungers. All the memories from years ago washed over him as he spoke. "My beautiful Claudette; at last, I've found you."

Recognising his voice immediately, she turned around and stared at him, a puzzled look on her face. "Alberto?" They walked toward each other until they stood within arm's reach. "How is this possible?" Taking her hands, he looked deeply into her eyes as she stepped forward. "All these years, I have looked for you without really knowing it. Subconsciously I tried to find you in many different places. I searched for you in other people, never finding what I was seeking. When I was happy, I wanted to share my excitement; when I was sad, I needed your love. I always knew something was missing from my soul, never really admitting to myself out of fear that it's always been you. When I began to help *Monsieur* Alistair find Villa Bonne Chance, I didn't know his whole story. He never mentioned Lola's identity, only that the villa contained something incredibly special for which he had yearned for many years. There was something so familiar in Jack's sad heart that I recognised in myself. I knew then that I would make it my mission to find you again. Amazingly, it turns out that it was Lola's grandmother, Delilah, who steered me back to you."

Jack and Lola watched as Claudette and Alberto stood in a tight embrace. They walked hand in hand and opened the door. Claudette was smiling as she and Alberto made their way through the villa. Lola waved at them, not wanting to disturb the moment. Then she suddenly remembered something. "Wait, you forgot this!" Walking over to the wine fridge, she pulled out a bottle of *Dom Perignon* and picked up the *Château la Nerthe* from the dining table. Placing them in a bag, she handed them to Alberto. "I think Champagne is definitely appropriate for this astounding afternoon." As they opened the front door, Claudette looked back at Lola for a few seconds. There was no need for words; both women knew the magic of this day.

When the door closed, Lola turned to Jack. "I think we should also open a bottle of Champagne." She selected a chilled bottle, and Jack opened it and poured two glasses. Deciding to take them outside, they eased onto the sofa. There was a slight chill in the air, so Lola put the blanket over her legs and snuggled up to Jack. They began to swap stories about Alberto and Claudette, agreeing that it added a lovely twist to their reunion.

As they reached a quiet respite, Lola plunged deeply into thought. "There's something I need to do." Jack looked at her, waiting. "I have to call my best friend, Ingrid Ashton. She started dating Max Valentine-Smithe after we ran into him at Scott's restaurant one Sunday. It was all too much for me at the time, but I know now she hasn't done anything wrong, especially because she doesn't know the connection our family has with him. When we go to London, I need to meet with her. It's weird, really, after so many years of running from the truth of who my biological father is, I feel incredibly calm about it."

"Can I ask you something?"

"Yes, of course, Jack."

"What about Ollie? Do you think he knows?"

"I hope he does because he has been the best dad I could have asked for, and I'm not sure how he would handle this kind of news after all these years. We should book our flights. How about leaving the day after tomorrow?"

"That sounds good. Why don't you call Ingrid, and I will go in and check my barrage of messages. I need to call back my assistant, Fiona, so she doesn't start to worry." Jack went inside, and Lola picked up her phone to call Ingrid.

CHAPTER THIRTY-FIVE

Ingrid waved goodbye as her mum pulled away from dropping her off at the Madrid-Barajas Airport. Wiping the goodbye tears from her eyes, she pulled her suitcase into the terminal and began to make her way to the check-in counter. The lines were long, primarily because business class had been sold out. Since Ingrid had plenty of time, she didn't mind waiting. While looking at the unruly children squabbling in front of her, the phone in her pocket suddenly vibrated. Pulling it out, she was completely taken off guard when she saw that Lola was calling! Feeling suddenly nervous, she answered and said, "Hello Lola, what a lovely surprise."

"Hi Ingrid, I think it's time we talked. I realise now that I have been very unfair. I hope you will forgive me." Lola waited for a response. From the background noise on the phone, it sounded like Ingrid was at the airport.

"As a matter of fact, I'm at Barajas Airport, and I have been so desperate to sort things out that I was planning to fly into Nice to surprise you. Crazy, right?" Lola could tell from Ingrid's voice she was very emotional.

"Wow, really? That would have been a surprise, and trust me when I tell you, it seems to be a good week for surprises, including one Jack Alistair who has walked back into my life."

"Jack Alistair?! I always knew he was much more important to you than you ever let on."

It felt so good to be able to chat with her best friend again. Thinking quickly, Lola said, "Would it be possible for you to change your flight? We are flying to London the day after tomorrow. I have a lot of unresolved issues I have to sort out with my mum. Why don't we get together at the end of the week?"

"Yes, of course. You called just in time, as I'm in the check-in line. It's so good to talk to you again. I've missed you so much," she said, as she stepped out of line and looked for customer service to change her ticket.

"Me too, Ingrid. I look forward to seeing you soon. I'll connect when we get to London." Hanging up the phone, she smiled, content that she had finally found the courage to start confronting some of her biggest fears.

Jack texted Fiona to say he was taking a couple of days of holiday before returning to London the day after tomorrow. He scrolled through his emails quickly. One jumped out immediately; it was from Christie's auction house. He was on their mailing list because he often went with clients to bid on paintings. Jack read the message out loud to himself. "The Ritz Hotel London to auction thousands of fine furnishings and artworks." But it was the following line that jumped out at him. "Included in this sale are the exquisite Brazilian rosewood Pleyel grand piano and bench used in the hotel's famous Palm Court from 1940 to 1950."

Jack couldn't believe it, the very piano Herb Gomes had played! He had to buy it. The auction was happening tomorrow, so he must have missed a previous email. Picking up his phone, he punched in his office number. "Hi Fiona, how's everything going?"

"Good. Just trying to locate the De Lempicka for Anais. I'm glad you are taking a couple of days off after everything that happened with Claude."

"Listen, I need you to do something for me tomorrow. Christie's is having a sale of historical Ritz Hotel furnishings. Included in the list is a Pleyel grand piano used in the hotel in the 1940s. I want to purchase the piano. It has a unique history attached to it that not many people know about." He could hear Fiona typing.

"I just looked up Pleyel, and apparently, Chopin was closely linked to this particular piano maker. There is even a quote: 'There are certain times when I feel more inspired, filled with a strong power that forces me to listen to my inner voice, and when I feel more need than ever for a Pleyel piano.' It all sounds intriguing. Can you forward me the details, please? Will we be on the phone during the bidding process?"

"Yes, absolutely. I just want to make sure I end up with the piano."

"Don't worry; I'll handle it."

Jack put the phone down as Lola opened the door. She still couldn't believe he was here in her house. The events of the last couple of days had been life-changing, and she knew when they got to London, there would be a lot of mixed emotions. As stressful as it would be, Lola knew it was the right thing to do. The years of running needed to finally come to an end.

Jack stood up. "How did the phone call with Ingrid go?" He had never met Ingrid but had read about her in various business journals, and she and Lola had been featured in a couple of fashion magazine articles together.

"It went well. We arranged to meet in London, which reminds me, we should book our flights. I will have my assistant Jill take care of it."

"I need to go to the Eden-Roc to check out and pack. Care to join me there tomorrow? We could have lunch."

"Sounds lovely." Finding Jack irresistible once more, she reached out to touch him. Their mouths met as he lifted her tee-shirt and placed his hands on the curve of her lower back; it was such a sensual, intimate moment. They stayed like that for a while, exploring each other's bodies. Jack was slightly distracted, thinking about the auction tomorrow. He knew he would need to tell Lola about the piano, but he was nervous that she wouldn't understand his reasoning. The last thing he wanted to do was upset her before they went to London, so he decided not to tell her for the time being. He would wait until he knew for sure the Pleyel was his.

CHAPTER THIRTY-SIX

Early the next morning, Jack got up quietly so as not to disturb Lola, who was sleeping peacefully with the two cats curled up next to her. He looked at them for a moment in the morning light and felt that finally, his own wounded heart was starting to heal. Gently closing the door behind him, he walked over to his phone, which was charging on the kitchen counter. It was too early to call Fiona, so he made some coffee and picked up the phone to check his emails. He was surprised to see one from Anais at the top of the list and noticed she had sent it this morning at six. So far, she hadn't reached out to him personally, as Fiona had been handling her. It was short and to the point.

Dear Jack,

I will be in London next week, and I would like to set up a meeting to discuss Rhythm No. 5. I have a personal connection to that particular De Lempicka; I'll explain when we meet. I promise I won't tie you up for too long. I'm just excited to purchase the painting as soon as possible for my new apartment because I will be moving in next month.

Anais

Jack read the email over, lingering on her choice of words. There had been something almost dangerous about her, and her sexual appetite was carnivorous, to say the least. He would definitely need to be careful.

Fiona's call interrupted his thoughts. "Good morning, Jack. Just to let you know, I'm ready for the auction today. Have you decided what your limit is?"

"Not really. I'm waiting to see how much interest there is. With this particular piano, there is a special story that goes with it that makes it more valuable. The good news is there are only a few people who know the real history."

Fiona was enthralled. "Can I ask what it is?"

"I'm sorry, but unfortunately, I can't divulge it, at least for the time being. I was told by a friend, and I feel like there is an unspoken confidentiality agreement in place."

Trying not to sound disappointed, she said, "I understand, and you can count on me to get you your special piano. I'll call you right before the bidding starts. I saw from the paperwork you sent that it's Lot Number 3."

"Great. Thanks, Fiona." As Jack put the phone down, he heard the bedroom door open, and Lola walked toward him wearing peach silk French knickers and a lace camisole. Following her were Domino and Solitaire, who were ready for their breakfast.

Jack whistled and joked, "Wow, what a lovely piece of crumpet you are."

She laughed at the comment and gave him a quick kiss before feeding the mewing cats. Pouring a coffee and topping up Jack's cup, she said, "Hey darling, I was wondering if you would mind if I didn't come with you to the Hotel du Cap today. I have some work I'd like to finish up before we go to London tomorrow. I just thought that if you go soon, we could spend the afternoon together."

That plan worked well for Jack in light of the auction starting in an hour and a half. If he left soon, he could get back to the hotel right before it started. "Okay, I will be back as quickly as I can. I have to say I am looking forward to changing my clothes," he said, laughing as he looked at his rumpled shirt and jeans. "I think I will leave now so I can get back to you in time for a late lunch."

"That sounds perfect. We will have the place to ourselves because, of course, I gave Claudette time off." They both hoped Claudette and Alberto were having a fabulous time together, again thinking how mind-boggling it was the way things had turned out for all of them.

*   *   *

Jack pulled up to the Eden-Roc, where the friendly *voiturier* greeted him as he handed over the keys. Looking at his watch, he walked briskly to his suite. Fiona would be calling him in a few minutes. He was excited and slightly anxious about the auction. What a coincidence that Herb Gomes' piano was up for sale. Closing the door of his suite, he sat down at the desk, and his phone rang; it was Fiona.

"Hi Jack, I'm at Christie's, and they are moving fast. I think the piano will probably be on the block in a few minutes. Do you want me to call you back?"

"No, I'll wait. I'm pretty nervous." He could hear the auctioneer in the background. Jack had been to Christie's often, and he enjoyed the energy of the room.

"So, Jack, how's your little mini-break going?" she asked to kill some time while they waited.

"Actually, very well, thank you. There's somebody I'd like you to meet when I get back to London."

Fiona was just about to ask who, but Lot 3 was up. "Right. Here we go, Jack. I'm going to put you on speakerphone. Are you ready?"

"Yep." He could vaguely hear the auctioneer in the background describing the piano and saying that the bidding would start at £500. Fiona held up her paddle, and the bidding began. It appeared that at present, about four or five other people were raising their paddles. It was moving very fast, and they were now up to £6,000, and Fiona quickly told Jack that she was now only bidding against one other person.

"Keep going. I have a feeling nobody else will go as high as I'm willing to go."

£10,000. Fiona held up her paddle, as did the other person. The auctioneer was going up in £500 increments. She tried to get a better look at the man bidding against her, but her view was obstructed.

"£25,000. Do I have £25,000?" They both bid again.

In a hushed voice, knowing that vintage pianos typically didn't hold their value unless they have a known historical story behind them, she said, "You must really love this piano, Jack. We are about to hit £40,000. Are you certain that you want me to keep going?"

"Yes, keep going." Jack's palms were sweating with anticipation as the bids rose quickly.

"£50,000." Fiona raised her paddle and looked in the other bidder's direction.

"£50,000. Do I have any other bids? All in at £50,000. Sold! The Pleyel piano and original bench sold for £50,000, ladies and gentlemen."

Jack let out a whoop. "Thank you, Fiona, you have just made my day. I will do a bank transfer as soon as we get off the phone."

Discreetly departing the auction room, she found a hallway where she could speak more freely with Jack. "Where should I arrange for it to be shipped, the Wapping office?"

"No, it's actually a gift for somebody. I will send you the address when we get off the phone."

"That's a very generous gift. May I ask who?"

"Yes, it's a gift for Annika Barinov."

Unable to keep the surprise out of her voice, Fiona said, "Annika Barinov?"

"Yes, that's right. She gave me the most life-changing gift, and I know this piano will mean a lot to her. You see, the pianist at the Ritz in the 1940s was Herb Gomes. He was a good friend of Kandinsky, and Herb inspired the painting *Piano Notes* that Claude wanted. There is more to the story that I will tell you at some point."

"Well, it sounds very mysterious," she said, laughing.

"Thank you, Fiona; I will send all the details right away." He put the phone down and immediately forwarded all the necessary information to Fiona before jumping in the shower and packing. After checking out, Jack waited for his car as he called Lola to tell her he was on his way and asked if she needed him to pick up anything.

"No, thanks, I ran to the market quickly and bought some steaks. It's such a beautiful day, I thought we could barbecue."

"Sounds fun. I should be there in an hour or so. I can't wait to see you. I've missed you this morning." They both rang off.

Jack was trying to figure out how to tell Lola about the piano, and he hoped she wouldn't be upset that he hadn't mentioned it before. He decided to be completely honest with her, and that would include telling her the history behind Kandinsky's *Piano Notes*. Pulling into Lola's driveway, he stopped to look at the Bonne Chance sign for a second to thank Grandmother Delilah privately for his good fortune.

Lola heard Jack's car and opened the front door, remembering how two days ago she had opened it and had the surprise of her life when she saw Jack standing there. They were at ease together; it just felt so natural. Waving as he parked, she gave him a long kiss before helping him with his bags. They walked together into the villa, and Jack wheeled his case into the bedroom.

When he came out of the bedroom, Lola was taking the steaks out of the fridge. Jack came around to help her and took her hand gently. "Look, there's something I need to tell you. Why we don't open some *rosé* and sit for a minute."

Nodding, Lola sat down on the barstool while Jack quickly poured them each a glass of wine. "What is it, Jack? You are making me nervous." He came around and sat down next to her, hating the fact that she was concerned.

"The thing is, I bought Annika Barinov a gift today as a thank-you present for all her help finding you."

Lola hadn't wanted to bring that up again, as she was slightly nervous about how Annika had gone about finding her. She assumed that Annika had some very high-up connections and was probably capable of using them whenever she pleased. "What did you get her?"

Jack knew such a lavish gift would seem over the top; he just hoped that she would understand when he told her the back story. "I bought her a piano from an auction at Christie's. They were auctioning off furnishings and artworks from the Ritz Hotel from the 1940s."

"A piano! That's quite a present."

"The thing is, there is something special about this piano and its connection to a Kandinsky painting that Annika owns called *Piano Notes*." Jack filled her in on the whole story, finishing with the fact that Herb Gomes had been sending secret codes via sheet music to a music shop in Paris. Noticing she looked confused, he took her hand. "Are you okay, Lola? I'm sorry if all this is a lot to take on. I just felt that you should know."

Standing she said, "You said Herb Gomes, right?"

"Yes, that's correct."

Lola walked over to the Steinway in the corner of the living room and opened the piano bench. Taking out a small pile of sheet music, she brought them to Jack and laid them on the marble island. "Here, look at this."

Picking up the sheets, Jack looked through them and noticed a single letter on the top right corner of every page and then the title under that. The first one was called *The Flustered Mallard*. Flicking through the rest of them, he saw they were all named after birds but with a twist to their stereotypical character. *The Ungraceful Swan, Pink Robin*. He smiled when he got to the last of the nine sheets, which was called *The Quiet Parrot*. "I'm a little confused about why you are showing me these, although the titles are amusing."

Lola took the pages and spread them out on the marble top, shifting the order around. Satisfied, she turned to Jack. "Look at the top corners. Now, do you see?"

He looked across at the neat line of the nine sheets and read the letters out loud.

"H E R B G O M E S. Herb Gomes!" Repeating it and looking at Lola, he said, "I don't understand; how do you have these?"

"My grandmother Delilah's family had a music shop in Paris in the 1940s called Cornell's. When I inherited the Steinway from my grandmother, it came with this sheet music inside the bench. I remember years ago she had told me about Herb Gomes sending sheet music from London. My grandmother took the sheet music out of the bench and showed me how his name was spelled out, just like I showed you. All she said was he wanted to keep his identity hidden from the Germans. I thought at the time it was quite mysterious and wondered if perhaps they had been an item at some time before she married my grandfather. She didn't go into the whole story like you just did. I suppose I was only a teenager at the time, so I wasn't overly inquisitive."

Jack was amazed. He could read music, but he wished he knew the code formula so he could decipher the content. "This is astounding! What a twist of fate. Do you know if the music store is still in Paris?"

"Unfortunately, not anymore, but I do know the address, as it was in the family until the late 1970s, and my mum talked about it, especially since its location is so unique. It was at 23 rue du Faubourg Saint-Honoré, sandwiched between Lanvin and Hermès. Today that whole street is home to all the luxury fashion houses."

"Do you mind if we take this music with us to London? I'd like to have a closer look at it."

"No, of course not. This is truly such a unique story that I can't believe it. I wonder if my mum knows all this history. I guess it's another thing to ask her when we have our talk."

Just to confirm, Jack asked her, "So, you understand the importance of the piano and why I wanted to buy it?"

"Yes, of course. I also know we have a lot of history to go over, and that will take time. I just want to get to know you again."

Jack stood up and took her in his arms, yet again so unbelievably grateful she was back in his life. They raised their glasses and toasted Herb Gomes and then Grandmother Delilah, whom they hoped was smiling at them right now, enjoying everything as it slowly unravelled.

CHAPTER THIRTY-SEVEN

The plane bumped down into London City Airport. It was a dreary day in London, especially noticeable after the bright colours of the South of France. They had already decided to stay at the St. Martin's Lane Hotel in Covent Garden. Lola thought it was too soon in their relationship to stay together at her parents' house in Montagu Square, and Jack said his Wapping pied-à-terre was more of a bachelor pad. They realised that they would need to sort out the logistics of their living situation in the near future. The Delphines were a little hurt when Lola told them she would be staying at the hotel instead of with them, but there would be an explanation tomorrow when she met with her parents.

The cab slowed down as it continued along St. Martin's Lane. Lola was happy to be back in London and excited to get to her office. She had arranged to meet Ingrid there this afternoon and hoped that everything could be smoothed out between them. It would be a very emotional week, but she knew that it was finally time to get the answers.

The cabbie came to a stop, saying, "Here we are then." Jack paid as they were met by the hotel's doorman, who welcomed them and automatically took Lola's case and wheeled it into the lobby. Looking around, Lola found the place familiar. She had been coming here for years and remembered the fun she had had in the hotel's Light Bar in its heyday. They checked in and took the lift to their suite; the bellhop followed with the bags.

Lola loved staying at the St. Martin's Lane even though there were more opulent hotels in London. The location was perfect, close to her office and many fabulous restaurants, including J.Sheekey, which had the best *fruits de mer* platter in London, not to mention her dad's favourite, fish pie. She had called her mum and told her she would be coming over the next day and said she would like to talk about something private. Roberta hadn't asked many questions; maybe she knew what was coming.

Lola quickly hung some clothes in the wardrobe and turned to Jack, who was checking his emails and texting Fiona. "I'm going to head to the office. I have a meeting with Ingrid at three-thirty, which I'm a little nervous about."

Jack stood up and took the coat she was holding and hung it in place on the rail. He took her in his arms as he spoke. "It will be fine, you'll see. Just be honest with her and open about why you were so upset. You two have been friends for a long time. I'm sure everything will turn out for the best."

Something Jack said reminded her of when Chase had come to dinner at Bonne Chance and the conversation they had when she confided in him about how upset she had been about Ingrid. Chase had sent her a couple of text messages, but she hadn't responded now that Jack was back in her life. Communicating with Chase didn't seem right, especially since she hadn't mentioned him to Jack for some reason. "Thank you. That makes me feel better." Their lips met, and they got lost in the long kiss that followed, both wishing there was time for more. Looking up at Jack's smile,

Lola turned and picked up the makeup bag that recently had been unpacked. "I'm going to freshen up a little before my meeting." She went into the bathroom, and he could hear her cleaning her teeth.

Lola's phone was on the bed, and all of a sudden, it pinged. He couldn't help glancing down at it and saw a man's name and a short message. It was from a Chase Campbell, and it simply read, "I've been thinking about you. How is everything going?" The name sounded familiar somehow. Jack couldn't help but feel instantly jealous, especially since she had not mentioned Mr. Chase Campbell.

Jack listened, and he could hear water running in the bathroom. Against his better judgment, he picked up his phone and typed Chase's name into the search engine. Instantly a long list of things came up; he opened the first one. Chase Campbell, American actor, fifty-five years old. There was a long list of films and television credits. The most recent one was a soap opera called *Balderdash* about a British butler working for a wealthy Californian family. If he hadn't been so perturbed, he would have found the name amusing. Accompanying this was a picture that Jack studied for a minute. Suddenly, he remembered Anais telling him that Lola had been with a film star at the wedding that she and Fabian Whitecliff had attended at the Colombe d'Or.

Lola opened the bathroom door and came around the corner to find Jack sitting on the bed. Something about his posture made him look slightly downcast. "Are you okay?" Sitting down on the bed, she put her hand on his arm.

Jack looked up at her. "Lola, who's Chase Campbell?" He pointed at her phone, which still had the message alert on its screen. "That name seems familiar somehow." He didn't want to give away that he had just looked up Chase.

Lola couldn't believe this. It was as if Chase could read her mind from across the Atlantic in Los Angeles. Quickly thinking about how to present the story to Jack, she decided to be entirely upfront about what happened. "Chase is an American guy, an actor from Los Angeles. I met him in the British Airways lounge in Heathrow. It turns out we were on the same plane flying to Nice. I ended up giving him a little tour of St. Tropez, and he came to Villa Bonne Chance a couple of times."

Looking at her, he knew she had left out the wedding for some reason. "What about the wedding in Saint-Paul De Vence?"

For a split second, Lola wondered how he knew about that, but then it just made sense. Anais had obviously told him during the lunch on Stefan van Carson's yacht. "Yes, and the wedding at La Colombe d'Or, which was, as I'm sure Anais told you, quite an interesting day." Taking Jack's hands, she looked deeply into his eyes. "Listen, Chase is a good friend now, that's all. I told him about you because as seemingly perfect as he was, I knew where my heart lay."

Kissing her again tenderly, Jack understood they both needed a lot more time to get to know each other, even though there was such familiarity from their past.

Lola looked at the time. "I better get going. Are you ready to leave now, too?"

"Yes, sure! Shall we meet back here at five-thirty? Where would you like to go to dinner tonight? I'll make a reservation."

"Why don't we just walk across the street and have an early dinner at the bar at J.Sheekey?"

"Great. I'll make the reservation for six-fifteen." They rode down in the lift together. Jack could see that Lola was slightly distracted, probably due to her upcoming meeting with Ingrid. He hoped for her sake that everything would be okay. They stepped outside and were reminded of the temperature difference in early October compared to that of the Côte d'Azur, which could still be quite warm.

"I'm going to walk to my office; it's only about a ten-minute walk."

A taxi pulled up, and Jack opened the door. "Wapping High Street, please." Turning quickly, he kissed her softly. "Okay, darling, I'll see you a bit later."

Lola shivered and tightened the belt on her grey cashmere Max Mara coat, watching as Jack's cab headed down St. Martin's Lane. Walking briskly, she had just turned down New Row when her phone started ringing. Pausing, she dug it out of her tote bag and looked at the number. It was Chase. The phone kept ringing while Lola contemplated whether to pick up. She decided she couldn't blow him off any longer. "Chase, what a nice surprise!"

"Lola, I'm so glad you picked up. I was getting a little worried when you didn't respond to any of my text messages. How's everything going?"

"I'm fine. I'm sorry that I didn't respond. It's just that there has been a lot going on lately."

"I was trying to get a hold of you to let you know that I just got the lead role on a new Stefan van Carson movie called *English Crumpet*." He could hear Lola laughing at the title. "It's a rom-com about a beautiful girl who works in a bakery while she's struggling as an artist. One day a famous musician comes in, and she's swept off her feet; it goes on a wild ride from there. This film is a bit of a departure in genre from what Stefan normally directs. I don't know if you saw the last one that came out recently. It was a horror story about a group of kids that lived on a haunted farm."

"No, I'm not a big fan of horror films. So, do you play the musician?"

"No, I play her long-term boyfriend, Jake Austin. Rumour has it Francis Williams may play the famous musician. I've heard he and Stefan are old friends."

Lola almost choked when he said that name, but thankfully she managed to keep it together enough to say, "So, when do you start shooting?"

"I arrive in London next week, and we will be shooting for around three months. At some point, we are heading to Venice, as some of the film takes place there."

Lola was still in a bit of shock at hearing Chase mention Francis Williams and went silent for a moment.

"Lola, are you still there?"

"Yes, yes, I'm sorry." At a loss for words, she said, "That sounds like a fun film. I like the title; it's very funny."

"I know. I had to take a crash course on British humour before I knew why it was amusing. So anyway, I'm calling because I really want to see you. It's simple; I can't stop thinking about you."

"Look, Chase, there is something I need to tell you." She could hear him say hello, hello like he had lost signal. Suddenly the connection came back.

"I'm driving up the coast to see my sister in Santa Barbara, and I keep losing you. Can we talk later?"

Before she could answer, the connection was lost again. She hung up and put it in her bag. Thinking over everything he had said, she remembered when they had lunch in St. Tropez, Chase had said something about knowing Stefan van Carson. It was interesting that Francis Williams knew him, too. Lola was so lost in that thought that she almost forgot the other part of the conversation when he had said he really wanted to see her. It was all getting too confusing, she thought, as she hurried along New Row, trying to switch over to the conversation she was about to have with Ingrid.

CHAPTER THIRTY-EIGHT

R ight over there, please." Jack pointed to a door on the right of the Captain Kidd pub. The cab rolled to a stop, and Jack gave him the fare and thanked him. He was glad to be home; it had been quite a wild time on the Riviera. After selecting his floor, the lift doors opened, and he was greeted by his receptionist Nicky, who said she had left a stack of mail on his desk. Crossing the polished white travertine floor, he stopped in at Fiona's office, which was next door to his. She stood up, smiling. "Welcome back!"

"I am glad to be back. I have to say it was certainly an interesting trip on so many levels."

"Do you want me to fill you in on what I've found out about the De Lempicka painting?"

"Why don't you give me an hour or so to catch up, and then we can go over it?" Jack turned and walked next door to his office and stood in front of one of the large arch-shaped windows looking out to the River Thames. A tour boat slowed down as they went past the historic Captain Kidd. He really did love living in London, and it was going to be a challenge trying to figure out the logistics of his and Lola's relationship. Maybe they could get a place here and just divide their time between the U.K. and France.

Thinking about it, it didn't sound too bad at all. He travelled a lot to Europe anyway, and Villa Bonne Chance was a beautiful place to live. It was a conversation they could have down the road. All he knew was that he was the happiest he had ever been.

The phone rang and brought him back to the moment. Taking it out of his breast pocket, he saw that it was from an unknown number. "This is Jack Alistair."

"Mr. Alistair, this Helga Petrov."

"Yes, how are you, Helga?" He said it almost in a jokey tone, knowing she wouldn't respond.

"Miss Barinov had me call you for security measures to make sure the piano that is down in the lobby is indeed from you. Everything is being inspected thoroughly before we have it delivered to the penthouse."

He would have thought she was a bit paranoid had he not experienced what happened with Claude. "Yes, it is from me. Can I talk to her, please?"

"Miss Barinov will be in touch, Mr. Alistair." With that, she clicked off, and the phone was silent.

Jack knew the piano would come with some kind of documentation explaining its provenance. He had overnighted it from London to Monte Carlo, and he just hoped she liked it and saw what a magical coincidence it was that it had come up for sale. As soon as he put the phone down on the desk, it rang again. Hoping it was Annika, he saw that indeed it was a call coming from France.

"Hello, this is Jack."

"*Bonjour, Monsieur* Alistair." He recognised her voice instantly. It was Anais. "I'm calling to check on the progress of my little

Rhythm No. 5." Her accent seemed stronger than usual, and her words were slightly slurred as if she had just finished a boozy lunch.

"How are you, Anais? I just got back to London, and your De Lempicka is on the top of my list. In fact, I am having a meeting this afternoon with my assistant, who has been on its trail since you contacted us."

"Good, good, do you have any idea where it is?"

"We think it is in a private collection in Montreux."

"Well, that's a good start." Jack was just about to end the conversation in a business-like manner when she said, "*Monsieur* Alistair, I have a proposition for you."

Oh no, here we go again, he thought with mild amusement and slight panic but decided to go along with it anyway. "Anais, what could that possibly be?"

"As I said in my email, I am going to be in London next week to do a Helmut Newton-inspired photoshoot for British *Vogue*." Jack almost commented as a flashback of Anais and Annika washed into his mind quickly. "It's going to be shot at the Lanesborough Hotel, and the models and crew are staying there. The magazine is throwing a special Helmut Newton-style party with a VIP list as long as your arm. I was wondering if you would like to join me. We could meet at the Ritz beforehand, have a drink, and discuss my painting. Of course, you know there is a Tamara de Lempicka hanging in the Rivoli Bar."

Not knowing what to say because she had caught him off guard, he just said, "Why don't you email me the details, and we can talk about it a bit later."

"Oh, and one last thing I forgot to mention. Annika Barinov is coming in for the party and staying at the Lanesborough. The

'Lord Guvnor' will be joining us, too." He almost coughed when she told him that but decided to put on a professional tone instead. "Thank you, Anais. Goodbye."

Jack's armchair was positioned in front of one of the enormous arched windows. He sat down and rubbed his hands up and down the tan distressed leather arms nervously and stared out to the river. What was it with this woman? She was so disarming, and he didn't know how he could turn down the invitation, especially if Annika were attending. Maybe he could bring Lola? No, that just wouldn't work. With the bizarre history he had with the two *femmes fatales*, who knew what could happen? They were just too unpredictable. Looking away from the Thames, he saw Fiona standing in his doorway.

"Hi. Please come in and take a seat. Guess who was just on the phone," Jack said as he moved from the armchair to the desk.

"One of the two vamps, I presume," she joked.

"Yes, it was Anais. She wanted an update on the painting, and she was also trying to coerce me into going to a party at the Lanesborough Hotel."

Fiona couldn't help but laugh. "I'm not going to say anything, but these women have you wrapped around their manicured talons."

Jack grinned at that. "Don't worry; I can handle myself. Let's get back to business. What did you find out?"

"Well, as I told you, the painting is in Montreux. It's presently owned by Contessa Suzette Florentino. She moved from Venice to Montreux after visiting the jazz festival one year. Apparently, she loves to volunteer her time during the three-week event. Of course, no one knows her status. From everything I could find, she seems like quite the humble contessa. She isn't married, but her boyfriend is the British jazz musician Casper Drake.

Jack had pulled her up on his screen, and he couldn't help but whistle. "Wow. She is beautiful in that very natural type of way."

Fiona laughed. "That hair looks like it needs a zookeeper, it's so wild!"

Jack looked at a picture of Suzette and her boyfriend. They seemed to be the subjects of a feature story set somewhere in the English countryside. They even had a Labrador puppy with them. She was tall with messy blonde hair and blue-green eyes, not typical for an Italian woman. He was very English-looking, wearing a tweed jacket and Hunter Wellies. Looking at the picture made Jack long for his native Hertfordshire.

"Don't be fooled by this. Behind the doors of her palazzo is an art collection that could compete with Annika's. She also likes to collect historical instruments from all over the world. She especially loves Asian instruments and plays the traditional Chinese *dizi*."

"Fascinating, but I hope she wants to part with *Rhythm No. 5*. Let's put together a game plan to approach her. I feel like I lucked out last time when I met the couple at the Eden-Roc bar who happened to be cabin crew on *Miroslava*. Maybe I should think about going to Switzerland."

"Maybe you should, Jack, and see what you can turn up."

CHAPTER THIRTY-NINE

Lola ended up popping into a *café* on Garrick Street for a quick cup of tea; she wanted to compose herself a bit before getting to the office. Looking at all the cakes on display, she was almost tempted, but they had had lunch at the Nice airport. Besides, she had a nervous tummy. Even though it was starting to drizzle, she loved being back in England. As much as France was her main home now, it still played a close second to the U.K. It made her happy to think she would be spending a lot more time here in the future. She and Jack would need to get a place sometime, or maybe it would be easier to stay in hotels. Anyway, there was no rush; it would be fun figuring it all out. Finishing her tea, she left the *café*, walked quickly toward Floral Street, and arrived at the Jetset Delilah offices. The lift doors opened, and Rebecca stood up to greet Lola.

"Great to see you, Lola! Ingrid is waiting in your office, and these just came for you. Oh, and Jill stepped out for a late lunch." Rebecca handed Lola a dozen beautiful white roses.

"Hi, it's wonderful to be back. These are gorgeous!" She would open the attached card later; they were from Doolittle's Flowers on Tavistock Street. Jack was so sweet. What a nice gesture, especially since he knew how stressed out she was this morning.

Ingrid stood up as Lola came in and closed the door; she looked like she didn't know how to greet her and glanced up through her eyelashes, almost like Princess Diana. Taking the lead, she put the roses down on the desk, turned to Ingrid, and gave her the biggest hug. Both women started to cry in unison.

"I've missed you so much, Lola, and I'm so terribly sorry about all of it—seeing Max and not honouring what you asked of me. I should have put that in front of an exciting night out."

"Why don't we sit down?" They sat on the long olive-green velvet Chesterfield and faced one another. Lola reached for a tissue from a box on the occasional table next to her. "I was in the wrong. You see, there is a big back story that you, of course, could not have known. I don't even know the truth at the moment, but tomorrow I'm meeting with my mother, and hopefully, she will be able to fill in the blanks." Ingrid waited for the story, almost scared to hear the truth. Lola continued. "This is one the hardest conversations I've ever had because I've been running from the heart of the matter for so long. I told you when you called from the airport in Madrid that Jack was back in my life again." Ingrid nodded. "He explained a lot to me, but he doesn't know all the answers either. We didn't talk for so many years because when I was around twenty, Jack overheard my mum and Max talking. Jack was hidden from view in one of the stables at Max's place. Basically, they were having a conversation about who my birth father is, and Francis Williams' name came up."

Lola could tell her best friend was in complete shock, and Ingrid simply said, "Oh no, what have I done?"

Continuing the story, Lola took Ingrid's hand and held it. "Anyway, as soon as they were gone, Jack jumped in his car and drove the short distance to our estate. I was getting ready to head out for a ride, but after he told me, I was devastated and galloped off, not wanting to hear any more. He jumped on Penny and chased me, which unfortunately caused my poor old Penny to have a heart attack. I used Jack as a scapegoat and blamed him for ruining my life at the time. I quashed all my emotions, believing the story had not been true, and convinced myself that he had just made up the story to hurt me. Of course, I know now that was never his intention."

"So, Max could be your father?" It was almost too much to consider. Now it made sense why Lola had told her to stay away from him. Ingrid didn't understand why if he was Lola's father, he had pursued her. Who knows, maybe Roberta didn't even know. Ingrid relayed these thoughts to her.

"I know. It doesn't make sense. Maybe Max doesn't know. It's all so confusing."

"What about your lovely dad, Ollie? Do you think he knows?"

Lola looked very downcast. Ollie didn't deserve any of this. The emotional weight of it was immense, and it was hard for her to keep it all together. "I have no idea; I guess I will find out tomorrow. I want to apologise to you, Ingrid. You didn't deserve how I treated you. I hope you will forgive me."

"Of course, Lola, you are like a sister to me; let's just agree never to let this happen again."

"That sounds like a plan." Lola looked at the time; it was four-thirty. "Why don't we call it a day and head over to J.Sheekey for a drink? Jack and I are planning on having an early dinner there tonight. We can catch up before he gets there, and then you can join us for dinner. This time we are not accepting any Champagne from strangers," she joked, trying to lighten the mood a little.

"A cocktail does sound good to me. I may need a *rebujito*, my favourite Spanish cocktail! I'll get my stuff and meet you in the foyer in ten minutes."

Ingrid stood up and turned to smile at Lola. What she had just heard was utterly shocking, but Lola needed her support right now. Ingrid decided to put her own emotions on the back burner until the whole tale had unravelled.

Lola shrugged into her luxurious cashmere coat, picked up the roses, and took in their scent. She slipped the small white greeting envelope into her pocket to open later, picked up her bag, joined Ingrid, and remarked to Rebecca in the foyer. "Bye, Rebecca. Would you mind putting my roses in a vase, please?"

"Of course. See you tomorrow."

CHAPTER FORTY

J ack checked the time. It was four-thirty. Time to finish up here and get back to the hotel to meet Lola. Maybe he could persuade her to come home early so they could give the hotel bed a test. He felt himself getting aroused just thinking about it. Lola had the most delectable body, and just thinking about it caused him to rise to the occasion.

The buzz of his phone snapped Jack back to reality. It was an unknown caller, but it wasn't hard to guess who was calling. He had already decided to keep private the fact that Lola's grandmother's family had owned the music shop and that they still had some of Herb's sheet music. Mostly, Jack wanted to try to figure it for himself first before getting Annika involved. "This is Jack Alistair."

"Mr. Jack Alistair, this is your favourite Romanian friend, Annika Barinov." She certainly was less formal than she ever had been. "I'm going to cut to the chase. That was a very thoughtful gift you gave me. I feel that the painting and the piano are probably secretly smiling at each other."

Jack was relieved that she liked it and understood how special it was that he had been able to purchase it. "I'm glad you appreciate it, Annika. When I saw it was up for auction, I simply had to get it for you, especially when I discovered the amazing history behind it."

"There's another part of it I want to tell you. It came with the original piano bench, and inside was a stack of sheet music. I don't know if it was Herb Gomes' because his name wasn't on it."

Jack froze; another twist of fate. Maybe there was some way to put Lola's sheets together with the ones Annika had.

"So, I'm intrigued. What happened with Miss Delphine?"

"We are both in London together right now, if that answers your question. Again, I cannot thank you enough."

"My pleasure. By the way, I'm going to be in the U.K. next week for business and, of course, a little excitement." She seemed to linger on the word. "Anais has invited me to a party at the Lanesborough. The business I'm doing is actually with you. Another Kandinsky painting has surfaced. It is said to be part of the same collection as *Piano Notes*, and I want it. Let's meet next week in London. And I want you to accompany me to the party at the Lanesborough."

This was the old Annika that he recognised, the one who would not take no for an answer. "Yes, let's meet. Please send me the details about the party." He didn't mention that Anais had already asked him. "What is the painting called? I can start doing some research on it."

Annika put the vodka on the rocks up to her lips. Jack could hear the ice cubes clinking against the cut-crystal glass. "The painting is called *Delilah*. *Misto,* I will be in touch." And with that, she hung up.

Jack couldn't believe the title. It had to be more than just an astounding coincidence, and he wondered why she needed him to find the painting. Considering how quickly she had delivered a fact sheet on Lola, it was obvious she had some serious connections. Perhaps it was the game she enjoyed, and what was it she had said in Romanian right before she hung up?

Looking up at the maritime clock on the wall, Jack did a doubletake when he saw that it said three thirty-three. His phone revealed it was actually just after five. Grabbing his peacoat, he quickly sent Lola a text saying he was leaving the office. Closing the door behind him, he stopped to chat with Fiona, who was busy typing and didn't see him standing in the doorway. After a gentle knock, he said, "So, you will never guess what. I just got off the phone with the lovely Miss Barinov, and she wants us to track down another Kandinsky. It's part of the same series as *Piano Notes*."

"Really? Wow, what is it called?" As Fiona waited for a response, she could tell that Jack was a little hesitant to tell her for some reason.

"It's called *Delilah*. Annika didn't give me any more information on it. She made it sound like it had just turned up somewhere. She is coming to London next week to discuss it. Can you see what you can find?"

"Yes, of course." Jotting down a few notes, she looked up. "It sounds to me like she doesn't want Anais to have all the fun! Could it be possible that these two like the competition?" There was a cheeky glint in Fiona's eyes.

Letting out a short laugh, he said, "Well, I have to say the thought had crossed my mind. See you tomorrow."

Jack jumped into a taxi just as his phone started to ring. "St. Martin's Lane Hotel, please," he said quickly before looking down at his phone and seeing that Lola was calling. "Hello, my love, how was your day?" He could hear a lot of background noise. It sounded like she was in a bar.

"Great! I'm actually at J.Sheekey with Ingrid. Why don't you just come here? I'd like you to meet her."

"Okay, I'll see you there. I'm in a cab right now, so see you soon!" Putting the phone back in his breast pocket, he leaned forward to tell the taxi driver the change of plans. Jack was happy for Lola and so glad she had reconciled with Ingrid. He knew the next few days would be extremely tough for her. So far, she had remained strong, but the issues were incredibly difficult and would take a while to sort out. On the other hand, Jack needed to figure out how he would handle the potentially complicated party at the Lanesborough Hotel. All that would have to wait. He couldn't risk upsetting Lola at the moment.

Jack walked into the restaurant, making a left to the bar. He immediately spotted Lola, who waved when she saw him walk in and stood up to kiss him.

"Hi darling, how are you? This is Ingrid Ashton." Ingrid stood up and took Jack's hand.

"Nice to meet you finally, Jack Alistair."

"So nice to meet you as well, Ingrid." They smiled at each other before settling down on the barstools. Ingrid was instantly taken by Jack's blue eyes. He was definitely a very handsome man, and she could understand Lola's attraction.

Jack ordered a bottle of *Perrier-Jouët*, which the bartender opened and poured into three glasses. Lola made a toast, and suddenly the emotion of the occasion got to her. Ingrid noticed tears on Lola's sad face as they started welling up, and one dropped on the menu. Ingrid put her arm around her friend to comfort her as she watched Lola look up with wet eyes and lift her glass.

"Here's to breaking down the walls, finally." They clinked their flutes together. "I'm sorry, I guess the realisation of everything just came down on me." Jack turned to her and pulled a grey silk pocket square out of his jacket. In a tender move, he gently patted the tears away from her face. Smiling up at him, she could feel the love at the moment and again felt so grateful that they had finally reconnected. Lola suddenly remembered the beautiful roses and that she had forgotten to thank Jack or look at the card. "Jack, I wanted to thank you for ...." At that minute, his phone started to ring, and he glanced down at it. "Oh, I'm sorry, but I have to take this call," he said, as he stood up and quickly walked outside, not mentioning who was calling.

Turning to Ingrid, Lola said, "I feel terrible. I completely forgot to thank him for those beautiful roses. I'll open the card right now." She reached around to her coat draped on the back of the bar seat and pulled the small white envelope out of the pocket. Tearing it open, she pulled out a small cream notecard, which read:

Lola, I have to confess, I've got a crush on you. Have dinner with me next week. I'm staying at the Lanesborough. Chase.

What a coincidence, Lola thought. She had been born there when it was St. George's Hospital. Ingrid noticed that Lola was a little flustered by the note and could tell something was up. "Is everything okay? Does the note say something weird?" Lola placed it down on the bar for her friend to see. "Who's Chase? Wow, you have been busy in the last few weeks," Ingrid joked.

"I nearly totally screwed up. I was just about to thank Jack for the flowers as I just assumed they were from him."

"So, hurry up and tell me before Jack comes back. Who is Chase then?" Now Ingrid was intrigued.

"He's a film star from L.A. I met him in the BA lounge at Heathrow. It turned out he was also flying to Nice for a wedding. To cut a long story short, I saw him a few times. He's a really great guy, but the whole time, I felt like my heart was somewhere else. It's really strange because I met him before I reconnected with Jack."

"A film star? Exciting! So, what are you going to do?" Before Lola could answer, Jack walked back in and sat down, apologising for being on the phone so long. Just in time, she discreetly slipped the card and envelope into her tote bag hanging on the back of the seat.

"So where were we, Lola? You were in the middle of saying something?"

"Oh, I can't remember now." She didn't dare look at Ingrid, who was looking bemused. "Why don't we order some food? I have a big day tomorrow, and I'd like to have somewhat of an early night." They ordered the famous *fruits de mer* platter and a side of fries. Lola soon conveniently forgot about the notecard in her bag as she sat between her two favourite people.

Just one oyster remained on the top tier of the seafood tower. "It's all yours, Lola," Jack said, taking the oyster and squeezing some lemon on it. Using a small fork, he loosened the juicy flesh from the shell and handed it to her.

"Are you sure now? Ingrid?"

Giggling, Ingrid said, "I'm stuffed like porky plumpsters; you go ahead." Lola tilted the oyster back, and it slid into her mouth. She looked so gorgeous, Jack couldn't help but lightly brush his lips over the side of her neck. Suddenly, Lola quickly brought the serviette up to her mouth and spat something out.

Slightly alarmed, they both said, "Are you okay?"

"Yes, yes, sorry. I just crunched down on something, maybe a piece of shell, and I didn't want to crack a tooth," she said, taking a big sip of Champagne. She opened up the serviette to inspect it but didn't see anything at first. Laying out the napkin on the bar, she saw it now—a tiny iridescent pearl. "Wow, look at this! Can you believe it? I actually found a pearl!" Picking up the pearl for a closer look, she used the corner of the serviette to clean it off a bit before passing it around. Suddenly, it reminded her of Claudette's book, *Une Perle Dans L'huître*. She smiled, happy to remember that Claudette finally had been reunited with Alberto. Turning the pearl around in his fingers, Jack couldn't help but think this was another good omen that had come their way.

When the bartender put the bill on the bar, Lola showed him her newfound treasure. Sitting back in her seat, she wrapped the tiny pearl in a paper cocktail napkin and put it in a small zippered pocket in her bag. For some reason, Edward Lear's poem "The Owl and the Pussy-Cat" came into her mind, and she smiled as she thought of the words. So many things had popped up from her past lately.

They all stood up together and prepared to leave. Both women thanked Jack for taking care of the bill. Lola gave Ingrid a big hug and said she would let her know the outcome of the meeting tomorrow with her mother. They stepped outside and walked the short distance to St. Martin's Lane and waited with Ingrid for a few minutes until a cab pulled up.

"Bye!"

"Goodnight. I'll talk to you tomorrow or the next day!" As Ingrid sat in the cab, she felt relieved that her relationship with her best friend was on the repair. Having decided not to bring up Max again until she knew the family meeting's outcome tomorrow, she prayed that Max was not Lola's father. It was too crazy to consider.

Jack took Lola's hand as they crossed the street and took a right; the hotel was just a few minutes away. "I have to ask you something that's been on my mind," he said. Thinking it was about the roses, she began to panic. Instead, he asked, "That night at the casino in Monte Carlo, who were you meeting? I don't know why, but it's been on my mind."

Lola was greatly relieved. "I was there meeting a friend who was visiting relatives in Monte Carlo. She lives in Switzerland, so I don't see her that often. She's Italian by birth, but I think of her as English because she has spent most of her life in the U.K. and seems so English. Funnily enough, she's kind of Italian royalty, in name anyway.

"Interesting." He wondered if he had heard of her in the press or something. "What's her name?" When they entered the hotel lobby, Lola was tempted to go into the Light Bar for a nightcap, but instead they headed for the lift.

"Well, her official name is quite grand. It's Contessa Suzette Florentino."

CHAPTER FORTY-ONE

Lola woke early after a restless night during which she went over different scenarios in her head about what her mum was about to tell her. It surprised Lola that Roberta hadn't asked many questions about the meeting. She suspected that her mother knew what was coming and had lived with the fact that someday the truth must be revealed.

Looking at Jack, who was sleeping peacefully on his back, she leaned over and put her hand on his chest. He stirred slightly as she gently massaged his shoulder area before moving her hand lower. There was such spellbinding chemistry between them; she had never felt anything like this before. Sitting up slightly before gently climbing on top of him, she started to kiss him lightly. Responding, he kissed her back in his drowsy state, whispering her name as she continued to make her way down his neck. She could tell from his astoundingly hard cock that he was indeed happy that she had woken him. Kissing him just below his muscular tummy, she lingered there for a while. Jack groaned in pleasure as Lola teased him, kissing her way past his hungry manhood and down one leg making sure her pert nipples grazed over him as she made her way down. Kneeling slightly, she took his left foot and brought it up to her mouth. Starting with the big toe, she licked it before parting her moistened lips and sucking lightly. Jack was watching her, getting more excited by the minute. The sensation was an incredible turn-on.

Lola sucked in and out, increasing the pace. He couldn't help but gasp slightly with pure lust as he imagined her wet lips wrapped around his cock. Lightly she released his toe from her mouth and performed a cat-like lick up his leg, pausing slightly on the base of his crown jewels. Deliberately teasing them with her tongue, she made her way down the other leg. She massaged his foot and licked every toe, letting them slide into her mouth slowly.

Taking her time, she worked her way up his body, skimming the tips of her nipples over his skin. Jack quivered in excitement and desire as she made her way up to his lips, kissing him with ferocious intensity. He said nothing as she made her way back down to his cock, which was ready for attention. She circled his nipples, taking time with each one. They rose to the occasion, needy for what would come next. Straddling him just above his navel, Lola said in a lusty voice, "Are you ready, Mr. Alistair?" Jack looked up, smiling in his aroused state.

"You are unbelievably sexy, Lady Delphine."

Lola took a sip of water and offered some to Jack, who sat up and took a gulp, never taking his eyes off her. Putting the glass back on the nightstand, she licked her lips and looked down at Jack's still rock-hard manhood. Easing her way down his body, she took the head of his cock into her mouth and circled it lightly. He groaned with excitement as she licked up and down, teasing him. The rhythm was increasing. Jack arched his back in anticipation as the sucking became more intense before Lola eased off and sat up, straddling him.

"More water?" Jack nodded, silenced in his heightened state of arousal. Picking up the glass, Lola dripped some into his open mouth and took a sip. He waited for what would come next as she seductively brushed his cock as she put the glass on the nightstand. Lola kissed and licked her way down the body she had regrettably missed for over twenty years. Her lips parted, taking him fully into her mouth. She sucked hard, wanting to feel the length of him deep in her throat. Exceedingly turned on herself, Lola licked her finger seductively. Taking him back in her mouth, she eased her finger delicately into his highly erotic and sensitive zone, gently easing back and forth. Probing deeper and deeper, she could tell Jack was about to reach his peak. Lola listened as Jack groaned, intoxicated by the moment, his eyes enticed by her erotic show. The sensation was simply one of the most sensual and intimate pleasures; he had never experienced such ecstasy.

In a flash, she tore her lips away and climbed on top of him, riding him deep and hard before squatting to change the position. Jack feasted his eyes as she slid up and down in a tantalising rhythmic motion on his iron-clad hardness. The intensity grew, as athletic Lola was able to hold the pose as she slid him inside her before ramming him deep with intense ardour. Knowing he was on the brink of exploding, she sat back down on him with such ravishment and rode hard in the most carnal way. They both cried out in rapture, reaching their highest peaks as the waves of pleasure engulfed them. The intense, indescribable mind-altering chemistry took over in a spiritual way.

Jack watched as she continued riding him faster, lost in paradise as the second transportive wave of ecstasy washed through her. Lola cried out his name as she was taken to a place so incredibly beautiful, quivering a little as the potent force was replaced with complete tranquillity. He wrapped his arms around her tightly, knowing he was finally home.

They lay entwined together for a while, enjoying the quiet moment. Lola stretched slightly, shifting her position before rolling over for a drink of water. She couldn't help but notice the bed was skew-whiff, appearing to have a weird dip in it. "Jack, I think we broke the bed." Turning over, he noticed the mattress was not quite right somehow, which made him smile. "I think that will go down in the record books. Lady Delphine, you were amazing!"

They dozed for a few minutes until she got up, noticing on the way back from the bathroom it was seven a.m. When she returned, Jack's eyes were closed. He had a look of total contentment on his face as if he had just received a box of Kipling's Fancies, found the Golden Ticket, and received free VIP tickets to the Royal Box at the Wimbledon Championships, all rolled into one. Grinning at Jack's smug face, she said, "Should I order some breakfast? All that excitement has made me hungry."

Smiling, he nodded. "Sounds good to me. I'll take a full English." Laughing at that, she picked up the phone and ordered a pot of coffee, full English, and a boiled egg and toast for herself.

"I'm definitely ready for something other than croissants, as much as I love them. I think I ate them every day in France. What time are you going to your parents?"

"I told my mum I would call her in the morning. To be honest, I would like to go first thing."

"Do you want me to go with you?"

"Thank you. I appreciate your offer, but this is something I need to handle by myself. What would be really nice is if we could meet afterwards."

Jack pulled her back into his arms. "Yes, of course, I will meet you wherever you like. I know I've said this before, but I understand how much courage this must take. I'm very proud of you for taking such a risk with your heart. It shows what beautiful strength of character you have. Many people can't confront their true emotions."

"Thank you, Jack, it's been a long time coming. I feel like everything is finally falling into place. As difficult as it will be, I know it's the right move for me going forward."

Twenty-five minutes later, there was a knock on the door. Jack got up and put on one of the hotel bathrobes. He returned a moment later, wheeling the service trolley into the room.

"Breakfast is served!" Lola sat up in bed, and Jack placed a tray with her breakfast and a coffee in front of her before settling down to eat his enormous full English. They ate in silence for a few moments. Jack thought back to last night when Lola had told him about her friendship with Contessa Suzette. He quickly decided that he would wait to tell Lola that Suzette owned a De Lempicka painting that was sought by his new client, Anais. It was all too convoluted, especially after Lola had met her at that wedding and knew what a man-eating temptress she was. However, the main reason was that he didn't want to upset her before she talked to Roberta.

Lola got up first, put her tray back on the room-service table, walked into the bathroom, and turned on the shower. She let it get super-hot before stepping in. The steamy water felt good as she rehearsed what she would say to her mum. After about twenty minutes, she stepped out and dried off. Wrapping the towel around her, she walked into the bedroom to call Roberta. Jack was up and checking his emails in his boxer shorts. It was eight-thirty. Lola dialed, and her mum answered immediately.

"Hello sweetheart, how are you? I can't wait to see you. What time do you want to come over?"

"Hi, Mum. How about in an hour or so?"

"Yes, that will work. Your father and I are just reading the morning papers."

"Okay, great! I'll see you then." And with that, she clicked off. Lola turned to Jack. "I'm just going to get dressed and leave."

He could tell from her voice that she was anxious. "Okay, I'm just going to finish up here, then head to the office. I'm dealing with a lot of demanding clients right now."

"I'd like to hear about them later."

Yep, that would be some conversation. He was a little nervous about how she would take everything. I will just have to cross that bridge later, he thought, especially when it came to the party at the Lanesborough.

Picking up her bag, Lola put on the grey Max Mara cashmere coat and walked over to where Jack sat, kissing him full on the lips. He stood up and looked into her eyes. Nothing else needed to be said. Saying just a simple goodbye, she left the room and felt like she had her sword, armour, and lance ready as she walked tall out of the St. Martin's Lane Hotel and into a waiting taxi.

"34 Montagu Square, please."

"Okay, luv, doing alright today?"

"Yes, thank you." As the cab made its way through the streets of London, Lola appreciated that they both sat in relative silence until they pulled up in front of her parents' house.

"Is this it? Red door, luv?"

"Yes, that's it." Lola paid him and stepped onto the pavement. As he sped off, she looked at the brass-lion door knocker. For some reason, it seemed almost ominous.

CHAPTER FORTY-TWO

Knocking on the door three times, Lola could hear Richard Chamberlain barking. The door opened, and her mum stood there holding Rich by the collar. He was excited to see Lola. The door closed, and Rich jumped up on Lola before circling around and around in happiness with half his body wagging.

"I'm so happy to see you, Lola. Come in." After giving Rich a good petting, mother and daughter embraced in the hallway before making their way back to the kitchen. "Would you like tea, coffee or something stronger?"

Lola could tell from the formality that her mum knew something unusual was coming. "I'd love a cup of coffee to start. Where's Dad?"

"Your dad went to the supermarket." Lola was glad in a way that her father was out; it would give them time to go through everything. Roberta handed Lola a cup of coffee, having quickly steamed some milk so that it had a frothy top, just the way she liked it. Looking at her daughter, she could sense some tension in the air.

"Is everything okay, darling? You don't seem like your normal self. Why don't we go and sit in the snug? Ollie made a fire this morning." Following her mother into a small cosy room that adjoined the kitchen, they sat in the two large grey-velvet armchairs that faced the Georgian fireplace. A large sash window looked out to the communal gardens in the centre of Montagu Square. It was such a nice room, and beside the two chairs, the only other furniture was a round, antique, French orange-marble coffee table in front of the two chairs. Today's papers and a couple of *Horse and Hound* magazines were stacked neatly in the centre. Rich walked in and put his head on Lola's lap before plopping down on the worn Persian rug in front of the fire.

Lola placed her coffee on the table and turned to her mother. There was no easy way to start this conversation, so she simply said, "Mum, there's something I have to ask you. It's something that has plagued me for years since that gut-wrenching day when Penny died. I am finally ready to face the truth. One reason is that Jack is back in my life. He told me he overheard you and Max having a conversation about my biological father that day. I feel like that day changed me entirely and sadly changed who I may have been had I not had to live with that haunting information."

Looking at her daughter's beautiful face, Roberta could see the pain she had caused. She felt horribly guilty that she had kept this secret for so long. Leaning over, she took Lola's hand. "You are completely right; it is time. First, I have to say I'm so sorry. I think at the beginning, I told myself it was the best way to protect you from the hurt of it all. In hindsight, I should have been honest with you and Ollie from the start."

Lola did everything she could not to break down as she looked into her mother's ashen face. "Does Ollie know?"

"He does. I told him when you were a teenager after we ran into Max Valentine-Smithe at the Stoneleigh National Horse

Show. I never made the connection between Max and his brother Neville, a distant business acquaintance of Ollie's. When I knew Max years prior, he simply went by Max Valentine, and besides, your dad rarely mentioned him."

Thinking back to that day, Lola remembered noticing how uncomfortable, almost petrified, her mother had looked when Max had come to the table. She had acted like she didn't know him. In a strange twist of fate, Ollie had met him some time back on a birthday hunting trip for Neville. Lola took a sip of coffee as her mother continued.

"Your dad was amazing about it all and said that he always thought the timing of your birth wasn't quite right. Also, after you were born, we tried for another baby, but due to some medical issue, he's unable to have kids. I think he knew at that time, even though the doctors said there was a very slim chance that more children may be in his future. Ollie always said he was fortunate to have his special Lola, and that was enough. After seeing the newspaper photo of Francis Williams, Max, and Ingrid, it all resurfaced, and he said it was time I told you the truth. But he wasn't going to push me, as ultimately it is my decision."

Lola thought about everything her mother had said. She realised what an amazing man Ollie must be to have accepted all of this. It could not have been easy.

Roberta looked at her daughter, her heart bursting in anguish at the thought that Lola might never forgive her. Looking down at the empty cup, she said, "Would you like another coffee?"

"Yes, please, how about we make it an Irish coffee? I have a feeling we both might need it." Her mum stood up and touched Lola's shoulder on the way out. Lola looked at the stylized nudes above the fireplace. Her parents had owned the painting for as long she could remember. It was called *The Chaise* and was of two nudes reclining on a turquoise *chaise longue*. The Delphines had been active art collectors, and she knew the stories behind most of the artwork in the house. This one was by a British artist named Sid Gimcrack. Apparently in the 1980s, he would often go to a Soho modelling studio on Brewer Street for inspiration and to sketch the models.

"Here we go, sweetheart." Rich looked up from his sleep and sniffed the air like he was hoping a tasty morsel might come his way. Roberta put the glass mugs with a floater of cream on the table. Lola took a small sip. The whisky immediately warmed her face, and she returned it to the table to let it cool down a bit.

"That's very tasty." Taking a deep breath while swallowing back the tears, she mustered up the courage to say, "Whenever you are ready, I would like to know who my biological father is."

"There is a story that I would like to tell you first because it will make more sense if I do. I will give you the shortened version today. Then, whenever you want, we can talk about it as much as you need. I want to make sure you have all the facts and are not left with any questions."

Lola could tell that her mum was being extremely stoic to get through all of this. Looking into her mother's blue eyes, she could see the hurt behind her brave face as Roberta began her story.

"I was staying at Villa Bonne Chance with my mum one summer. I was just twenty-two years old, and Ollie had come to visit me. We had been together for about a year at that time. One evening he wanted to take me to the Hotel du Cap-Eden-Roc for dinner, which I thought was very romantic at the time. We had a lovely dinner, and then afterwards, we went up to the Champagne Lounge. Well, out of the blue, Ollie got down on one knee and proposed to me. At that age, I felt like I wasn't ready for marriage, so I asked him if I could wait a while to make that decision. His response completely shocked me. He basically asked me what was the point of us being together if we were not getting married before storming off and leaving me sobbing alone in the bar. I didn't know what to do, but thankfully, a very kindly waiter gave me a tissue and tried to calm me down. I even remember his name; we kind of bonded because he was around my age and said he had just broken up with his girlfriend in Paris."

Lola couldn't believe it; she had to interrupt. "Was his name Alberto?"

"Yes, that's right! How do you know that?"

"He still works at the hotel, but more importantly, there is another big story I have to tell you later. It's a very sweet love story, and our family played a part in it."

"What a lovely coincidence. I look forward to hearing about it and how you know him." Roberta picked up the story where she had left off. "So, Alberto went to fetch me another glass of Champagne, and I just sat there, tears rolling down my cheeks. Suddenly two Englishmen appeared in the bar and invited me to join them. At first, I was hesitant, but they insisted on cheering me up. It turns out that one of the men was Francis Williams, who, as you know, is a famous musician, and the other was his tour manager, Max Valentine, as he called himself then. Francis had just played at the *Jazz à Juan Festival* in Juan-Les-Pins. They were staying at the hotel and thankfully had their driver take me home afterwards because Ollie had not cared about my being stranded. The three of us became fast friends, and I ended up visiting them on tour in various places in Europe. One time, your grandmother went to London for a couple of days, so they came to Bonne

Chance. We drank a lot of *rosé*, and Francis played the guitar. It was all so much fun."

Lola hadn't picked up on any hints of romance from her story. So far, she made it sound like they were all just good friends. She was beginning to realise there was a lot she didn't know about her mother. Roberta picked up her coffee and took a long drink, nodding. "Mm, that is good; we may need another one after this! So, as I said, I'm leaving out a big chunk of detail because it's not very relevant, but of course, I will share that with you whenever you want. One day, I got a phone call from Max and Francis inviting me to a party on a yacht docked in Monte Carlo. They said they would send a car for me and gave me all the details. I remember being very excited about it. The timing was perfect because my mother had been called away for a few days to visit a client who wanted to commission a painting for his villa in Capri."

Lola sat very still listening to the story, one she had been denied hearing all her life. Knowing the struggle it must have been to bear the weight of such a huge secret, she wasn't sure if she was angry at her mum or just felt compassion for her. Besides, she knew she had been angry under the surface for years. It was all dressed up on the outside with the image she portrayed, one that most people couldn't see with all her business success, confidence, and beauty. Her mother interrupted her thoughts. "Are you alright, Lola dear?"

Looking at her mother, she could see tears in her eyes, so she took her mum's hands and held them tightly. "It's going to be okay, mum; please don't worry."

Roberta managed a small smile before carrying on. "So, I arrived at Port Hercules to be met by Max. A tender was waiting, and the trip was about thirty minutes to where the superyacht *Rumpy-Pumpy* was anchored. I remember the name because it was so amusing." If Lola hadn't been so engrossed in Roberta's admission, she would have had a laugh at the name. However, she was utterly spellbound as she listened to her mother's story unfold.

"Max told me that Stefan van Carson, who owned the yacht, was the youngest person ever to win a director's Oscar for his film, *Fur Coat and No Knickers.* To celebrate, he bought his first yacht, which would be considered quite modest by today's standards. As you can imagine, the party was amazing. Waiters were walking around with *Cristal* Champagne and delicious *canapés.* The crowd was made up of well-known celebrities and models. It was all incredibly glamorous, to say the least. Max introduced me to Stefan, who was talking to Francis Williams. Francis greeted me warmly, as we hadn't seen each other in a while. I noticed that Stefan seemed to be paying particular attention to me, and of course, I was extremely flattered as the *soirée* was full of stunning women. Francis and Max could tell that there was some chemistry between us because they excused themselves and went to chat with some other acquaintances."

"Well, we ended up spending the evening together. I have to say I was mesmerised by him. He was so enchanting, and it was hard not to be hypnotised by his charms. Toward the end of the evening, guests were getting on their tenders, and the party was coming to an end. Stefan took me in his arms and asked if I would care to join him for a few days as they were cruising down to Portofino the next day. Of course, I couldn't resist. At that time, I was someone who liked to go for it when an opportunity arose. Plus, I think it was a good distraction from my broken heart. We just kind of fell head over heels in love overnight. I ended staying on the yacht for a week. When I reflect, I think about how excited I was by the glamour of it all. He bought me a bikini and a couple of dresses, and I was good to go! Luckily, my mother had decided to stay longer in Capri, so I didn't have to explain my whereabouts until later. Before I carry on, should I bring us a couple more Irish coffees?"

"Yes, thank you. This is all quite astounding, and I could do with a moment to re-group." All of this was flabbergasting, just imagining her mother as a beautiful ingénue. However, she knew her mother was neither naïve nor innocent. Lola stood up and kneeled by the fire to rub Richard Chamberlain's tummy. In his sleepy state, he automatically rolled over and put his paws in the air. "Good boy," Lola said.

Roberta came back in, laughing slightly, as she looked at Rich while Lola sat back down in the comfy armchair. "Here we go; I made this one a little stronger. So, where was I? Oh yes, so the glorious few days went by, and we sailed back up to Monte Carlo, where he dropped me off and had his driver take me back to Villa Bonne Chance. We agreed to meet the following month, as he was set to direct a new film in London. I was completely infatuated with him, and of course, when my mother returned from Capri, I told her how besotted I was."

"Stefan called a lot, and we wrote letters. Even when he was in pre-production and super busy, we still talked on the phone a few times a week. As time went on, I didn't notice the tiny changes I felt in my body. I put it down to being infatuated, but I suspected something was up when I started getting sick in the mornings. At first, I didn't tell anybody because I was terrified. But then one day, Max called, and I broke down on the phone and confided in him. He said he would do anything to help and persuaded me it was a good idea to tell Stefan as soon as possible. For some reason, I just couldn't tell him. Still to this day, I don't know why. Instead of doing the right thing, I ran from it all and quickly ended my relationship."

"Shortly after that, Ollie called and wanted to make things right and get back together. At that time, I was only about four weeks pregnant and not showing at all. We reunited and got engaged shortly after when I told him a terrible lie. I said I was pregnant, but I hid the fact that he was not the father. If I could do this all over again, I would. I behaved atrociously, and I'm very ashamed of all the hurt I have caused you and Ollie. As soon as I got back with him, I felt like I needed a fresh start, so I avoided Max and Francis. Somehow, it seemed to be an easier way to forget. In fact, I didn't see Max for years and still have not spoken to Francis, who gave up trying to contact me after many months. All that came crashing down at the Stoneleigh Horse Show. That's when I decided I had to tell Ollie the truth. And the truth is that your biological father is Stefan van Carson."

Lola sat in silence and disbelief. She remembered that when she looked at the picture of Stefan on his yacht, he had seemed slightly familiar. The question was, what to do now? She wondered how he would take the news that he had a forty-three-year-old daughter. It would be the strangest news to receive. Then she remembered her conversation with Chase yesterday about how he was starring in the new Van Carson film and that they would be in London next week. Roberta looked at her, concerned. "Please tell me what you are thinking. I know this has to be very intense."

"To be honest, I don't know what to think. I'm completely shocked because I was so sure it would to be Max or Francis. I thought when you told me I would break down, but actually I feel amazingly calm. I think it's going to take some time to process it all. Thank you for telling me. I would like to hear more about it all down the road. For now, I just want to get used to the fact that I have a Dutch father who is a famous film director. Do you know if he has any other children? I suppose I should look him up," Lola said, picking up her phone.

"I don't know if he does because all these years, I deliberately never tried to find out anything about him. It was all just too painful."

Lola typed in his name and opened the first thing that came up. She studied the picture for a while, trying to see any resemblance. He was blonde with blue eyes. It was hard to tell more because it seemed that she was looking into a stranger's face. There was a list of all his film credits, and then she jumped down to his personal life.

Looking up from the phone, she turned to her mum. "He does have children, three in fact, two boys and a girl from two different women. They only talk in any kind of detail about the youngest one. His daughter is twenty-five and an up-and-coming artist named Violetta Martini Vos-van-Carson. It says here she dropped Vos-van-Carson from her name, preferring to be a little incognito. I guess Martini is her middle name." Lola continued to read the explanation. "Wanting to carve her own success instead of relying on her famous parents' names, she dropped Vos-van-Carson. Her mother is a Dutch model named Skylar Vos. It's strange to know I have siblings out there."

They stood up and held each other tightly. The tears finally came as they sobbed in unison. At that moment, Rich looked up as Ollie stood in the doorway, nodding slowly as he looked at his two favourite women entwined in this tender moment. He instinctively knew that Roberta had finally unravelled the truth. Lola signalled for him to come and join their embrace. It was all that was needed to reassure Ollie that he was Lola's real dad regardless of her new insights.

Ollie wiped away a tear with the corner of his sleeve before suggesting they move into the kitchen. Lola paused for a moment to look into her dad's sorrowful eyes. Her immense love for this man was unquestionable. He was the best father anyone could have. She simply said, "I love you, Dad, and that love will never be replaced, I promise. All of this has been exceedingly emotional, and I need some time for it all to sink in. I'm exhausted, and Jack said he would meet me as soon as I was ready."

"Jack Alistair? I haven't heard that name in a while." Ollie looked confused.

"Yes, we have reunited after a very long journey. I realised that he is my true soulmate." Both parents smiled at her, knowing that she had finally found true love.

"That is such wonderful news," Roberta said. "We can't wait to see Jack again. You must bring him for dinner soon."

Putting on her coat that was draped over a dining chair, Lola smiled and walked into the hallway, giving her parents one last embrace. Opening the front door, she waved goodbye as it shut behind her. Walking down the steps of the Georgian townhome, she flagged down a taxi before quickly texting Jack to ask him to meet her at the hotel. He replied promptly and said he would jump in a cab immediately and rang off.

CHAPTER FORTY-THREE

Suddenly Lola's phone rang again. Thinking it was Jack, she answered without looking at it. "Hello?"

"Hi Lola, this is Fabian. How are you?"

"Fabian! How are you? Is everything okay?" She was taken entirely off guard and not expecting him to call, especially since they rarely talked on the phone.

"Yes, fine. I'm actually calling you from Houston right now. There is something I wanted to tell you."

"Okay, I'm in a cab in London. I just left my parents' house. There are some things I need to tell you at some point. It's nothing to worry about, just some Delphine family history that has surfaced after being hidden for years. Oh, and you should know Jack Alistair is back in my life. Maybe the next time we are in the same city, we can get together!"

Fabian sounded surprised, but he answered, "Absolutely."

"So, what is it you wanted to tell me?" She could hear him take a few deep breaths before he answered.

"Lola, I realised that all these years I've been holding a piece of my heart in your court, and to be honest, it's prevented me from truly loving someone else. I always knew you didn't feel the same about me, even though I feel that we have mutual affection and chemistry. After I got back from that atrocious wedding in Saint-Paul de Vence, I was going through some of Anais's things. I came across some old modelling photos and unraveled a few things about her that led me to believe that she had quite a traumatic childhood. For some reason, it shook me up and forced me to look at my own heart and soul. It helped me realise that I, too, have let the past control who I am today. It's time for me to move on and put all that behind me. Suddenly it struck me that I needed to face the facts. You were in love with Jack from the beginning, and I guess part of me hoped that with time you would change your mind about me."

Lola wished she could reach into the phone and take Fabian's hands, knowing this was not an easy thing to say. "I'm sorry, Fabian. I don't know what else to say. I understand where you are coming from, and I'm sorry if I have done anything that led you to believe that at some point, we would be together or something."

"No, Lola, you didn't. It was always just a fantasy of mine, that's all. I want us always to be friends, though. There's something else. Remember Scarlett from the wedding?"

"Yes, of course, how can I forget? That Riggs was a complete piece of work." She didn't want to tell Fabian what Anais had ended up doing, especially since it meant mentioning Stefan, which she wasn't ready to do yet.

"Well, she lost her pearl earring at the wedding, and somehow I found it. The earring was important because it belonged to her grandmother. Since I was coming to Houston for business, I contacted her; we had dinner the other night, and I was able to hand over the precious heirloom. I think there's hope here; I really like her a lot. The good news is Paris will most likely be in her future because it looks like she will end up taking ownership of Galerie Raphael in the divorce settlement."

"That's great news, Fabian. I'm happy for you. I just want to say I do love you. It's just not that kind of love. Jack stole my heart all those years ago, but it's taken me all this time to acknowledge it." Lola's cab was now at the top of Saint Martin's Lane. "I know that now."

Lola was glad when his tone lightened. "Thank you for sharing all your thoughts with me; it means a lot. I have another call coming in from Paris, so I better take it." Fabian said goodbye before hanging up and switching calls. Lola just had a couple of minutes to compose herself before the cab pulled up at the St. Martin's Lane Hotel.

Fabian didn't recognise the number, but he decided to answer anyway, thinking it was a business call. "Hello, this is Fabian Whitecliff."

"Fabian, this is Anais. How are you?"

Stunned, Fabian didn't know how to respond for a second. "Listen, Anais, what do you want? To be honest, if I'd known it was you, I probably wouldn't have picked up."

"Yes, I understand. The thing is, I wanted to thank you for sending my things."

"I told you I would. Is that all?" He sounded irritated as he waited for her to respond.

"I found the note you slipped in with the old Polaroids, and I think I would like your help." Fabian couldn't believe she was reaching out to him like this. He wished now he had not had a moment of empathy and left it alone.

"I have to think about it. You and Riggs behaved horrendously. The reason I put that note in there was I had a moment of sympathy when I looked at those sordid photos. Was that your twin sister?"

"Yes, that was Clara and me. My birth name is Esmee. Changing my name to Anais helped me run from the shame and guilt of it all." Her voice seemed to change. She seemed so vulnerable all of a sudden.

"Anais, I'm sorry that you had to go through all that. I just don't know if I can help you after what happened at the wedding. If I change my mind or have any ideas, I will let you know."

"I understand, and Fabian, I'm sorry." With that, the phone call ended.

CHAPTER FORTY-FOUR

Opening the door to their suite, Lola noticed that Jack was pouring two glasses of wine. Lola walked toward him, and he immediately stood up to embrace her in a tight hug. "How was it, sweetie?" Feeling his muscular arms around her body, she was silent for a moment, enjoying the cuddle while gathering her thoughts. Handing her a glass of Sauvignon Blanc, Jack guided her to a seat on the sofa.

"You know, it went all right." Lola filled him in on what her mother had told her from beginning to end, finishing with, "So, my biological father is Stefan van Carson." Jack tried to hide his shock. He couldn't believe it, especially after the afternoon he had spent on the *Lekker Kontje*. The two naked blondes, Giselle and Kitty, came back into his mind. Knowing that he had met Stefan, Jack was sure Lola would eventually want to know the details of the day. "Another crazy thing is I have three half-siblings. One of them is an up-and-coming artist; her name is Violetta Martini."

Jack was gobsmacked. The name was so unique it was hard to forget. He had met her that night at the casino when he had met with Claude. It was the same evening he had seen Lola for the first time in years. Seeing that his face had changed, she said, "Jack?"

"This is so strange. I met Violetta that same night I saw you getting out of your car outside the casino. What's bizarre is I recall thinking that she seemed so familiar at the time, and I didn't understand why. Now it all makes sense, of course. I was meeting my client Claude Laurent, and he introduced me to her because she wanted some connections to the London art scene. At the time, I thought they were having an affair, but I was wrong. It turns out that Claude was having a fling with Annika Barinov."

Lola didn't know what to say. This was simply astonishing. All she could muster was, "What is she like?"

"To be honest, after seeing you that evening, I was kind of in a trance." Lola spontaneously kissed him; she could tell he was in a state of confusion.

"Listen, let's put this to sleep today; there is so much to go over. It has been a big crazy day for me, and all I want to do is have a late lunch somewhere fabulous, then climb into bed and watch films or something else, if you know what I mean."

"Sounds good to me. Where would you like to go?"

"How about The Wolseley? We could split the chateaubriand." He was glad to see her happy face.

"That sounds perfect!" he said, as she walked into the bathroom to freshen up a bit. Thinking back to everything she had just told him, he was a little concerned for her moving forward and wondered if she would decide to contact Stefan.

Jack heard a light knock on the door over the sound of running water coming from the bathroom. Putting the wine glass down, he wondered who it could be. Housekeeping? Looking in that direction, he noticed an envelope on the floor. Swiftly, he opened the door to see if the messenger was still in the hallway, but no one was there. Looking at the small cream-coloured envelope, he instantly recognised the perfect calligraphy. It was the same beautiful penmanship as the last note slipped under his door at the Du Cap-Eden-Roc. Jack paced back and forth as he quickly tore open the envelope. The card, just as before, had her gold initials, A.B., embossed on the top. He began to question how she had found him at the St. Martin's Lane, but of course, she had her means. Thinking about that, he questioned again why she needed him to find the Kandinsky. It was confusing because if he could get the deal done, it stood to make him a lot of money. Pushing the thought out of his mind, he read the short note.

Mr. Alistair, let us meet for dinner at Frenchie on Henrietta Street to talk about my new Kandinsky, Delilah. Afterwards, you will accompany me to the party at the Lanesborough Hotel. Lara Lenkov will contact you with further details.

Jack slid the note into the pocket of his laptop bag just as Lola emerged from the bathroom, looking refreshed. He felt slightly guilty about not telling her that Anais and Annika had become clients. It just didn't seem like the right time to bring them up; he was torn about how to approach it. The conversation would have to come soon, though, as he didn't think he could get out of the meeting with Annika. "You look gorgeous, darling. Are you ready? I did make a reservation, and thankfully because of the time, they can accommodate us."

"Do you mind if I go into the other room and call Ingrid? It won't take too long. I feel that I should give her a quick explanation, so she doesn't have to worry about Max anymore."

"Yes, of course, and I need to call Fiona about a couple of things." Lola walked into the bedroom and shut the door. She told Ingrid what had happened, cutting the story into the shortened version. Then she added that she would give her blessing if Ingrid wanted to date Max.

Meanwhile, Jack dialed his office. "Hi Fiona, how's everything going? Any word on the Kandinsky whereabouts?"

"As a matter of fact, I found that a man called Sid Gimcrack owns the piece. He is a London-based artist specialising in nudes. It has been challenging to track down because it was actually discovered hidden between two walls during a remodelling project in his Bethnal Green studio. My online search found a newspaper article about it. Apparently, there was also a stack of old sheet music with it."

"Really? A stack of sheet music?" Jack couldn't believe it! What was the connection with the sheet music? He wondered if Annika would bring the ones she had found in Herb Gomes' piano bench. Opening his laptop bag, he pulled out the sheet music that Lola had handed him at Bonne Chance and laid them out on the coffee table.

Fiona could hear him shifting through papers. "Jack, are you there still?"

"Yes, sorry, this is all getting more mysterious by the minute. Do you have an update on the De Lempicka? Anais is in London next week and will require some information."

"As I told you, *Rhythm No. 5* is owned by the Contessa Suzette Florentino. The good news is that her boyfriend, Casper Drake, is on a short tour of the U.K. before wrapping up in Paris. He just happens to be playing at Ronnie Scott's in two weeks. I get the feeling, just from looking at their press coverage, that Suzette typically travels with him. I read an article about them in *Jazzwise* magazine. The contessa was included because of her unique international collection of historical instruments. The article went on to say she started collecting a few years ago after combing through markets and curio shops on a trip to Tokyo."

Jack was just about to pull up Ronnie Scott's website to purchase tickets when Fiona said, "I already took the liberty of buying you two tickets to the show. I was afraid they might sell out."

"Great! Thank you, Fiona. Looks like things are moving along nicely. I'll be in the office tomorrow, and we can talk more about it then."

"Okay, I will continue my research into both paintings. See you tomorrow."

Putting his phone on the table, Jack glanced over the sheet music. This must be only a small part of the puzzle. Maybe if he could put the ones that had been discovered together, he could decipher the code. Should he tell Lola right now? It was very likely Suzette would contact her if she were in London with Casper. He would cross that bridge when the timing was better. She had so much going on that he didn't want to add to it, especially by bringing Anais into the picture. Jack decided to wait a few days until they had gotten back into the rhythm of being with each other. Also, it would give her some time to recover from her mother's admission. He was so lost in thought that he didn't hear Lola coming up behind him until she put her hands on his shoulders, bending down to kiss his neck before sitting.

"How did it go with Ingrid?"

"It went well." Yawning a little, she said, "I'm finding it all very surreal. I expected to feel completely different when I found out, but at the end of the day, I'm still me, with two parents who love me the same as they did yesterday. I am not in a mad rush to contact Stefan. Of course, Ingrid will keep this private. It turns out that she and Max are crazy about each other, and she understands why he couldn't tell her about my mum and Stefan. It's pretty admirable that he has honoured Roberta's secret all these years."

Lola thought back to Chase's phone call the other day. It was strange that Stefan would be in London soon to start filming *English Crumpet*. Chase's floral note was left unanswered, tucked away in the pocket of her tote bag simply because she didn't know how to handle it right now. It was all pretty exhausting, and the weight of it was a lot to bear.

Jack looked at her tenderly as he said, "I'm glad you are beginning to resolve all of this. I have some work stuff that I'd like to discuss with you at some point when you aren't so burned out."

As he kissed her lightly, she gazed deeply into his eyes and kissed him back passionately for a minute before leaning back slightly. "I've just realised how tired I am. How about we order room service?"

"Great idea, and look, it's just started to pour down. Standing up, he went to grab the lunch menu and brought it back. Sitting next to her again, they put their heads together, deciding what to order. The rain was now thrashing the floor-to-ceiling windows, and a rumble of thunder could be heard in the distance. Lola shivered slightly, so he automatically put his arm around her. Turning to him, she gazed into his smiling eyes as he looked deep into her soul. Jack was the only man she had ever known who really knew who she was. He accepted the whole package and was willing to take all of her into his heart, and this is where their magic began. It was the most beautiful surprise that they had found each other again, and she knew she had finally found her soulmate. It had been a very long journey of self-discovery and searching for who you are and what you want.

"Lola, I have always loved you. I think it's time I gave you something back that I have held onto like a precious pearl in an oyster." Reaching down, he pulled the small box he had purchased at the Eden-Roc boutique out of his bag and handed it to her.

Taking the box in the palm of her hand, Lola undid the ribbon and placed it to the side. Before opening it, she looked up into his eyes. They both felt highly emotional. She slowly took off the lid, and there it was, the golden horseshoe pendant. The symbolism of this pendant and what it represented was so powerful. Carefully taking it off the tiny velvet cushion, she held it up, not believing he had kept it all these years.

"Here, let me." He took the horseshoe necklace. As she swept up her hair, he fastened it behind her neck. They both had tears in their eyes. As he placed his hand in hers, they stood up facing one another. Lola was the first to speak.

"Jack Alistair. What a lovely surprise."

"Lola Delphine. You take my breath away."

Thank you for reading *Lola Delphine.*
Next is a preview of the prequel, *Annika Barinov,*
the second book in the *Lola Delphine* series.

ANNIKA
BARINOV

CHAPTER ONE

Annika listened as the countdown to 1985 started: 10, 9, 8, 7, 6, 5, 4, 3, 2, 1. Happy New Year!!! "Auld Lang Syne" played, and the tipsy patrons sang. She daydreamed for a minute about what the new year would bring for her and hoped that things would improve. She was sad in a way that she wasn't on the streets of London's Soho to enjoy the festivities.

"Come on, luv, get us another pint, would ya?" Quickly going back into automatic pilot, she grabbed a glass and poured the man another lager as he ogled her in his drunken state. The Intrepid Fox was hopping that night. Glancing outside, Annika could see Wardour Street was cram-packed with revellers. Making her way down the bar, she served one drink after another. Her hands were sticky from all the spills, and she occasionally felt a tinge of pain as a lemon slice hit the paper cut on her finger. As much as she despised this job, it just about covered her minimal expenses, as she lived above the pub and often ate for free at a local restaurant, where the bar manager had taken a shine to her. Arriving at the end of the line of punters, she was happy to see one of her favourite regulars, Finn O'Malley.

"Happy New Year, Finn. What can I get for you?" Finn smiled at her and raised his glass.

"I'll have a pint of Guinness, please. How are you doing tonight, Annika?"

Annika talked to him as she carefully began to pour his Guinness, knowing that you certainly didn't want to mess up an Irishman's champagne. "I'm doing fine. As you see, it's super busy, so I haven't stopped all night." Out of the corner of her eye, she could see rows of people waiting for a drink. Finn was writing something on a piece of paper.

"Hey, listen, if you know anyone who is looking for a room to rent, my sister lives just up the street opposite the *Pathé* Building, and she's looking for a lodger," Finn said.

He handed her the scrap of paper with a number on it. Annika took a quick look, put it in her back pocket, and waved at Finn before quickly moving on to serve the hordes of people waiting. Looking down the bar, she noticed that the pub's landlord, Monty Knight, was talking to someone. He kept looking her way as if they were talking about her. Ignoring it, she carried on making drinks without pausing for the next hour.

Since it was New Year's Eve, they had extended hours and were closing at one a.m. Annika was exhausted and couldn't wait to get to her bed in the eaves of the pub. Finally, the last-call bell rang. Annika poured one more pint and started to wash the mountain of glasses, letting the other barmaid Stella handle the last few drink orders. Keeping her head down and focusing on the tedious task of cleanup, she didn't notice Monty making his way toward her.

Monty tapped her on her shoulder. She turned as he said, "I need to talk to you after you're finished with that." He stood so close to her she could smell his breath, a combination of whiskey and cigarettes. As Annika turned to him, nodding, she felt his hands on her hips. When he squeezed past her, she felt the buckle on his belt graze the back of her tight jeans. Although Monty repulsed her, Annika didn't question his behaviour out of fear of losing her job. Thankfully, he never took it any further. Maybe it was her five-foot, ten-inch commanding frame that held him back. She had also learned to fight in the orphanage and knew she could put Monty on the floor if he tried anything more.

Stella came over and helped with the glasses. Both of them were silent as they dried, too weary to chat. Annika liked Stella, who was from the East End of London and had a no-nonsense attitude about her. When the clear-up was nearly finished, Monty signalled for Annika to come around the other side of the bar. She put the dish towel down and gave Stella a weak smile, almost expecting what would come next. Standing in front of him, she was easily a good four inches taller than he was. With her grey-blue, almost wolflike eyes and Slavic cheekbones, she was a commanding presence. Monty seemed nervous. Shifting from one leg to the other, he looked her up and down before saying, "So, Annika, it has been brought to my attention that you are only fifteen years of age. Is this correct?"

There was no point in lying. She stood tall, holding herself proudly so as not to let him see how terrified she was of losing this job. "Yes, that is true."

"Well, I'm going to have to let you go. It's illegal for me to hire minors in this particular pub due to my license agreement. If the snitch decided to go to the authorities, I could get into trouble. You can stay here until Wednesday, and then you will need to find other digs."

Annika said nothing. She waved weakly at Stella as she made her way upstairs to the top floor of the building and her cell-like room. She needed to think and quickly. Tomorrow, Tuesday, was, of course, New Year's Day. After walking down the narrow hallway to the very basic bathroom, she washed her face and scrubbed her hands and forearms in soapy water, trying to wash away the stench of beer.

This was Annika's second sacking in the last couple of months. It was tiring moving from one place to another. She walked back to her chilly room, quickly undressed, and climbed under the scratchy blankets. Lying there, she told herself things had to get better. Sometimes, when she let the curtain drop, she liked to imagine what her mother was like. It was as if her mum were some kind of mythical being or something. Silently asking her for help, Annika said a little mantra that she relied on in times of stress, which seemed all too often. She repeated it three times. The last time, she said it out loud: "When one door closes, another one opens."

For whatever reason, these few words brought peace to her, and she immediately felt more centred and powerful. As she was about to switch off the lamp, she noticed her jeans on the chair in the corner. A piece of white paper was poking out of the back pocket, and she suddenly remembered Finn's giving her his sister's number because she was looking for a lodger. She decided right then she would call first thing in the morning, not knowing, of course, how she would pay rent, but it was a start. With that, she thanked her mum for sending a sign and said her mantra once more before drifting off into a troubled sleep.

* * *

Annika woke early the next day. Her muscles felt stiff from the chill. Leaning over, she switched on the kettle by the side of her bed and looked at the Mickey Mouse alarm clock that sat next to it. Seven-thirty. She was glad to have woken early because she had a lot to accomplish today. After the kettle clicked, she filled up a mug and tossed in a teabag. There was no milk and no bread for toast. Perhaps she could treat herself to a small breakfast at Bar Bruno on the other side of Peter Street.

Sitting up and taking a sip of weak tea, she lifted the corner of a small rug that ran the length of the single bed and retrieved an envelope. On it, she had written *The Great Escape* in reference to her favourite film starring Steve McQueen. Smiling a little, she emptied the contents, which turned out to be exactly fifty pounds, her life savings. Swinging her long achy legs out of bed, she made her way to the bathroom, splashed cold water on her face, cleaned her teeth, and brushed out her waist-length blonde hair. Blinking the water away, she looked in the mirror before heading back to the room and dressing quickly, trying not to think about the cold.

First, she would head down the street to the phone box to call Finn's sister. Then, a quick stop at Bar Bruno for breakfast. She hoped that nine was not too early to ring. Gathering up the money, she put it back in the envelope before hiding it again under the rug and looked around the small room she had called home for the last six weeks. She wasn't sad to leave the depressing, dark space. It was just the unknown that was scary. Her suitcase sat in the corner; she would need to pack later that day. Her meagre possessions consisted of a few items of clothing, a French for beginner's book, the Mickey Mouse alarm clock, and a Russian doll.

The matryoshka doll sat on the makeshift nightstand next to the kettle. Sitting back down on the bed to finish the tepid tea, Annika picked up the colourful wooden doll and began to open the different figurines, positioning each one in a line. Arriving at the last one, she took out the baby, which was wrapped in a piece of paper with a worn string attached to it. Cradling the tiny treasure, she gently unravelled the cord and looked down at the paper. It had been at least five years since Annika had dared to open the doll. For some reason, something drove her to read the scrap of what looked like parchment. It was her only pathway to the past and where she had come from. The orphanage had told her that at three-months old, she had been dumped on the steps outside wrapped in a burlap sack. The only clue to her heritage was the string tied around her neck with the writing "7.7.70 Romania" on it.

Studying the handwriting for a minute, she wondered if her mum had written it. There had been many Romanian girls at the orphanage. She had made some close friends and had sworn to them that she would come back and help them when she found her fortune. Due to the number of Romanian children, part of their school curriculum had been to learn Romanian, which Annika did without an accent. Strangely, when she spoke English, she had a slight Slavic tone. She definitely had a talent for languages and was very close to becoming fluent in French, which she constantly studied in any spare moments.

Staring hard at the only thing that connected her to her past, she carefully wrapped it around the miniature wooden baby and put the eight dolls back inside the mother matryoshka. Standing up, Annika picked up the old suitcase in the corner and put it on the bed. She placed the Russian doll and Mickey Mouse alarm clock in the bottom of it, along with the French language book. The rest could wait until later.

*   *   *

Slipping into the man's oversized tweed jacket she had bought in a charity shop and tying a silk paisley cravat around her neck, she was ready to hit the streets of Soho. It was a frosty first day of the year, and she looked on in envy as a couple came toward her on the pavement holding hands. The woman wore a long camel-hair coat and carried a designer purse. The man was very well dressed in a three-piece suit. Annika noticed his gold watch as they got closer. For some reason, she was almost mesmerised by the glamourous couple. As they passed her, they kindly wished her a Happy New Year; the woman gave her a friendly smile. Annika turned to have one last glance, at that moment swearing to herself that she would be like that tantalising woman one day. She would work hard as if there were a gun to her head and not stop until she had made her millions.

*   *   *

The phone box smelled like urine, and she noticed a condom on the floor, so she decided to go to the next closest one in front of St. Anne's church. Thankfully, it didn't have any offensive odour or rubbish in it. Annika dug some change out of her pocket along with Finn's piece of paper. Taking a deep breath, she fed the telephone some change and waited as it rang.

"Hello, this is Nora."

"Hello, Nora, my name is Annika Barinov. Your brother Finn told me that you are looking for a lodger." There was a short silence as if Nora was thinking.

"Yes, that's right; it's thirty pounds a week."

Annika thought for a moment. Could she really afford that? She had to make it work somehow.

"Would it be okay if I came to have a look at it today? You see I have to be out of my place tomorrow. I am just down the street from you in a phone box outside St. Anne's. Would it be convenient to come right now?"

"Yes, that would be fine." Nora gave her the address, and Annika thanked her before putting down the phone.

She walked up Wardour Street and passed Bar Bruno, glad they were open today. Her mouth watered at the thought of hot buttered toast. Annika arrived at the right door and pressed the buzzer. Almost immediately, the door clicked open, and she walked up to the first floor. She knocked twice, and the door swung open.

"Come in, come in." Annika followed Nora into the living room, which had windows overlooking the street. The kitchen was in the back. Nora walked back into the hallway and opened a door. "So, this is it."

Annika stepped inside the room, which had a single bed and a small wardrobe. On the end wall was a sash window. It was very simple and plain but certainly nicer than her room at The Intrepid Fox.

"What do you think? Of course, you will have use of the other rooms as well."

"Would it be okay if I paid you weekly?"

"Well, I don't really like to do that. Maybe we could do that the first month as kind of a trial period for both of us. After that, I will need four weeks' rent at the start of each month. By the way, how do you know my brother?"

"I was a barmaid down the street at The Intrepid Fox, and he is a regular there."

Thankfully, Nora did not question that Annika had said "was" a barmaid. "Okay, well, normally I ask my lodgers to fill out some paperwork, but since you know Finn, I suppose I can let that slide. Just show up tomorrow morning before ten with your thirty quid, and the room is yours. We will take it from there."

Annika didn't know if Nora had taken pity on her, but she was grateful not many questions had been asked. As they walked into the hallway toward the front door, she turned to Nora. "Thank you. I'll see you in the morning."

Nora nodded and smiled as she closed the door. Annika's tummy rumbled as she ran down the flight of stairs and into the black-and-white-tiled hallway. Pulling open the front door, she exited to Wardour Street, which she crossed and walked the short distance to Bar Bruno. The smell of bacon hit her as she walked into the *café* and up to the counter.

"*Ciao, bella*, how are you today?"

"Morning, Riccardo, I'm good, thank you. Can I have a cup of tea and some toast, please?"

"Of course, darling, please take a seat. I bring it to you."

Annika liked his sing-song Italian accent, wondering for a moment if she should also learn Italian along with French. She sat in the window, enjoying the warmth of the place. It felt cosy in there, as if her troubles had disappeared for a minute. Unfortunately, as she looked across Peter Street to The Intrepid Fox, that thought immediately vanished. Riccardo interrupted her troubled mind.

"Here we go. How did everything go last night at the pub?"

"Oh, you know, busy."

He could sense something was wrong. Riccardo liked Annika; she came in often, always for the same thing, tea and white toast. Usually, the staff didn't like it when customers sat for a long time nursing one cup of tea, taking up table space. They let her do it, however, because she seemed so lost, sitting in the corner studying her French-language book. It also didn't hurt that Annika was extremely beautiful, made even more so by the fact she didn't seem to realize it. She took a sip of the steaming tea and looked up at Riccardo sadly. "The honest truth is, I got sacked last night. I don't suppose you know anyone who is hiring, do you?"

Riccardo thought for a second. He knew the landlord, Monty, and what a slimy bastard he was. He came in the *café* often, always boasting how he had his pick of barmaids. Riccardo, of course, knew the truth—that he was a complete letch. He wondered if Monty had tried something on the mysterious beauty. The thought made him shudder a little, and he said kindly, "Let me ask around, see what I can come up with. Why don't you pop back in a couple of days, and I can let you know." He turned around, noticing someone waiting to order at the counter.

Annika thanked him quickly as he went to help the new customer. Looking outside, she noticed that the sky had darkened, and rain had begun to hit the window. She watched as the drops of water raced each other down the glass. Taking a bite of buttery toast, she heard the door swing open and turned to see two girls probably not much older than her step into the *café*. They stood for a moment, running their hands through their damp windblown hair before making their way to the counter to order.

For some reason, Annika couldn't help but watch them. Both were very tall and thin and had identical long hair and similar mannerisms. She looked away shyly as they turned in her direction, giggling and whispering as if they were talking about her. As Annika took the last sip of her tea, she wished she could afford another one, especially since she didn't fancy her other options. She could either go back to her frigid room at the pub or pound the pavement in search of a job, which almost seemed like a waste of time on New Year's Day. Lost in thought as she watched people outside hurry along in the storm, their colourful umbrellas a nice contrast to the grey wash of the street, she didn't notice the two girls approach her table.

"Do you mind if we join you?"

Now that they were standing in front of her, she instantly saw they were twins. She thought she detected a French accent. Not really knowing what to do because nothing like this had happened before, she said, "Eh, sure, why not?" Annika couldn't help but smile at them; it was uncanny how identical they were.

They sat down opposite her and introduced themselves. "I'm Esmee, and this is my twin sister, Clara." Esmee was the first to reach her hand out to shake Annika's.

"I'm Annika," she said as she shook Clara's hand next. The chatter was put on hold as Riccardo put a tray down on the table with a large pot of tea and a rack of toast cut into triangles. Plus, there were four plump sausages on a plate.

"Would you like some more tea and toast and a greasy sausage?" Esmee speared a sausage and put it on Annika's plate. Clara began pouring the tea for all of them.

"That is very kind of you." Annika felt a little shy in front of the two confident glamazons.

After the tea had been poured, Clara spoke. "So, do you work and live around here?" The twins looked at her, waiting for a response. For some reason, their kindness broke down some kind of wall in Annika as she sat with her hands wrapped around the warm cup. Looking down at the steaming tea, a giant tear rolled down her cheek. Esmee stood up and came around the other side of the table. Sitting down next to her, she put a friendly arm lightly around Annika. "I'm sorry if we upset you." Nobody said anything for a few minutes, as Annika cried silently with her head down. Esmee handed her a tissue, and she seemed to pull herself together again. After taking a big gulp of tea, she looked up. "I just got fired from my job over there." She pointed at The Intrepid Fox. "I found somewhere else to live this morning, but I only have one week of rent money. You see, I'm only fifteen. When the boss finds that out, he always lets me go. I don't know what I'm going to do."

The twins nodded in unison; it certainly was curious how alike they were. Annika excused herself for a minute. "I'm going to the loo; I'm sure my mascara is halfway down my face by now." Standing up, she managed to smile at both girls before walking away.

Clara turned to Esmee. "What do you think? Should we introduce her to Reggie?" Esmee thought for a moment. Reggie would certainly like Annika's looks, and with her bone structure, she would certainly photograph very well. "Well, she is very young, but I do think she could handle Reggie and take care of herself. There's a certain toughness I can't put my finger on." She spoke fast, knowing Annika would be back shortly. "Do you detect a slight accent?

Clara agreed. "Yes, with a name like Annika, she sounds Polish or Swedish to me." She was just about to continue when Annika returned to the table.

She could tell that the twins had been talking about her by the way they quickly shut up and stared at her with wide, almost excited eyes. Esmee, who seemed to be the leader of the two, spoke first.

"So, Annika, we have a proposition for you." After taking a small bite of sausage, she continued. "You mentioned you needed a job?" Looking up from her second piece of toast, Annika smiled at the sisters, encouraged by their enthusiasm. Before she had time to answer, Clara chimed in. "How do you feel about doing some modelling?" There was something about the way she lingered slightly on the word modelling, as if she wasn't sure that was the right word. They waited for her response, which came almost nervously.

"What kind of modelling?"

Clara nudged her sister as if she didn't know what to say, so Esmee took over the conversation again. "Well, there is a photography studio just around the corner on Brewer Street. We could take you to meet Reggie."

Annika thought for a moment; she knew about these so-called modelling studios. The girls could see her hesitation, so Esmee took a softer tone as she answered the question. "Well, you see, it's pretty simple—mainly lingerie, some topless. We just pretend like we are lying on a beach somewhere. Reggie takes the photos and sells them on to other people."

Annika shuddered slightly at the thought of it. This was certainly not what she had in mind for her future. She stared into the teacup, searching for an answer. For a second, her curiosity got the better of her, and she blurted out, "How much does it pay?"

"Twenty pounds per picture and thirty pounds for girl-on-girl stuff. Sometimes we do three of four different shoots a day, which of course, pays a lot more."

Thinking hard about her predicament, Annika knew it would certainly help sort out her financial issue. Also, she knew it was unlikely she could find another job that would pay so well. "Okay, I suppose I could try it."

The girls clapped their hands together in unison. Clara was the first to speak. "Why don't you meet us tomorrow afternoon at one? The address is 16 Brewer Street. Just buzz on the left door-bell. We will introduce you to Reggie, who owns the studio. Don't worry about makeup or lingerie; you can borrow ours to start with."

Hoping she could trust the twins, Annika said, "I will see you there." They clinked their teacups together in an impromptu toast. "Well, we better get going. Looks like the rain has finally stopped." Standing up together smiling, the twins said, "Bye then, see you tomorrow at one."

Annika waved as they made their way out of Bar Bruno and down Wardour Street. Sitting back in her seat, she couldn't help but think that although this wasn't her first choice, it would get her through until she had a better offer.

Riccardo walked over to the table and started to clear away the plates. Looking at Annika, he said, "So, are they friends of yours?"

"No, not exactly. I just met them today. Why? Do you know them?"

"They come in here often; rumour has it they are Reggie's girls."

Annika nodded. "Yes, that's what they told me."

Riccardo looked a little concerned. "Just be careful, okay?"

"Thank you, Riccardo. I will." With that, she stood up and smiled at the friendly barista and made her way onto the streets of Soho. She considered walking down to Leicester Square to see what films were on at the Odeon cinema. Instead, she decided to go home and pack.

After crossing Peter Street, she opened the side door of the Fox and walked up the narrow staircase to her room. When she opened the door, the small space smelled damp, and the chill hit her hard, especially after sitting in the cosy warmth of Bar Bruno. Rubbing her hands together, she began to pull her clothes out of a small chest opposite the bed. It took no time at all to place her few belongings in her suitcase.

Lost in thought as she tended to the task of packing, Annika suddenly heard the hallway door slam. Strange, she thought, who could that be? Turning, she cracked open the door to see who it was, and in the gloomy light, she could make out the landlord, Monty Knight, stumbling drunk in the dim hallway swinging a bottle. Thinking quickly, she pushed the mostly empty chest of drawers in front of the door. Swiftly she sat down with her back against the hardwood and wedged her feet against the end of the bed. The sound of broken glass leaked through the crack under the door.

"I know you're in there. Come out, pretty girl." Monty's words were slurred. She listened as he turned the door handle. Annika braced herself as he tried again, saying, "If you don't come out, I'm coming in there to get you." Monty was shouting now and pounding on the frail door, which seemed to flex under his weight. Terrified and using all her strength, she managed to keep the door firmly shut.

His fists were now pounding harder on the door, and he was roaring drunken abuse. Surveying the room in a flash, Annika looked for anything she could use as a weapon if he broke through her barricade. The only thing that might work was the old lamp stand or the kettle, neither ideal to beat off a man weighing fifteen stone. She listened for a second and could no longer hear anything, which made her more nervous. Then suddenly, as if he were standing an inch from the door, he said in the most chilling, almost robotic voice yet. "I'm coming for you, Annika; I want that sweet teenage muff of yours. You owe it to me."

She mustered every single last bit of strength she had as she waited. Nothing happened for a few moments, but then Monty rammed into the door like a bull hitting a matador. Everything happened quickly after that. Right then, as her weight gave in and the door opened a foot or so, he screamed out in pain. There was a thud and the crunching of glass, then silence.

Annika sat quietly, listening until she thought she could make out heavy breathing. Taking a chance, she quietly eased herself off the floor and peaked through the opening in the door. Monty was lying in somewhat of a mangled mess. She could see a pool of blood forming above his ear. The smell of whiskey wafted from the array of broken glass. Looking down at him, she wondered if he was still breathing. Then she saw his hand twitch slightly. As silently as possible, she closed the door and stood for a minute, thinking about what to do. She certainly could not stay here. Who knows what he might do when he woke up? Something snapped in Annika as if her survival-mode button had just been pushed.

Spinning around, she threw the rest of her clothes into the suitcase. Next, lifting the rug, she retrieved the envelope with her fifty-pound savings in it. She put it in the breast pocket of her tweed jacket, which she put on. Thankfully, there was just enough change in her pocket to make a phone call. Annika's head spun around, double-checking to be sure she had everything. She zipped up the case and put it on the floor before gingerly cracking the door open again. The chest of drawers shifted easily without her weight behind it.

Monty was still lying in the same position, the pool of blood now the size of a dishtowel. As quietly as possible, she eased the chest out of the way and picked up her case. His legs were spread wide, so it made more sense to step over his chest in one motion instead of two. As she lifted her light suitcase and stepped over him, she was grateful for once at her lack of possessions. One foot, then two. Nearly there, she thought, as she made it over his bloody body.

In a split second, everything changed. Monty suddenly reached up and grabbed her ankle. "I've got you now, you witch." Annika's adrenalin kicked in at just the right moment, and she slammed her case down on his hand with such velocity that even she was surprised. Monty yelled and let go of his grasp. He struggled on the bloody broken glass, trying to get up.

Annika took that moment to run down the hallway and downstairs onto Peter Street. Not turning back, she ran all the way to St. Anne's Court and the sanctuary of the phone box. She sat down on her case to catch her breath, almost not believing the events of the last hour. As she pulled the scrap of paper out of her pocket, she prayed that Nora would pick up.

The phone rang and rang. Annika willed someone to answer. Just as she was putting the phone back on the receiver, she heard a weary voice say, "Hello?"

"Hello, Nora, this is Annika Barinov. I met you this morning."

"Yes, did you change your mind or something?"

"No, not at all, it's just I was wondering if I could move in today…well now, actually."

There was silence on the other end of the phone. "Well, I suppose that would be okay, so long as you're quiet. I've been working night shifts at the hospital, so I'm exhausted."

"Of course, quiet as a church mouse. Can I come now?"

"Sure."

Annika was very grateful. Putting down the phone, she picked up her suitcase and lugged it onto Wardour Street, quickly scanning up and down for any sign of Monty. She walked the short distance to the flat, pressed the buzzer, and the door clicked open.

Nora stood in the doorway to greet her. "Hi, come in." Annika followed her into the hallway and paused at the kitchen. "I made some soup earlier if you are hungry. As I said on the phone, I'm exhausted, so I'm off to bed. My shift at the hospital starts at seven tonight."

"Thank you for letting me come early and for the soup. I promise I won't disturb you." Reaching into her breast pocket, she took out three ten-pound notes and handed them to Nora.

Nora studied her for a moment. "Are you alright? You look all kinds of shook up."

Annika nodded. "I'm better now," she said, looking around.

"Okay then, I'll see you later." With that, she turned and went into her bedroom at the other end of the hall and shut the door.

Annika picked up the case and walked the few steps to her new room. She lay the case on the floor and unzipped it. Deciding to unpack properly in the morning, she pulled out her Mickey Mouse alarm clock and the Russian doll and put them on the narrow nightstand. Glancing at the time, she couldn't believe it was five already. Sitting on the bed, she took a deep breath and thought about the horrors of the afternoon. There was no doubt in her mind that Monty would have inflicted some serious harm. She would need to be very careful she didn't run into him again on the streets of Soho.

Her tummy rumbled, so she walked into the kitchen and saw a big pot on the stove. Lifting the lid, a waft of rich, savoury flavours hit her. She found a spoon and a bowl and filled it, halfway conscious not to eat too much of Nora's Scotch broth. Standing at the counter, she wolfed down the delicious hot beef and barley soup. She washed the bowl and spoon and put them away.

Yawning fully, she realized how tired she was. The flat was very basic, but the one thing she did notice was how warm it was. Closing the door to her room, she undressed and climbed under the covers, not forgetting to say her mantra three times. "When one door closes, another one opens." She had barely mouthed the last part before sleep engulfed her.

CHAPTER TWO

Annika woke up with a fright and sat straight up in bed, gripping the bed covers. She listened for a minute as she glanced around at the shadows of the dim room. A bead of sweat ran between her breasts as the panic subsided and her nightmare evaporated. In her dream, Monty was smothering her, and she was crying out for help, but no words came. She could almost smell his rancid repulsive odour. The taste of blood was present in her mouth, and she realized she must have bitten her lip in the night.

Sitting still, waiting as her pounding heart slowly calmed down, she picked up the Russian doll and wrapped her hands around it. Annika rocked back and forth, clutching the doll, the motion bringing some kind of inner calm. She placed the doll back on the nightstand and picked up the clock. It was impossible to make out the time, so she switched on the small lamp. Blinking as the sudden glow almost stung her eyes, she looked down at the clock. Mickey's white-gloved hand was pointing at seven. Surely not?

Sounds were coming from the hallway and then she heard the clink of cutlery as the kitchen drawers were opened. Annika wondered if Nora was getting ready for her night shift. She felt very disoriented, so she pulled the covers back and swung her legs out of bed. Her ankle felt sore where Monty had grabbed it. Looking down, she noticed that there was a bracelet-like purple bruise. It felt a little puffy; thankfully, there seemed to be no hindrance in motion when she turned it left and right.

Standing carefully to test the level of pain, she walked the few steps to the suitcase and pulled out a nightdress, which was really just an extra-long tee-shirt. There was a picture of Lady and the Tramp on the front. Tracing the outline of the two dogs, she remembered the shirt had been given to her the Christmas before last. The orphanage received gift boxes from a local charity around the holidays, and that year, Annika received the Mickey Mouse clock and the nightshirt. Looking down as she put the shirt over her head, she contemplated again if she should have run away in such haste after all. Quashing the thought, she opened the door and heard music playing. As she neared the kitchen, the Radio 1 jingle came on, and the DJ began wishing everyone a good morning. Annika was so confused; surely she hadn't slept that long. Thinking back, it had been around five-thirty when she had climbed into bed. Never in her life had she slept that long. She stood in the doorway, yawning.

The kettle clicked, and Nora turned, sensing her presence. "Oh, hi there; I hope I didn't wake you."

"No, not at all; what time is it, please?"

"The guy on the radio just said seven-thirty."

"In the morning!?"

"Yes, of course, silly. I just got home from the hospital. What a night I had. Lots of mess there tonight."

"What is it you do?"

"I'm a clinical assistant, which basically is just a fancy title for ward housekeeper. You will never guess who they brought in last night."

Annika could almost guess what was coming next. She just kind of shrugged her shoulders, not knowing what else to say.

"Your old guvnor, Monty Knight."

Her body stiffened at the sound of his name as she remembered the pool of blood and the lacerated body. Not knowing what to say, she just stood there waiting for Nora to continue with the details.

"He was brought in by one of the barmaids who had gone to work at five and arrived to a locked pub. Apparently, she waited for an hour or so for Monty to show up. Finally, she decided to try the back entrance, which led her upstairs. She found him in a pool of blood, unconscious and lying on a bed of broken glass."

Automatically holding onto the counter for support, Annika hoped her fear hadn't shown. She only managed to ask, "Is he going to make it?"

Nora stood looking at her in the Lady and the Tramp nightshirt with her long elflock air. There was something about this girl she couldn't put her finger on. At this moment, she seemed so childlike and lost, but when she looked behind the coltish physique, she could see an unbelievable resilience and toughness.

"They think so. He lost a lot of blood and has a broken arm. When he came to, he was muttering all kinds of abuse to the matron and claimed someone had tried to kill him. Nasty piece of work that one. It's a shame the assailant failed."

Nora peered at Annika intensely as if she were trying to read her mind. She had heard of Monty Knight's lecherous reputation from a friend of a friend's daughter who worked for him years ago. Could this young girl have had anything to do with what happened last night? The thing was, she didn't want to get involved. Rumour had it Monty had connections in the East End, along with the fact that his brother ran the notorious Blind Beggar pub on Whitechapel Road. If Annika was involved, there was not a shadow of doubt that Monty would come after her. Nora noticed her looking nervously at the kettle. The poor girl looked terrified, she thought. "Would you like a cup of tea and some toast?"

Annika's face lit up. "Thank you, that would be very kind of you."

Nora set about refreshing the kettle and took some bread out of the cupboard, putting a couple of pieces in the toaster. She made the tea and handed Annika a plate with buttered toast and jam. She gestured for her to sit at one of the two wooden stools that sat at the end of the counter. While Annika ate and took big gulps of the tea, Nora looked at her beautiful long blonde hair. It was certainly an eye-catcher. Monty, for sure, would notice her in a second. Also, he would probably put the word out on the street to look for a girl with waist-length blonde hair. It was highly recognizable, that's for sure. Nora's mind was spinning.

"Listen," she said. Annika looked up from her toast. "Have you ever thought about cutting that hair of yours? I think a shoulder-length bob would really bring your cheekbones out. Also, with those beautiful grey-blue eyes, a lovely auburn colour would go down a treat."

For a moment, Annika was shocked. She took her hand, pulled the mane over one shoulder, looked at it and then looked back at Nora. Annika knew in a heartbeat the reason behind the somewhat bold suggestion. Nodding sadly, she said quietly, "He tried to attack me, you know; he came up to my room late afternoon yesterday. I barricaded myself in, but then he rammed the door, and I guess he slipped or something and landed on his broken whiskey bottle." Annika showed Nora the bruised, swollen ankle. "As I was escaping, he grabbed my ankle. I hit him with my case and ran up the street to call you."

"Shhh! Please don't tell me anymore. I can't know, as these people are dangerous. First, we need to cut that hair of yours and give it a different colour."

A big tear rolled down Annika's cheek as she realized the danger she could be in. Nora took pity on her; she couldn't help but feel sorry for this young woman. "It will be okay. We will change your appearance a bit, and I'll talk to Finn later to see if he has any ideas. Your hair will grow back after all this dies down, and the colour will grow out."

That thought made her feel better. Hopefully, if Annika was super vigilant, she could outsmart Monty.

"When I go to work tonight, I'll find out the extent of his injuries and see how long he'll be in hospital."

Annika was grateful for someone else to take charge. Nora stood up and walked out of the kitchen, returning a minute later with scissors and a box of hair colour. "Just so happens I quite fancied a bit of auburn myself and bought this the other day." Looking around the kitchen, Nora picked up yesterday's paper, which was sitting on top of a pile of bills. She spread a large square of newspapers on the floor before placing the stool on top of them. "Sit here." Taking a comb out of her back pocket, she untangled Annika's hair. Now it hung deadpan straight. It was a crime to cut such beautiful flaxen hair, but it was Annika's only hope of not being caught. Taking the scissors, she cut in a straight line just above her shoulders. The cut hair hit the newspapers, its weight making a noise as it hit the ground. Next, Nora came around and faced her. "I think we will give you a fringe that will give you a really different look. To be honest, I think you are going to look quite stunning."

That was a very nice thing to say, Annika thought. She hoped Esmee and Clara would still want to introduce her to Reggie this afternoon with her new look.

Finally, it was almost done. Nora turned off the hairdryer and sprayed some product, using her fingers to style Annika's fringe. She stood back to admire her work before saying, "Hold on, I know what will finish the look." She dug around in her handbag, which was on the counter, and pulled out a red lipstick. "Look at me." Annika looked up, and Nora skilfully applied the lipstick. She stood back and whistled.

"Well, you look at least twenty-one now and a lot more sophisticated." Taking her hand, she led her to the bathroom and placed her in front of the mirror. Annika stood there, not recognizing the new woman in front of her. She had to admit it was a dramatic change, one she hoped would keep her safe. Turning away from the mirror, she took Nora's hand. "Thank you so much for helping me."

"Just keep your wits about you and never let your guard down. One last thing. I think you should drop your last name, as it's too recognizable. Okay, I'm heading to bed. I'm back at the hospital at seven tonight. I will find out more about Monty's condition and let you know tomorrow."

Annika nodded and watched as Nora made her way out of the bathroom. She listened as the radio DJ announced that it was ten a.m. There was some time before meeting the twins. She decided to unpack before venturing out to pick up some basic food items. Her head felt lighter without the weight of waist-length hair. Glancing down at the Lady and the Tramp nightshirt, then back up at her new shiny hair, it was as if the metamorphosis had paused halfway.

A hot bath suddenly sounded so good, but it would have to wait until later, as she didn't want to disturb Nora with the sound of running water. Instead, she walked back to her room and took a small wash bag out of the open suitcase. That would have to do for now.

Annika finished unpacking in no time, pushing the suitcase under the bed. She sat down for a minute while deciding what to wear. It looked like a nice day today—chilly, but the sky was blue. Wishing she had something new to wear, she decided on black Levi's 501 jeans and a tight black polo neck. She cinched the jeans with a wide leather belt and pulled on some suede ankle boots. Nora had given her the red lipstick, so she reapplied it in the hallway mirror before heading out.

Annika walked down the flight of stairs. Suddenly the main door clicked open, and Annika nearly jumped out of her skin. Thankfully it was just another resident carrying a couple of shopping bags, and they greeted each other. Before stepping onto the pavement, she looked nervously up and down Wardour Street as if someone were waiting to grab her. It felt like a covert operation getting from the flat to the small supermarket a few streets away. Sensing people were staring, she kept her head down. Finally reaching the store, she ducked in quickly.

* * *

Annika put her goods, which consisted of bread, milk, tea, eggs, two cans of beans, and some cheese in front of the cash register.

She paid and picked up the plastic bag of goods and stepped back out into the hustle and bustle of Soho. A police car with its siren on was making its way toward her, and cars and black cabs were stopping to let it pass. Annika shrunk back into a doorway, immediately thinking the worst—they were coming for her. As the siren got louder, she braced herself, cowering when the police car was almost parallel to her. Turning away, she shielded her face, waiting for the screech of brakes, but none came. She stood there frozen as she listened to the blaring noise trailing off. The street resumed its normal activity.

Letting out a sigh of relief, Annika hurried on, finally turning onto Wardour Street. Weaving around people, she was very near the flat when she spotted the glamorous woman in the camel-hair coat from yesterday. Even from behind, she knew who it was. The long coat swung from side to side as she walked, and she had long chestnut hair that flowed down her back. Annika was almost mesmerised by the woman's confidence. She automatically slowed down and decided to mimic the poised stride, following closely a few paces behind.

As the lady continued, she reached her hand into the side pocket of an expensive-looking handbag slung over one shoulder. Annika noticed the crimson, perfectly manicured nails as she retrieved a folded piece of paper from her bag. As the last of the folded sheet came out of the pocket, something else happened, which she didn't notice as she continued down the street.

A folded wad of pound notes wrapped in a rubber band almost landed on Annika's foot. Quickly she stopped and glanced around to see if she was being watched before scooping up the neat bundle. After a speedy observation, she realized there had to be at least a thousand pounds in her hand. Next came a decision that

Annika made without thinking twice. As much as she knew this money could take her far, far away from her hellish predicament, she also knew in her heart the right thing to do. Ramming the notes into her coat pocket, she hurried after the woman, who was completely oblivious to her valuable loss.

Passing the entrance to Annika's flat, the woman was crossing Wardour Street and nearing Bar Bruno. Annika picked up her pace, not really wanting to get closer to The Intrepid Fox. She could see Riccardo standing outside talking to a delivery driver. They moved out of the way as the woman continued, passing the Fox.

Riccardo and the delivery man's heads turned, silenced by the beautiful swish of chestnut hair. There was no choice but to continue by them as well. She didn't dare look at Riccardo. As she passed him, the men stopped talking, and one of them let out a low whistle.

Annika was a short distance from them when she heard Riccardo say loudly, "Wait, is that you?" Pretending not to hear him, she quickened her pace to almost a run, passing the pub and disappearing out of sight behind a group of tourists looking at a map. When Annika had almost caught up with the woman, she felt in her pocket to double-check the money was still there before calling out.

"Excuse me!" The woman didn't turn or slow down, so Annika ran a few steps until she was beside her. "Excuse me, but you dropped something way back there, and I've been trying to catch up with you for a while." Finally, she stopped, and Annika looked at the confused woman.

"Listen, do you mind stepping over there?" she said as she pointed down a small side alley. "I don't think I should hand this to you on this busy street." The woman immediately felt in her handbag pocket, realizing what was missing. She nodded suspiciously as they walked and waited a minute to make sure no one was around. Annika reached in her pocket and handed her the bundle of money. "Like I said, you dropped it back there. It happened when you pulled a folded paper out of your bag."

The suspicious look on the woman's face went away as she flipped through the money, confirming it was all still there. "Thank you so much." She looked Annika up and down, surveying the thrift-store jacket and scuffed suede boots. The girl struck a chord with her. Many people would have pocketed this amount of money without thinking about it. There was something familiar about this drop-dead gorgeous young woman with the wolflike eyes and Slavic cheekbones. Annika looked to be the same age the woman had been when she moved to London all those years ago. Knowing she probably shouldn't get involved, she couldn't help but ask, "Have we met before?"

"Not exactly, but yesterday you were walking down the street with a man, and you wished me Happy New Year." The woman thought back a second and looked at Annika, slightly confused. Unable to stop herself, she blurted out, "I had long blonde hair then." She knew she shouldn't have said it, but there was no way this elegant woman would ever know the slimebag Monty and his gangster friends.

"Oh, yes, I remember now." She didn't question the hair change, seeing how terrified the young beauty was. Annika didn't know what to say. She shifted her eyes from side to side, wondering if anybody was paying them any attention. Finally, she spoke up. "Well, I better get going then."

"Wait, what's your name?"

"Annika."

"Well, Annika, I really appreciate your being so honest, so I want to give you this." She opened her hand that held the cash and eased a hundred-pound note out of the band. Annika shook her head.

"No, it's okay. I didn't do it for a reward."

"I know that, but I think you need it right now. I sense you are in some kind of trouble," she said, surprising herself that she had asked.

Instinctively Annika touched her dyed auburn hair, the woman's kindness bringing a lump to her throat as she swallowed back the tears.

"Listen, take the money. I'm not taking no for an answer." She placed the hundred in Annika's hand and put the rest inside her bag this time. Before zipping it up, she handed Annika a business card.

"Listen, I was like you once, running around the streets of Soho trying to find my way. If you ever need any real help, you can call me. My advice to you is walk tall and don't show fear. Confidence translates into power, and that will bring you respect. It can be an illusion, and that's okay because one day it will turn into reality."

Looking down at the most money she had ever had in her life and the business card, Annika smiled gratefully. She secured them both inside her breast pocket. When she looked up, she was standing alone, and all that remained of the fateful meeting was a whiff of spicy perfume.

It was unbelievable what a twist of good luck this was. If she were careful, she would have enough money to survive until she made more. Annika remembered every word the woman had said and decided that from now on, she wasn't going to cower in the shadows. That would be letting Monty win. No, she was going to hold her head high and walk tall and strong, just like her new friend had said.

It was like a light switched on in her head as she made a left back up Wardour Street. A magic shield had suddenly appeared along with her new presence. Even in the short distance to her flat, people stepped out of the way as she commanded the pavement.

An unusual feeling of hope lightened Annika's mood as she opened the door. She turned to the hallway mirror and looked at the new person staring back at her. It was amazing how a few words of encouragement had made her feel that everything would turn out fine. The woman had no clue what a special life-changing gift she had given her.

*   *   *

After putting away the few grocery items, Annika went to her room and sat down on the bed. She took the hundred-pound note out of her pocket along with the business card. The Great Escape envelope now had a lone twenty in it after giving Nora the week's rent. It felt good to add the hundred to the small stash. Looking around for a suitable hiding place, she remembered the lining of her suitcase was coming away in the corner. Kneeling on the floor, she eased it out from under the bed and flipped it open. Using her finger to make the hole bigger, she was able to slide the envelope in and smooth the lining back into the corners. She inspected it quickly before sliding the case back under the bed.

Annika glanced at the clock. It was twelve-thirty, so she would need to leave soon. There were mild butterflies in her stomach, which usually would have gotten the better of her. She remembered the woman's advice, however, and the butterflies settled. She almost forgot the business card. Picking up the thick glossy card, she traced her finger over the embossed gold lettering. She was surprised that there was just the woman's first name and a telephone number. She read the name out loud.

"Miroslava."

ACKNOWLEDGEMENTS

Writing this novel has changed my life and whisked me away emotionally to the places I love most in the world. I have been fortunate to have visited most of the settings that help make this story as authentic as possible. None of this would have been achievable without the help of friends and family who shook me dirty martinis (with blue cheese olives), shucked oysters, and poured red wine while listening to me talk endlessly about Lola and her friends. I would like to thank the fabulous locations that helped inspire me to write this book, especially Ronnie Scott's Jazz Club, The Ritz, La Colombe d'Or, Hotel Du Cap-Eden-Roc, and the Lanesborough Hotel where, just like Lola, I was born when it was St. George's Hospital.

A big thank you to my editors Donna Tennant, Scarlet Neath, Terrell Hillebrand, and Henry Hunt. This journey would have been more challenging without all of you. Thanks also to my dad, Colin Barker, who designed the cover, and my mum, Sandra Barker, whose motivating spirit was always perfect at the right time.

A very special thanks to my friend, London-based artist Will Martyr, who kindly allowed me to use his magnificently exquisite and captivating painting *Inspired Completely* for the book cover. A very special thanks also to my friend, British jazz pianist and composer James Pearson, for creating a seductive, transportive, and thought-provoking music score for the audiobook. Both of you were exceedingly generous in contributing your incredibly creative expertise and brilliance to this project. If you have enjoyed James Pearson's score, you will love his new soundtrack album, *Lola Delphine*.

A big thank you to Lori Freese, my amazing public relations and media guru. Thank you also to my super-talented producer and sound engineer Scott Szabo, and many thanks to sound editor Chris Bourque and everyone at Szabo Sound and Music.

Lastly, I want to thank London and the Côte d'Azur for being awe-inspiring backdrops to the tale of *Lola Delphine*.

ABOUT THE AUTHOR

NAOMI BARKER is a British writer who has lived on four continents but currently resides in the U.S. Naomi comes from a creative background and has a history in equestrian sports. A love of art, music, travel, fashion, and all things rock and roll have inspired her to make her first novel, *Lola Delphine*, as genuine as possible.

Made in the USA
Coppell, TX
05 May 2023

16452595R10224